I0607482

PHANTOM IN THE DESERT

A Michael Case Novel
Book one of the Proliferation Files

Books by Damon Nomad

Phantom in the Desert

Coming Soon!
Nuclear Proliferation Trilogy
A Dangerous Test
Russian Puppet Master

Nuclear Mafia Trilogy
Playing with Nuclear Fire
Hidden Forces
Nuclear Reckoning

Nuclear Flashpoints
(a short story collection)

For more information
visit: www.SpeakingVolumes.us

PHANTOM IN THE DESERT

A Michael Case Novel
Book one of the Proliferation Files

Damon Nomad

SPEAKING VOLUMES, LLC
NAPLES, FLORIDA
2022

Phantom in the Desert

Copyright © 2022 by Michael Cash

All rights reserved. No part of this book may be reproduced or transmitted in any form or by any means without written permission.

ISBN 978-1-64540-640-2

To a beautiful soul, a spring flower,
my wonderful wife.

Acknowledgments

Thank you to the staff at Speaking Volumes, especially Erica and Kurt Mueller for their patience.

PART ONE

Transitions

Chapter One
Someone Took Their Eye off the Ball

He threw his cigarette butt to the ground just outside the small factory building as he looked out towards the sea of sand dunes. They were on the edge of the city in this industrial area, there was nothing out here, no decent markets or restaurants. It was steamy hot already at 8:00 am, he hated this place. It had been three years since the general had sent him here. He missed the seasons back home, they insisted it was not a punishment, but he knew better. He had not made sufficient progress in adapting the warhead design for riding in the small space of a missile reentry vehicle, they simply did not have the computational tools to make the warhead design that efficient. He knew what the problems were, the rate of compression of the core, the complex interface issues with the tamper and the timing of the source neutron burst. So, they put his young protégé Park Yo San in charge in Pyongyang and sent him to design and fabricate a warhead for these fools in the desert. None of them had the slightest clue about the technical challenges and the science behind a nuclear warhead, but they were rich and paid his government good money for his knowledge and services. The one who thought he was in charge was the biggest fool of them all. He would swagger and complain about the lack of progress. The rumor was he was a smuggler with no college education. The general told him not to worry. There were others really running the show. As long as they made progress, he would be able to come home, when they were satisfied it would work. He was using a variant of one of their old designs. He had spent most of his time the last three years setting up the fabrication facilities and working with the fools on the explosive lenses.

He lit another cigarette; he was surprised when they actually delivered a sample of enriched uranium metal. It couldn't have come from the smuggler and his pals. The general would not tell him where the core material was coming from. When he saw the chemical analysis, he knew it was not from home. The general said it was from a regional partner, that's all he needed to know. He knew the known sources in the region, and they weren't friends of these people. That meant a new player. Somebody the Americans might not even know about, he laughed at the thought of that. The first samples were not suitable, too many chemical impurities, but the quality was improving. The general told him to be patient, they should have a sufficient supply. He hoped so, then they would be ready to begin the fabrication process for a warhead, and hopefully he would be able to get out of this place. They still had some work to do on the explosive lens; the symmetry of compression was not quite there. There wasn't a lot more he could do until he had enough uranium metal for a complete core. He shook his head, as he stamped out the cigarette butt. How had these fools been able to hide this from the Americans, someone must have taken their eye off the ball. That was the idiom the Americans would use. He opened the door and headed back to his office.

Michael sat down in a visitor's chair in front of Andrea's desk. Andrea was settled into the large office of Deputy Inspector General in the executive suite. Quite a step up from her investigative supervisor's cubicle which was now Michael's office. Andrea saw Michael was slightly limping.

"What did you do to yourself?"

"Twisted my ankle hiking in West Virginia last weekend."

"Let me guess, you didn't go to a doctor. I will never understand someone as smart as you afraid of doctors."

"It's not fear, it's an irrational phobia. Anyway you wanted an update on the status of the team."

The organizational changes went the way Andrea had described to Michael. Andrea Jacobs became the new Deputy Inspector General in February, and he became the new investigative team leader for X-ray in March. The new X-Ray team formed quickly after Michael was selected as team leader. The previous six years the team had become well known in the IG community and beyond in US government. Nine major reports on breakdowns in nuclear proliferation, some getting newspaper headlines and spawning congressional hearings. Word spread that the new team leader was instrumental in those investigations and the team had two positions to fill; there were more than 30 applications for each position. The team was fully staffed by early June. Sheri Landry was still with the team as a senior analyst, the only other original member besides Michael Case. Allen Dressler had replaced Randy Wright two years ago. Allen had been an FBI analyst for fourteen years before joining the OIG, with a master's degree in computer science and expertise in computer forensics.

Andrea put her reading glasses down on the desk, "Kate Bucci, you made a good choice with her."

"George Malley recommended her; he calls her the human lie detector. She mostly worked complex fraud cases at DCIS and NCIS, but they also had her on major classified leak cases. I hate to tell Tom Bradley that there is someone at the OIG who is a better interviewer than him."

"Yea, I have a friend at NCIS who said she is a master with the polygraph, most times she uses it like a prop, getting targets to confess before she even turns on *the box*. They call her the confessor; you know like a priest hearing confession."

Kate had a persona when she did target interviews using her petite frame to her advantage. For high profile leak investigations, she even took on a different look, less makeup, put her hair back, kind of frumpy clothes and always wore her glasses not contacts. She was more soft spoken, almost meek during target interviews. Kate told Michael, most people who had given classified information to foreign governments were tortured inside, many on the verge of tears as she would empathize with their financial difficulties, drug problems or moral outrage about US government. Many were sure Kate understood them and would help them. Telling her their secrets, confessing and feeling relieved until they realized she had captured their words for prosecutors. She was hyper-acute in monitoring body language and very effective at baselining an interviewee, a skill she was rumored to use in poker. Michael didn't play, but George told him that she was legendary at beating agents all over the defense investigative agencies. Michael had heard the term human lie detector and thought it was absurd. He reconsidered his views after watching Kate Bucci.

"What about Brandon Eller in your old position as senior technical advisor, how is he working out?"

"It's still early, but he has a solid foundation; bachelors and master's degrees in Chemical Engineering from Carnegie Mellon, and worked five years for Guardian Chemical in designing countermeasures against chemical weapons, and a master's degree in criminology while he worked at Guardian. Then he spent five years at Department of Homeland Security monitoring chatter and looking for signs of WMD. But they did not involve him much in investigative field work or interviews."

"You know the importance of interviewing. Has he been to FLETC?"

"DHS sent him to the same course I went to; it still has the intensive interviewing modules, but he needs more practical experience. I have already asked Kate to work with him."

"But he understands the job is a specialized investigator; he will not be a law enforcement officer."

"Yes Andrea, not everyone wants to carry a gun and badge. We wouldn't have hired him if we didn't have that clear."

"Okay, Okay, just making sure. That ankle seems to have made you a bit snippy."

Andrea knew that Brandon would be a good fit to move the X-ray team beyond nuclear weapons proliferation. Michael had the background in nuclear technology and Brandon the foundation for chemical weapons. They covered the waterfront from the perspective of technology. Michael had no investigative background when he started working for Andrea when she was the team leader, right out of Purdue with a degree in nuclear engineering. The FLETC course gave Michael the fundamental background in investigative plans, evidence collection and control, investigative report writing and interviewing. Kate could coach Brandon the same way that Tom had helped Michael develop. But Michael had a natural gift for the investigative world, far exceeding her initial expectations.

It wasn't like Michael to be testy, she hoped it was the ankle pain and not stress. He was the first investigative supervisor in the OIG who was not a law enforcement officer and the youngest team leader, younger than the people he was supervising. He had a group of people that still needed to come together as a team and move into a new focus area. She hoped she had not set him up for failure; IG Ross supported the promotion, but it was really her idea. There were a lot of challenges facing Michael, and Steve Thomas was making noise.

"Have you heard Steve Thomas has been making some noise? He has some senior people at the intelligence agencies and even congress worried about our shift in direction. The agencies have benefited from our reports on nuclear proliferation, program improvements and better budgets and the State Department takes most of the heat because that's where our reports focus. He is reminding people of the threats out there, especially Iran and North Korea and the possibility of emergent nuclear weapons programs." Andrea didn't tell Michael about a private meeting with one of the congressmen on their oversight committee. He told Andrea and IG Ross that it was a waste of time to look into chemical weapons. They had nothing to do with this country, and if something happened with nuclear weapons while they were wasting time, he would personally call for both of them to be investigated for malfeasance of office. IG Ross was not bothered he told Andrea the guy was a blow-hard; she should not worry and not to tell Michael or anyone in the office about the threat.

"Sorry, Andrea far above my pay grade, I'm focused on the team and the investigative work that is for you and the Inspector General to deal with. Steve is always talking; you know he is a good guy. He helped us getting started, nuclear proliferation is his professional obsession. He is right, there could be another hidden nuclear weapons program out there, but there is only so much we can do as the Inspector General at the State Department. Have you changed your mind about shifting our proactive initiatives to focus on chemical weapons?"

"No, but it worries me. We made a positive impact. The State Department is pressuring other countries to follow through on changes resulting from our investigations. There is only so much we can do, and chemical weapons represent a hazard. But if something were to happen with nukes and we aren't watching . . . You know better than me how horrible a single nuclear strike would be or the destabilizing effects of a

7

new program in unstable regions around the world. Crap, I sound like Thomas."

Michael did know, and he remembered what Steve Thomas told him years ago, a nuclear weapon was likely to be used in Michael's lifetime. Michael thought it might be dramatic hyperbole, now he knew the potential realistic scenarios. It wasn't the cold war era his parents had grown up with, the US and Russia facing each other with the threat of all out nuclear war. It was less predictable and more unstable. A small country anywhere in the world could go nuclear, lose control of a nuke, and it could end up in the hands of criminals or terrorists. A small country involved in a regional conflict with poor command and control and an "accidental" nuclear strike, results in a nuclear counterstrike from another small nuclear power, then things really spiral out of control. They were only one piece of the network of agencies trying to reduce the threat from nuclear weapons. Andrea was right. It would be horrible, and if it happened when they had their eye off the ball, it would be personally traumatic. Now he was one of the guardians.

Chapter Two
Poor Man's Nuclear Weapon

Michael learned watching Andrea as she organized the team and prepared them for nuclear proliferation investigations. Michael and Brandon discussed the assignment Brandon's first day on the team. Brandon would prepare a basic briefing for the team on chemical weapons and proliferation controls. The team would use this information to develop investigative strategies. Brandon had read the primer on nuclear weapons that Michael had written years earlier to prepare the team for those investigations. Brandon knew very little about nukes before reading Michael's background report. Brandon knew this detailed technical approach was not necessary for chemical weapons. Nuclear weapons were complex machines; investigators without a technical background would have no idea of what made a nuclear bomb work and why things like high-speed switches needed to be controlled as dual use nuclear equipment. There was a lot more to nuclear weapons than the uranium and plutonium fuel; some basic knowledge of the elegant physics necessary for detonation was important to understanding the dual use items in nuclear proliferation.

Chemical weapons were easier to understand; they were poisons. They had been around since ancient times in simple forms. Advanced weapons in use since World War One, weaponizations of different and more sophisticated poisons. Everyone knows that some things in certain dosages can be safe but poisonous in higher doses, it's something people teach their children. The briefing on chemical weapons would be simpler than the nuclear weapons briefing; it would essentially come down to covering the classes of chemical weapons, the concept of precursors and the three schedules in the Chemical Weapons Convention

(CWC). The most complex aspect of chemical weapons proliferation was the wide variety of things that could be used to produce chemical weapons, the large volumes in commerce and the complex legal controls to try and stop proliferation. Michael agreed with Brandon, there was a big difference, and the briefing should look very different than the one he gave years ago.

Brandon knew that Allen and Kate hated chemistry. They had both gone out of their way to tell him he better go easy on the science. They had struggled with Chemistry in high school and were lucky not to have to take it in college. Michael told Brandon he didn't mind a small "prank" so long as it did not get out of control. The meeting notice was sent out in early June for the briefing on Chemical Weapons fundamentals in the conference room two weeks later. There was no reference document for the briefing. Kate saw the email, no reference document, she smiled. She saw Allen at the coffee pot a few minutes later, she smiled and whispered, "No chemistry manual to study for the briefing".

One day before the briefing, Brandon sent an email in the afternoon, *some background information to refresh you on the basics of chemistry for tomorrow's briefing.* He attached a PDF of a textbook *Inorganic Chemistry;* it was a graduate school textbook. Brandon was gone the rest of the day, and Allen and Kate could not hunt him down. He came in early the next morning, wrote a long series of chemical reactions on the white board, along with some definitions and terms. He was out of sight again until the briefing was ready to start.

The entire team was in the conference room at 8:55 ready for the briefing. Michael could see Kate fuming as she looked at the white board.

She went after Brandon as he walked into the room, "Ok buddy, you sent us this textbook to study at the last minute. I have not even looked at it, so we better reschedule this briefing."

Allen jumped in, "I agree that was very nonprofessional, you could have written a primer like Michael, not dump some textbook on us."

Michael asked, "What did Brandon's email say yesterday?"

They looked at Michael puzzled, and he looked at Brandon, Brandon read the email out loud.

Michael finished, "I haven't looked at the textbook. It was background not required to be read for the briefing."

Kate pointed to the white board, "You expect us to understand this!"

"Oh no that was just for myself, I was trying to recall some of my work on my masters project," Brandon chuckled while erasing the white board.

"You jerk, you pranked us; beware revenge is a dish best served cold."

Brandon led off the briefing with a quote from a former director of a chemical trade association, "The challenge of chemical weapons is that the technology is relatively simple. Equipment for making fertilizers, cosmetics or industrial chemicals can be used for weapons production. Any country that has the desire to use these industrial resources for weapons will eventually be successful."

Brandon continued, "This statement is from more than 30 years ago. Technology and equipment have advanced significantly. It's not just countries, but any entity with sufficient resources and willpower can develop chemical weapons, including highly toxic nerve agents. You have all read Michael's primer on nuclear weapons, chemical weapons and proliferation of chemical weapons is a totally different proposition from the perspective of technical sophistication, industrial capability and financial commitments. Chemical weapons have been famously called, the poor man's nuclear weapon; it is difficult to achieve high casualty rates, but it is not difficult to cause loss of life, panic and fear. Nuclear weapons are complex machines, we all knew that uranium and plutonium could be used to make a nuclear weapon; but before this work, none of us had any idea how the devices used these materials to generate the energy of a nuclear blast."

"The challenge for chemical weapons proliferation is the large numbers, the number of manufacturers and suppliers, the large quantities of materials produced, processed and transported and the large numbers of chemicals involved in potential chemical weapons. The Chemical Industry in the United States is much larger and more diverse than the nuclear industry. These practical factors create proliferation challenges. The size of the industry, the diversity and number of products and the enormous quantities of materials being produced are difficult to track with many opportunities for diversion schemes. The U.S. chemical industry converts raw materials into more than 70,000 products for business and home use. The facilities cover a range of uses from manufacturing of specialized products to very general widely used chemicals. These chemicals are manufactured, stored, transported and delivered through a complex, global supply chain. There are approximately 11,000 chemical manufacturing facilities in the United States with nearly one third owned and operated by small and medium enterprises."

"The Scheduled Chemicals Database is a tool that the Organization for the Prevention of Chemical Weapons, called OPCW, maintains to assist government and industry with the identification of chemicals covered in the Chemical Weapons Convention, CWC for short. The database includes a key number, the Chemical Abstracts Service Registry Numbers, the CASRN, this number is an easy way of tracking chemicals. Much easier than the long complex chemical names, chemical synonyms and the acronyms commonly used in industry. This database contains more than 34,000 scheduled chemicals including more than 2,000 scheduled chemicals in the OPCW Handbook on Chemicals. Tracking more than 34,000 chemicals manufactured at more than 10,000 facilities transported and sold throughout the world presents quite a challenge."

Brandon continued with the background and historical overview, the first large-scale use of poisonous gas was on April 22, 1915, in Ypres, France, during World War One. Greenish, yellow-colored clouds of chlorine gas choked scores of allied troops to death. The Germans used 168 tons of chlorine gas released from 5,730 cylinders. World War One was the peak of the use of chemical weapons in warfare, used by both the Allied and German forces. The horrific effects on soldiers also led to the first treaties on the use of chemical weapons, but it did not stop their use in warfare, including the Japanese against Chinese in World War Two and Iraq against Iran in the 1980s. He continued going through the categories and classes of chemical weapons and their basic physiological effects.

Then he turned to precursors, "To understand the proliferation of chemical weapons, the concept of a precursor is important."

Kate spoke up, "Way ahead of you buddy, I know all about precursors."

"Ms. Bucci, why don't you please take over at this point." Brandon was curious.

"A precursor is a building block chemical, not a chemical weapon in itself but something that can be converted into a chemical weapon with some processing."

"That is correct." Brandon was staring at Kate waiting for an explanation.

"Six months on a Department of Defense and Drug Enforcement Agency task force, I learned about precursors for crystal meth. Pseudoephedrine, PSE is the most common precursor used in the US for meth production. The diversion of PSE from legitimate suppliers to the illicit market was a problem on several military bases, there were massive quantities being smuggled into the United States through military bases. The PSE was being used in super labs; labs capable of cooking at least 10 pounds of meth per batch. At the time there were dozens of super labs in California, lots of PSE was coming in from Asia especially on Naval vessels. Traffickers realized that soldiers and sailors could get PSE overseas cheaper than domestic sources with less exposure to law enforcement. They don't have to go through customs when they travel on military planes or naval vessels. The black market price was skyrocketing, tempting for servicemen being paid too little to protect their country. So, I figure a precursor for making illegal drugs likely means the same for chemical weapons, just making a chemical weapon and not a drug."

"Kate is correct; the diversion of precursor chemicals to make chemical weapons is at the heart of the challenge of chemical weapons proliferation. They are particularly challenging because most of them have many uses in commercial applications and can be diverted separately and come back together in another location to create a chemical weapon. The equipment to combine and process them can be found in any laboratory or commercial facility that makes legitimate products, like pharmaceuticals, lubricants or pesticides. Hence the fundamental challenge of chemical weapons proliferation. Try and determine whether an individual shipment or portion of a shipment of one the hundreds of precursor chemicals being traded by the ton in commerce is intended for a legitimate commercial or illicit purpose."

"Let's look at the precursors for a chemical weapon a dangerous nerve agent, Tabun. One method of production only requires four chemicals, phosphorous oxychloride, dimethylamine, ethyl alcohol and potassium cyanide—in a two-stage process. Ethyl alcohol is not subject to export controls, but the other three are; however they have a wide range of commercial uses. Dimethylamine is used in various products and processes including pharmaceuticals, detergents and pesticides and is traded in very large quantities in international commerce. Phosphorous oxychloride is used in the production of hydraulic fluids, insecticides, flame retardants and plastics. Potassium cyanide is used in pesticides and electroplating. You see these chemicals have many commercial uses."

"Can anyone think of a scheme for covert production of Tabun nerve agent, with these four chemicals?"

Allen answered, "Not that hard to imagine, like many smuggling enterprises, shady brokers and shipping agents. They work together; divert portions of four separate legitimate purchases and direct them to a bad actor. Could be four different producers and four different customers. At the production end the broker adds a bit to the original order with a legitimate producer. At the shipping end, the broker directs the shipping agent to make a separate stop in route and pumps the extra into another tanker truck. They do this for each precursor and deliver the over orders to the bad guy setting up a small factory with equipment from a series of brokers. It looks legitimate at the origin and legitimate at the point of delivery at the port and to the final legitimate customer, getting the quantity they ordered."

"Thanks Allen, definitely realistic, I'm sure we could come up with dozens of schemes that can evade routine monitoring and reporting. So can the bad guys."

Brandon moved on to a real-world example, involving sarin a potent and sophisticated nerve agent. Its production had been considered too complex for use by non state actors. Aum Shinrikyo was a religious cult in Japan established in 1984 that was able to manufacture sarin. The organization raised money by various means: membership fees, selling "religious" items and various businesses including a noodle factory. The means of delivery was notably low tech. Members carried plastic bags of sarin and broke them open with sharpened umbrellas on five subway trains in Tokyo. The sarin naturally diffused through the air without any forced means, in the confined spaces of the subway train and underground spaces at stations. They were expected to simultaneously break their bags at 8:00 a.m. targeting the train and time to target police and government workers. More than 5000 people went to hospitals complaining of eye burns and difficulty breathing, 12 died as a result of the exposure. The sarin was low quality, it could have been much worse.

The last segment of the briefing was on the Chemical Weapon Convention (CWC) and the outline of the proliferation controls. The Chemical Weapons Convention outlaws the production, stockpiling, and use of chemical weapons and controls their precursors. This would be their investigative focus the effectiveness of CWC controls; the State Department was the national authority responsible for the CWC. Chemical weapons were effectively banned with the treaty.

Brandon summarized, "In reality the system of compliance relies primarily on paperwork, with a small number of inspections at declared facilities. The system of controls does not rely on inspections during export, import or verification inspections of end users. It is not practical to chemically test all of these chemicals moving in transit in these large quantities. Commerce agents and Customs officials have insufficient resources or skills to conduct on-site checks at ports, airports and other points of export and import. The same is true in every country around the world. For the shipments that are checked, there is no time or skill for complex laboratory analysis, the shipments that do get checked rely on labels, shipping paperwork and documentation. It is very unlikely that any shipment will be stopped in route unless there is suspected terrorism from intelligence or law enforcement sources. Compliance relies heavily on good faith efforts of producers and intermediaries to follow the export and import laws and reporting requirements for chemical facilities.

Clever bad actors can exploit these systems, including deceptions of legitimate producers and suppliers."

Brandon finished his presentation and asked for questions, Sherri and Allen wanted to know where they could find the databases and reference documents.

Michael closed the briefing, "Thanks Brandon, now that you know the basics, work together to develop some proactive investigative strategies. You also have the experience of the nuclear proliferation case files, there are some similarities in diversion schemes of dual use items. Bounce your ideas off me when you have a concept you want to pursue as a preliminary investigation."

Chapter Three
New Case Work

In August Andrea Jacobs came into the X-ray conference room where Michael, Kate and Brandon were discussing strategies for initial investigations into the effectiveness of Chemical Weapons Convention controls; Andrea sat down and listened, "Don't let me interrupt."

Kate finished explaining her idea using watchlists; looking to see if entities involved in import and export were being properly screened against watchlists. She was working with Sherri on the databases and methodology. Brandon had a more complex strategy, looking for undeclared facilities in the US, chemical companies looking to avoid compliance inspections and reporting, with production, transfer and inventory manipulation. There were similar schemes used to avoid environmental regulations. He was working with Allen on the database and investigative methodology.

Michael wrapped up after they finished describing their strategies, "These are both good approaches, keep working together in teams and do some preliminary analysis before we decide to open a case, see what initial searches reveal."

Andrea got up to leave, "Sounds like you are making progress. Let's see where you get with these ideas; we need a real case in this area." She was hearing rumors; there was nothing to find they should have stuck with the nuclear cases. They might find minor gaps and problems, some illegal transfers but not a big case. A waste of resources was the rumor that was starting to circulate.

Allen and Brandon were working together on their initial investigation of chemical weapons controls, searching for manipulating inventory, production and processing to avoid reporting requirements. Allen knew it would be challenging after he saw the volume of data and reports he would need to structure in a database. "Brandon, we are going to be digging through a lot of data."

Allen went back through Brandon's briefing. He wanted to organize the categories of chemical agents into classes, and he wanted to have drop down filters for industrial sectors including pesticides, pharmaceuticals. He also knew CWC schedules were very important. The materials were risk ranked based on toxicity and how common they were in commerce. Schedule 1, the most dangerous, included 8 toxic chemical classes; the first three classes included O-alkyl Sarin and Soman were included in class 1; Tabun is included in class 2 and VX in class 3. Lewisite's, Sulfur Mustards and Nitrogen Mustards are also included in the 8 toxic chemical classes on schedule 1. Schedule 1 lists 3 classes of precursors Schedule 2 contains 3 toxic chemical classes and 11 identified precursors and Schedule 3 lists 4 toxic chemical classes and 13 precursors.

The CWC reporting requirements were complex, described at a high level in the Bureau of Industry and Security (BIS) regulations which were 50 pages long. There was a handbook on declaration that was more than 300 pages to assist national governments in the aggregate reporting for the country as well as the operators for facility specific reporting. Brandon and Allen studied the regulations and regulatory guidance together, to help them structure their investigative strategy and database structure.

Brandon found the requirement for facility annual reports. He summarized the requirements for Allen, "Look at these annual reporting requirements they cover past production, consumption and processing as well as anticipated activities for the upcoming year. These key words are defined; for example, consumption means the conversion to another physical form, processing meant no change in chemical nature but physical changes like extraction, dilution or purification. We definitely want to track these domestic transfers. The regulations say they have to track movement of Schedule 2 or Schedule 3 chemicals in certain quantities and concentrations transferred from the facility to any destination in the United States, for any purpose. So, if a company has multiple facilities and they are trying to shuffle things around, these domestic transfers could be helpful."

"Yeah, I get it, we can load in these reports from different companies and search for any of these fields, and I can organize the database to connect facilities with common ownership. This is going to take time; this is more complicated than I thought. Thousands of facilities and chemicals and thousands of reports. This is going to be a complex sorting and filtering algorithm. We still need investigative steps to know what is really going on; the database isn't going to give us a final answer."

Brandon knew the database analysis would only reveal anomalous trends indicative of potential production and inventory schemes. "You're right, it's surprising the lengths some companies will go just to be off the government's radar screen. The database results will only indicate potential reporting schemes, manipulating concentrations and shifting product from year to year or from facility to facility to stay below a threshold for reporting and avoid possible inspections. But there can be legitimate reasons for anomalies in the data, significant changes in product demand and even honest errors in the data, incorrect CASRN codes, using the wrong units for weight, wrong facility identifiers. The database will only flag suspect facilities, we will need to review the data more closely and select facilities for field investigation. I will develop the investigative steps for the field. But the end result could be identification of facilities cheating the chemical weapons declaration requirements, and the United States Department of State falsely reporting to the international community."

Allen laughed, "Or we create a massive database that reveals nothing."

By September the work was starting to pay off, Allen had finished building the database, populating it and testing the methodology. They organized facilities with common corporate ownership, using corporate filings and other governmental databases. It was a lot of data, using all of the reports from the last eight years, along with the OPCW chemicals database applying the reporting thresholds and rules. They broke the country into four geographical regions, in the first two weeks in September their analysis showed no anomalous data for the northeast.

The next two weeks they worked on the southeast. They met in the conference room as they finished their final review; Brandon summarized, "We agree four facilities owned by Crown Plastics in Georgia, three facilities owned by Triumph Cleaning Solvents in Mississippi warrant field investigative steps."

Then they finished the southwest; they identified three companies in Texas for field investigation. In the last week of October, they were almost finished with the northwest, with no suspicious data. Then they discovered a strange anomaly in Washington state. Brandon told Michael they needed to meet with him to discuss something suspicious in the data, "We have found something very unexpected in the data."

Michael asked Kate and Sherri to sit in, "Let's get everyone's views on what Brandon and Allen have come across."

Brandon covered the short presentation he and Allen prepared, "We organized facilities into groups based on common ownership using SEC and other federal and state filings. The algorithm searches for facilities working together manipulating production levels, concentrations and intracompany transfers to try and prevent any facility or minimize the number of facilities that would meet the declaration requirements for the chemical weapons regulations. The analysis is not conclusive, it indicates anomalies in the data. Then we review the full reports and determine where a field investigation is necessary. We have a field work plan to investigate the most suspect facilities."

Brandon summarized what they found for Crown Plastics, "They had a declared facility for dimethylamine for three years but has not been declared in the last four years, and there are indicators that it was a result of manipulation of production concentrations and transfers with other facilities owned by the same parent company."

Kate spoke up, "This is like shell companies moving money around, using multiple transactions below thresholds and shifting it from country to country trying to hide drug money."

"Yea, same general idea. We found similar patterns for Triumph Cleaning Solvents in Mississippi and three companies in Texas near the Mexican border; Lone Star Solvents, Prairie Grass Pesticides and Four Squares Limited. So possibly five facilities that should be declared under the CWC that appear to have avoided declaration through these schemes. We need to move forward with further investigation including field inspection of detailed records and interviews of facility staff. There may be legitimate reasons for the patterns of transfers and production variations."

"We really wanted to talk about a facility in Washington State, near Sedro-Wooley, an old logging town. There are six facilities owned by Stellar Industries throughout Washington state. The company is one of the largest makers of pesticides and insecticides in the Northwest. There are three facilities that have dropped off of the declared facilities list, but they came back onto the list later. There is Richland Enterprises near Richland Washington that was a declared facility for phosphorous oxychloride for three years, not declared for two and declared the last two years. There is Spire Processes, LLC near Kent Washington that was a declared facility for dimethylamine for four years, not declared one year, declared the last two years. Finally, there is Stellar-Pinnacle near Mount Vernon Washington as a declared facility for potassium cyanide for two years, not declared for three years and declared the last two years"

Sherri interrupted, "I don't get it, all of these facilities are now reporting as declared facilities, couldn't this be the ups and downs of production? They don't seem to have been very effective at avoiding reporting requirements."

"Your right, it doesn't look like a reporting scheme for these three facilities. But the algorithm flagged the facilities for review. I noticed something strange when I reviewed the detailed reports. These three facilities sent those three chemicals to another facility owned by Stellar Industries near Sedro-Wooley the last two years and a lot last year. The facility near Sedro-Wooley is Stellar-Storage and Disposal, and it has never been a declared facility. According to the company website, Stellar Storage and Disposal is a non-revenue generating facility for decontamination, temporary storage and processing for disposal of products. Allen checked other sources of information."

Allen picked up on the point, "I checked the Washington State Department of Transportation, State Environmental Protection, US DOT and US EPA records. There are no records of transport permits or permits for storage of materials for Stellar-Storage and Disposal for the last four years."

Brandon looked at the group before he went to the next slide in the briefing, "What are they doing with these three precursors in large volumes? They aren't reporting them as processed or consumed under CWC regulations, they aren't reporting that they are transporting, disposing or storing them under state or federal environmental or transport regulations."

It clicked with Michael when Brandon used the word precursor, "Those are three precursors for Tabun nerve agent, from your briefing those three and ethyl alcohol. You said a simple two stage process and they have Tabun."

Brandon went to the last slide listing the chemicals for Tabun nerve agent. "Exactly right and a large volume, quantities sufficient for attacks on sports arenas, concert halls and similar venues. Potentially thousands of fatalities."

Kate was clicking rapidly through files on her computer, the work she and Sherri had been working on, she remembered Stellar. "Brandon let me connect my laptop to the room display. Stellar Industries is on a classified watchlist for imports or exports of CW precursors, it is a privately owned family company of the Seward family. Randall Seward is one the owners, Sherri found a short FBI summary about him, a white supremacist, suspected of funding hate groups and an anti-government hate monger. Never convicted of any crimes but suspected of being involved in bombing the homes of two state judges about twenty-five years ago."

Michael knew they needed to act on this information as he looked at Kate, "Develop a few slides summarizing Stellar Industries, why they are on the watchlist and about Randall Seward."

Then to Brandon, "Strip out the slides about the other facilities, keep the methodology and background and the slides on Stellar Industries, then add the slides from Kate on ownership and the watchlist at the end. Add a Title Slide, potential threat domestic terrorism Pacific Northwest, make the slides Confidential—Law Enforcement Related."

Brandon asked, "When do we need these?"

"Now, we are going to brief the IG, everything in the briefing is correct, isn't it? Kate is your information correct?"

Kate answered "yes but . . ."

Brandon finished her sentence "Yes, but we don't have reviewed work papers."

"We aren't going to wait for writing and reviewing workpapers, not in these circumstances so long as your confident enough to brief the IG. They could have Tabun nerve agent now, isn't that correct Brandon?"

"Yes, if the data they reported is accurate, they could have a lot of nerve agent." Brandon looked at Allen.

Allen was shaking his head in agreement "Our information is good."

Kate looked at Sheri and Sheri spoke up, "we are good, Stellar is on a CW watchlist and our information on Randall Seward is from an FBI summary report."

Michael picked up the phone in the conference room and called Andrea Jacobs. "We have just uncovered credible information involving a potential domestic terrorist threat; I think you and IG Ross should hear this as soon as possible."

"He is in his office. We will come to your conference room in ten minutes."

Michael looked at the team, "who is going to brief IG Ross and Andrea?"

They looked at each other but said nothing.

Michael looked at Brandon, "This was your idea, you developed the concept. You will brief the IG."

The slides were ready just as IG Ross and Andrea walked through the door. Michael introduced the purpose of the briefing.

"The team has been looking at potential proliferation control gaps associated with Chemical Weapons. Brandon and Allen were reviewing data looking for potential production and inventory manipulation schemes to avoid reporting requirements. Kate and Sheri have been reviewing effectiveness of watchlist implementation in imports and exports. Information from both of these reviews point to a potential threat of domestic terrorism, that cannot wait for work papers and routine reporting. We are confident what they have in their briefing is accurate although not conclusive."

Brandon took over from Michael with his presentation, describing the basic methodology, the transfers of three precursors to a facility that supposedly is for storage and disposal but never seems to have shipped or have permits for storing anything. Brandon added a slide of the four components and a brief summary of the process needed to make Tabun a nerve agent. The quantities of precursors were sufficient for major attacks with significant casualties. He covered the ownership and the reason they were on a watchlist, noting that this information came from the work of Kate and Sherri.

IG Ross waited for Brandon to finish, "What are the odds that this is just a common business operation that we might find in many places?"

"Extremely unlikely, these three precursors end up at this facility, no clear business purpose and not reporting them to any state or federal agency. They are either making Tabun, planning to make it, or are illegally disposing of these chemicals by means which they do not want authorities to know about."

Andrea added, "My gut goes with nerve gas, given the little we already know about Randall Seward."

IG Ross was satisfied, "I agree this is good work. We need to get this to the FBI Assistant Director of the Counterterrorism Division immediately."

IG Ross picked up the phone in the conference room and asked his executive assistant to get the Director of the FBI on the phone it is urgent. Three minutes later the phone in the conference room rang, IG

Ross picked up the phone. "Director we have come across a potential nerve agent manufacturing facility in the Pacific Northwest, through some database analysis, the team led by Michael Case. The facilities are controlled by the Seward family, one of the family members is on a domestic terrorism watchlist, putting some of the company's facilities on a classified watchlist for chemical materials controls."

Ross responded, "That's correct Randall Seward, the facility is near Sedro-Wooley. Yes, I can hold"

Ross looked at the team in the conference room, "The Director is checking to see if they already have this place on their radar, he knows who Randall Seward is, so he must be a person of substantial interest."

IG Ross was back on the phone, "Yes Director I can send a briefing team over immediately, where should they report?"

He hung up the phone. "Okay make us proud. FBI Director's office as soon as possible, they are gathering and waiting. Have one of the state department drivers take you and give you a ride back. Michael you and Andrea are known commodities with senior officials over there; I want you to accompany Brandon and Allen there, introduce Brandon and let him do the briefing. Allen can answer any questions on how the database was created, sorted and collated; they will do a little due diligence on our methods."

There were eight senior officials in the FBI Directors conference room waiting for the State OIG team. Brandon plugged in his laptop as the senior officials introduced themselves and the OIG introduced themselves. Michael was ready for skepticism; how could a group of State Department IG investigators find a chemical weapons threat in the United States. However, they all knew Michael's reputation as well as Andrea, so they were willing to give it a listen. Michael introduced Brandon and Allen, one of the officials knew Allen was a good analyst who had worked for the FBI. Michael described what Allen and Brandon had been working on. Brandon developed the investigative model and Allen built the database searches. Michael handed off to Brandon, this was his first briefing to the most senior officials in law enforcement. Michael was impressed he went slowly, spoke clearly and covered each of his speaking points thoroughly not reading but talking in an authoritative manner. Michael could see their body language; they were taking this seriously and it was important. Brandon finished and Michael asked for any questions.

The Director of the FBI started, "First of all, thank you for immediately contacting us. This is solid preliminary investigative work, and this place is not on our radar screen or at the counter terrorism center. I will let our Supervisory Agent for Chemical and Biological Branch go first. Bryan Flanigan."

"This is a clever approach looking for production and inventory manipulation schemes using their annual reports. I cannot imagine any legitimate reason why all of those precursors would be at this Sedro-Wooley facility, without any reporting. I agree with OIG, if the company reports are accurate, they are either making Tabun, planning to make Tabun or involved in illegal dumping. I also agree with OIG these quantities are sufficient for large scale domestic terrorism, seeking thousands of fatalities not a handful, if dispersed efficiently."

The Director asked if there were any questions on the database collection and analysis, one of the Office Directors spoke, "a little more description from Allen Dressler would be helpful. We know his work, he was with us for several years." Allen went through the structure of the database and how the queries, sorting and filtering were done. The FBI Director went to the Deputy Director of Counterintelligence, for recommendations.

"We have confirmed the facility is part of the Seward family owned business enterprise. It seems likely that Randall Seward may be involved with this place, he lives in the area. His rhetoric and involvement in white supremacists groups and antigovernment groups have become more volatile in the last few years. We have been monitoring him, we believe he is funding extremist groups, but he works with cash and has avoided leaving a paper or electronic trail. His potential involvement given this information from the OIG should be sufficient for warrants for his financial records, wire taps and monitoring his computer accounts. I recommend an immediate investigation out of the Seattle Field Office, led by supervisory agent Bryan Flannigan, and we would like the support of Mr. Eller in the field. Eller is responsible for the preliminary investigation methodology and his assistance would be helpful."

Bryan Flanigan was relieved. He could see Brandon had more expertise in this technical area than he did; they could definitely use his assistance. Andrea Jacobs responded, "I have discussed the possibility with IG Ross. We are happy to support the FBI."

The FBI Director brought the meeting to a conclusion, "Very good, thanks again to the OIG team. Agent Flanigan, we should plan on being on the ground next Monday. Please provide updates on anything of significance and if you need any additional support. I will direct the Seattle office to go ahead and get eyes on this place, until you arrive. They will stay out of sight, but if they see vans or trucks leaving, they will be instructed to seek SWAT assistance, and we will stop them."

After the briefing Andrea Jacobs introduced herself to Bryan Flanigan, "I hope you are good with Brandon coming onto the team in the field."

"I would have requested the assistance myself; I can see he has some real expert knowledge in this area; I have a BS in Chemistry and some basic training from DHS and the FBI."

Andrea smiled, "Brandon has a strong technical background, a master's degree in chemical engineering, and he worked in CW countermeasures at Guardian Chemical, and he has time at DHS on WMD. We are trying to further develop his investigative skills, we want him to be a top-notch investigator, please involve him in the investigation to the extent you can."

"I understand, a specialized investigative model like you guys set up for Michael Case in the nuclear proliferation cases the OIG ran. No problem, he seems to be on the right path, this is good work."

FBI Special Agent-In-Charge (SAIC) in Seattle, Carol Wood, answered her phone "Yes sir." She saw the number, it was the Director; it was 4:00 in DC and 1:00 in Seattle. The Director laid out the last few hours, a credible threat of a nerve gas facility near Sedro-Wooley; the facility inventory could support a large-scale domestic terrorism attack. A team at the State Department IG uncovered it and briefed them in DC in the last two hours. The facility was owned by Stellar Industries, she knew what this meant, the facility was likely controlled by Randall Seward.

When the Director used her first name, she knew this was serious, "Carol you need a top-notch team monitoring the site, by the end of the day. They should be ready to stay for the duration, under the supervision of Bryan Flannigan head of the Chemical and Biological weapons unit. He will arrive with the IG investigator who uncovered this facility on Monday. They will brief you on further details and then dispatch to Sedro-Wooley. Tell your team to keep their distance from the place until they get properly briefed by Flanigan. I think this is a substantial threat, the team needs to be invisible in Sedro-Wooley, choose them carefully with a basic cover." She chose Clara Spalding as the lead agent for the group from the Seattle office, they would all report to Flannigan when he arrived on site.

Chapter Four
The Rotten Apple

Murray and Flynn finally had the facility producing quality Tabun, and Murray asked Seward about the target. Seward looked around the restaurant making sure no one could hear, "The head of the cabal, Francesca Rains that dirty bitch; she is the head of the snake, she leads a group of shadow government Feds, looking to take over local government, town halls, take our guns and take personal property for the federal government. They want to redistribute land to darkies, Hispanics and Indians. She will be speaking in Seattle in January. You need to determine the amounts to kill everyone inside that speaking hall, that is our first target; we will cut the head off the snake along with those in league with her. Then we will find the next target and keep going until we eliminate every member of this secret shadow government." That was okay with them, they hated the liberal former secretary of state. There were rumors she might run for president.

Cameras the FBI team had put inside the facility weeks earlier allowed them to identify the six felons working inside, including two former chemistry professors Murray and Flynn. The six were living in rented homes in Sedro Wooley and had arrived a week after the FBI team. Brandon went with the team one night and collected chemical samples of the precursors, developed detailed diagrams and took photographs proving the facility was a nerve agent factory. Seward was careful and stayed away from the place and there was no electronic communication.

***

Clara told Brandon "Bryan wants us to find someone who will give up Randall Seward. It has to be either Murray or Flynn, the other four are just low-level help." Bryan Flannigan and SAIC Carol Wood knew time was running out to get Seward. The facility was fully operational and ready to start producing large quantities of Tabun.

They studied the files of Murray and Flynn closely for another hour. "Okay Brandon what do you think?"

"It needs to be Murray."

"Okay make your case."

"Basically, Flynn is a lost cause, starting with his crime it must have been racially motivated. The prosecution could not find direct proof of it at the time, but the university had complaints from several black students. And his victims, he wanted those people to suffer from the poison, enough so they would suffer but not be killed. His rhetoric on online sites had become more extreme and more frequent in recent years. Randall Seward found six true believers, but Flynn was by far the most outspoken and extreme in his views, and he previously used poison to torture people. Murray stole lab equipment and sold it to drug lords cooking meth. He is bad but much less extreme than Flynn. He is fifteen years younger and would be more interested in a deal that might shorten his prison time. I wouldn't be happy with him getting a deal but to get Seward it seems necessary; he is a better choice than Flynn. The other four have no direct dealings with Seward."

"I agree, we need to see if the Attorney General is willing to offer Harold Murray a plea bargain for cooperation. We will see what Bryan and the rest of the team think when you brief them, you will cover the proposal for a plea deal for Murray and the reasons."

Brandon finished the briefing; the team was all in agreement that was their best shot at getting Randall Seward. Bryan agreed, he had gotten an email from SAIC Wood that morning, she had six agents working on two shifts monitoring cell phones and computers around the clock. Her email was clear. She didn't think this was going to help them get Randall Seward; they were going to need something else. Bryan knew the plea deal was the best option they had given the urgency.

"Okay Brandon you write up a summary memo of what the charge would be and the supporting evidence to arrest and charge Harold Murray. A request for the Attorney General to provide a written plea bargain to get Murray's cooperation."

"Are you serious, this is really important."

"Absolutely, you wrote the affidavit for the search warrants, you should be able to do this. Have Clara review it before you send it to me for approval. We should send it to the Director of the FBI tomorrow by noon for urgent processing. You focus on this. There isn't anything going on at the facility."

Brandon did some research after dinner and started on the memorandum; he had the workroom to himself. He found the appropriate statutes and he summarized the elements for violations of 18 USC § 2232 which prohibits *uses, threats, attempts or conspiring* to use WMD including *any weapon that is designed or intended to cause death or serious bodily injury through the release, dissemination, or impact of toxic or poisonous chemicals, or their precursors* and also 18 USC § 842 *which prohibits the teaching or dissemination of information for the production of WMD* including the same definition for section 2232 for chemical weapons. Brandon described the factual basis of Harold Murray's violation of the statutes, his activities in the facility, manipulating controls, giving directions and he described the facility with the same evidence he used in the affidavit for the warrants. He summarized Murray's education and prior criminal record, the evidence of his white supremacists and anti-government views. Brandon knew that they need not wait for the actual production of the nerve gas to prove the crime of "attempt," it was sufficient to demonstrate actions beyond mere planning to support attempt charges under both statutes. These two violations, especially section 2232 and his felony record would result in severe penalties for Harold Murray. Sunday morning Brandon reviewed and finalized the document and made some edits and collected the evidence into a folder on the server.

Clara reviewed it, "this is really good, this is better than I could have done myself."

Brandon sent it to Bryan for review at 10:00 a.m. Bryan reviewed it, he made a few modifications and edits. Brandon had all of the essential elements. Bryan strengthened the evidence a bit for 2232 and signed the signature page, a memo to the Director of the FBI, copy the Assistant Director of the Counter terrorism division and SAIC Carol Wood. Urgent request for written plea offer, for Harold Murray.

Monday morning at 10:00 am Bryan received the email from the Director, a plea offer for Harold Murray signed by the Attorney General was attached. It was twenty pages long describing the charges and summarizing the evidence. It contained the sentencing recommendation of the Attorney General for Harold Murray, life in prison no parole before twenty years served. The recommendation was the top of the range of the sentencing guidelines for attempted use of WMD in domestic terrorism for someone with a previous felony. The document described the required full cooperation through the trial of the other five and Randall Seward. The last portion was the offer of a reduced sentence, ten years in protective custody and an offer for witness protection. The signature page was signed by the Attorney General with a line for Harold Murray's signature. Bryan thought this seemed like a good deal for Mr. Murray, they just needed to get him to bite.

Bryan brainstormed with Clara and then talked over their idea with SAIC Wood. She agreed. They sent a short text message to Harold

Murray on Monday afternoon titled debt relief, *the punishment for illegal manufacture of chemicals, life in prison. Get debt relief, see the red hat at Sedro Cafe & Market Tuesday 7:30 a.m.*

***

Murray told Flynn he was going into Sedro Cafe & Market. He wanted to get some breakfast and pick up some of his coffee blend. He would swing back around 9:00 and pick him up. There was a newspaper setting next to the man with a red hat and a coffee. The man got up as Murray approached. The man was Bryan Flannigan; he left a note on the paper, *gray SUV in five minutes if you want a deal.* By 8:30 Murray had signed the plea deal and had the two tiny microphones, one in the ball point pen they gave him and the other would activate using his cell-phone.

Flannigan told Murray to try and get Seward to reveal his target when the time was right. They didn't have time for detailed questions at the time, only to ask if Tabun had been shipped offsite. He said none had been sent offsite. They gave him instructions on using the listening devices and how to get the recordings to them using his laptop in the evenings when he was away from Flynn.

The investigators listened to the dinner meetings between the professors and Seward starting that Tuesday in small restaurants across town as they reported on testing. They heard Randall Seward demand a test killing cats; he wanted real proof. None of them were happy as they watched the preparations for the test and watched the animals die. They knew they finally had Randall Seward. After Seward watched the video of the animal killing on a mobile phone, they heard the recording as he named Francesca Rains as a target. They all laughed as Brandon spoke "we finally have that dirty rotten apple."

Clara looked at Brandon, "pretty harsh Brandon, dirty rotten apple really."

35

Chapter Five
What Do We Do Next

After days of planning, the FBI was ready with the arrest warrants. Along with US Marshalls, they were carried out early in the morning without incident. A few hours later the press release came out from FBI HQ. *The Federal Bureau of Investigation in cooperation with an investigator from the US State Department Office of the Inspector General arrested seven individuals involved in the production of Tabun nerve agent in Sedro Wooley in Washington State.* The press release gave the names of the seven in custody to be arraigned in federal court later that day and announced a press conference in Seattle at 10:00 a.m. SAIC Carol Wood spoke to reporters; there were lots of cameras. "Bryan Flannigan is the FBI supervisory agent in charge in the field from Washington DC. He has been working with six agents from the FBI Seattle Office and an investigator from the OIG at the Department of State. There was a large SWAT presence during the arrests; no shots were fired no injuries or casualties during the arrest. The US Marshalls have all seven individuals in custody. The facility was under surveillance for an extended time ensuring that no harm could come to the public as the team collected evidence against the group headed by Randall Seward. The Director of the FBI asked me to express our thanks to the US Marshalls service for assisting in the arrest and the US State Department Office of Inspector General. An investigative team at State OIG initially identified the threat and collaborated with the FBI, a model of federal agency collaboration."

Everyone in the State OIG was proud of Brandon, a written letter of commendation from the Director of the FBI came to the Inspector General. Bryan Flannigan called and gave Andrea Jacobs an overview of Bryan's role during the investigation, and he sent a follow-up email to Andrea and Michael Case thanking them for the support and praising the role of Brandon Eller. The entire IG community and federal law enforcement community was buzzing with the shocking news of the discovery of a nerve agent factory. Andrea Jacobs knew this was their breakout case for chemical weapons proliferation.

Kate Bucci had a moment of revenge during the team meeting when Brandon was back in the office. "I have a short presentation; I have some pictures from the agents in Sedro Wooley, Brandon Eller in action in the field."

She cut and pasted pictures of Brandon's face over the faces of pictures of famous fictional police from television series and movies with clever catch phrases from the characters. Everyone had a good laugh. Kate finished, "Good job Brandon, we are glad to have you back. We have been working on our reports, let's get back to work."

While Brandon was away, they had continued to work on the reports, but they were still not complete. The report on watchlists was issued in March; OIG identified 39 cases where entities on watchlists for potential links to terrorism had been granted import or export licenses for chemical precursors, without supporting justification. OIG reported that the watchlist being used by the State Department and Commerce Department were inconsistent, not updated on a frequent basis and the guidance to staff was unclear. Some staff members used public databases and never consulted classified watchlists. State Department officials said the primary responsibility for the watchlist review was the Commerce Department, and Commerce officials said the primary responsibility for watchlist reviews was the State Department.

The report for the production and inventory control schemes was issued in May; the interviews and field work confirmed what they had discovered during the preliminary investigation. The report identified

Crown Plastics in Georgia, Triumph Cleaning Solvents in Mississippi and Lone Star Solvents, Prairie Grass Pesticides and Four Squares Limited in Texas as manipulating production schemes to avoid facility declaration requirements under the Commerce Regulations for the Chemical Weapons Convention. The corporate officials essentially admitted the scheme was intended to stay below reporting thresholds but claimed the regulations did not prohibit the manipulation. The State Department and Commerce Department acknowledged that the facilities were receiving chemicals for which there was no business purpose, and reporting should be required. This would be further clarified in regulatory guidance. The Commerce Department was considering civil enforcement measures against the companies for reporting violations. The report summarized what was found at Stellar Industries in Washington State concluding that the Sedro Wooley facility had produced Tabun nerve agent in violation of the CWC, and that the US government had failed to declare the facility. Neither State Department nor Commerce officials reviewed the annual declaration reports to verify potential violations of reporting requirements. The report stated that individuals involved with the Sedro Wooley facility had been referred to the Federal Bureau of Investigation for criminal investigation. The individuals were not named in the State Department report or their specific charges, the OIG did not want to interfere in the criminal prosecution.

Michael Case felt the momentum for the chemical weapons proliferation investigations, the same as happened after the Pakistan nuclear proliferation report years ago. It was different now, he was the team leader. Brandon and Kate were working together like Michael and Tom Bradley had in the old X-ray team. There was one more big chemical weapons report before year end, the diversion of American chemicals to Syria and Libya, through a broker in Malaysia that was traced to Sarin production in both countries by US intelligence. The report was widely reported in the media, and there were congressional hearings. The report was recognized as the top investigative report of the year for the entire US government's inspector general community.

Inspector General Ross, Andrea and Michael were at the award ceremony as Brandon and Kate received the award for the office. There was a small reception in the OIG executive conference room; it was a prestigious award for the office. Andrea found Brandon, Michael and Kate in the X-ray conference room late that afternoon. Andrea sat down, "Quite a day, Inspector General Ross is really pleased with this investigation and what you all have done in the chemical proliferation area. People didn't expect much, supposedly everything was under control, but there are clearly countries who want these weapons."

Michael nodded, "Yes, the poor man's nuclear weapon proliferated to countries that want WMD's but cannot afford a program to develop nuclear weapons. Unfortunately, chemical precursors from the US are making their way to these places. Quite a job by the entire team, especially you two Brandon and Kate."

Kate smiled, "We had a good role model Michael. Andrea do you mind taking a picture of the three of us together."

Andrea smiled, "sure, right over there in front of the OIG seal." Kate and Brandon left after the picture, leaving Michael and Andrea alone. Andrea was proud of Michael, he had become an amazing team leader. She knew someone would probably offer him a bigger opportunity maybe sometime soon.

"Does this remind you of a time a few years ago, another time like this?"

Michael thought, "I'm not sure what you mean. We won three of these awards for our nuclear cases."

"I was thinking of the time when you and I met, in this conference room, and I talked to you about being team leader. The work we had been doing with the nuclear cases was the talk of the IG community then, and we talked about moving on to these chemical proliferation cases. You have really done a great job leading this team Michael, we need to think about the future for this team. It's been almost three years since we touched a nuclear proliferation case, what do we do next?"

Michael had been thinking about the nuclear proliferation cases as well, "I have been thinking about that a little bit. It makes me nervous sometimes. Remember what we said about taking our eyes off the ball? Now it's been almost three years. There is still a lot to do with the chemical proliferation cases. Maybe we develop a mixed profile of proactive cases next year."

"Okay that makes sense, do you think Brandon might be able to take your place if you were to leave?"

"Are you trying to get rid of me?"

"No, of course not, Michael. You are well known in government investigative circles now as an investigative leader, first with the nuclear proliferation cases now leading the team in the chemical proliferation area. You saw the article in the New York Press a few weeks ago about the work of the State Department Inspector General's Office. It was all about the Xray team and a lot about you. There were quotes from several inspector generals across the community and even the FBI director. Don't be surprised if someone comes to you with even a bigger opportunity to serve. IG Ross and I will not stand in your way."

Michael smiled, "Brandon would do well; I don't have any plans to leave. It would be good to give him; a nuclear case to help develop him, let me think on that for next year."

Two months later in February, Michael was in the office on a Saturday morning working in the X-ray conference room. He was trying to finalize a proactive investigation plan for the second quarter; he wanted to find a nuclear proliferation angle. He was struggling and was looking back through old case files; he didn't want to repeat anything they had already done. Andrea came in, "I thought I saw you earlier coming down the hall; working on a Saturday something big?"

"No, just trying to come up with a proactive nuclear angle for next quarter. Thought it would be quiet, and I could look through some old files. I'm just about done. I have some rough ideas. What about you?"

"I have a briefing on Capitol Hill next week for the Office. I needed to brief myself up on the budget information. I was just getting ready to leave. Okay if I have some coffee, just half a cup?"

"Sure, let me get it."

"Thanks Michael. Did you see the announcement yesterday from that Yale professor, Larson, going to run for president? I'm not a political junkie, but it would be good to see a little more civility in the campaign. Maybe an outsider from academia will help."

Michael nodded, "I don't pay much attention to politics. I did see the announcement, talking heads said he doesn't have a chance."

Andrea laughed, "You are getting ready to marry a congressman's daughter, and you don't pay attention to politics."

Andrea remembered Michael's engagement, "I still can't get over you proposing in the south cafeteria like that; that was not something I expected from Michael Case. You two dated in college, right, and then she moved back to DC years later, and you started dating again, what are the odds of that, not very likely."

She finished her coffee, "Well I need to get out of here. Don't stay much longer; see you Monday."

"See you, have a good weekend, Andrea."

Michael thought about what Andrea said; what were the odds of that. He drank his coffee thinking back to how it started with Marion in May two years ago, only two months after he had become team leader. Michael had not seen Marion Bartley for four years; there she was sitting across the table from him in the South Cafeteria at the State Department. He thought she was living in Chicago, a lawyer for a big law firm?

She looked at him, "Aren't you even going to say hello."

Marion was wearing a visitor's badge; she reached over and took a French fry off his plate just like she used to do at Harry's at Purdue. "Sorry Marion, I'm just surprised to see you. What are you doing here?"

"I'm living in DC now; here at State for a meeting. I haven't seen you since you moved out of my parents' house four years ago."

Congressman Bartley had insisted Michael live in his garage apartment when he first moved to Washington DC when he first went to work at the OIG, he lived there for nearly two years. The Bartley's would have been happy for him to stay, but he needed to move out onto his own. He had lived with them when Congressman Bartley got him an internship on Capitol Hill two summers in college.

She continued, "I went to work for Trawley and Smith in their Chicago Office after law school; I'm specializing in immigration law and international property rights. I transferred to the Washington DC offices a few weeks ago. There is a public meeting on some new state department regulations for transfer of intellectual property. I'm living with my parents for a few months until I can find my own place. Maybe you could come over for dinner this weekend, we can catch up. Mom and dad would love to see you."

She stole another French fry as she got up and gave him a business card, "Do you have one?"

"Investigative Supervisor, very good Michael."

He noticed she wasn't wearing a wedding ring, and she noticed he wasn't wearing one either. Michael called Marion that Friday; he would like to see her parents again, it had been a while. Lydia and Raymond were excited when they heard Michael was coming over. Lydia hoped there was still a spark between those two. Marion needed to settle down now she was nearly thirty. It would be nice to have a grandchild some-time in the near future. There was still a spark. They would get married in Bloomington Indiana in April nearly two years later, nearly ten years after they first met in college.

Chapter Six
Son of a Cleric

Feisel Mohammad Ramul was born in Tehran, the son of a Shia cleric, a follower of the radical Ayatollah Khomeini who had published a book "Clarification of Points of Sharia." His father Feisel Abdul Ramul stayed behind when Khomeini was exiled to Iraq in 1965. His father was a young man and had just obtained the rank to collect some of his own followers; he would never make the rank of Ayatollah. Feisel Abdul became important not for his mastery of theology or great oratory skills, he was not so gifted. He did coordinate a large cell of Khomeini's followers while he was in exile from 1965 until February 1979. For those 14 years his father would hold secret meetings, teaching from the Clarification of Points of Sharia to audiences of around 20, but they really came to listen to the smuggled tapes of the lectures of the Ayatollah. He traveled all over southern Tehran with the tapes, putting himself at risk that the Savik might capture him and throw him in jail.

Feisel Mohammad had studied the Quran in his childhood, from when he was eight years old until he was fifteen with tutors from friends of his father. He didn't get the same messages that his father and his followers constantly espoused; they talked about the importance of women covering themselves, the grave sins of homosexuality, sex before marriage, the gateway sins of dancing and music. They preached fear and punishment and seemed to enjoy it, castigating their followers to be careful of the path to face Allah at judgement day. They also were obsessed with the Shah, the evil form of government, the foreign influences and their country and the need for Islamic rule taught by the great Ayatollah Khomeini. Feisel went to Tehran University to study physics and lived on the campus. He loved his mother, she was a gentle soul.

When she talked about the Quran, she talked about the messages that appealed to Feisel, not the fire and brimstone of his father.

When he was in secondary school, his mother was always awake before him. He would find her reading the Quran, and she would have him sit and eat breakfast. He walked to school, it was close, and she insisted on a good breakfast to start each day, and she always gave him a verse for the day. She would write in on a piece of paper and put it into his snack bag, with fruits and small sweets. She said snacks for the body and food for his soul to enrich his life. As an adult he remembered many of the passages that were favorites of his mother. Even as a grown man he had many of these original small sheets of paper, some of the favorites he had saved in his mother's own written hand. *Do not confound the truth by mixing it up with falsehood and do not knowingly conceal the truth.* This one in particular he carried in his small change purse. Since his college days he was sure that Ayatollah Khomeini, his father and most of the radical clerics and leaders in the Iranian government had failed to heed this important mandate.

His mother had many favorites, messages of love and hope. *"Kind and forgiving words are better than charity followed by harm. God is self-sufficing, most forbearing." "Good and evil are not equal. Repel evil with good and you will find that your enemy has become your close friend." "The true servants of the merciful God are those who walk on the earth in humility and when the ignorant people address them, they reply, peace be upon you"*. Feisel was sure that his father and his followers were wrong, the Imams and the Ayatollah were not infallible, and he was sure the teachings in Clarification of Points of Sharia was mostly nonsense, a selfish attempt to grab power by Khomeini. He never told his father about his views other than once late in his first year of university, he had read some lectures of a moderate Imam written years earlier, critical of Khomeini, he baited his father when he was home one weekend. He asked his father if the Quran actually instructed that Imam's were infallible; his father spouted off the cherry-picked verses and the Hadith's that supported this view. He then asked his father about the teachings of the moderate Imam's who opposed the views of Khomeini; asking how can they both be infallible when they are in such disagreement, they are both Imam's. He knew that his father had a bad temper, but this was the first time he saw the explosive nature of his father's temper, he threw a glass pitcher of water across the room shattering and called him a heretical liar. His father came at him with a piece of the broken glass screaming curses. They scuffled as he knocked the glass from his father's hand. Since secondary school, he had come to see his father as someone obsessed with the sins of others, but not violent or evil in any sense. Once Feisel went away to university his father's personality seemed to become darker with outbursts of temper, and when he would come home his father would spend his time locked in his study and in town at meetings with Imams under his supervision.

His first year of graduate school he was home on the weekend and saw that his mother had a blackened eye. She would not say why; he found out from a neighbor that his father had beat her for going into the courtyard without covering her face. His father had begun to lose control of his temper, and he was starting to hit Afshan more frequently, and it was beginning to damage her. Feisel tried to talk to her, but she denied it and said she was getting old and falling down. She had a broken arm and cracked ribs that were never treated in a hospital, and he began to fear for her life. He filed an anonymous tip with the local police. They came by the home and saw it was Imam Feisel. If she was being punished, that was the work of Allah, who were they to interfere. He confronted his father and told him he needed psychiatric treatment. His father said that these were the words of Satan, the same as his mother his father was screaming saying the two of them were being controlled by demons. He could see his father was becoming more irrational, and he was becoming dangerous.

His mother's family was not in Tehran. She had met her father while studying in Tehran. Afshan was very close to her older sister Jasmin, and she came to stay with them for a few days when Feisel was in graduate school. Jasmin was like Afshan deeply religious, but her views of the Quran were not those of Afshan's husband; she had always been uncomfortable with his support of the radical Khomeini, but they held the power in the country now, it was not wise to speak up against them. She was disturbed, her normally cheerful sister seemed depressed and her sister's husband's behavior was strange. She never liked him, but now he seemed to be somewhat unstable, brooding and locked himself in his small study for hours and went out late for meetings. Afshan finally confessed to Jasmin what had happened, when Feisel Mohammad went to university his first year. Her husband had been given the authority of southern Tehran, reporting directly to the Ayatollah Rasmani responsible for all of Tehran, a close ally of the Ayatollah Khomeini. Rasmani had come to their home to meet with her husband, but he was running late, he called to say he would be another 40 minutes. She went to the kitchen to make tea; Rasmani came behind her and threatened her with a knife and fondled her in the kitchen. He told her no one would believe her; he would say she had offered herself to him and he had rejected her. She laid in the bedroom crying while Rasmani and her husband met in the study. She went to her husband after Rasmani left, her husband refused to believe his wife. He accused her of adultery saying that Rasmani was a good man, Allah's servant, he said Satan had possessed her and Rasmani had been seduced, it was her sin. There was no one they could go to, the police were controlled by the clerics. When Feisel Mohammad came home that weekend to see his Aunt Jasmin, she told him the story, although she had promised Afshan she would not. Jasmin hoped that Feisel Mohammad may be able to convince her sister to leave her husband. Afshan refused to leave her husband and live with Jasmin's family.

His mother's torment ended his last year of graduate school, his father was robbed and stabbed on the way home one evening and died in the streets. Feisel was contacted in his dorm room on campus by the local police the next morning; he needed to come home, there had been a terrible attack on his father. The police never caught the man. People said they saw someone on a bicycle riding towards the west out of the city. His wallet and watch were taken as well as the collections purse for the mosque, which was probably the reason for the robbery. Feisel felt guilty for his emotions after his father's murder; he mostly felt relief, relief that his mother was safe and would not be subject to any more physical abuse. His father had kept a large silver frame in his office, a picture of his father with Ayatollah Khomeini and Ayatollah Rasmani. A week after his father was stabbed, Feisel Mohammad stayed to work late in the metallurgy laboratory, he had already burned the picture and had carried the broken silver frame in his backpack. He sawed the frame into small cubes and melted the sterling silver into a crucible in the furnace. He poured it into a mold shaped in Farsi calligraphy عدالت (Justice). He had bought the mold at a local artisan's shop. He would keep this paperweight with him for his entire life at his desk and pray to Allah that he would find justice for what had happened to his mother. He also believed his father had suffered mentally, for what had been done to his mother. Feisel graduated later that year and went to work. His mother's health was better, and she was more cheerful. As the physical and mental scars began to heal, she moved away to live with her sister Jasmin. When Afshan was safe at her sister's home, Jasmin called and filed an allegation with the Tehran police; she did not give her name only that Imam Rasmani was sexually assaulting women in Tehran. The police traced her phone number, some old lady 300 km away, they wrote her name down and filed the document as not credible and did nothing to investigate.

Feisel Abdul Ramul was mourned as a martyr and his mother received a widow's allotment and Feisel Mohammad was labeled the son of great cleric, the son of a Martyr. Feisel Mohammad listened to the praise of Ayatollah Rasmani, for his father on the local radio, the man who had molested his mother. Feisel had long felt uncomfortable with his father's brand of Islam. Focused on sin and retribution, he had not lost his faith, he accepted a different version of the faith. He knew there were radical Sunni zealots and radical Christian and Jewish zealots as well. It was not unique to Shia Islam, driven by blind simple-minded literal reading of ancient documents or manipulation of religious text for personal power and benefit. The struggle for his journey of faith was the admonition to forgive. He could not bring himself to forgive Rasmani and Khomeini. He saw Rasmani to be a product of Khomeini and the government radical clerics, who chanted about the great Satan of America. Certainly, the Shah and Americans had done great damage to Iran, but Feisel was sure that the system created by Khomeini their rigid moral views, their meddling in government and their criticism of Sunni Muslims was as bad as the Shah. He could not forgive he would find retribution, he realized this would be his biggest barrier on judgment day, his stubborn insistence on revenge he would need to find a way to make it just. He would be patient and find the means and opportunity.

PART TWO

Phantom in the Desert

Chapter Seven
Another Story from a Whistleblower

Michael was in early on Monday, he wanted to study through his notes from working the past Saturday. He needed to come up with a proactive nuclear case for next quarter. Andrea and he had agreed they needed to get the team back into some nuclear cases this year. He looked through his notes from the old nuclear cases and the ideas he had for new investigative angles. Brandon and Kate were working on two new chemical proliferation cases, and Sheri and Allen were busy developing a large-scale database to support one of the cases. He put his coffee down thinking of the best direction, he saw the brochure for cabin rentals on the corner of his desk. He needed to make plane reservations for the honeymoon, get a rental SUV and reserve the cabin. They had agreed on a relaxing honeymoon in the mountains in Maine and Michael promised Marion he would take care of the details. It was February, he only had two months he didn't want the good cabins to be gone; he would take care of it before he left today. He put a yellow sticky on his computer, *reservations before leaving.*

The phone rang, "Michael Case, OIG Investigations."

"Yes, Mr. Case I have information involving a middle eastern country and leaks of classified material."

"Okay, what can you tell me?"

"Not over the phone, can we meet, somewhere outside of government offices?"

"Okay, what's your name?"

"Can we wait till we meet please sir?"

"Okay, do you know the bookstore grill near Georgetown university, 1:00."

"I will find it, thank you sir."

Michael hung up the phone, just what I need another whistleblower, secret information and a clandestine meeting. What will it be this time, another crackpot or disgruntled employee?

The man came to the table "Are you Michael Case?"

The guy looked familiar, Michael shook his head, "Yes".

The man sat down, "can my identity remain confidential?"

"Yes, you can give information to me confidentially."

"My name is Arthur Larson, I'm an officer in the US Navy in the Judge Advocate General."

It clicked the son of the guy who just announced he was running for president last week; he had seen Arthur Larson in the news clips of the announcement. "Your father just announced he is running for president, the professor from Yale."

"That's right, I am especially concerned about confidentiality with my father in the public light. If it is absolutely necessary for me to come forward in a hearing, I will do my duty. I just cannot imagine it will be necessary."

Michael nodded, "okay let's order some coffee, I will take notes and you tell me what you know. I will use our confidential sources system to protect your identity, but you realize that it is possible others may discover you have given us information."

"Yes, I understand how it works, I have been careful coming here. I have been TDY in Bahrain 5th Fleet working with NCIS agents on allegations of leaks of classified information. Last November I was approached by a naval officer who claimed to have information involving a state department employee and energy department employee, he had met them on leave in Abu Dhabi. This was not part of the leak investigation. The officer claims to have met the two guys at the beginning of two weeks leave, they ended up as drinking friends hitting the same expat bar. One evening they went back to the hotel where these guys are staying, to drink and watch basketball on SportTV. According to the naval officer, the energy department guy passes out as soon as they get to the room and the state department guy starts bragging about the trips they take to a big villa in the desert every time they come to Abu Dhabi. Says they meet with some Saudis at some huge villa in Abu Dhabi, relatives of the Saudi King. Says there are prostitutes, and they shoot rifles and handguns in the desert behind the villa, an awesome party. The naval officer thinks it's just bull. Why would Saudi Royals be hanging out with these guys, so he asks how they met the Saudis. The state department guy says they want the files, the specifications and drawings and stuff, all on external hard drives. The navy officer is curious, and asked drawings for what? The state department guy tells him everything they need that's what the secretary of state wants, give them everything they want for enrichment centrifuges. The Navy officer doesn't ask anything else; he is worried about what these guys may be up to, and he gets out of there; he doesn't go near that bar again. He found me when he gets back to Bahrain because I am in the JAG. He gave me the story and the names they gave him; he said he doesn't know what they are doing, but it didn't sound right, and he knew enrichment centrifuges are nuclear."

Larson took a drink of coffee and sat the cup down, "It took me a while, but I found out who they are, Franklin Williams—Department of State and Shawn Harrison—Department of Energy National Nuclear Security Administration. Williams is a senior policy adviser who reports to the chief of staff for the Secretary of State, and Shawn Harrison-Department of Energy National Nuclear Security Administration, working on special assignment at the Department of State assigned to Secretary of State's office."

"I tracked down the navy officer and showed him the two guys personnel pictures, he confirmed that's who he met in Abu Dhabi. I confirmed all three were in the United Arab Emirates the last two weeks of October just like he told me. Here are their names and pictures, including the naval officer. This is everything I know about this. I know that centrifuges can be used to enrich uranium, but this isn't my jurisdiction, and I have heard about your team. Like I said I prefer to be left out, but if I need to testify to what I have heard under oath, I will do it."

Michael Case looked through his notes, "I cannot think of anything else; you have done a good job of covering the essentials. I will track you down if I need more information from you, but it doesn't seem likely since you have everything second hand anyway, and you have given me the key details. Thank you for coming forward with this information; I will advise you of the results when we complete the investigation."

"Thank you, Mr. Case, it's my obligation to report this. I couldn't just ignore it. I realize it's really thin. I don't need to hear the results of your investigation."

Michael nodded, "It's our process, and I feel obligated to close the loop."

Michael thought as he sat in the metro on the way back to the office, this guy wasn't like most whistleblowers; he doesn't seem to have any agenda, but there isn't much to go on. Michael got back in his office. It was still early afternoon when he confirmed the navy officer and the names and positions of Williams and Harrison and their personnel photographs, matched what Larson gave him. This is really thin, some drunks telling a navy guy that two men who work for the Secretary of State are giving drives full of drawings and specifications for centrifuges to Saudi officials in a villa in Abu Dhabi. Michael knew this wasn't something to charge into; he went directly to talk to George and used his notes to replay what Arthur Larson told him. George set up a meeting with Andrea and Inspector General Ross immediately, that afternoon. George did not attend, he knew this was sensitive. The IG would decide if he needed his help on this issue. Michael replayed the conversation again with his notes and the little bit he had confirmed.

Inspector General Ross leaned forward, "Hmm, this is thin really thin, it doesn't seem like a JAG officer like Larson is going to lie. What did he seem like to you?"

"A JAG officer obligated as a naval officer and attorney to provide this information to a competent authority, very credible."

Ross continued, "we don't know about this navy officer that went to Larson and who knows about a couple of government employees drunk in Abu Dhabi. The Saudis after nuclear technology covertly, doesn't that sound strange?"

Michael had been thinking the same thing, "Yes sir, there is not a whisper about the Saudis pursuing nuclear weapons, which is the only reason they would pursue enrichment technology covertly. It doesn't make sense to me. But you know we haven't been watching the nuclear proliferation area with proactive cases for almost three years."

IG Ross shook his head in agreement, "Potential misconduct of senior State Department Officials is squarely in the jurisdiction of this Office and the Energy Department employee is detailed and working at State. I do not see how we can simply ignore this, if there is anything to this at all it could be significant. We cannot start a formal investigation, Michael, I want you work this under the direction of Andrea, a preliminary investigation to determine whether a credible foundation exists to initiate a formal investigation. Document your work outside the investigative database, let's see if there is anything to this story. Keep this very quiet, we don't want word out that we are investigating people in the

Secretary of State's office for leaking classified nuclear information and Saudi Arabia is our regional ally."

Michael and Andrea walked into Andrea's office and went to the sitting area putting their cups down on the coffee table, Andrea got the coffee pot and freshened their coffees, they both were thinking of the next step. Michael went first, "Well all we have are these two in the Secretary's Office, I can't start there. Maybe the best thing to do is evaluate the credibility of the underlying story, could Saudi Arabia be pursuing nuclear technology covertly. I need background and a historical perspective. I need to talk with Steve Thomas."

"Okay, but Thomas cannot know the specific allegations, we cannot have a State Department Official involved in an OIG investigation of potential wrongdoing involving senior officials at State. We don't want him to know we have anything specific on the Saudis. I will tell George we are handling this outside the formal case reporting structure for now, we will involve him, if necessary, the fewer people involved the better."

Michael finished the allegation intake memo and generated a confidential source identification for Arthur Larson. He was ready to leave when he saw the yellow sticky. He sat back down and looked at the brochure and got on their website looking for cabins, they wanted something kind of remote but well-furnished. They weren't looking for a camping experience for their honeymoon.

Chapter Eight
Saudi Arabia and AQ Khan's Network

Michael called Steve Thomas the day after briefing the IG and Andrea. "Steve, I have something very confidential, I'm interested in the history of any efforts of Saudi Arabia for a nuclear weapons program."

"Bloody hell Michael, you guys haven't touched nuclear proliferation for three years, and you call me out of the blue with a strange question like that; now if you asked me about Argentina starting back up or the Russians giving weapon components to Bulgaria I might understand, but really Saudi Arabia."

"Steve I wasn't looking for a fight, I just had a question and was looking for some information from a historic perspective."

"Okay sorry, I just wish you guys would get back in the game on nuclear. I know chemical weapons are important, but we need your team. Anyway, back to your question about the Saudis, nobody has been talking about a credible concern in Saudi Arabia for more than a decade, kind of ancient history going back to the Khan network. I did read an interesting paper by a lady here at the State Department last year. I have met her, Dr. Gulshan Wallace. She is a historian and an expert on the region. She bases her views on international relations and a historical perspective, very smart with original ideas. Her paper acknowledges there is no supporting intelligence for some of her views that challenge the mainstream. I heard it ruffled some feathers at CIA and DIA."

"I wrote a briefing paper a few years back on the history of proliferation and there are some mentions of Saudi Arabia. I can send that to you, I wouldn't spend too much time on this. It seems unlikely to be a current concern."

"Okay, send me your paper Steve, I will get back to you if I need more information."

Steve Thomas hung up the phone puzzled by the query from Michael. The OIG team had moved away from nuclear proliferation the last few years, Thomas thought it very curious indeed. He was getting near the end of his career. He was struggling to remain optimistic about proliferation, hoping that breakthroughs in policy or politics would help reverse the trends in proliferation. The most positive progress in the last decade was due to the IG team with Andrea Jacobs and Michael Case. Their reports prompted a number of important improvements in US procedures. They had moved on to chemical weapons proliferation and did good work, but Thomas wanted them back in the nuclear game. The technology and capability for proliferation seemed most likely to accelerate in the future, and the US could only do so much. He had told many colleagues over the years he had expected to see the use of another nuclear weapon in his lifetime, 50-50 chance if he lived to be 85; nothing had changed his views on that assessment.

Michael opened the email from Thomas with a copy of the briefing document. The email directed Michael to focus on sections throughout that implicate potential Saudi involvement and the hub of activity in nearby Dubai. Michael had not remembered these aspects of the AQ Khan network. He noted the details, AQ Khan travelled to Dubai 41 times during the nuclear proliferation network, illegal nuclear financial transactions were coordinated in Dubai, delivery and fabrication of enrichment equipment and designs in Dubai, presence of highly enriched uranium in Dubai, a nuclear warhead design in a Dubai apartment, Saudi and Emirati royalty meeting with AQ Khan and interacting with the network. This was a lot of circumstantial evidence pointing to Saudi interest in nuclear weapons and Dubai as an important hub of illicit nuclear trade dating back more than 20 years. He needed to meet with

Steve Thomas to discuss this further; he also was interested in what Dr. Gulshan Wallace might have to say. He went to see Andrea. He wanted to have a meeting with Thomas and Wallace.

Andrea knew who Dr. Gulshan Wallace was, "She has an excellent reputation; we can trust her. Make it clear to both of them we want this to remain completely confidential. We don't want anyone to know we are even looking at the background of nuclear weapons in Saudi Arabia."

Michael called Dr. Gulshan Wallace; she was worried, "Inspector General's office. Am I in some sort of trouble Mr. Case?"

"No Dr. Wallace, I am doing background research. I would like to meet with you and Steve Thomas, but it is highly confidential. It will probably take a half day or more. Do you know Steve Thomas?"

"Yes, well I have met him. He is very well respected and he is very direct I like that, he will be there? Are you sure I am not in some type of trouble? I really don't want to be a source; I am not aware of any wrong-doing or crimes."

"Listen, call Steve, I have worked with him on background research before; ask him what his experience has been."

Gulshan talked to Steve Thomas. She felt better Thomas assured her that Michael Case was a straight shooter. He said Michael led the team that did the nuclear proliferation reports. She thought she had heard the name, the nuclear proliferation investigator; she heard they were working on chemical weapons now. She wondered why Michael Case would want to talk to her.

Gulshan Wallace had never been in the Inspector General's office. Michael Case was younger than she expected, probably ten years younger than her. The conference room in the executive suite of the OIG was very comfortable with nice views out large windows. There was coffee, tea, diet sodas and donuts. She felt more relaxed this didn't look like an interrogation. A few minutes later Steve Thomas came in, and they were all sitting at the table ready to start.

Michael explained, "This is not part of an active investigation. I am doing background research; however the subject matter is very confidential and, I need your agreement not to discuss the subject of this meeting with anyone. Do you understand Dr. Wallace?"

"Yes, I understand, please call me Gulshan."

"Okay and call me Michael. I will take notes as we go. We also have a white board and flip charts. Think of me as your student and you are my professors."

Steve Thomas laughed, "Well I might be old enough, but not Gulshan."

"Okay my tutors then. I would like this to be an interactive dialog. I am interested in both of your views about the possibility Saudi Arabia has pursued nuclear weapons in the past, and whether they still may be pursuing them."

Gulshan was excited but surprised, "Awesome, really you are interested in the Saudis and nuclear weapons. But I am not technical, Steve can tell you all about the technical history of what they have done. Do you really want to hear my views based on international relation dynamics and the history of the region?"

Michael smiled, "I definitely want your viewpoint, Steve suggested we get your views. As an investigator I am always interested in motive, why people do things. I suspect your insights will reveal much about the possible motives of the Saudis."

Steve Thomas nodded in agreement, "I am interested in hearing your views Gulshan. I read your paper from last year, characterizing Saudi and Iran as a regional cold war on the verge of going nuclear. Maybe you could walk us through that outline, to get started, if that's okay with Michael."

Michael agreed, "Sure, sounds like a great place to start."

Gulshan, walked to the white board, "where do you want me to start; how much do you know about the history of the relationship between Iran, Saudi Arabia and the US; how much time do we have?"

Michael could see her enthusiasm, "We have lots of time, you can assume I don't know anything I'm not sure about Steve."

"I have always regretted how little I learned in high school world history and am ashamed of my own ignorance. What I know I have gotten through the filter of the media. Take us back to school Gulshan."

She wrote on the board *Regional Power Struggle*, as she introduced her thesis "Saudi Arabia and Iran each see themselves as the natural regional power in the middle eastern region from the Mediterranean in the west to Afghanistan in the east. Iran's national identity built on their great Persian history, one of the great ancient empires in the world. Saudis national identity is much different, a short history of Bedouin cunning and survival and their relationship with the world's superpower the United States."

She wrote *Religion—the Shia and Sunni Divide.*

"I cannot emphasize how much this drives the relationship between Saudi Arabia and Iran. Iran is majority Shia and Saudi majority Sunni, an underlying divide helping fuel a regional cold war in the last few decades. Similar to how communism and ideological differences between the US and USSR drove the early days of the global cold war for forty-five years after World War Two. There was a growing intensity of the competition, with conflicts in proxy wars in surrounding countries."

Steve Thomas was interested, "Is it okay if I ask questions as we go?"

Gulshan shook her head, "Michael is it okay with you; this is your meeting?"

"Yes, absolutely I am interested in the full picture and a dialog."

Steve Thomas continued, "I have never really understood, why is it so intense and what is the background of the religious aspect of the relationship between the two countries."

"First of all, both countries are very different than the United States; there is no separation between church and state; Islam is part of the government; it is imbedded in their policy and politics. Are you willing to hear a bit of old history?"

Thomas was shaking his head, "Absolutely." Michael was nodding in agreement.

"The Prophet Mohammad Peace Be Upon Him died in 632, Abu Bakr was selected by the prophets trusted circle of followers as the one to be the leader, the Caliph of the faith, but he died only two years later of natural causes. Abu Bakr had nominated Omar ibn Khattab as his successor. Abu Bakr's cousin Ali ibn Abi Talib was favored by one group of supporters. They were disappointed by the selection as was Talib, but he accepted the decision. In 644 Omar was stabbed by an Iranian slave; before dying Omar named an electoral college of six to select the next Caliph. The council first approached Ali Talib and required as one condition that he honor all previous precedents and religious decisions of the Caliphate; Talib refused saying that only the Quran should serve as the basis of faith and not these decisions of men. The council went to Uthman ibn Affan. He accepted the condition and was named leader of the Caliphate. In 656 soldiers attack Uthman at his home and he is killed, rebels and local supporters endorse Ali Talib as the new head of the Caliphate. They call themselves supporters of Ali the Shia Ali the founding roots of the Shia. Another large group of followers of the prophet rejected a Caliph *born of murder* and demanded that the Caliphate be led by a lineage of Abu Bakr Omar and Uthman. They advocated for a leader that was close to Uthman, and they referred to themselves as Ahl al Sunna, People of the Path, the early Sunni."

"This divide and the *murder* are still engrained in modern Iranian and Saudi relations. There are an estimated 1.6 billion Muslims worldwide, only an estimated ten percent Shia feel castigated by the majority, as heretics ever since the *murder*. Nearly ninety percent of all Shia's are in Iran and the religious leadership of the country believes they have an obligation to protect the religious minority throughout the region. The Shia and Sunni creeds share three principles: monotheism, communication to Allah through the Prophet Muhammad and the resurrection and judgment of souls on the last day. There are also some significant doctrinal differences between the Shia and Sunni creeds. The Shia creed holds that only those in the lineage of the Prophet can govern on behalf of Allah, and Imams are divinely inspired and infallible. Sunni's see these principles as heretical, only Allah and the Quran are infallible. For some Sunni's even the Prophet Muhammad's Hadith's are subject to question, only the Quran was the direct word of Allah to the Prophet."

"These doctrinal differences affect the structure of government and the role of religious clerics in each country. The Ayatollah Khomeini exaggerated the original Qur'anic teachings, to create a theocracy with the Ayatollah as Supreme leader supervising and guiding the government in Iran. In Saudi Arabia, the religious leaders work in partnership with government, with leading positions appointed by the King of Saudi Arabia. The general view is the clergy works at the direction of the government in Saudi, if they want to keep their appointed positions. The Iranian Shia clergy preaches that the government headed by a King is heretical. The hardliners in both countries claim the other to be heretics, sometimes boiling over into rhetoric from senior officials, more frequently from the religious leaders in Iran. There are also many public statements from high-ranking Saudi Royals and clerics repeating common caricatures of Shia, with forked tails hidden under the robes and mixed sex religious meetings being used for orgies, giving birth to disciples of Satan. Although both countries claim Islam as the national religion, the specific sects are identified in their legal documents."

She sat down and drank her coffee.

Michael heard several things that piqued his interest, "Gulshan, you mentioned Ayatollah Khomeini and the Shah. I remember some of that from Modern American history class in high school; they took over the US Embassy. Before then Iran was our ally."

Steve Thomas laughed, "My gosh you are a youngster, I was a teen-ager when the embassy got overrun, and I didn't understand it at the time. I remember one of my teachers saying they were crazy religious fanatics. I have never really understood what drove them to take our embassy; diplomatic relations have never been restored since then. I suspect it was more than just religious zealotry."

Gulshan shook her head, "You are right Steve. Most Americans don't realize religion was only a small piece of what drove that revolution with the overthrow of the Shah and the boiling anger at the United States. It was really a middle class uprising. Michael not only were they our ally, they were our biggest ally in the region. President Nixon called them our policeman in the middle east, what a difference from today."

Michael was interested, "How about a little on this. This must be relevant to the relationship between Saudi Arabia and Iran right?"

Gulshan got up and went back to the white board, she wrote *Americans and the Iranian Revolution,* "You are correct, the dynamics between the three countries, Iran, Saudi Arabia and the United States is the defining force in the Persian Gulf. Iran is like Egypt, with millennia of history of the Persian empire and its proud culture of architecture, language, art and science. By the early 1920s the country was suffering from decades of incompetent and corrupt rule of the Qajar dynasty; some believed that the country was on the verge of collapse. There were many young proud patriotic and nationalist leaders who felt that foreign powers, especially Britain had exploited the country as well as Russia. Reza Khan Pahlavi prompted by British diplomats led a coup starting in February 1921 he occupied Tehran leading 1200 men in revolt. In 1925 Reza Khan was named Shah-en-Shah (king of kings), and he started on a path to modernize the country and reduce the authority of religious leaders seeking a secular state. He inaugurated Tehran University in 1934. His son would even more aggressively advance development in the country and focus on a secular state. Reza Khan was forced out in 1941 by the allied forces, his son Mohammad Reza Pahlavi succeeding him in power, he would rule until the Iranian revolution in 1979. He is the one commonly referred to as the Shah. In 1947 legislation was introduced into the Iranian parliament the Majli', it called for securing national rights including the natural wealth of the southern oil fields."

"There were growing feelings of nationalism and concerns about British exploitation. Then stories came out in 1947 about the profits from the Anglo Iranian oil company, approximately 110 million USD in revenue with Iran receiving only about ten percent. The growing middle class was enraged, and the National Front coalition headed by Muhammad Mussadiq led the push for nationalization of the oil resources of the country. Mussadiq was elected to the Majli; he succeeded in leading the effort in nationalization of the oil industry and the formation of National Iranian Oil company. The Majli chose him as prime minister and the Shah reluctantly appointed him to office. Mussadiq influence continued to grow, and he was seen as a challenge to the Shah. The potential for a coup forced the Shah to flee to Rome in August 1953. The United States CIA and British Intelligence coordinated a coup with military loyalist of Reza Khan, placing Mohammad Reza back on the peacock throne only three days after he left. The United States denied involvement in the Coup until about twenty years ago. But the Iranian middle class at the time believed the American's had interfered in their domestic politics, and they were right."

"The Shah approved a new agreement in 1959 allowing increased US intelligence access in Iran and greater intrusion of American influence into Iranian life, working in collaboration with the Shah and his advisers. This was a foothold for the American government in the middle east to oppose Soviet influence, the most important ally along with Israel and Saudi Arabia. In the early and mid-1970s the Iranian military was growing in strength, and economy was growing. The Shah had visions of grandeur declaring the Iranian security perimeter covered the entire Persian Gulf and extended into the northwestern Indian Ocean. US policy makers in the 1960s made a decision that Iran was the stronger of the potential allies when compared to Saudi Arabia, with five times the population, better educated and more skilled workforce. This is how Iran became the closest ally of the US in the region, our policeman, but it would come crashing down in less than twenty years."

"In the middle and late 1970s religious messages were merging with complaints about the Shah's government. These views appealed to the huge middle class, frustrated with foreign influence in the country, oppression of religious practices, the Shahs political corruption, oppression and abusive secret police. Demonstrations and strikes began cropping up. The media under the control of the Shah began to attack Khomeini which further inflamed the middle class; the unrest grew as the economy slowed down. The sermons and lectures continued, and the Shah's cabinet announced a 6-month curfew. A large crowd had gathered in Saleh square in southern Tehran, not aware of the announcement of the curfew. They were confronted by soldiers in September 1978, and tear gas and live ammunition was used by the soldiers to put down the protest, 1600 dead in the streets and another 2300 died of injuries over the next several days. The Iranian government claimed the protestors had been killed in a stampede by the mob, however pictures emerged of police with firearms and the CIA reported back to Washington confirming the use of live ammunition on the crowd. By the end of the month more than 2 billion USD had been transferred overseas by wealthy Iranians; the elite believed the Shah's regime was ready to fall. Khomeini was expelled to France from Iraq at the request of the Shah, in an effort to prevent his message from making it to Iran. It did not work. Strikes and demonstrations grew in size with 2 million people marching in Tehran in December 1978 with the military deserting in support of the protest."

Gulshan took a drink of tea; she added to her points on the white board *The Ayatollah Returns and The Embassy is Attacked*. "In January 1979 the Shah left for a vacation in Aswan, never to return seeking Asylum in Egypt. Later in January Ayatollah Khomeini and supporters returned to Iran, and he appointed Mahdi Bazargan prime minister of a provisional government. In February the commander of Iranian military forces announced the neutrality of the military in the struggle for political leadership, and four hours later on February 11, 1979, national radio announced it had been secured by the forces of revolution. Never in modern times had there been a change in power like this in the middle east, the rising up of the middle class to take power away from a ruler, it was not a military coup but a peaceful revolution. The American public at the time, did not understand the revolution was a middle class revolution, it was seen most commonly as a radical religious revolution due to Khomeini. Months later the US allowed the Shah into the United States for medical treatment infuriating Iranians, the Americans had brought him to power in a coup, supported his oppressive and corrupt government. This anger was also incited by rhetoric of Khomeini helping drive the anger of a group of students who over ran the US embassy."

"I should also note, Saudi Arabia did not fully understand the change believing the Islamic government would be more aligned to it than the Shah. The Saudis had not been paying attention to the radical Shia doctrine being preached by Ayatollah Khomeini, antagonistic toward their monarchy as against Islam and despising their treatment of Shia minorities."

Michael suggested they take a break, "You have been going for about an hour, the restrooms are in the hall just outside the executive suite."

Steve Thomas went to the coffee pot, "Fascinating and embarrassing. I really did not know the details of these rivalries and anger at the US. I am going to hit the men's room, I will be back in a few."

They were all back and Gulshan started. She wrote *Saudi Origins House of Saud,* "Maybe we should move to the Saudis and their motivations for nuclear weapons. Which is what your request was really about."

"Critical to an understanding of Saudi Arabia is the house of Saud and the founding father Ibn Saud. The Ottoman general Ibrahim Pasha attacked and captured the Diriyah Emirate in 1818, near modern Riyadh, the early predecessor to the Kingdom of Saudi Arabia known as KSA. Abdullah Al Saud surrendered and was taken to Constantinople and convicted of heresy and beheaded in the Sultans palace and displayed in public. Abdullah's son Turk gathered a small army and took back control of Diriyah in 1824 and established the Emirate of Najid, later named the Saudi State."

"The founding father Ibn Saud was a towering figure, six feet four inches and renowned as a powerful and brave warrior, born in 1876 he became a leader of the Najid around 1902 and began to organize the Nomadic tribes in the region. He also sought religious volunteers to teach Islam to the pagan Bedouins. He established three pillars of his emerging colony, Islamic Education, Enforcing sharia law and protection of public morality. These three pillars have remained as foundations to the house of Saud, notably the protection of public morality grew into the religious police, more than 5000 strong at its peak, later reduced by Prince Mohammad bin Khalid, known as MBK. His younger brother Rashid, a leader of the police would use this as one piece of evidence to convince the King to choose him to replace MBK as crown prince a few years ago. Rashid became the King on the recent death of the King, the most recent of the brotherly struggles for power in the Royal family."

"Saud took in a religious leader Muhammad bin Abdul Wahhab teaching a fervent brand of Sunni Islam with extreme anti Shia views at the core. The teachings became the core of Saudi Wahhabism and sought to ban music, dance and even poetry in its puritanical view of anything judged not pure for the soul. The colony founded by Saud grew and nurtured other similar colonies across the Arabian Peninsula, spreading Wahhabism as it moved across the landscape. The Ottoman empire fell at the end of World War One and Saud consolidated control over the region. The British recognized him as the ruler of Hijaz and Najid in 1927 and in 1932 he consolidated control over the new Kingdom of Saudi Arabia naming himself King, controlling more than 1 million square miles of territory."

"Saudi Arabia grew from this history of the house of Saud, with the discovery of oil by Americans at Damman in 1938 and early partnerships with American oil companies and alliances with US administrations. Generally, the succession of Kings have maintained the three pillars first laid down by Saud in the early 1900s. The flag of KSA capturing the Islamic creed, there is no God but Allah and Muhammad is his messenger. The first five-year plan for the country wasn't developed until 1970-1975 an 8 billion USD plan, the explosive growth of oil revenues propelled the next five-year plan 1975-1980 to grow to 142 billion USD. The country needed basic infrastructure, roads, ports, communications, power and water. There was a massive influx of foreign workers used to support the growth. The literacy rate in 1970 for Saudis was fifteen percent for men and two percent for women there was no way to modernize without foreign workers. Saudi oil production rapidly grew under Aramco, it was later nationalized as Saudi Aramco and would grow to supply nearly twenty five percent of world production and put Saudi Arabia into the position of a swing producer, it could modulate its output to control world price."

"Saudi and Iranian relationships worsened after the Iranian revolution of 1979 and the alienation of Iran from the United States pushed the US to a closer alliance with Saudi Arabia. The antagonistic messages regarding the Saudi royal family continued and competition turned into conflict wherever there were Shia minorities, Pakistan, Syria, Iraq and Afghanistan and Yemen. The Iranians claimed religious persecution of Shia minorities by a heretical series of Saudi Kings from Khalid, then Fahd, Abdullah, Salman and now Rashid. The influence of the United States and the soldiers' presence on Saudi soil also had many internal Saudi critics and was a source of criticism by Iran. Generally, the entire period of Iranian-Saudi relations for twenty years following the Iranian revolution was a transformation to a regional competition for power with proxy conflicts all across the region making the conflict more and more severe. After the second Gulf war, the Shia majority was able to gain power in Iraq, and there was a power shift in favor of Iran. The Saudis were angry at the Americans for the invasion and more so when the US failed to appreciate the impact of allowing the Shia minority to gain power and influence."

"There was another dynamic at play, one involving religious extremists in Saudi Arabia, a bombing of the US air force base in 1996 in Saudi Arabia, the bombing of the USS Cole and then in September 2001 the deaths of thousands of innocent Americans as 19 Saudi Arabian citizens collaborated to crash airplanes into the US pentagon and twin towers in New York, and a third plane crashed believed to be headed towards the capitol. The trigger of the global war on terrorism, Iran was considered a backer of many extremist groups and while not responsible for 911 became one of the countries that was a sponsor of terror. Most Americans do not remember that the Iranian president condemned the 911 attacks and the new Ayatollah as well. Most Saudi royal family members and elites believed the conspiracy theory that it was a Zionist frame-up to get the US to attack Islamic countries. The two most significant acts against America from the middle east came from these two countries, Iran's attack on the US embassy in 1979 and the Saudi citizens involved in the terror attacks of 911. Setting up a very complex triangular relationship between the three countries."

"The revelation that Iran had been hiding a secret enrichment program sent off alarm bells in Saudi Arabia as the possibility of an Iranian nuclear weapon forced Saudi Arabia to pursue several routes for acquiring nuclear capability. The proxy wars continued, with Syria, Iraq and Yemen all disintegrating as world powers and regional powers fought in the region, destroying homes and displacing millions of people. Sanctions by the US began to create more desperate circumstances in Iran. Iran got more aggressive with drone attacks on Saudi oilfields and Saudi oil tankers. Concerns grew and early this year was the most aggressive strike by Iran, six small sea-launched missiles struck near the Barakah nuclear plant in the UAE, less than 100 km from the Saudi border. US intelligence leaks confirmed that satellite imagery showed the strike came from boats of the Iranian Revolutionary Guard. It is believed the missiles were a threat not intended to strike the reactors, all six struck a gymnasium for workers at the nuclear plant, about a kilometer away from the reactors. A brazen threat."

"The relationship between the United States and the Saudis has eroded for more than twenty years, they no longer have confidence in us for a security umbrella. The Saudis previously pursued a nuclear umbrella agreement with Pakistan as well as attempts to purchase warheads from Pakistan. US intelligence has confirmed these efforts but judged that no final transfer of a nuclear warhead has ever taken place. Iran has become more aggressive in their attacks, and the Saudis have known for several years that the Iranians were on the verge of an operable nuclear weapon. They have connections with our intelligence community, the forces for Saudi Arabia going nuclear have become overwhelming and the primary driver is not Israel, it is their close neighbor Iran."

Gulshan smiled as she concluded quoting Steve, "It is a regional cold war on the verge of going nuclear, as Dr. Steve Thomas has said proliferation begets proliferation."

Steve Thomas sat back, "It's very compelling, you know your paper frustrated some senior officials at the CIA and DIA, it is rationale and believable, but there is no direct evidence of nuclear weapons, of course they, cannot prove it to be impossible. The difficulty of your position I am sure you know is that moving towards nuclear weapons is a bit ambiguous. It could mean a graduate student in the basement of King Saud University separating out a milligram of enriched uranium or a warhead sitting in a warehouse waiting to be installed on an intermediate range Dongfeng missile, or anything in between. It's hard for the intelligence community to prove that nothing exists in that range."

Gulshan had heard some rumors last year when she issued her paper for interagency review the intelligence community didn't like this portion of the paper, formally there was no comment. "I understand the frustration and you are correct about my assessment, but it is for the technical elements of the intelligence community to answer that question. With all due respect to my colleagues in the IC, I think my paper makes them uncomfortable because I bring the question into focus and they do not deny the premise, that the Saudis have probably moved down the road. Whether they have gone only a single step or coming to near the end of a long journey, I do not know. My instinct is they are much further down the path than we are aware."

Michael had not read Gulshan's paper; he knew little of this important regional competition and the underlying history. He had thought there was no reason for the Saudis to have any interest in developing nuclear weapons, Steve Thomas was right this was rational and believable. But the practical consequence was not at all clear.

Michael knew they needed a break, "Well it looks like it's time for lunch. We can either order some sandwiches and carry through with Steve's piece or come back tomorrow. Gulshan, are you interested in Steve's background involving the AQ Khan network as it relates to Saudi Arabia? What would you both like to do?"

Gulshan went first, "Well I opened my schedule for the day, and I most definitely want to hear about AQ Khan as it might relate to Saudi Arabia. I would prefer to take a short lunch here together and finish up today."

Steve Thomas responded, "Same for me, I cleared my day for this."

They had sandwiches delivered to the lobby; the IG's executive assistant agreed to pick them up. Gulshan asked Michael, "What is your background Michael; you're an investigator, but I understand you're not a law enforcement officer. You specialize in these complex investigations involving nuclear proliferation and now chemical weapons?"

"I have a degree in nuclear engineering. I went to the Federal Law Enforcement Training Center, FLETC and had basic investigative training, but it's mostly on the job training."

Steve Thomas smiled, "Why do you always leave something out?"

"Yes, I have a law degree, and I passed the bar, but I have never practiced law."

Gulshan nodded, "Interesting, and what do you think of as your professional identity, an engineer or lawyer?"

Michael thought, "I am an Investigator, that is at the core of what I do and what I enjoy, but I have a keen affection for engineering and law."

Steve Thomas went to the white board, *Saudi and the Network*, "I will start with some background on AQ Khan, and then I will cover what we know about operations that have relevance to Saudi Arabia."

"In 1972, ZA Bhutto organized a clandestine meeting in Multan near the Indian border to announce to a select group of military and scientific officials his intent for Pakistan to develop a nuclear weapon and tell them that those assembled in the room would build it for him and for Pakistan. He had only been prime minister for a few weeks. Most of the experts in the room with experience and knowledge were skeptical that Pakistan had the technology and skills to build a nuclear weapon. At this time Pakistan had a small research reactor from the US located in Rawalpindi near Islamabad and a Canadian power reactor being constructed near Karachi, which was subject to IAEA controls."

"Bhutto embarked on a tour of 20 countries mostly in the middle east advocating for the need for a nuclear bomb for the Muslim world and seeking financial support. Bhutto organized an Islamic Summit which has sideline efforts to raise money for the "Islamic" bomb, not long after oil prices have spiked high and oil revenues were surging in many middle eastern countries. Bhutto had a vision that Pakistan could be the primary weapons supplier for the Islamic states, including nuclear capability. Libya agreed to participate and shortly afterwards delivered $200 million in cash by courier reportedly requesting the first bomb. Saudi Arabia provided funding and sought arrangements to be part of a

Pakistani security umbrella backed by nuclear weapons. Many Arab leaders saw the effort as necessary especially given the widely held view that western backed Israel had nuclear weapons."

"Abdul Qadeer Khan known as AQK, was considered the founder of the period of proliferation that emerged from the Pakistani nuclear program. He would transform proliferation from nation state diversion of civilian technology to what experts refer to as Market Based Proliferation Networks or marketplace proliferation. AQK was born in 1936 in Bhopal British India; he modeled himself in early adult life on his impressions of his father, focusing on humility and politeness. He also took on his father's fervor for the Islamic state of Pakistan and his hatred of India. In August 1947 Pakistan East and West was created as an Islamic haven and refuge for Muslims. Free India separated the two Pakistans and was created the following day. This division of British India deteriorated rapidly into communal warfare with tens of thousands of Muslims killed in riots as they tried to leave. AQK was eleven years old, and the violence and chaos were seared into his mind, he remained a Nationalist with a deep hatred for India throughout his career."

Steve Thomas went through the early work of AQ Khan as he graduated from university, went on to graduate school and got his first job in Europe. He had access to advanced centrifuge designs and began to steal the designs and made contact with the Pakistan government to bring the technology home. He described the collapse of the Libyan nuclear program under pressure from the United States, the subsequent investigations. The US and British governments had uncovered AQ Khan's role, the network had been operating for nearly twenty years. Subsequent investigations revealed the wide-ranging procurement network including its connections to Saudi Arabia and Dubai in the United Arab Emirates. He summarized in detail the many activities in Dubai and the interest of members of both the Saudi and Emirati Royal families.

Steve Thomas finished, "There is no direct evidence that the Saudis were a customer of the AQ Khan network. There were suspicions and circumstantial evidence, and there is all of this activity in Dubai in the United Arab Emirates next door. The broad consensus is that the missing customer was Iran. In my opinion it is unlikely that the Saudis were an AQ Khan customer. They were curious and had money to stay involved in Pakistan's so-called Islamic bomb project, keeping their options open."

Gulshan was fascinated, she never knew these details, "Steve for the sake of argument, assume they were the customer, and they had enrichment components, fabrication specifications and warhead designs years ago. With their money is that enough time to build an enrichment plant and fabricate a warhead; I really am not sure about the timelines?"

"Well, that's very speculative, with their money, if they were highly motivated, yes, it is enough time. It would be difficult, and it is very unlikely they could have stayed covert for so long. But it is within the realm of possibilities. Hiding a small research project or even a small pilot enrichment plant seems possible, but a weapons program is big with a lot of pieces. The US intelligence community would be embarrassed, there would be some significant lessons learned, investigations to find answers as to how it was missed for so long."

Gulshan took a drink of coffee, thinking that over, "If that were the case, the diplomatic and military postures of the United States would need to be completely reformulated, a fascinating and frightening thought. But as you say hypothetical."

Michael thanked Steve and Gulshan for their time, he had to think about his next step. He had the weekend to think this all over.

Chapter Nine
The Missing Link Database

Early Monday morning Michael answered the phone. It was Steve Thomas.

"Hey Michael, sorry I guess I'm getting old I didn't think about this on Friday when we met, it hit me over the weekend. There was a guy at the CIA who had kind of an unusual interest in the AQ Khan network. I hadn't thought about this for years. I heard about Russ Nixon at the CIA; he was organizing all of the AQ Khan files in a database a pet project. This was six or seven years after the network was uncovered, no one was talking about it anymore. I made an appointment back then, I wanted to review the warhead design papers; it was amazing what Russ Nixon was intent on doing. There was a large, classified storage room with all of the documents, thousands of pages in hard copy, hard disks and USBs everywhere; Russ was cataloging and building a relational database of everything. He was complaining he only had part time staff support for scanning the hard copies. This was his own pet project; his boss let him devote about 20 percent of his time; nobody was interested in what he was doing."

"Did he tell you why?"

"He said that intelligence that was collected should be collated and analyzed and not lay in storage. He didn't know what they would get from it, maybe just confirm what everyone suspected, but they might find something new, some missing link."

"I reviewed the warhead documents, which were in a special cabinet in the room for Top Secret materials. I asked Russ to give me a call when he finished the database, but I never heard back. I forgot about it, he probably gave up; it would have taken him another five to ten years, and he was about ten years older than me."

The next day Michael called Steve Thomas, "I'm going to the CIA to meet with Hugh Willet, he was Russ Nixon's last supervisor; Nixon retired about six years ago and passed away a short time later. Willet said Nixon worked the last three years after being diagnosed with cancer and had focused more time on his pet project. He says the database is still there, almost complete. You interested in making a trip to Langley?"

Willet took Michael and Steve to the storage room, Willet explained "no one has worked on the database since Russ retired, but it is nearly complete. The library Russ was building had US intelligence files, law enforcement reports, IAEA documents and reports and everything the US had recovered from Libya. Russ was an unusual kind of analyst, the kind that you give the 10,000-piece jigsaw puzzle of an all-white background with no picture. Russ was relentless in slowly building and organizing structured databases useful to many analysts. Russ would say they were like secret treasure maps; it took work to extract hidden treasure. I became Russ's supervisor a few years before he got sick and I agreed to allow him to continue the work, but nobody was interested in completing it when Russ retired. It has to be complete, tested and verified with some test cases before it can be put into the system certified for use by analysts."

They looked around the room, very well organized with the binders describing the cataloging system and database design. All of the hard copies stored away with one small box, probably 3000 pages that were unscanned.

Willet looked at the high-speed scanner, "I got this for him when he was diagnosed with cancer so the work would go faster. I really wanted this project to complete while Nixon was still alive. The two desk top computers are still working with the database on each one. I have controlled access to the room and made sure that no one disturbs Russ's work, maybe someone will finish it someday."

Michael looked at the computer, "Can I look at the database?"

"No problem; the database on the desktops are classified secret, not under any special controls, anyone with a Secret clearance should be allowed access. The warhead drives are top secret, and we keep those in a separate cabinet."

Willet had already verified Michael and Steve had Top Secret clearance before he had agreed to show them the storage room. Michael turned on one of the computers and brought up the database, he saw it could be searched in many ways with drop down filters for many categories. Michael did a simple search typing in Dubai, more than 32000 hits in 2341 different documents.

Michael looked at the results, "How much longer would it have taken to finish the scanning and the database?"

"It's really heart breaking, I brought in a few clerks and Russ said he would be done in another three months, but he was too weak. He retired a week after the clerks arrived and died three weeks after retiring."

Michael walked over and looked at the documents that had not been scanned, "What if there were three more scanners with dedicated staff?"

"A week or two, but I never could have received the budget for that when Russ was alive."

Steve Thomas knew what Michael was thinking, Thomas was thinking the same thing. It would be worth a look, only a few weeks to get the database complete.

For two weeks Sheri Landry and four contractors with security clearance worked in the storage room using four high speed scanners to finish building Russ Nixon's Database; "MissingLink." Hugh Willet was glad to accommodate Michael's proposal, Russ's project would be complete and turned over to CIA IT as an agency database. The Deputy Director of Intelligence agreed to give the US State Department OIG a copy of the Secret version of the database in exchange for their assistance. Sheri never understood the purpose of the database, Michael had it placed on a special laptop locked in classified storage under his control. Hugh Willet told Sheri the story of Russ Nixon; he had worked on it as a pet project for nine years but had not been able to finish before he died of cancer. That was enough reason for Sheri; she did not need to know the purpose of the database. Sheri developed and ran test cases, Willet reviewed the work and certified it for release as an official database.

Michael knew that the database would not answer any questions about the allegations he had received from Arthur Larson. After listening to Steve Thomas and Gulshan Wallace his investigative instincts told him it was possible the Saudis were a customer of AQ Khan years ago. If that were true, they may have gone on searching for a new supplier after the AQK network was shut down or worked with domestic development of what they had gotten. If this were the case, they might find leads relevant to the allegations they had recently gotten about centrifuges. Nothing was lost in analyzing a database, just to see if there was something.

Andrea and IG Ross agreed that Steve Thomas could continue working on the historic review using the database, but Thomas would have to sit on any results waiting for Michael to complete the investigation into recent allegations. Thomas readily agreed, he didn't like working in partnership with the OIG, people in the State Department could see him as an informant if it got around. The chance to investigate the riddle of the AQK networks missing customer compelled him to go forward. Andrea also brought Tom Bradley into the investigation, Tom went through intense Arabic language studies in OSI and was proficient as an Arabic translator. He used this skill in some OIG cases. Many documents in the database were in Arabic with only English translations of titles and keywords searchable by English in the database. Clever Russ Nixon had built the system to allow for Arabic searches, with menu structures in Arabic.

Tom, Michael and Steve were splitting their time between this investigation and their other assignments. Michael looked through Russ's database manuals, he found there were documents from another unstructured CIA database, signals intelligence, diplomatic cables and other sources all collected by CIA staff immediately after the AQ Khan network was revealed. The CIA staff had been anticipating a large-scale investigation looking for the other customer. They sucked in a massive number of documents from various intelligence gathering platforms; they had not been collated and catalogued and the investigation for the missing customer never materialized. The raw database was forgotten until Russ Nixon discovered it and migrated it into the structured MissingLink database. Many of these documents were in Arabic. None of these documents had ever been used in an AQ Kahn investigation; the addition of Tom was a great help.

They had a dedicated office secured for them in the basement of the State Department; they had three computers with external hard drives with the database, and Tom focused on Arabic searches, and he started with the ones that had never been reviewed as part of any AQ Khan investigations. They met and worked there, sometimes half a day together sometimes a full day. If they had other pressing work, they would skip a day, this wasn't high enough priority to drop other work.

The first day Tom looked around, "Michael couldn't you do any better than this? This place is nasty, looks like it was for storage."

Michael covered the objective looking for ties between Saudi Arabia and nuclear weapons through the AQ Khan network. He summarized what he had learned about the databases studying the manuals, they had copies on the manuals on the shelves in the small office. "The documents cover almost fifteen years, up to the time the AQ Khan network was discovered in 2003. We don't have any more recent documents than that. Tom, do you see what we are after?"

"Yes, I haven't gone brain dead buddy. I remember dual use items and the basics; I worked proliferation cases with you for more than six years. I understand what we are after. You need to get a new coffee pot for this place, and a water cooler, I'm not using the water out of that tap, a small fridge with some sodas and water and a white board. These desks and that worktable are ancient, but I guess they will do."

Michael laughed, "Okay Tom my gosh its only for a short time."

Michael finished describing the database, "There are nearly 20 million documents in the database. The vast majority from the hard drives and USBs that the US had taken from the Libya and the separate database that Nixon had loaded into his system. There were also documents and electronic files from locations in the UAE that the Emiratis allowed US access to while investigating AQK."

Michael had briefed Tom separately on the allegation from Larson and how that led to the historical search into the Saudi Arabia decades before, Tom understood the connection Michael had made. Tom knew that countries pursued these programs for decades to achieve their goal of joining the nuclear club. Michael explained that Steve Thomas was walled off from Larson's allegation.

Steve Thomas had an idea, "I have come up with a series of initial filtering searches; this will reduce the volume of documents we are searching through, and we can avoid reviewing documents that are not relevant. Let me work on this, Michael. Maybe you can take care of the coffee pot and Tom's other requests; Toms right this place is like a storage closet."

In April it looked like they finally found something. Tom tapped his fist on his desk, "I am the man. Say it Michael, Tom is the man."

"Okay, Tom you are the man, what does the man have?"

Michael and Steve turned their chairs around and watched as Tom walked to the white board and began writing. "I have found Arabic code words being used in Emirati government and customs documents. I kept seeing these words mostly in intercepts by US signals intelligence. The sentences didn't make any sense. But if I have the code correct then it becomes interesting."

Michael and Steve read what Tom had written in Arabic and English: Code for AQ Khan (Khayat—the tailor), Code for warhead (al-badhour—a seed), Code for enriched uranium (alasmada—fertilizer) and Code for centrifuges (hadhne—incubator).

Tom continued, "Let's use these codewords for searches both in English and Arabic."

Steve Thomas smiled, "Do you know the story about how the warhead designs were discovered during the IAEA investigation in Libya after the AQ Khan network was discovered?"

Michael shook his head, "Not me."

Tom didn't know, "Certainly not me."

"A general in charge of the Libyan nuclear program had them in shopping bags in his office; he had stored them there for two years, nearly complete designs of nuclear warheads. He said that AQ Khan had given them to him as a good customer gift. Bags from a tailor shop."

Later that week Tom finished collecting the documents where he came across the code words, he had fifty-three documents. Communications between UAE security service officers and customs officials tracking the tailor into and out of Dubai. "Michael and Steve, I've got something now from these messages with the code words"

They sat together at the worktable, "These communications are from surveillance by UAE security services, the tailor supplying incubators to Iran and Libya. Then there are a series of messages, suspicions that he was carrying technical information about seeds in and out of Dubai. Then a message, Emirati security services reporting to two senior Emirati officials they have taken a seed from the tailor, from an apartment on Gamal Street."

Steve Thomas stood up and stretched, "So the UAE security services figured out that Khan had warhead designs, and they have taken them or copied them. We know from the IAEA investigation that he stored these in his Dubai Apartment. They must have broken in when he was out of country and made an electronic copy of the warhead design. That is very curious, why did the Emiratis want these designs? This is before the network was exposed. I am sure they never told American intelligence they had found these in AQ Khan's apartment, very curious indeed."

The next day was Friday, Tom jumped up "Bingo, very interesting."

Michael was waiting, "Well come on, out with it."

"A short text message later the same day of the previous message about taking the seed from AQ Khan, another text message from a member of the Emirati royal family, says they have a seed lost by the tailor."

Michael shrugged, "what else does that give us?"

"It's from an Emirati to a Saudi official, both low level princes in the royal families."

Steve Thomas was surprised, "Really you have members of the Emirati ruling family communicating with Saudi royals in code about nuclear weapons."

Michael was surprised as well, "They could just be sharing intelligence about the activities of AQ Khan but why, they don't tell the Americans, but they tell the Saudis, why?"

None of them knew the answer to that.

It was late in the day, Michael shrugged, "Maybe we can find the answer to that next week."

Tom and Steve both laughed. Tom looked at Michael, "Really dude next week?"

Michael was embarrassed, "oh yeah, well in two weeks after I am back from the honeymoon and Tom not a word to Marion that I said I would be working next week."

Steve Thomas patted Michael on the back, "Have a good time on your honeymoon, you said Maine hiking right. I have some work to catch up on, see you both in two weeks."

Two weeks later they were back in the basement workroom, Steve Thomas came in last. "Hey, Michael, how was the wedding and honeymoon, was the weather good for hiking?"

"It was great Steve, thanks."

"Well congratulations and best wishes for your future together. How was it for you Tom?"

"I got to see Pumpkin Center Indiana, quite a nice place actually and I saw some old clippings from newspapers, Michael's baseball prowess at Silver Creek high school."

Michael laughed as he sat down with his coffee, "Let's get back to work."

In late May Michael and Tom knew Steve Thomas was on to something. He had stayed late for three straight days working in the basement. That Friday they came in early in the morning, and he was there at the worktable, "Okay guys grab a cup of coffee, this is really interesting."

They circled their chairs around the small worktable as Thomas started, "I have a large number of US diplomatic wires and cables, discussions about a new joint air base the Saudis were building southwest of Riyadh in 1995-1998. There are underground hangars and munitions storage areas. The Americans believe the underground facilities are oversized, and they don't like the configuration, but the direction from the Pentagon is not to complain the Saudis aren't asking for any

US funding. There are messages and communication monitoring the plans and the progress being made on finishing the air base."

Thomas gets up and gets another cup of coffee and brings some papers with him, "I printed these four US cables from the Abu Dhabi CIA station to Langley and to the State Department intelligence bureau. They say they have some unusual Saudi and UAE messages from signals intelligence. The cables describe 90,000 square feet construction for incubators and processing for fertilizer, updates on a project southwest of Riyadh in the immediate area of the new airbase. The cables are asking for any views about the meaning of these communications and direction. Finally, two weeks later there is a response from Langley, nothing of interest, must be some plans for agricultural processing in the future. Tell me I haven't gone crazy, what does this sound like to you?"

Michael looked at the cables and the Langley message, "Holy crap, we already know the Emiratis and Saudis are using Tom's code words. But the Americans looking at these communications back then didn't know the Emiratis were using code. Using Tom's code words, it's an enrichment facility."

Steve Thomas finished the thought, "Not just an enrichment facility but a large-scale facility, they are talking about 90,000 square feet of centrifuges for processing enriched uranium. I cannot believe this is here in these old cables. That's all there is from the English language search."

Tom Bradley jumped up, "I am on it. Today you are the man, Steve. I will do focused searches on the airbase using the code words."

By the end of the day Tom had found dozens of Arabic messages between Emirati and UAE officials about the air base. It was clear what the messages described, 90,000 square feet of underground caverns constructed at the edge of the new airfield, housing three banks of centrifuge farms, 10,000 centrifuges per bank for a total of 30,000 centrifuges underground, less than a kilometer away from hangars with US and Saudi jets.

In early June Michael found another piece of the puzzle, paperwork and invoices, from a previously unknown AQ Khan network member, a South African (Lars Stoller). Michael found references to his work for the "incubators" and the "fertilizer business." Michael realized he had found a whole new piece of the AQ Khan network. Tom knew Michael was on to something; he was working at the white board drawing a diagram, a complex hierarchy of companies, with blue and black boxes and transaction arrows in red and green. His diagram covered the whole white board, listing transaction numbers and dates. Steve Thomas was walking over to look at the board, Tom grabbed him by the arm and whispered, "Let him finish he is focused on this; he will explain when he is ready."

Michael stepped back and looked at the white board, "I think that is it, hey guys I have something here, it's kind of complicated; it involves this player Stoller and his companies." He gave them a summary tracing out the relationships and transactions he had drawn on the white board, describing Stoller and his companies. It took more than an hour to go through the structures and transactions.

"You can see, there are dozens of large shipments flowing for the AQ Khan network that looked like they were part of the supply for Libya. There are a group of shipments all for three years right before the network was shut down. The shipments flowed into Dubai from the same suppliers for Libya, but these all have reference to a fertilizer plant in Saudi Arabia. These are all tied to the Dubai shell companies under Stollers control. They are the only ones that cannot be traced to ship-ments to Libya, they end up on trucks for Saudi, for the southwestern fertilizer plant Riyadh Saudi Arabia. This includes the so-called missing shipment that IAEA investigators had discovered long ago, from Malaysia, it was boxed into another shipment and sent on to the fertilizer plant."

Steve Thomas was dumbfounded, "I'll be dammed; you found the missing AQ Khan customer, it was Saudi Arabia. No doubt about it, after all of these years. How did you find that buried in all those financial documents and transactions?"

Tom laughed, "Scary smart right."

Michael shook his head, "Not me, we all worked to find the missing customer."

Tom asked, "So are we done? Can we get anything more from this database?"

Steve Thomas sighed, "There are still missing pieces of a weapons program."

Michael thought, "The UF6 where were the Saudis going to get the uranium hexafluoride for their centrifuges."

Thomas added, "and the smaller facilities for converting the enriched uranium to metallic form, and finally weapons design and warhead fabrication."

They worked for several more days. They had exhausted the leads in the database, there were no answers about a UF6 supply or the other pieces of a weapon's program, but they had the evidence of the purchases of a pilot sized enrichment cascade and plans to build a large facility in Saudi Arabia and possession of the stolen warhead designs.

The next Monday they reviewed the status, Michael summarized. "So, we are done with the database, right? Any further investigation would have to be by other means."

Steve Thomas shook his head in agreement, "The Saudis have substantial uranium deposits and the conversion plant to create the UF6 is not so complex and far less substantial than an enrichment facility. The other smaller facilities, the carbonator-calciner for converting the UF6 to metal and warhead fabrication facility are also relatively small operations, but important to pursue if you wanted to claim they were after a weapons program."

Michael wrapped up, "Okay we are in reporting and briefing mode now. We need to finish our document, review memos and develop a summary memorandum to bring all of the pieces together. We need to cross-check each other's work; Tom you will need to triple check the translations. We are going to make sure we have accurate facts before we brief Andrea Jacobs and Inspector General Ross on the Saudi-UAE nuclear program."

They worked the rest of the week, finished the briefing and went through it together in a dry run in the work room.

Steve Thomas did not know IG Ross very well, "Ross will understand this right, he will understand the significance of this? I don't want to underplay this, but I don't want him to think we are saying Saudi Arabia has a nuclear bomb sitting on a missile. To be honest, I am not sure what to conclude about all of this, it's all historical; I am conflicted as to what it means for today."

Michael shook his head, "He is not technical, but he has seen our briefings on these proliferation cases, he is smart he will understand. We lay it out and see where we can go next."

The briefing was given in IG Ross's executive conference room in July, Michael gave the briefing with Tom and Steve in support for questions. Andrea and IG Ross listened without interrupting.

After Michael finished Andrea spoke, "I have already reviewed the supporting memorandum and looked through some of the supporting evidence. Everything in the presentation is based on solid evidence."

Inspector General Ross sat back in his chair, "Okay, compelling circumstantial evidence that the Saudis and Emiratis were working together and had enrichment components shipped to Saudi Arabia, possible construction of an enrichment facility near an air base and possession of stolen warhead designs. As of about twenty years ago. Does that about sum it up?"

Steve Thomas was impressed, that was an excellent summary of the forty-five-minute briefing.

Michael shook his head, "yes sir."

IG Ross continued, "So let's bracket the interpretations of what this circumstantial evidence could be indicative of within reason. The least significant implication first. I would guess, enrichment components sitting in some warehouses at a Saudi airbase and warhead designs in a storage vault somewhere. Sound about right?

Michael nodded in agreement, "Yes sir, I agree."

IG Ross got up and filled his coffee cup and sat back down, he smiled "That's as far as this old secret service agent can go; I need you to bracket the most significant implication. I know they have money and resources."

Michael shook his head, "I would prefer to let Steve Thomas respond to this since it is a very complicated technical question. Steve, if we assume the Saudis are motivated the way that Gulshan Wallace described, compelled to counter an Iranian threat, what would you estimate the greatest progress the Saudis could have made given the evidence we have?"

Steve Thomas didn't expect to be answering such a difficult question, "I understand your objective IG Ross, you want to reasonably bound the interpretation of this evidence. I have been struggling with that myself. You are right, they have money and resources; the direct implication of this evidence is that they were pursuing a covert nuclear weapons program at that time. They also have substantial security forces and control over information. If you assume, they have been highly motivated for this long period of time; they have had enough time to make centrifuges operational as well as the other facilities necessary for warhead production. They could have a small number of warheads, not more than ten. There is no evidence to support that, but it is technically feasible; it seems very unlikely they could have actually produced warheads and kept the program covert. Michael has put his finger on the key factor, and it is beyond my area of expertise, more for you, Andrea, Tom and Michael and experts in international relations. The key factor is the motivation of the Saudi regime. Sir you understand that the intelligence community would require an incredible level of proof to convince them that there is a nuclear program in Saudi Arabia. For some of them nothing short of a picture of a warhead with a Saudi Flag on it would be sufficient."

IG Ross shook his head, "thanks Dr. Thomas, your opinions are highly valued in this office. You remember our agreement, please keep this information in confidence. We are finished with this background investigation. We appreciate your assistance. Michael and Tom, we would like to meet with you both after lunch."

The briefing broke up, Michael walked Steve to the corridor, "Thanks Steve. If anything else comes up that we can share, I will get in touch."

"Okay Michael, it has been interesting to say the least."

After lunch Michael and Tom were back in the conference room with IG Ross and Andrea Jacobs.

Andrea led off, "okay you two, any investigative strategies from here? We either have useless parts sitting in a warehouse outside Riyadh or nuclear weapons in Saudi Arabia less than 100 miles from nuclear Iran. How do we determine which it is, or something in between and how this relates to the original allegation of Americans giving the Saudis enrichment designs?"

Michael shook his head, "Sorry Andrea and to you IG Ross, I have been thinking about this the whole time we were preparing the briefing. Tom and I kicked it around a little, we do not have any recommendation. It's too big, nothing like any of our proliferation investigations; this is not about State Department programs, its whether or not Saudi Arabia has a covert nuclear weapons program, its beyond our capabilities. We still cannot go charging at the Secretary of State's office. It looks like I have not really advanced the case for us."

IG Ross and Andrea had talked during lunch, she smiled as Michael talked. She waited for IG Ross to respond; she knew what he was going to say.

"Michael, what does your instinct tell you, drop it or keep going?"

"Sir, I was very convinced by Gulshan Wallace's views on Saudi motives; they have strong motivation to pursue nuclear weapons. They must know that Iran is nuclear capable. Given this and what we found, I would definitely want to keep going if I knew how to investigate."

"I agree, don't beat yourself up, this is excellent work by the three of you; you followed the facts and your investigative instincts. Your right, you found something that exceeds our resources and capabilities. It's still relevant to our mandate; it could be related to the original allegation you had. There could be a connection. I have an idea of how to advance this, but I need to discuss it with a colleague.

David Ross had known Inspector General AJ Reyes of the Director of National Intelligence (DNI)since Reyes was appointed by the president five years ago. They had met through the IG Council, Reyes sought out IG Ross for advice on developing the IG at DNI. The State Department OIG under Ross was considered one of the most effective in government.

David Ross sat down in Reyes' office. "Good to see you AJ; how is everything going?

"Everything is going well; there isn't a better job in Washington DC than inspector general. What do you need David?

"Well, it is unusual and significant; it comes from some work by Michael Case in the nuclear proliferation area. Here is the background briefing I got from him, Agent Tom Bradley and Steve Thomas. Do you know Steve Thomas?

"I know of him; the intelligence community holds his views in high regard."

"The investigation started out with allegations that two government officials working out of the secretary of state's office had given information on enrichment technology to the Saudis. Michael Case decided to look at the history of potential Saudi interest in nuclear weapons before charging into the Secretary of State's office. We got a database from the CIA, and the three of them used it as evidence for this background investigation."

"Okay, I heard you guys worked with the CIA to finish the database. Mr. Nixon was a valued analyst; he passed away before he could finish it. I was curious about your interest, but stayed out of the way. Seemed like it was good for the Agency and not my business what you might have been looking into."

Ross summarized the briefing as Reyes looked through the presentation. Ross gave the assessment of worst case from Steve Thomas. A small number of warheads but Thomas did not think it likely they could have done that covertly. "Thomas sees it as a judgement call at this time. It comes down to their motivation and desire. We want to go forward, but this is beyond our capabilities. I thought you might have some ideas of how we might collaborate with the intelligence community. I don't want to put you in a difficult position."

Reyes listened to Ross as he looked through the briefing slides with the summary of supporting evidence; it was a compelling case even without reading the detailed work papers. If the Saudis were working on nuclear weapons that would be a great concern and contrary to current intelligence assessments. Actual nuclear weapons or near that stage of development would set the intelligence and diplomatic world on fire. There would be a lot of questions about how the community missed this for so long.

"You know the general stated policy is limited intelligence gathering on the Saudis and even less on the Emiratis. We get a lot of bad press about this, and intelligence and diplomatic senior officials complain. But I have an idea of how there might be some collaboration for something this important. I need to discuss it with the CIA Director. I will get back to you within a week."

What Reyes planned to recommend to the CIA Director was not in his capacity as the IG of DNI. He was not aware of any request for this type of CIA support for an investigation, much less one from another agencies OIG. Support using one of the most secretive and productive intelligence gathering platforms in the United States intelligence community in one of the most sensitive regions of the world to investigate something opposing the current views of the entire intelligence community. He wasn't even authorized to tell his colleague IG Ross about the existence of BLACKHOLE. The CIA Director was a straight-shooter and would hear him out, and it was warranted in his opinion.

Chapter Ten
Blackhole in Abu Dhabi

Blackhole was the brainchild of Michael Thomas a former United States Army four-star general, former Director of the National Security Agency and former Director of the Central Intelligence Agency. The United Arab Emirates (UAE) began recruiting operations seeking to hire former CIA operatives and NSA operatives, to try and build their own spy operation. The initial reaction was to stop the Emiratis, but Thomas had a better idea. His idea was approved by the National Security Council and the president in a Top-Secret Presidential Directive, authorizing Blackhole. The gang of eight in congress had a limited scope briefing on the program. It was a carefully guarded special access program under the control of the Director of the CIA working in collaboration with the NSA Director. In the State Department and Department of Defense only the Secretaries were read into the program unless others required access for limited periods of time. The program allowed employees and the retirees of the CIA and NSA to be recruited and go to work in Abu Dhabi for the companies that were popping up there as consultants for the Emirati government, helping the UAE build their own spy agency. Stories began to appear in newspapers about a UAE based company Dark Energy and other similar companies in the UAE, filled with rogue former employees of the NSA and CIA helping the Emiratis spy on citizens and dissidents across the UAE. Senior officials in the Department of State began to complain as well as senior staff and working level analysts and clandestine officers at the intelligence agencies. There were also stories circulating that the US intelligence agencies had taken a hands-off approach with the Emiratis and also the Saudis, while partly true, it was not the full story.

The Americans heading these four companies in Abu Dhabi, Lodestar, Triangle, Eagle Eye and Talon were officially retired or resigned US intelligence officers. Talon and Triangle operated training similar to the CIA farm, clandestine tradecraft training Emiratis to be clandestine operators. They were based in a massive villa complex, a former small palace, a cousin of Sheikh Abdulla Bin Zayed (ABZ) the Abu Dhabi Crown Prince. Talon was headquartered in the Western half and Triangle in Eastern half; to make training more realistic they would operate against each other across Abu Dhabi, and Dubai as if they were competing national clandestine services, trying to run operations against each other. Eagle Eye and Lodestar were run out of two separate buildings, in MASDAR near the Abu Dhabi airport. Eagle Eye was focused on video surveillance, drone surveillance and mobile networks for monitoring and tracking. Lodestar was the internet vacuum cleaner, sweeping in everything on the internet within the UAE. The presidents of these companies two former CIA (Triangle and Talon) and two former NSA senior officers (Eagle Eye and Lodestar) were despised by former colleagues, and they were subject to harassment when travelling under directions from mid-level state department officials; delays at passport checks, baggage searches other ways to irritate them. They were each making between 1 million and 1.5 million dollars per year and the teams of experts they brought on board were making salaries ranging from 250,000 and 400,000 per year, three to ten times what they made in the US. The Emiratis were happy the Americans were sticking with them even as the US government harassed them and complained to the Emirati government about their presence in the country. The US Ambassador frequently registered complaints; he was not part of Blackhole and like most Ambassadors did not fully know what the CIA and NSA people in his Embassy were doing. They were not State Department personnel and not under his direct authority when it came to intelligence operations.

The US Ambassador in Abu Dhabi was shocked when he learned of the size of the CIA station, the staff and physical size of their facilities; he could only imagine what they were doing; he suspected they were the tip of the spear spying on Iran. He also knew they ran limited operations against the Saudis, they provided him support as he needed, but he knew the station chief was not going to tell the Ambassador more than he had the need to know.

The concept developed by Thomas was an enormous and brilliantly devised deception of the UAE. The presidents of each of the four Abu Dhabi companies were CIA and NSA assets and a small select group of individuals in each of the companies were CIA and NSA assets. The entire set of electronic and computer spy tools built in Lodestar and Eagle Eye were all derived from NSA and CIA platforms, the Emiratis believed their friends had "stolen" these to help build their own toolkits. All of the platforms contained sophisticated trap doors and leakage paths to feed everything to the US Embassy in Abu Dhabi. The Americans also had the ability to modify and manipulate intelligence data that the Emiratis had in their electronic storage systems. These human and electronic assets were becoming the biggest US intelligence gathering platform in the middle east. There was a Faustian bargain in the development and implementation of Blackhole, the Emiratis did use the tools to spy on citizens and residents in the UAE, but they also used the tools to track Iranian activity, the massive smuggling and money laundering operations that were functioning in the Emirates, and they were developing it to spy on all of their neighbors, especially Saudi Arabia and Yemen. As the American consulting companies made the Emiratis' spy networks more effective, they increased the success of US intelligence gathering. To a great extent the Emiratis were spying on themselves and others for the US intelligence community.

Chapter Eleven
The Truth Shall Make Us Free

The CIA Director was convinced by IG Reyes and the briefing materials; the evidence was supported by a database the CIA had developed. He knew the story of Russ Nixon. The potential for a Saudi–UAE cooperative nuclear weapons program was a grave threat to regional and US security, and the possibility that US government employees were assisting was very troubling. "This is good work; we aren't going to ignore the possibility just because we may have missed it for decades. The truth will make us free; we will support them in their investigation. If there is nothing then fine, but if there is something, we have a lot of work in government to respond to this regional threat."

The CIA Director met with AJ Reyes and David Ross. "IG Ross we will support your investigation; I understand this is a bit speculative at this time, but the possibility that the Saudis have a nuclear weapons program is clearly of great national security interest. You and your two investigators will be read into a highly classified surveillance program run out of Abu Dhabi station. Your investigators will need to deploy to work in Abu Dhabi in collaboration with the CIA Station Chief. Your investigative lead will establish the evidence requests and the priority, but the Station Chief will determine the modalities and ensure operational security. Will this be a satisfactory arrangement?"

"Yes Director, we very much appreciate your assistance."

The CIA Director sent orders through the deputy director to CIA Station Chief (Melvin Randolph) in Abu Dhabi. Mel Randolph read the orders; he was surprised he had never received a request like this. Two OIG investigators, Michael Case and Tom Bradley would work in the CIA station in the UAE embassy, as trade representatives for the nuclear power industry. They would work in collaboration with the CIA station using assets of the Blackhole operation. The CIA station had a staff of eight NSA analysts and technicians and six CIA clandestine operators. He was directed to assign two NSA analysts and three CIA officers to work with Case and Bradley. He was directed to assist in intelligence collection at the direction of Michael Case as well as planning any covert activities to support Case and Bradley. Michael Case would brief Randolph on the investigation when he arrived, it was urgent and sensitive. Mel knew that it had to be very important if they were using BLACKHOLE to gather evidence. He would make sure Case and Bradley got exactly what they needed, he had top notch operators and analysts. The orders from the Director were clear, the investigation was led by Michael Case; Mel was to make sure Case had the assets he needed to collect evidence and make sure they did not put Station intelligence operations at risk. Mel had a lot on his plate beyond this, to keep the rest of the ongoing operations going and respond to requests from the Ambassador.

Michael Case, Tom Bradley and David Ross met with the Deputy Director of Clandestine Services, he read them into Blackhole. The US was using the Emirati intelligence network that was being built by American consultants to spy on the Emiratis, Saudis, Iranians and anyone else. There were a large number of former NSA and CIA staff working for companies in the UAE, a select number of these people were CIA and NSA assets working to develop and deploy the tools and monitor the Emirati development of its own spy organization. Virtually any form of surveillance, monitoring and covert intelligence gathering could be supported with Blackhole assets, including covert human intelligence using CIA operators and assets. The Emiratis had no problem allowing them to deploy to Saudi Arabia or other countries; it was more difficult to use them in the UAE, but it was possible.

Deputy Director Sweigart explained the practical details, "orders have already been sent from the Director to the CIA station chief Melvin Randolph. The CIA station will provide investigative support and Michael Case will lead the investigation, and you prioritize your request for evidence collection through Randolph or his assigned lead. Melvin Randolph leads the Blackhole operations in Abu Dhabi and all other Station operations. He will assign NSA analyst and CIA covert operators for full time support of the investigation. The analyst and operators can clarify and assist in defining evidence collection methods, but everything needs to be cleared through Randolph to ensure Station covert operations are not compromised. Michael Case will brief Randolph and the supporting Station assets on the investigation on arrival. They are expecting Case and Bradley to arrive September one as nuclear power industry trade experts of the State Department expected duration of the assignment is four months."

IG Ross thanked the Deputy Director for the briefing and assistance, "State OIG will handle all travel and logistics for Case and Bradley."

The IG had a driver outside waiting. Michael and Tom were quiet on the drive back from Langley, Ross knew they had not expected to be TDY to Abu Dhabi for four months; it was short notice. "You two have a big decision to make, and we need to know next week. Are you deploying accompanied with your families?"

Michael and Tom were still processing everything they had just heard, thinking about working in the CIA station in Abu Dhabi. It had not hit them yet, four months away from home.

"The CIA Director gave me a heads up that you would work from the CIA station; the Secretary of State knows you are deploying as State Department Staff; he knows you are working in the CIA station, but he does not know why. They have an official who can help you both with all arrangements when you decide."

Ross handed a business card to Tom and Michael, *Ms. Regina Pritchard Director Foreign Support Services*, "The Secretary says you can call her directly. She understands this is urgent, and she knows you may need help arranging for family. The Secretary says she handles their Ambassadors and senior staff in the middle east, she will make it happen. Your wives can also call her if they want information."

Ross knew that Michael was a newlywed, Congressman Bartley's daughter and Tom had school age children and his wife was a school teacher. That weekend Michael and Tom were going to hit their wives with the news. Michael and Marion spent a lot of time with the Bradley's the next four months. Usually getting together for dinner one night on the weekend, which was Friday and Saturday, the workweek starting on Sunday, Friday was the Muslim communal day of worship in the UAE. They usually went together to the Evangelical Community Church service on Friday mornings. Marion thought Amanda was an amazing cook, and she had a good sense of humor like Tom. Sometimes they would go shopping together at Abu Dhabi Mall or Al Waddah Mall. Mall Shopping was the national pastime in the UAE, with Dubai Mall and Mall of the Emirates in Dubai the mega malls. The Mall of the Emirates had the ski slope and Dubai Mall the enormous fish tank. They did the tourist things, the Burj Khalifa tallest building in the world in Dubai, a desert safari dune busting with belly dancers and a cookout in the desert. They went to Al Ain and saw the traditional oasis and took the kids to the zoo and went to the Green Mubazzarah park.

Chapter Twelve
Going to Work with the Spooks

Melvin Randolph was uneasy about the tasking allowing Michael Case and Tom Bradley to work an OIG Investigation out of the Station in Abu Dhabi, especially the use of the Blackhole intelligence operation to help them gather evidence. He checked with contacts in DC. They both had good reputations; Case was leading a team that investigated government programs involving nuclear and chemical weapons proliferation. They both had worked the case revealing a diversion of US nuclear equipment from Pakistan to North Korea. Bradley was a federal law enforcement officer, and Case was an investigator, a nuclear engineer and lawyer, by education. Neither had experience with covert operations as far as he could determine; he would give them the benefit of the doubt and give them the lay of the land. Given their background it seemed likely their investigation had something to do with the Iranian nuclear program. Mel had lived the last twenty years all over the middle east, he rarely went back to the United States, his parents were divorced, one of his brothers was a drunk living off of disability payments from a logging accident, the other was living off the grid somewhere in the Cascade mountains. What a messed-up family.

Mel was born in Port Angeles, Washington, a little fishing town on the Juan De Fuca strait. His parents were both alcoholics; they were functional with jobs, but they argued constantly. His father left on a commercial fishing job in Alaska when Mel was a freshman in college and never returned. His mother went into default on the mortgage and lost the home. She worked as a waitress at a series of small restaurants around town. He paid for college with student loans and money he made in the summers; he worked as a mountain guide in the Cascade mountains in the areas around Mount Baker and Mount Shuksan. He got a degree in Anthropology thinking he would get to see the world; he found out there weren't any jobs like that unless you went the long haul for a Ph.D.

He worked for two years after he graduated from Western Washington University. He worked as a mountain guide in the summers and a substitute teacher and handyman around Bellingham. He met Elliott Clancy the first summer after graduation; Elliot came on a guided climb on an alpine course on Mount Baker. Elliott came back again the next summer and asked to be in one of the small-group Shuksan classes led by Mel. Elliott took a nasty fall, Mel administered basic first aid, he had a gash on his leg from his crampons. Mel applied butterfly bandages and made sure Elliott was safely off the mountain. Mel went to the hospital with Elliot to make sure he was ok.

Elliott was grateful; they talked, and Elliott asked Mel about his long-term career plans. Mel told Elliot he wanted something better than this; he had always been interested in traveling. Mel knew that Elliott worked in Washington DC, then he learned that Elliott worked for the CIA in Langley, Virginia. Elliott knew that Mel was smart, he was resourceful and could think on his feet. He was outgoing, probably a good candidate for the clandestine service. Two weeks later someone called Mel for an initial interview in a small office in downtown Bellingham. Then he went to Seattle for three days, for more interviews and written examinations and had a psychological evaluation. The next week he was invited to Washington DC; he stayed at a hotel for two weeks in McLean, Virginia. He had intensive interviews every day, another psychological evaluation and then a polygraph interview, a lot of questions about drugs, gambling, involvement with anti-government organizations. Three weeks later he got a letter with an offer of employment in the Operations Directorate as an analyst.

Mel felt like he had found a home in the CIA when he came into the lobby of the Langley HQ that first day, the statue outside of Nathan Hale, America's first spy to die in the line of duty. He learned years later that Hale had been killed because of inadequate planning and poor tradecraft. Then there was the statue inside of General William "Wild Bill" Donovan, the founding father of the CIA across the lobby from the nameless marble stars, one for each CIA officer who had died in the line of duty. He immediately felt a sense of pride standing in the lobby that day looking at those stars. Unknown American heroes, he thought it would be an honorable and important career. Most of his first year was in training, classroom and the field, split between "spy tradecraft" and paramilitary training. The training focused on targeting and recruiting assets, covert surveillance, planning and conducting clandestine meetings and communications. The paramilitary training focused on basic weapons training and survival, mountain, desert and jungle. They also learned basics of using explosives. He enjoyed the training especially when they would go out into the real world and practice tradecraft, brush pass and conducting a clandestine meeting. It was all about operating in the open, sleight of hand and misdirection.

His first assignment after training was in Langley in the Middle East Operations Group as a Clandestine Support Officer; he was enrolled into the intensive Arabic program. His first overseas posting was in Amman Jordan. He was a natural as a clandestine case officer; he knew he had found his career and he would see the world, or some of it. He was in Jordan when the terror attacks hit the United States, and he saw the front lines of the war on terror. Then he was in Cairo for several years, then Riyadh for years as Deputy Chief of Station. Then Chief of Station in Abu Dhabi for almost ten years and the assignment to run the Blackhole Program, considered one of the most important postings in the Clandestine Service. It had been an honorable and important career; it also had been difficult and challenging. He learned many important lessons from his first Station Chief, Brad Clay. He remembered one of the first things Brad told him. He told Mel he should be prepared to feel a little dirty like everyone else who served as a field officer in the clandestine service.

Tom had worked with CIA covert operators a few times when he was in OSI years ago. The weekend before the first day working at the embassy, Michael and Tom were in the Starbucks on the ground floor waiting for their wives and the kids to come down. They were all going to Yas Mall and Ferrari World amusement park, something to do indoors in the oppressive heat.

Tom wasn't sure how Michael would react to the rough edge of these operators. "You ready to go to work with the spooks? These covert operators have a bit of an edge, don't expect a bunch of Ninjas or special force operator types."

"What should I expect?"

"Con artist trying to steal your retirement savings."

Michael was puzzled, what a strange thing to say. They were scheduled to meet with Melvin Randolph the station chief at 10:00 a.m. on Sunday morning. He met them in the lobby; he was a little older than Michael expected dressed casually, no tie sport coat and dress pants. Michael wasn't sure what he expected, military fatigues or a tuxedo. Melvin looked like a regular guy. He had their security access badges for the embassy and showed them the way to Abu Dhabi Station. Through a plain secured door "Restricted Area Authorized Access."

They met in Mel's office. It was not grand, no windows with a desk and a round meeting table, bookshelves and a white board; it was functional. Mel got them coffees, asked them about the trip and where they were living.

"Nice Reem Island Wind Tower, they gave you VIP housing. I'm not too far from there, a villa near the Eastern Mangroves; I can see Wind and Breeze Tower from the second floor of the villa. You have already been read into Blackhole, maybe it would be better if you were to brief me first, then we can talk about the next four months."

Michael gave Mel a copy of the briefing, he started with the allegations about Franklin Williams—Department of State and Shawn Harrison—Department of Energy National Nuclear Security Administration giving sensitive nuclear related materials to Saudis. Then Michael went through the briefing on the Saudi nuclear activities from years earlier. Mel listened looking through the briefing slides as Michael finished.

Mel got another cup of coffee, "This is very interesting. I haven't heard anything about Saudi-UAE nuclear weapons since I have been in Abu Dhabi. Seems kind of unlikely they had a hidden nuclear weapons program for decades."

Michael thought it was a reasonable response, "Yes, it is a bit of a long shot, but if there is something there it would completely shift our regional security and diplomatic stances."

"You're right about that, it would change the neighborhood. So, it's possible the Saudis picked back up from where they left off sometime after the AQK network went down. We have the right platform here to see if something is going on now."

Mel was generally familiar with the network and what had happened, but not the details; he was in Jordan when it was exposed, but they were not focused on nuclear issues in Jordan. "We will run this under a Project; there will be supporting tasks authorized to support the Project. Each task will be assigned a code word. I hadn't given the Project a name, I was waiting to hear what it was about; how about Phantom, an elusive presence hiding in the desert."

"Let's talk about work inside of an intelligence organization. The orders from the CIA Director are clear. This is an investigation under Michael's supervision, but Phantom and tasks to gather evidence to support the investigation will be under my direction as the Chief of Station. It is important you understand some of the basics of how we conduct intelligence. You will have two NSA officers and three CIA clandestine officers assigned to Phantom. I will introduce you to them when we are done meeting. Craig Collins will act as the senior member of the intelligence team working with Michael and will help structure the intelligence tasks."

"It's important to understand that clandestine officers, myself and the CIA officers you will be working with have jobs very different from what you are accustomed to when searching for evidence using law enforcement techniques. When I started in my first posting in Jordan, my first boss had a cartoon on the wall, two filthy pigs beside a man covered in mud with his head poking out of the muck. The caption said, if you wrestle with pigs you are going to get dirty. Some of what we do and what we might do to support you might seem dirty and disgusting; I have blackmailed people, using embarrassing sexual information and other personal secrets; coerced people telling them family members are in danger, lied and tricked people, betrayed assets who became a risk. These are all things we are trained to do and is sometimes necessary to get foreign assets to betray their own country."

Michael knew this is what Tom meant, they operate by a different set of rules, like people who might try and con you out of your retirement.

Mel continued, "There are limits, I have never been asked to physi-cally torture or physically abuse anyone. I will never allow or authorize some of things that happened in some circles of the CIA after 9/11. People were extremely angry, under incredible stress and lessons have been learned from that experience. Not my responsibility to judge others in the service, but that is where I draw the line for myself and the people who report to me. We operate more by the law of the jungle and not the rule of law, this is foreign covert information gathering not law enforcement. But our methods and means have things in common. We both want facts; you want reliable evidence, and we want accurate information useful in the development of intelligence."

Michael remembered the carving in the lobby of the CIA headquarters, "and the truth shall make you free."

Mel smiled he knew Michael must have seen the carving in Langley "exactly and we have systematic procedures and methods as you do in your investigative work. Most of what we do covertly is subtle, sleight of hand and deception."

Michael knew what it was like to trick a witness; it wasn't a frequent technique, but he could not imagine blackmailing or coercing someone. He understood how this could be a dirty job. Michael was glad there were people like Mel Randolph who were willing to do it and also willing to draw a line at torture.

Mel continued, "staying covert, working in plain sight while hiding what you are really doing is the tradecraft of clandestine officers. To pass information to someone in public without it being observed, the brush pass and dead drops. You will need to understand some of these basics to help maintain our operational security."

"Let's talk about surveillance as an example."

He knew that Tom Bradley was a federal law enforcement officer and had likely conducted surveillance using cameras and video, standard federal law enforcement procedures and protocols to develop evidence for court. "Tom, what do you think are the best ways to conduct covert surveillance?"

"For a fixed location, operate in plain sight, a surveying crew, gas line repair crew or even better trash collection."

"You've been to the school haven't you."

Tom smiled, "Yes but of course that's only in my classified personnel materials."

Michael had no idea what they were talking about, "what is the school?"

Mel shrugged, "go ahead and tell him, the existence of the school has been out there in the public domain like the farm, the CIA just never acknowledges its existence or exactly what it does, and they are always changing and morphing."

Michael knew Tom he could see from his expression; this was going to be an interesting story.

"The school is run by the CIA, but it's not a school in a fixed location; it moves across the country always in larger cities. It is a training program on how to conduct surveillance covertly using limited and simple technology. The emphasis is on how to hide in plain sight. Not hidden away in some van, room with two-way mirrors or an apartment across the street with the shades pulled down. The CIA offers a few slots in some sessions to federal law enforcement officers. I went when I worked for OSI years ago, in Charlotte North Carolina."

Mel explained, "The school operates completely under the jurisdiction of the CIA. Local law enforcement and even federal law enforcement agencies in the area are not aware the school is present and functioning in their jurisdiction. There are no weapons involved, so no safety issues are created in this arrangement."

Michael wanted to hear more, "Come on Tom, I know you. There is a good story about what you did in Charlotte."

"The first month we were at a compound rented by the CIA on Lake Norman north of Charlotte, it was used by companies for retreats and had lots of facilities; there were classroom sessions and practice sessions, learning the basic trade of surveyors, cable repair, power line, gas company and my favorite garbage and rubbish collection. There was no technical lingo to remember, no fancy tools to carry around, just clean stuff up. The class was broken up into teams of three. Each team had to decide on their cover. I was lucky I was with two CIA classmates who also favored trash collection. The CIA had all the equipment, uniforms for each cover, and then we were sent out for one work week of surveillance. We even had a truck exactly like the municipal crews had for neighborhood clean-up."

"Our *target* was a family home in the south-central side of Charlotte middle class neighborhood with a mixture of residential and small business, near Freedom Park. We decided to play it like we were on a special project team for the neighborhood to get all the eyesores out of the neighborhood. Each team had to remain covert for five working days. In the evenings we lived at the compound near Lake Norman."

Michael was surprised by this interesting training, "What happened if the police or someone approached you?"

"The team was on its own. They told us to be quiet if we were put in jail for some reason; they told us the local FBI would have us out in a few days; they would be told it was an FBI operation from Washington DC; nobody other than a deputy director in the FBI and the director of the FBI would know it was the CIA running the school."

"What about the family?"

"All the pictures were deleted each evening after the instructors reviewed them to confirm our work. It was just a regular family. Their house was just chosen as a target for training purposes."

Mel asked, "How did your team do?"

Tom laughed, "This is the good part of the story. On the last day, Friday, a local newspaper reporter showed up toward the end of the day. Several people had called the newspaper about the amazing cleanup being done by the city around their neighborhood. The picture ran on

Saturday. A short article said city officials could not find which crew had done the job and could not identify the city workers in the photograph, and the names did not match names on the sanitation crews. The guy running the school gave us grief; he was upset we allowed our picture to be taken, but he admitted we passed because the article did not run until Saturday. We maintained cover for five working days. We thought it might drive that reporter crazy trying to find the mysterious work crew."

Mel went to the white board and drew a small circular diagram, "This is the intelligence cycle. Directions-coming from senior officials and policy makers, which leads to Collection-tasking to collect specific information, the next step Collation-collecting and organizing the information into structured databases, then Interpretation- analyzing the information and turning it into intelligence products, Dissemination-sharing the intelligence products and then the cycle continues in a loop. In this model, Michael is essentially responsible for the directions, what you need for the investigation."

Mel drew a tabular matrix and wrote in some titles and information "This is a simple example of an intelligence collection plan, the essential elements of data necessary in the far-left vertical column, along the horizontal rows are intelligence sources and modes of collection, including SIGNIT-signals intelligence, HUMINIT-human intelligence, IMINT-image intelligence, OSINT-open source intelligence and Diplomatic-Government. For example, an element how many tanks are deployed with sources and modes coming classically from IMINT using satellite, element-number of soldiers called in from reserve, sources and modes human intelligence and possibly also signals intelligence. Through a structured process we identify the modalities of collecting intelligence (evidence) of the key elements you and the team identify."

Mel moved on, "The same type of table used for the collection plan can be used to provide an Indicator/Warnings Matrix. If you were looking to assess how likely an enemy is going to attack, large number of tanks deployed red, few reserves called in would be green, and you can start to see visually through a scorecard like this what the likelihood is of an attack; the more red the more likely. For an investigation like this, an indicator matrix is not so important, but it is one way to balance conflicting information."

Michael and Tom saw strong parallels with the investigative process they used, an investigative plan to collect evidence, analyze and evaluate the evidence and make decisions for collecting more evidence, before summarizing the evidence in a report.

Mel was finished, "That's it for me, any questions?"

Michael had something on his mind from the past, "Can I ask a difficult question about 9/11?"

"Sure shoot."

"I was in grade school at the time. It had made a strong impact on me watching my parents and teachers in the days and weeks later. I heard adults and reporters on the news say, there was general information about a threat but no information about how an airplane could be used as a weapon to attack. Even when I was a kid that didn't make sense. Surely someone had thought that such a thing could happen."

"You are absolutely correct; there was a massive failure of intelligence. Investigations in the months and years following 9/11 found that there were more than thirteen specific intelligence references collated into the Counter terrorism centers databases specifically identifying terrorists' use of commercial aircraft to attack high profile American buildings. There was a failure in dissemination and sharing; the information was not fully evaluated through the intelligence community for further analysis. There were indicators waiting there to be displayed in a threat matrix, and it would have been flashing red, if it would have all been done correctly. Too much bureaucracy and operating in informational and organizational silos. I was at the very beginning of my intelligence career in Jordan; it was professionally humbling. Many professionals in the intelligence community still carry some sense of guilt for the lives lost, our failure as guardians."

Mel took Michael and Tom to a small office suite that had been set up for their team; the team was there ready to get to work. Mel quickly introduced them, he smiled and said its time for the Phantom Project to get to work and he left. Mel had other work to attend to including a meeting with the ambassador, he would be curious about the two trade representatives in the embassy detailed to the CIA station. The Ambassador knew Mel would not tell him; he did not have a need to know. The Phantom team had Shane Harmon (NSA) analyst 12 years in NSA, the last 7 in Abu Dhabi, most experienced with the Blackhole platforms; and Lisa Higdon (NSA) 8 years NSA, the last 4 in Abu Dhabi; Craig Collins (CIA) 14 years in the CIA, last 8 in Abu Dhabi; Tim Rogan (CIA) 8 years in CIA, last 3 in Abu Dhabi; and Jamila al-Fatoon (CIA) 10 years in CIA, last 6 in Abu Dhabi.

Michael and Tom were wearing suits; he noticed that the two from the NSA were dressed in para-military tactical clothes and the CIA covert operators were dressed like Mel, business casual. "I expected you all to be dressed like Lisa and Shane; how should we dress?"

Craig answered, "Lisa and Shane work here in the station, they do not go into the field so they can wear anything appropriate, they like to look like special forces operators."

Lisa shook her head, "Very funny Craig. These clothes are comfortable."

Craig continued, "Tim, Jamila and I are listed as technical IT support staff, so we wear typical Abu Dhabi western business casual for lower-level employees. We will also alter what we wear for operational tasks."

Lisa spoke up again, "Wait till you see Jamila full on Emirati in an Abaya, very convincing."

Jamila laughed, "Yes, an alluring Arabian beauty, only my beautiful almond eyes visible." Jamila was Christian born in Jordan, but her parents came to the US when she was three years old.

Craig answered Michael, "You two should stick with the suit and tie. It would be expected for trade representatives. If we want to deviate in the field, we will discuss it. Tom, you speak and read Arabic is that correct?"

Tom shook his head answering in Arabic "I do pretty well."

Craig nodded "All of us as well. We may use that skill if we are in the field, and it will definitely help with document reviews and surveillance."

Michael took the team through the briefing on the case. They asked a lot of questions.

When Michael finished, Craig asked, "Do you have any background briefing materials? None of us have any background in nuclear. We need to understand what this equipment looks like, how big are these things, a breadbox or the size of a ship. We will need a crash course."

Michael had anticipated this, "I have some background briefings we could cover those tomorrow."

Tim Rogan spoke up, "You understand our basic collection planning process and how we organize our work?"

Tom answered, "Mel gave us an overview, it is parallel and similar to how we do investigative planning and Mel also cautioned us about the importance of protecting covert operational security."

114

Tim continued, "It sounds like the collection plans start with the enrichment equipment; is it installed and in operation? Then look for the conversion equipment and determine whether the design and fabrication are in the UAE or Saudi Arabia and find those locations. Lastly, the role of these two clowns from the US, are they handing out nuclear secrets?"

Michael was nodding in agreement, "Those are the major pieces we have been outlining in the Investigation Plan. Tom and I will use our investigative software on our laptops; it's called Cross-Cut. We can import and export files in different formats."

Craig agreed, "We will use our standard software platforms and tools, and we can coordinate the investigative planning and evidence collection with the intelligence collection and cycle working together as a team and exchange files between the systems."

Lisa asked, "Now let's talk about something important, where are your accommodations?"

Lisa responded like Mel, "VIP accommodations, very nice."

Craig continued, "You are deployed with family, correct?

Michael answered, "My wife is with me, and Tom has his wife and two children."

Craig shook his head, "We need to keep that in mind if we are building any type of narrative around you in the field."

Jamila laughed, "No hookers for Michael or Tom, too bad boys."

Michael was surprised, Jamila had a wicked sense of humor. Surely there was very little prostitution and seriously underground in a Muslim country with strong security services.

Chapter Thirteen
Getting a Little Dirty

Mel came by that Thursday, he wanted to take Michael and Tom on an orientation session. "Okay this evening at 5:30, tell your wives you will be home around 10:00, it's a business dinner. I want you to meet a few of the assets in one of the American consulting companies. An introduction, if we work together on this project. Take a taxi, tell the driver Danara Hotel its near Abu Dhabi mall; they will know it's a landmark for the taxi drivers. The penthouse level, it's called The Saloon, it's a bar and restaurant with good live music. A group from the Philippines sing American pop music, they start at 9:30. Several of our Talon assets like to meet there on Thursday evenings around 7:30 and play darts. No suit, same as you might wear out for a casual dinner back home."

Mel didn't tell them the full story, he wanted to watch and see how they reacted and gauge what kind of situational awareness and poker faces these two had; this would help him judge if they had any skills for going into the field with his team.

Michael and Tom got out of the elevator in the Danara at the penthouse level, it was 5:25 and Mel was there waiting for them. Two Nigerian men were at the door, to collect the cover charge, one man smiled "Friends of Mr. Mel you don't need to pay." The bar was done in a western theme, there was a stage to the right for the band, the bar to the left was actually quite large. There was no one in the bar except them and the workers who seemed to be getting ready for a crowd. The small restaurant was towards the left and there were five couples in booths, westerners eating. Mel didn't look at the menu, "The steaks here are quite good, I come here twice a month. I like the food and the atmosphere, and I work assets here as well."

He gave Michael and Tom a copy of his business card, Mel Fisher Director IT Services US Embassy. "I'm just here showing two new arrivals the Abu Dhabi night scene."

Michael understood that this was like a training session. Working in plain sight, "Yes, thanks Mel."

Tom said quietly, "Two new trade representatives from the embassy."

Mel smiled, "Two new trade representatives in Abu Dhabi with your wives, happily married, is that correct?"

Michael answered quickly, "Yes definitely."

Tom shook his head in agreement, "I intend to keep it that way."

Mel picked up his beer, "Keep that in mind."

Mel was right, the food was very good, Michael would come back here, he had a T-bone and baked potato.

They finished dinner around 6:45. Mel took them towards the very back of the bar, there was an open area, two dart boards with a white board beside each board for keeping score. Michael had thrown darts a few times in college, it was OK, but not like billiards. They sat at one of the round tables with high stools in front of the boards and ordered a round of beers. Mel had two sets of darts in small leather carrying cases. He suggested they practice a little. At around 7:00 people started coming in, well more precisely women. First a group of 4, they looked Arab or middle eastern. Michael saw them as they sat down together at the bar near the restaurant. They started smoking, Michael noticed, they took off the thin shawls, revealing lots of cleavage. They took off their flats and got stiletto heels out of their large bags. Then there was a group of six women. They looked central Asian, maybe Kazakhstan or Uzbekistan, they had a spot at the bar in the middle section. By 7:30 the bar was filling up, very few men, the largest proportion were Asian women, Thailand, Vietnam and Malaysia in groups of three to five at a time. The

117

bar was filling up with attractive women, but there were almost no men. Tom and Michael knew what was going on, it was like a supermarket. The women were waiting to be selected, or as Michael would find out they would search out a customer. Michael could not believe it, this was a hooker bar, the women were all attractive maybe 30 to 40 years old, clean and polished looking. They looked like attractive housewives looking for a good time on the town. He would wait to get the story about this later, it would break cover to quiz Mel here at the bar.

Mel's contacts arrived around 7:40, and Michael and Tom were introduced to Bob Franklin, Keith Sampson and Byron Hilliard.

Mel introduced them, "This is Michael and Tom, two new members of the team at the embassy."

The three men knew "members of the team" meant Michael and Tom were working inside the CIA station, and they would know that the three of them were assets.

Mel was talking not loudly but not in a whisper, "These guys work for Talon training Emiratis finest to be covert operators, they handle the paramilitary training. All three are former Delta operators. Bob, Keith and Byron." This was all true.

They all shook hands.

Bob spoke as he put the flights onto his darts. "What do you guys do at the embassy?"

Michael started, "Trade representatives for the nuclear power program. We are here to check in with the two biggest American suppliers on the project and make sure everything is going well on their end. The Emiratis are talking about building more reactors. We will also meet with officials from the Emirati company operating the nuclear power plant, see if they are satisfied."

Tom chimed in, "there are also some big maintenance contracts coming up, maybe we can get some more business for other US companies."

Mel was pleased, Michael and Tom fell right into their roles.

Michael had seen all three men come in with three Asian women, the women had gone to the bar and ordered drinks and finger food. They were now sitting with the three Talon men at the table next to them at the other dart board. The men were 40 to 45, fit but not big muscular types; looked more like middle distance runners, lean. He thought Delta guys looked like linemen in football, these guys looked more like lean line-backers or defensive backs.

Keith introduced Michael and Tom, "This is Yu-Yu, Lin-Lin and Pin-Pin they are from Vietnam," the three ladies smiled and waved. They were dressed attractively but not like the hookers. Moments later a very attractive woman came and put her hand on Mel's shoulder. An Elegant looking lady about 35, a little cleavage showing and a knee length red dress. She asked Mel, if she could play darts tonight, he said sure and introduced them to Don-Don from Malaysia. Two other Malaysian women quickly moved in, one next to Tom and one next to Michael.

Michael felt her hand go onto his thigh under the table and give a slow squeeze. "I'm Li-Li friend of Don-Don can we be partners?"

Michael answered quietly, "Sorry I don't need a partner."

"Sure, you need a partner, you ask Mr. Mel, very good massage, very good service."

She was pushing her breast into his side. Michael answered again quietly "No thank you, I have my wife in Abu Dhabi, she is a very jealous woman, she takes very good care of me."

Li-Li looked at Mel, "His wife is in Abu Dhabi is this sure?"

Mel shook his head, "Yes both Tom and Michael have their wives with them."

Li-Li got up, "You two miss a good time, maybe you should send your wives home."

The two women retreated, and the word spread to the Asian network the two new friends of Mel had wives in town. Men started to come in around 8:00 and slowly selections were made, and people left the bar together. Michael noticed the women and men were cautious; there was no kissing, and any touching was very subtle.

They played darts and talked and drank beer, sharing stories about where they had grown up back in the States. Michael and Tom left around 9:15 along with Mel with Don-Don following them. Mel said he didn't usually stay for the music. Michael and Tom saw Mel get into a Taxi with Don-Don. Michael and Tom got into a taxi. They didn't say anything about Mel, it was his personal business. When he got home, Marion waved her hands, "Oh my you smell like smoke."

"Yeah, it is a restaurant and bar, and they allow smoking inside."

The next Sunday Mel came by the Phantom office to talk with Michael and Tom, "You both did pretty well, I wondered if one of you would freak out, what did you think of Abu Dhabi's nightlife?"

Michael was curious, "How does it work? Why do the Emirati officials allow this? They are so religiously conservative and they have lots of security and police."

"Emiratis actually run the prostitution business in Abu Dhabi and Dubai. There are four bars in Abu Dhabi, they are all like the Danara, not the big expensive tourist hotels, just a little bit seedy. You will be hard pressed to find a hooker anywhere else, certainly not on the streets. The Nigerians, Russians and Lebanese occasionally try and set up local rings and the Emiratis find them, shut them down and throw them in jail with big stories in the local newspapers. The Manwari family runs the business in Abu Dhabi. Abdulla Manwari is a senior security official, he is in charge, three of his brothers run the business through local companies. The women hear about the business through networks of friends in their home countries, the Emiratis screen them making sure they do not have criminal records; they have local contacts in the countries. The women are given a fake job offer with one of the Manwari companies, typing clerk, warehouse attendant, the women know the deal. The women pay the Manwari contact about $5000. The women get a legitimate two-year Residence Visa, with a Manwari company as their sponsor, but they never have to show up at work. They have local coordinators who help them find a cheap place to live and then they are on their own. The rules are simple, only work in one of the four bars, dress modestly in public, no stealing and no violence. The bars check them the first time they come, to make sure they have a Manwari residence visa. The men looking for some action in the bars are all expats with residence visas, and the women are all working ladies with residence visas. To get a residence Visa requires a health check and blood test, a primary reason for the health check is to test for STDs, somewhat safe sex but most people insist on condoms to be safer."

"Some of the central Asians, Russians and Nigerians try and run some scams on the side, usually with friends in the country. Stay away from them, the women from Vietnam, Thailand and Malaysia are different. They usually have been abandoned by a husband or divorced with no support; they need to support their parents or children or both and are not well educated. They can make ten times what they can make at home if they can even find a job. They usually last two or three visa cycles, in six years they can bank enough for a small home and have enough to live off for ten to fifteen years, enough time for their children to get out of school and support them. The Emiratis see it as a practical need. There are large numbers of men in their country expat workers many without their wives, they figure a safe outlet for sex is better than criminal enterprises and sexually transmitted disease. The difficulty is the labor camps, they don't get access to women. The labor camps are almost like prisons, they give them three-year work visas then send them home and get a replacement. The working women are a bit tribal, between the different ethnic groups, sometimes frictions arise if a regular customer is poached by a competing tribe."

"These Asian women are survivors, they can't find a way to feed their children or parents and they are doing what they can. There are a few bad apples, but most of them are decent people in my book. They learn just enough English to get by, they live together, the groups you see, four or five women in a small rundown apartment. The Asian women have several buildings they like, usually with Asian groceries and restaurants nearby. There are cash transfer companies all over Abu Dhabi, certain ones cater to their currency. They send most of their money back home through the transfer companies."

Tom asked, "What's the deal with the women with the three guys from Talon."

"Abu Dhabi wife, that's what the ladies say. Those three guys are a little bit older; they aren't looking for a new woman every week and they are all divorced. They make a deal with the girls, they pay them a fixed amount each month, the girls call it their salary. They don't work the bars or service any other men, and they live with them like wives, taking care of the homes and cooking. For the girls its more stable income and a better life, they get to live in a comfortable home. I have never been married, Don-Don and I have been together for about four years, she lives with me. I wanted to see how you were going to react to the scene, so I had her come over after we arrived yesterday. I'm not cheating on anyone, the Emirati security services are not going to mess with a CIA station chief, the top officials in Emirati government know who I am, there is no hazard or risk to the operations."

Michael was surprised by all of this, "And these bars, this is common knowledge?"

"Any expat with any sense and who has been in Abu Dhabi for more than a year or two knows what goes on at these few bars, and they steer clear if they don't want to be around it."

This was not the kind of place Michael and Tom were accustomed to spending time. They wouldn't want Marion and Amanda to see a picture of them when Don-Dons friends got in close. This was common knowledge; they would need to tell their wives about the Danara hotel restaurant and bar; they would tell them what goes on there. That's where their new boss had some friends, and they would need to go for some meetings.

Tom wanted to be truthful, "We need to tell them the right way, consistent with investigative work. We say undercover meetings with confidential sources. That is true, we are acting covertly, and Talon assets are confidential sources. Amanda and Marion are going to ask us about our boss. We tell them the truth, he has a regular lady. He has lived with her for several years, and he isn't married, and he seems like a good guy."

They knew they would be back there with Mel on occasion and their wives were smart women, they would hear the stories about the Danara hotel. Marion was surprised when Michael told her about the hooker bar and restaurant. A US official, Michael's boss was living with one of the women, very strange. Michael said the women looked like housewives dressed up provocatively. Michael told her the story he had been told; the Emiratis controlled the entire thing, and the women in this place worked like free agents, it wasn't a forced sex trade. Women with difficulties supporting themselves, children and their families. Not a happy story, people trying to survive and get through life. Michael told Marion the full story about the place. Marion listened, "okay I understand, no touching right, it sounds a little bit dirty."

Chapter Fourteen
Hunting for the Enrichment Cascade

Michael and Tom had worked with Craig to lay out an investigative and intelligence collection plan, Mel had reviewed and approved the collection plan and the initial tasks. Michael had already given the overview briefings of the equipment and systems necessary for a nuclear weapons program. They were starting with the largest, the enrichment facility where they had a suspected location. They knew what they were looking for, piping and valves and thousands of the cannisters which contained the high-speed centrifuges inside of them. Spinning the uranium hexafluoride gas so fast the lighter atoms of U235 and U238 become stratified from each other. The U235 enriched stream sent on to the next centrifuge, where the separation continues thousands of times to go from less than 1% to more than 95% U235.

They would look for the other facilities later, a conversion plant to turn uranium ore into uranium gas. The greatest hazard was chemical not nuclear. The fluorine gas, if it was released to the air, it would form hydrofluoric acid. This was a relatively simple industrial facility. There would be truckloads of yellow cake arriving from the processing site at the mine. There was another chemical processing plant to produce uranium metal from the enriched uranium. This would be a small facility but with significant nuclear safety controls because the uranium was capable of a chain reaction. Then an even smaller facility to fabricate a warhead, with precision digital machine tools for the uranium metal, high-explosive lenses and other internal components of the nuclear weapon.

They were starting on the work for the enrichment facility; the base was only about a hundred kilometers from the UAE-Saudi border.

Shane and Lisa had worked through the intelligence databases collecting imagery from satellites during the construction. There were enough images for a good overview but not thousands. The satellite platforms were valuable assets, why spend time doing surveillance on an airfield being constructed for joint use by Saudi and American fighter jets. Lisa gave a briefing to the team going through the imagery over time, from initial construction through a recent image only two years ago.

Lisa described the facility as she went through the images, using a laser pointer to trace out the feature. "There are two long runways, each about 5000 feet long by 100 feet wide, capable of handling large transport planes if necessary. They intersect each other almost in the shape of an X, but not crossing at the mid-points, but about 1000 feet near the ends at the northern end of the field. This runway runs NW to SE and this one NE to SW, then there is this large southern pie shaped area between the two runways. This is where the massive underground hangars are with the munition bunkers on the far southern edge. Here are some images during construction. You can see the deep cutout of the shape of the large bunkers clearly visible. Here it is complete. The bunkers are all covered again with sand. Here are the entrances and a network of paved jetways and truck roads connecting the bunkers and hangars to the runways and a roadway system inside the perimeter of the base. The total area inside this security fence is about nine square miles, just about a square three miles on a side. Here is an entrance gate near the northwest corner and another entrance gate on the southeastern corner. There are security gates and guard houses at each gate. There are above ground buildings in the northeastern quadrant of the square, including housing accommodations for permanent base staff."

Lisa focused on an area near the southeast portion of the base, "This is about a hundred yards away from the southern end of the runway running northwest to southeast. You see there was another excavation area separate from the main hangars and munitions storage. It seemed strange to me and Shane, why have this separate underground not connected to the large pie shaped area near the intersection of the runways? Why have another group of hangars and munitions so far from the central area of air operations? This excavated area in this rectangle is about 400 by 300 feet, 120,000 square feet, large enough for the 90,000 square foot cascade facility. This image shows the final configuration. There is a roadway leading into the storage area on the southern end, and it connects to the roadway system around the base. If there was an enrichment cascade it would most likely be here, separated from the main logistics and aircraft operations and large munitions storage areas. It was covered with sand after construction. She showed the final image of the base and surrounding areas, this is two years ago looking much the same as an image from ten years earlier, with some additional buildings on the northern portion of the base."

Mel approved the tasking request (FalseFalcon) two weeks of daytime surveillance and analysis from RQ-4A "Global Hawk" drone flights from Al-Dhafra air force base in Abu Dhabi. CIA analysts in Langley were tasked with reviewing the drone footage, analyzing traffic to and from the Saudi base focused on the storage area in the southeast corner of the base. Shane and Lisa received the report from Langley in the middle of September.

Shane briefed the team on the results, "In this two-week period there were only two trucks that entered the southeast storage area, about one week apart. One from Riyadh was traced to a military supply depot, uniforms, tactical gear, consumables like toilet paper and soap. The other truck was traced to the Al Jabeer small munitions factory NE of Riyadh. CIA Langley reports that the Saudis have manufactured some of their own tank artillery and gravity drop bombs in this facility for several years. Nothing indicating the delivery of uranium hexafluoride."

Craig and Tim were hitting the local bars in the evenings, at Al Danara and the Al Ain Oasis, bars frequented by Americans working at the Saudi Air base coming to Abu Dhabi on the weekends. Saudi Arabia had none of the creature comforts of Abu Dhabi, no bars and nothing like Al Danara or the Oasis. They were glad to see Reggie in The Cage on the mezzanine level of the Al Danara, a smaller and livelier place than the penthouse. The Asian women ruled the penthouse bar, and the Nigerian and Ethiopian women ruled the smaller and rowdier Cage on the first floor. Reggie was in his favorite corner booth near the small stage with two Ethiopian women. He was as loud as always with two South African friends he stayed with when he was in Abu Dhabi. About a year earlier Craig and Tim found out that Reggie was stealing supplies from the airbase, small tools, electronics nothing of military value, and he was bringing them to his South African friends. They would sell them in Dubai to shops at the Dragon Mart free trade zone. Reggie was in supplies and logistics, and he knew how to alter inventories and records to cover his tracks. They made a deal with Reggie; if he stuck to these small things, they would not turn him over to the military, but he would need to help them out when they needed information about the base.

Now they needed information, Craig and Tim sat with Reggie. These girls spoke very good English. Craig ordered drinks, "Reggie the ladies need to take a break. Give them some money for some dinner. They can go to the place in the lobby."

Craig continued when the women were gone, "We want to know what is in the underground southeast storage area, and whether there are passages or doorways in the walls or floors."

"It's not open to US personnel, I have never been in there, but I can get in, just tag along with one of my Saudi comrades. I will be back in Abu Dhabi next week."

***

Reggie saw his friend Ahmad that next week, "Ahmad can you help me out? I understand you guys have some of that landing gear lubricant in the southeast storage facility, can I tag along to get a case?"

"Sure Reggie, I don't know why they don't just give you guys access, there is nothing special in there it's mostly empty." Reggie was always helping him out.

***

Reggie sent the women upstairs for dinner when he saw Craig and Tim, he slipped the USB to Craig. "I got pictures when my buddy wasn't paying attention. Its big, maybe 50 yards wide and 50 yards long, the ceiling height was probably 30 feet. There is an overhead crane for large deliveries. It's mostly empty, there were maintenance tools and consumables, some spare parts, general consumables and some test equipment used by maintenance crews for aircraft. Inside there was a side rollup door, the size of a garage door. It leads into a munitions area, and there was a personnel access door. The door was not locked, I looked in the small munitions storage area, there were some gravity drop bombs in there. There were no other doorways on the other walls or the floor, no seams for a hatch or anything like that."

Craig thought about the spinning centrifuges possibly behind some hidden access, "could you hear any noise, rotating machinery or motors?"

"No, definitely not, I walked all around the inside, and it was only me an Ahmad. It was like a Church it was so quiet. It does seem strange, why it is so deep and why the access is so controlled, nothing there seemed that important, it must be 50 feet underground. Maybe they had plans for storing some sensitive equipment there, nothing unusual there now."

The last week of September Michael called a team meeting to review the status of the centrifuge hunt. Craig led the discussion, "The location seems correct, it seems strange to locate a warehouse so deep in an out of way spot. There is nothing there. We have pictures and a good source. There are no other potential large locations on the base, we confirmed that with our source. The global hawk surveillance didn't reveal anything unusual, consistent with the area being a general-purpose warehouse and small munitions storage area for Saudi gravity bombs. Maybe it was intended for the centrifuges, and they got cold feet later and abandoned the effort, sold the stuff, buried it in the sand or they found another location."

Shane remembered something. "The CIA station had a monitoring task underway when I arrived in the station. The State Department and DOE NNSA had asked the station to monitor shipments intended for the Barakah nuclear power plant. Apparently, there was some concern that the Emiratis might divert equipment and materials to other Arab Countries. Dubai had a bad reputation when it came to illegal trade, and I heard there was even illicit nuclear traffic in the 90s."

Michael was nodding in agreement, "You're right, the AQ Khan proliferation network operated out of Dubai for many years. There would be people in the intelligence community familiar with that history."

Shane connected his laptop to the large screen display in the conference room, "Here is the summary report when the work was complete. One of the monitoring points was this truck road that leads from Abu Dhabi directly by the nuclear plant and then on to the Saudi border. There was a twenty percent increase in large truck shipments on the truck road leading from Abu Dhabi-Dubai to the nuclear power plant site these five years when construction was getting underway for the first four reactors. This was a time frame when commerce was generally trending downward, detailed analysis supported the view that the increase was mostly associated with the nuclear plant. But look at the analysis of the traffic along the truck road crossing from the UAE into Saudi. It trended downward three years before the nuclear plant construction as the economy was dropping off with substantial drops in imported goods. Then these two years the truck traffic from the UAE into Saudi Arabia along the truck road that passes the nuclear plant increased ten percent for two years during the peak of nuclear plant construction. Then the truck traffic along the road trends downward again, following the general trend in the Saudi economy and imports was still trending downward for several years. We delivered the data but never heard anything about it and were never requested to follow up on any possible diversions."

"It seems strange, truck traffic into Saudi Arabia along this truck road is on a continuous downward trend for a period of about seven years matching general economic and import trends. Except for two years right at the peak of the UAE nuclear power plant construction project. It doesn't prove anything, but it is a data point we should capture it in our database."

It was sinking into Michael, it looked like the Saudi-UAE nuclear weapons effort never moved past buying materials and equipment for a few thousand centrifuges. If it had gone forward, it wasn't at this airbase it was somewhere else in Saudi Arabia, and they had no idea where to look in the 900,000 square miles of sand and desert. Like IG Ross said maybe there were some centrifuge parts in boxes in the warehouse on the air base.

Michael thought of something, "Lisa can you bring up the last satellite images, the most recent one that shows the wide area view."

Michael used a laser pointer, "There it's a large electrical switchyard."

"Bring up the same view a few years after the base was finished." They saw the airbase, but there was no switch yard.

Tom knew where Michael was going, "Centrifuges consume massive amounts of electricity, follow the juice."

Shane got it, "The UAE nuclear plant is not far away, that could provide a lot of electricity. The Saudis and UAE interconnected their grid systems starting about a decade ago. They will be instrumented to track power flow. It will all be digital stuff these days, we will be able to get inside with Blackhole."

Craig opened up the intelligence collection matrix and intelligence plan, and was building task descriptions as they were talking, "We need tasks for evaluating the electrical power grid flow into the Saudi airfield and the UAE interconnect; we will use the Blackhole platforms to tease out the data."

Lisa added some details, "We can work through the servers and map the network of SCADA instruments recording power flows all accessible through Blackhole. Since the Saudis have connected their grid system with the UAE, the Saudi network of instruments was also accessible to us. Collect raw data voltage, current, frequency and power factors from the hundreds of instruments for say the last two months from the historical data. They should have archived data for hourly averages on the servers, that will be accurate enough for what we need, looking for a long continuous draw of power"

Craig was shaking his head "Okay got it, keep going."

Shane picked up, "We bundle and ship it back to Langley. We will need them to do some computer modeling, it will take them some time; we will need to lay out the local grid topology. They will have to build a model of the local grid and power system and analyze the power draw for the airbase."

Michael nodded, "Well it's a gamble, it will take them a few weeks to build a model and analyze the data. But if they have a few thousand centrifuges operating anytime in that two-month window, they will be able to see it in the electrical demand."

Mel approved the tasks for POWERSURGE, it would take a while. They had other work to do. Williams and Harrison were coming to Abu Dhabi next week, they had been monitoring their government email and looking for travel plans. Craig had been working on the collection plan for monitoring Williams and Harrison while they were in Abu Dhabi, Michael and Tom would see another aspect of the Blackhole operation.

Mohammed Bin "Aziz" Gamal was excited. Williams and Harrison would be in Abu Dhabi the next two weeks. Aziz had been working with two of King Rashid's cousins from Saudi Arabia for several years, starting when Rashid was still the Saudi crown prince. Rashid's cousins Salem and Waddah were like Aziz, big thinkers looking at the big picture. Aziz had met Williams and Harrison, they were in the UAE to help with the nuclear program, and they were working directly for the Secretary of State, looking to help Saudi Arabia start a nuclear power program. The US congress was trying to block it, but Williams and Harrison had orders to make it happen, offer assistance, connect them with American suppliers. Aziz knew it was a goldmine, the UAE was monitoring the American's email and mobiles when they were in the UAE, these new monitoring systems that the Americans had helped the Emiratis build. Aziz decided that Williams and Harrison could help get American enrichment technology, they could use the design information for a weapons program. They would scam Williams and Harrison, letting them think the Saudis were in the market for commercial contracts.

Those plans had already been cancelled, but they might be able to get these designs for advanced centrifuges.

Aziz was disappointed how slow things were moving with the nuclear weapons program, they needed American help. His cousin Dubai Sheikh Gamal and the Abu Dhabi Sheikh were moving too slow. They also did not give him credit for everything he had done for the last ten years. The idea of (Al-mukhvih Nawah) Hidden Nucleus was his and he started it up, it wasn't his fault if they were moving so slow and would not scale up his enterprise. Salem and Waddah were also sure their cousin King Rashid would be pleased if they could get this American technology for the nuclear program, it would really start producing results. Salem and Waddah liked Aziz, they hadn't gone to college either, and met him through smuggling, perfume, watches, costume jewelry, fake designer bags and especially pornography that was very profitable on the black market in Saudi Arabia. Aziz knew a good business; he was right this nuclear stuff was just smuggling; you didn't need to be a scientist.

Aziz ensured the Baniyas villa was cleaned and ready, the swimming pool was cleaned, condoms in the bedrooms, the freezer and refrigerator were full. Frank and Shawn would live at the villa this trip, he had convinced them it would be more fun. He even had a driver with an SUV take them into Abu Dhabi to the bars and they could choose the women they liked, bring them back to the villa, and the driver could take the women back home. Aziz had saved their previous deliveries of hard drives in a safe in his home, waiting to surprise the Sheikh when it was complete. Salem and Waddah liked to party with Frank and Shawn when they were here; Saudi Arabia didn't have the same opportunities as Abu Dhabi and Dubai.

Franklin Williams and Shawn Harrison knew this might be their last trip to Abu Dhabi, maybe one more; they got the news from the chief of staff. The Secretary of State would be moving on before the president left office, the end of his second term was approaching. They hoped they would be able to finish their mission. The Secretary was very clear when he first met with them. Congress was trying to block American nuclear companies from getting tens of billions of dollars of Saudi business. He wanted to make sure the Saudis could get everything they needed. The Secretary was loud and clear we should give them everything, we should supply them reactors and enrichment equipment, help them build an entire nuclear power industry based on American nuclear technology. He wanted Franklin and Shawn to help support this effort, and they found Saudi contacts through some UAE contacts. Franklin Williams knew the Dubai Sheikh's cousin Aziz and he had found important contacts with relatives of the Saudi King, and according to them they wanted to go big into the nuclear fuel cycle.

Craig briefed Michael and Tom about the next phase, "Every word that Williams and Harrison speak once they turn on their cell phones in Abu Dhabi will be captured by Blackhole. Every email and text message, their location will be tracked. We can activate the camera on their laptop to get a photograph or video. We can use their phones to record conversations in the car or bars."

"We have emails with directions for them to stay in this Baniyas villa. They have been communicating with Mohammed Bin "Aziz" Gamal, the cousin of the Dubai Sheikh Gamal. We have his cell phone under surveillance as well. We know there are two Saudis, Salem and Waddah, but we don't know who they are yet."

Craig brought up pictures and a map, "Tim and Craig will install cameras and microphones there and also Aziz's apartment in Abu Dhabi. Lisa and Shane are responsible for the surveillance monitoring; they listen actively sometimes, and they use key word activations to flag them. They stand down when the subjects go to bed; they can check the overnight for any key word activation. They rotate time, its tiring work when they are monitoring. There is an extra monitoring computer there, next to Lisa's monitoring station, you two can listen in if you want."

Within a day of the American's arrival, they were capturing everything from the Americans and Aziz, Salem and Waddah. They got pictures of Salem and Waddah and found their identification accessing the database of Saudi national ID cards. It was connected to the UAE immigration database. Salem and Waddah were cousins of King Rashid in Saudi Arabia, senior officials in Saudi Customs. The third day Michael saw Lisa taking a break. He got a cup of coffee and sat down beside her in the small lunchroom. "How's it going, anything yet?"

"Nothing useful, the Emirati and two Saudis talk a lot about smuggling; fake watches, purses and perfume when they aren't around Williams and Harrison. When they are all together in the villa it's just sex with hookers, shooting guns outside in the desert, playing video games and drinking."

The next day Lisa was getting ready to leave for the day, all four subjects were all in the villa watching SportTV. Then she heard Harrison "We should talk some business now."

They turned off the television, Lisa focused and was ready to type in comments, the surveillance software had a dialog box, Lisa and Shane typed their observations. The software would automatically tag the comments in the dialog box to the proper location in surveillance video or audio file. Later the comments could be reviewed and exported for summary memos and, if you clicked on a comment, it would go to the correct location on the surveillance video or audio.

Lisa typed centrifuge business discussion into the dialog box as Shawn started, "I have lots of drawings and manuals, about 2000 files this time, Aziz here is the drive."

Aziz connected the drive to his computer, and he looked through the files as Shawn continued, "There aren't too many more files we need to give you to get started with bidding; can we talk about the scope of program that you are contemplating?"

Lisa accessed Aziz's laptop through the villa wi-fi and downloaded the files on the external drive he had just connected to his computer. She typed, hard drive files downloaded, given from Harrison to Aziz.

Aziz kept looking through the files. He wasn't quite sure what the information meant, but it looked technical, and the files were marked confidential. He thought about what he had talked about with Salam and Waddah, they needed something big to hook the Americans on the scam. "The leadership is interested in about fifteen or twenty reactors, so I think 100,000 centrifuges, maybe 50,000 to start and then 50,000 five years later. The country that agrees to supply the enrichment facilities will get the reactor business."

Williams and Harrison knew that was a lot, but they weren't experts on this stuff, degrees in accounting and political science, they both knew that would be a huge business opportunity for American companies. That many reactors would be huge business, they could probably sell them the enrichment plant at cost. Shawn smiled, "really good we should begin to think about a price structure and terms and conditions, we will talk with some companies when we get back to DC."

Aziz smiled they were buying the scam, "Okay but we need to have complete design information before we make a deal, we have some engineers and scientists that need to confirm these designs meet our needs."

Lisa waved Michael and Tom over when she saw them come in, "We got something yesterday. Here listen and I downloaded the files in this folder from the drive they gave Aziz."

Lisa opened the dialog box and clicked on her comments from yesterday. Michael and Tom listened, and Michael looked through the files.

Michael was done listening, and he was scanning through the files, "This doesn't make any sense; these drawings are for spare parts and the manuals are maintenance manuals for general plant components valves and motors. This information looks useless, it certainly is not secret centrifuge information. That number of centrifuges, that is three to four times what a small country like Saudi Arabia would need, these people don't seem to know what they are talking about. They aren't talking about weapons, they are talking about a commercial nuclear power program."

It was the middle of October, the team could see that the investigation was not going to find a nuclear weapons program, no centrifuges in Saudi Arabia and the American connection was a couple of party animals wasting time and US taxpayer money for trips to the UAE. They were talking about commercial nuclear reactors for enrichment, not nuclear weapons. There are prohibitions against transfers of this technology, but it's not why they came to Abu Dhabi. They would interview others in the State Department and Williams and Harrison when they got back.

Michael was disappointed, but they would go with the facts; they would keep digging, they had time. It would be good news if there was no nuclear weapons program in Saudi Arabia, but investigators were disappointed when their preliminary investigations were off the mark. Inspector General Ross and the Director of the CIA had invested big in using Blackhole for this work, Michael knew his reputation would take a hit for missing the mark so badly with his preliminary investigation. This would be the first big miss of his career, but he needed to keep digging. He still had a feeling deep down, he laughed to himself Agent Jethro called it his gut on the TV classic Navy Yard Investigations. Tom used to call him Agent Timmy when they first worked together, well maybe Agent Timmy had a gut instinct.

Chapter Fifteen
Hidden Nucleus

The rest of the stay for Williams and Harrison continued the same, lots of partying and the little discussion about the nuclear business was not useful. Williams and Harrison wanting to talk commercial but Aziz refusing at this stage, not till they did technical due diligence. Shane and Lisa listened to about 70% of the surveillance, the rest they relied on extensive key word recognition triggers in Arabic and English to key them to listen to something.

Lisa heard a puzzling discussion between Aziz and Salem late in the day in Aziz's apartment in Abu Dhabi. The software system flagged a key word during the discussion "Iran", she put on her headphones and listened to the playback. She typed, *Hidden Nucleus* in the dialog box. What are they talking about? I need to get Tom to listen to this tomorrow.

Lisa saw Michael and Tom come in, "Tom come here and listen to this. It's something but it doesn't make any sense to me, it's Aziz and Salem in Aziz's apartment late yesterday afternoon."

Tom and Michael walked over, Tom put on Lisa's headphones. Michael got a cup of coffee for Tom and one for himself. He sat at the extra monitoring station; turned the seat around watching Tom, thinking he should have studied Arabic or any foreign language.

Tom took a sip of coffee as he listened to Aziz speaking first, he knew their voices from earlier conversations.

"You know Salem, I do not understand Sheikh Abdullah and King Rashid, why are they satisfied with so little progress. I built hidden nucleus from the ground up, it took us years of work. Then we had more than ten thousand incubators and kept making progress with more than twenty thousand. Why did we stop; we could have more? Now we only have one seed after years of work, one seed. They seem happy with this; I do not understand."

"Yes brother, you are right. I do not understand why King Rashid is satisfied with this; he says there is no more need for more procurement. I know ABZ is cautious, he is very concerned about the nuclear power program and upsetting the Americans. We should be accelerating, ten to twenty seeds a year. We need to be worried about Iran and Israel."

Michael saw Tom as he jumped up with his coffee cup in his hand, coffee spilled all over the floor. "Crap . . . Lisa play that again!"

Tom was cleaning up the coffee, everyone came into the monitoring room. Tom stood back up, explaining, "When we did the initial investigation on the historical database, we identified some code words. They are very disciplined in using the terms, fertilizer is enrichment, an incubator is a centrifuge, and a seed is a warhead."

Lisa bolted out of her chair, "oh crap, Aziz says they have a seed."

Lisa translated the conversation for Michael as she played it for the rest of the team through the speaker. Craig shook his head "These idiots think they are moving too slow; that's what they want from Williams and Harrison; they want to scale up from what they have. They want to build more centrifuges and are looking to steal the American designs. They are scamming Williams and Harrison to give them the design information for American centrifuges."

That morning the power analysis came back to Mel from Langley. He rushed to the Phantom Project office. He saw they were all in the monitoring room.

Craig saw Mel come in "We have something you need to hear."

"Hold on, I have something you need to see first about the power consumption at the military base."

Mell logged onto the computer where Michael was sitting and brought it up on the display mounted to the wall. He opened his email. He went to an email marked SECRET. They saw it was from the Director of the CIA. They read the short message from the Director: *The national security council will be briefed on the attached SECRET report, the power consumption of the military base is grossly above anything necessary for the facility. You are onto something, but there are a lot of skeptical voices here in DC.*

Mel brought up the summary page of the classified power flow report; the power draw from the switchyard to the military base switchyard for this past August and September is sufficient to operate 20,000 to 30,000 centrifuges above the base needs of the airbase. The paper cautioned, *The power estimates are high confidence as well as the range in number of centrifuges. There could be other covert activities in particular high-powered lasers, electromagnetic pulse or hypervelocity railguns or some type of electric smelting process these can consume large amounts of electricity. The steady consumption of power however is very consistent with continuous centrifuge operation. Analysts warn that errors in grid topology from the field could significantly affect the accuracy.*

Shane sighed, "They think we may have gotten the grid topology wrong; they are saying the numbers may be nonsense if we gave them bad data. Our grid topology is solid. I hate it when HQ people do things like that; do they think we are stupid?"

Mel looked at them, "Don't worry about that; we know its correct. Aren't you guys excited, this is substantial evidence?"

Lisa clicked on the surveillance file, "Listen to this." Tom explained the code words to Mel.

Mel's reaction was like Tom's; he stood up when he heard the number of centrifuges and said "woooo . . . game changer" when he heard there was a warhead. In the course of 2 hours, they had two pieces of intelligence pointing to operating centrifuges at the base and a possible warhead, totally reversing the trajectory of where the evidence from the last five weeks had been pointing.

Mel looked at Michael, "What do you think?"

"I'm still trying to process all of this, I cannot understand how they could have so many centrifuges. We only identified a supply of about five thousand about twenty years ago, but from this it seems like they were putting new ones in service for several years and may have upwards of 30,000 in service. I think Craig is right. Aziz, Salem and Waddah are scamming Harrison and Williams, telling them they want commercial reactors, but they want to scale up warhead production. I don't think what the five of them are doing is a priority for us anymore. The information looks to be useless and the number of centrifuges they are talking about is absurd. Aziz mentioned something we had never heard before."

Tom knew what Michael was thinking, "Hidden nucleus we never came across that term before."

Mel headed toward the conference room, "Everybody grab a cup of coffee; Michael you need to think of your new priorities; Craig bring your laptop; we are going to need some new collection plans."

Everybody was ready, Craig started "Okay if they are operating centrifuges, they must have UF6 coming from somewhere."

Tim and Jamila were mostly quiet during these technical discussions, but Tim was concerned, "We have no idea where to look for that; Michael said that this was a small facility, that would be like looking for a needle in a haystack. We need some clear direction."

Mel stopped them, "Okay, let's hear what Michael thinks, it's his investigation, he sets the priorities."

Michael went to one of the whiteboards, the one that had an outline of Saudi Arabia and the UAE. "Okay, the uranium ores in Saudi Arabia are in these areas. We think we have an enrichment facility here, so somewhere we have a conversion facility to produce UF6, and a metal fabrication facility and a warhead fabrication. We will put them here off the map for the moment. The streams of materials get smaller and smaller and more difficult to trace as you go from ore to a warhead."

He drew arrows tracing out the flow, "There will be large trucks moving processed ore yellow cake to the conversion facility, then large cannisters of UF6 gas going to the enrichment facility, then large cannisters of enriched UF6 going to the metal fabrication plant, then we are dealing with small shipments of metal for warhead fabrication. We need to follow the flow and document evidence of the entire processing route. We need to find the locations of the other facilities and exactly where the centrifuges are; they must be under the warehouse. We don't know how they got so many centrifuges. But Shane has already given us a good idea of when the new centrifuges were delivered, and possibly the other materials. We know a time frame to look."

Shane smiled, "The truck road monitoring anomaly, the increase in truck traffic to Saudi when the nuclear plant was receiving all of its equipment while all Saudi imports were dropping like a rock. Bring in the stuff hidden in the stream of things being brought in for the nuclear power plant. That's consistent with the time frame given by Aziz."

Mel knew the next step for Blackhole assets, "You getting all of this down Craig, for collection tasks?

"I'm tracking Mel, but I haven't heard anything really specific yet."

"Okay consider this, these facilities were probably built out sometime in the last ten years."

Shane picked up on Mel's idea, "Blackhole has been in place for nearly a decade, everything will be in the archival files on Blackhole server farms back in the US. We can query them with new searches through the archives. We have the names of the players that Michael and Tom found from their earlier work and Salem, Aziz and Waddah and these code words."

Mel nodded in agreement, "Okay work out a collection plan, dig deep and wide."

Michael was moving in the same direction. He was working in the cross-cut software system, "We will finish an investigative plan and compare to make sure we are synched up."

The full story became clear as they worked through the database over the next two weeks, filling in some of the gaps from the initial investigation from the MissingLink database and picking up the story after the AQ Khan network was shut down. Michael was impressed, Shane and Lisa were incredibly fast using the blackhole database. The database had sophisticated sorting and querying schemes including artificial intelligence informed algorithms. They went through the vast sea of data much faster than Tom, Michael and Steve Thomas when they had sifted through the missing link database back in Washington. Shane and Lisa were putting in long hours, Michael and Tom were helping formulate search filters and reviewing the documents and files. Tom and Michael were developing summary files in the investigative system on their laptops.

They were ready to brief Mel. The whole team was gathered in the conference room the first week of November. Michael led through the narrative the team had developed working together the last two weeks. It was pieced together using thousands of documents from the blackhole database, including phone call transcripts, text messages, documents, cables, diplomatic wires and emails. Michael combined this information with the findings and evidence he and Tom had from the initial investigation. They had those files with them on their computers.

Michael traced out the complete story with the briefing, "The nuclear weapons program was initially conceived in 1995, an agreement between Zayed bin Sultan Al Nahyan in the UAE and King Fahd of Saudi Arabia. They were fearful of the twin threats of Iran and Israel. Iran was the bigger threat, more likely to use nuclear weapons against Saudi Arabia and the UAE. The Emiratis knew what the AQ Khan network was doing, and the Saudis became an AQ Khan customer, with the Emiratis a silent partner. The Emiratis monitored the AQ Khan networks movements in the UAE, they stole copies of the warhead design that AQ Khan had stored in his Dubai apartment. The Emirati and Saudi Sheikh's agreed to a division of labor, the UAE would develop the warhead design, manufacturing and final construction of warheads. Saudi Arabia would develop uranium enrichment and later plutonium from a research reactor. The Saudis would deliver highly enriched uranium metal ingots to the Emiratis and the completed warheads would come back to the Saudis for storage, along with the bomb housings."

"The Saudis were confident the uranium enrichment was hidden in plain sight from the Americans. In 1995 they began the construction of a new military airfield southwest of Riyadh close to the UAE border. The airfield featured underground hangar facilities and underground munitions storage. In the far end was a large munitions storage area that was in fact built for an enormous centrifuge facility. The Saudis got nervous and decided to modify the facility configuration; the possibility of an American pilot or technician coming across the facility was too great of a concern. The original design and configuration called for three 30,000 square foot enrichment halls side by side, each housing 10,000 centrifuges 50 meters below the surface, accessible through cargo and personnel access. The final design had only two cascade halls side by side each with 12,000 centrifuges 90 meters below the surface, 30 meters below a general warehouse storage area above. The storage area above was 30 meters below the surface not quite as deep as the original design. It was constructed to look like a warehouse with a small munitions storage area. The total footprint is about 20,000 total square feet, 5000 square feet in the rear is hidden behind a large, concealed cargo door, the door was in the northwest corner driven by motors, there are no visible seams. This explains the observations of our source in the warehouse, they built it carefully to conceal the centrifuges deep below."

"The Saudis plan was to store limited supplies in the front of the "warehouse." They also had plans to manufacture dummy munitions for storage there. Gravity drop bombs, they were going to tell the Americans they were making these at the Al Jabeer munitions factory."

Michael described a diagram of the facility layout, "The UF6 cannisters and staff can be moved into the hidden back portion of the facility through the cargo door. They have the overhead cranes and the UF6 can be injected or extracted when it was enriched in this area. Here are elevators and industrial lifts to the lower levels."

"The first centrifuges were under construction starting about the time the AQ Khan network was shutdown, enough to fabricate the first three thousand centrifuges. They planned to install and operate these as a large pilot for a few months and when they were operating properly, they would move forward with the fabrication and installation of the remaining 21,000. There was no more supply after the exposure and collapse of the AQ Khan network. The work was slow and without the support of the AQK network it took them years to get the three thousand complete and operating. There were a few remaining centrifuge components, and the operations were not going well with the ones they had in service. They no longer had the consulting experts from AQ Khan to guide them in operations and maintenance of the centrifuges. They were damaging centrifuges, having leaks and very inefficient enrichment levels. They weren't sure if the problems were in the fabrication, the control systems or some other technical issue. The Saudis and Emiratis had become more cautious immediately after the AQK network was exposed and the Libyan program collapsed; there was no other supplier like AQK. The UAE-Saudi weapons program was struggling, the Emiratis did not have any engineers or scientists who could do anything with the warhead design. Then there was a major restart of the program. I will come back to that; I will summarize the development of the UF6 plant."

"We found a new player, in the AQ Khan network, Hans Freeland a friend of Lars Stoller and like Stoller undetected for any role in the AQ Network. He joined the network later than the others, for the Saudi scope of supply and he was not known with the intelligence agencies who were suspicious of activities of the AQ Khan network. The other reason the Americans and others didn't find him is the Emiratis didn't want him to be found, it would reveal the Saudi-UAE nuclear program. Stoller had quickly escaped when the AQ Khan network blew up. For some reason Freeland decided to stay."

"Shane and Lisa picked up Freeland about three years after the AQ Khan network was shut down, he was contacted by Aziz, another Emirati senior official and a Saudi. They wanted him to supply a UF6 conversion plant components and equipment. This was a limited scope of equipment, and we suspect Freeland didn't really have a choice. They paid him well and they could just throw him in jail or turn him over to the Americans. The small chemical processing plant, Al Jabeer Chemical Operations, was operational a year before the centrifuges were operational processing ores into UF6 gas near a military base 100 km northwest of Riyadh. It has a hardened security perimeter with a front as a Saudi military facility. The Saudis told the Americans they were trying their hands at making simple munitions for tanks and gravity drop bombs based on US designs. It is a pretty simple plant to operate. They hired a Russian as the plant manager along with two Bulgarian chemical engineers. The cannisters are hauled to the enrichment cascade in large military trucks marked as munitions. The initial output demanded was very low; to make sure the factory remained operational, they also stockpiled cannisters."

"The blackhole data showed nothing of Freeland since the UF6 plant went operational, we guess he left Dubai. This is about the time the UAE announced their civilian nuclear power program with the four massive reactors supplied by the Republic of Korea. Mohammed Bin Aziz Gamal is a first cousin of Sheikh Gamal, the Dubai Emirates leader, conceived of the idea for Al-mukhvih Nawah, Hidden Nucleus. Aziz had been a smuggler and money launderer his entire life. That's how he really made money for himself and the Gamal family enterprise. He was also the Head of Dubai Customs Authority which greatly facilitated his smuggling business. He is not well educated and never attended college, but he is clever, and he knew a good scam when he saw it. He hired educated and clever people to run a sophisticated internet platform for trading and disguising transactions, mostly South Africans and Australians. Aziz knew the story of the AQ Khan network and what they had done in Dubai. He had been the head of Customs during some of it and before him his father, another smuggler. They knew some of what the network was doing, and they did not care, they got paid their import and export fees. Aziz went to his cousin, a way to restart the program what he called, Hidden Nucleus."

"We used text messages, emails, cell phone transcripts to reconstruct a meeting between the Gamal's and Sheikh Abdulla Bin Zayed (ABZ) in Abu Dhabi. ABZ was the ruler of Abu Dhabi and the President of the UAE, for more than a decade. Aziz outlined his idea for Hidden Nucleus. They would develop a procurement network in Aziz's organization in Dubai. He would bring in some talented South African's who knew about nuclear procurement, and they would build a sophisticated modern logistics software platform to acquire equipment and resources. They would have things shipped into Dubai falsely labeled and boxed from the ROK and American suppliers who were shipping the hundreds of tons of nuclear equipment for the reactors to be built in the western region of Abu Dhabi. The equipment shipments to the nuclear plant were expected to be very high during early construction. They would move equipment along the same route along the truck road that leads to the planned nuclear plant along the shores of the Persian Gulf; some of the trucks would continue to Saudi Arabia with equipment to complete the enrichment plant, also equipment for a calciner-carbonator plant to be built next to the UF6 plant at Al Jabeer to convert the enriched uranium to metal. and a small amount of equipment would stop in Musaffah on the outskirts of Abu Dhabi to complete a fabrication facility for warhead production, using the uranium metal from Al Jabeer. The only ones who might detect the movement of these illegal shipments of nuclear technology would be UAE and Saudi customs officials, so there was no way they would be caught. It was all under their control."

"ABZ liked the idea, but text messages and phone calls between ABZ and Sheikh Mohammed after the meeting revealed ABZs view of Aziz. ABZ knows that Aziz is clever, but he had no college education and was not sophisticated enough to run this without some strong support from experts in the Dubai group he wanted to create and others throughout the program. ABZ wants people to resolve production problems with the centrifuges, make sure the other equipment worked and properly design and fabricate an operational warhead. ABZ had a meeting with the Saudi King about a month later; we have been able to reconstruct what was discussed and decided during the course of that meeting. ABZ laid out the plan, he is confident it could be done covertly, but he wanted it done correctly. This wasn't black market perfume. We also identified two new players; the Saudi King had his nuclear adviser Haitham al-Abdullah and ABZ had Faisal al-Kaabi his adviser for the covert nuclear program. Haitham and Faisal had been sent to the United States together and both had bachelors and masters degrees in nuclear engineering, returning to help run the covert nuclear program."

"ABZ suggested that the North Koreans could fill the gap and supply technical competence to run Aziz's network. The North Koreans approached the Saudis several times since their first successful nuclear test offering missile and nuclear technology and know-how. The Saudi King agreed, a team of North Korean experts finalize the procurement specification requirements, testing and development of the enrichment cascades and the warhead design and fabrication and oversee testing and operations. Pay the North Koreans a relatively modest fee, a fortune to the North Koreans upfront and salaries and living expenses. They would have a team of North Koreans working on hidden nucleus; it will just look like a few more South Korean engineers from the outside. Faisal al-Kaabi had brought estimates for the meeting. He estimated it might take a decade to have the facilities operational and the first warhead ready following this path. They would need dozens of North Korean experts in different parts of the program; the numbers would taper off over time. The Saudi and Emirati leaders agreed. A hidden supply and procure-ment network hidden under the UAE ROK safe and peaceful nuclear power project, it was a perfect plan; the first new large-scale nuclear weapons network since AQ Khan."

"Within a year Aziz was setting up the network, and the Al Jabeer metal fabrication facility was ready about six years later. The first small ingots ready about two years ago delivered to Musaffah on the outskirts of Abu Dhabi, the warhead fabrication facility. There are ten North Korean experts that have been working in Abu Dhabi for several years on warhead design and non-nuclear detonation testing of the explosive lens at the Al Dhafra air force base. They are responsible for the war-head design and setting up the warhead fabrication facility which is in the same compound as the design facility in Mussafah on the western edge of Abu Dhabi. The first warhead was complete this past June, the second is scheduled for completion in December and the third scheduled for completion in April next year. Each final warhead package is shipped separate from the cores. The cores are shipped in two segments, shipped one day apart. Abu Dhabi staff accompany the shipments marked as munitions for transportation to a safe storage facility in Saudi Arabia at the Abdul-Aziz air force base. The agreed plan is one warhead per year for the next five years, and then evaluate the long-term plans. North Koreans designed the gravity drop bomb housings, brought into the country through the procurement network, with the electronics for arming and detonation circuits, all in the safe storage facility. The North Koreans do not yet have a missile capable design; they promised it this year. That sounds like a false promise; their technology is not nearly that sophisticated. Final assembly of a bomb would take several hours in this storage configuration for delivery by F-16 Falcons. The plans call for the Saudis to begin leaking hints of a nuclear program late next year to US intelligence, and then establish a position of ambiguity with the US on a promise not to test. The Emiratis will remain silent partners. They want to protect their large commercial nuclear power program which would be under intense pressure to shut down if they were found to be involved in nuclear weapons. That brings us to where we are today, a covert functional Saudi-UAE nuclear weapons program with one complete warhead and more in the pipeline."

Mel was impressed, "Outstanding work everyone. The story holds together. I like how you organized the briefing as a chronology, easy to follow. You have all of the references to the supporting detailed intelli-gence, that will be very important for senior intelligence officials. But it is still just a history lesson, nothing from boots on the ground today. People will not believe it without solid and concrete evidence."

Michael nodded in agreement, "Thanks Mel, this has been an amazing team effort; these last couple of weeks Shane and Lisa have put in a lot of hours. You are right, there is no physical verification of anything. Craig has been working long hours along with Tim and Jamila to develop an intelligence collection matrix and tasks, focused on physical confirmation of what the evidence suggests, a UF6 plant, enrichment cascades, metal fabrication plant, warhead design and fabrication and movement and storage of warheads."

Craig picked up, "Well, Tom and Michael have also been working long hours reviewing raw intelligence documents. Michael did an amazing job converting this evidence into a coherent presentation. It's Wednesday, we all could use a break this weekend. We are still in the preliminary stages outlining the collection plan. We will have something early next week. I can already tell you we will need some operational support, either Delta or our local assets."

Mel expected that would be the case, "This is big. We will see if we can get the Talon team, and we might have to play dirty to get access to these places, we need to get physical evidence."

Craig agreed, "This requires a full court press; we may need to get into the mud and roll around."

Mel got up, "Michael and Tom, a business dinner at the Danara hotel tomorrow night. I want to see if the Talon team might have connections that have heard anything. They have close ties with UAE military and security services and also some Saudis. I would also like to get their operational support to go into the facilities and collect evidence."

Tom smiled, "I am up for some darts."

Mel laughed, "But you're just looking right."

"Absolutely."

Craig rubbed his eyes, "Tim and Jamila, we need to get the surveillance equipment out of the Baniyas villa and Aziz's apartment. We aren't going to need anything more from these sources."

Chapter Sixteen
Operational Support

Thursday morning Mel came by to discuss the meeting for that night with Michael and Tom

"Okay, the three Talon operators have a close working relationship, they served together in the same Delta Unit for several years. Bob Franklin was the team leader of the unit, and he makes the final call on what they will offer as support as assets for the CIA. We occasionally need covert military skills, that is not part of our skill set, we are not soldiers. One of my options as Station Chief is to use the Talon guys or another group of three guys in Triangle. This avoids tasking through DOD channels for US special forces operators, they are in high demand and that takes time. But its Bob's call; if he thinks it will place them in too much risk for what he sees as the value, then he can beg off. They are assets and not employees of the Agency. We want to give Bob just enough information to see if they have the skill set we need and are willing to penetrate the airbase, UF6 facility and uranium metal processing plant next door was well as the Abu Dhabi location. I don't understand this well enough to lay this out for Bob. Michael, I want you to take the lead for the discussions with Bob; we want to know if they can do it and will they do it. You have to offer him just the bare minimum of what we have so he gets the picture. Can you do this? Do you understand what I'm asking?"

Michael thought for a moment. "You want me to explain in vague terms that there is a Saudi-UAE nuclear weapons program in a highly advanced state. We want to know if they have any experience with covert entries for these types of facilities and if they are willing to collect evidence. I need to do it playing darts in plain sight so that no one knows what we are talking about. I can do that. What about the women they are with?"

"Don't worry, their English comprehension listening skills are not so great. They are okay with small talk and with their *husband*s. If you are vague, they will not have any idea what you are talking about. By the way, you will see Jamila at the bar tonight. There are two Saudi officers from the airbase, she will try and see what they do and what they might know."

After Mel left Jamila came over, "So, tonight you boys don't know me. I'm Leila from Jordan, a high-dollar working girl. I'll be by myself near where the Lebanese women hangout."

Michael was surprised, "You have to do this for your job?"

Jamila laughed "Don't worry farm boy. Every clandestine operator chooses where they draw the line; Mel gives me the task, but the means are up to me, and he will not ask me to do something I do not want. I knew long ago that I could not cross the line of sex or allow myself to be violated, so my methods are seduction and drugs. I might let them see a little cleavage in the hotel room as I start to strip tease, but they are unconscious from a little spray within minutes of getting into the room or something in their drink. I accidentally spray a little perfume in their face, as I give them a little hug or kiss on the cheek or put something into a drink. Then it depends, what we are after; scarching them, maybe some nude pictures, I can bring in women and men for a few thousand Dirhams and get some compromising photos. Craig and Tim may come in as American spies ready to take them to a secret prison or assassinate them, so many options."

"I'm glad there are people like you guys. Don't get me wrong I have no objections to what you are doing. I just could never do your job."

"Like Mel says, you have to get dirty; the moral judgment is that the compromise in ethical behavior is warranted based on the evil you are trying to stop. Mel has told us where he draws the line for our Station, no physical torture only physical force for self-defense. Let me tell you something else about Mel, you have seen him at the bar, you know Mel lives with that Malaysian woman, goes by Don-Don. Don't you dare tell Mel I told you this, but he has helped a few of these women; if Don-Don knows about a woman that cannot survive, he tries to find another option for them. I met a woman that told me about this, one of her friends. Mel found a construction company that gave the woman a job. Mel paid for her to go to English classes. She was smart and hardworking and was going to starve in Abu Dhabi and had little money to send her family. She could not adjust to the lifestyle. She got a job as a translator with paid housing, and she was able to send money back to support her son. The Asian women at the bars call Mel the lifeboat. If they see someone who cannot make it, they steer them towards Don-Don and the lifeboat. A good man in my book, I don't care what anyone else might say about his lifestyle. He has been with Don-Don for years, pays for her to go to English language classes and supports her family."

Michael shook his head in agreement, "Mel is a good man, even if he wasn't the lifeboat. You are all heroes in my book."

Tom agreed, "Amen to that."

Tom and Michael got out of the elevator on the Penthouse at the Danara. The big Nigerian doorman recognized them, "Hello gentlemen long time no see, Mr. Mel is waiting."

They saw Mel as they walked into the restaurant; he had already ordered the beers. "Are you guys ready for the evening?"

Michael smiled, "Yes definitely, we are ready."

He didn't tell Mel the plan, but they had already mapped out how they wanted the evening to go.

Mel took a drink, "I will tell Bob that Michael is leading a new project that he might find interesting, it involves security systems. A new project means we are seeking Talon assistance and Bob will know that Michael has the lead for discussing the project. Security systems means high national security interest of the United States; I have never used the code before in any of our previous work together. That will get their attention."

Michael and Tom had already worked out their general strategy for the clandestine meeting. Tom was going to be a monitor watching for any sign that they should watch their words more carefully and would let Michael know with a loud cough and excuse me. He would also watch the three operators and their body language and listen carefully looking for anything that might assist Michael. Michael and Tom had brought their own dart sets. They bought them on the way to the bar at Abu Dhabi Mall at the big sports store on the second level. Michael had something inside he might give to Bob depending on how things went.

They finished dinner and they went to one of the tables for playing darts. Mel saw Michael and Tom get out their own set of darts in small leather carrying cases. "Very nice, gentleman you came to play, very good indeed." Michael went to the other table; Mel knew Michael planned to play at the Talon dart board, good idea.

Like clockwork the bar began to fill up. Michael and Tom saw Jamila come in; she took off her shawl and got her stiletto high heels out of her large purse and put them on. She was made up very much like the Lebanese women with lots of eye makeup. Tom whispered "wow."

Mel looked over, "Yes very attractive bait."

The Talon guys arrived along with their three *wives*, and shortly after Li-Li and Don-Don came to the table, they wanted to play darts with Tom and Mel. Tom explained to Li-Li "500 dirhams to play darts, if you find someone for work, you can leave and keep the money."

She smiled, "only darts Mr. Tom, you sure?"

"Yes, only darts."

As Mel predicted, Michael and Tom could see the interest of all three men as Mel spoke, waiting to hear about the new project with national security implications. Bob threw a practice dart, "It would be interesting to hear about Michael's project."

Mel was relieved Michael didn't jump right into it,

Michael threw a practice dart, "We can talk about work later, let's play some darts."

Tom picked up the initial conversation as they had discussed, "Bob, how were the Emiratis stacking up in their paramilitary training, did they have some skills?"

It was relatively safe conversation, no one was around, they had the end of the bar to themselves, the occasional Indian or European man would wander down and realize it was a closed game and walk away. The other women saw there was no business there and stayed away; the occasional Malaysian or Vietnamese lady would briefly chat with one of the women and would move on.

Bob asked Byron, "What do you say about the Emirati skills in par-amilitary training?"

"They wouldn't last a day in US basic military training much less special forces training."

Tom sensed the harshness, "That sounds a bit harsh, every Emirati is that bad?"

"No of course there is the exception maybe 5 out of 100 that could make it in a real military training program."

Tom continued as they played darts, "Why is it that they all perform so poorly?"

"Keith and Bob, do you agree; am I off base in my assessment of our trainees' military skills."

Keith answered first, "Have to agree."

Bob shook his head, "Well I have to agree as well."

Bob asked Mel, "You have been here a while, what are your views."

"You guys are right; the Emiratis are building a society spoiled with entitlement. They expect and receive promotions in government employment not based on merit, 90% of Emiratis work in government jobs. Free university, free healthcare, free land for homes, loans forgiven if they cannot pay. The Emirati schools and universities are rampant with cheating and teachers being paid for grades. The typical Emirati home has four domestic workers: two cooks and two maids who care for the home and children, many also have a driver. That is a typical middle class family, four domestic servants. When they enter the workforce, they expect and are often hired into entry level positions as managers, not working their way up through the ladder based on merit. They do not expect the manager to be qualified to lead the work or a competent decisionmaker, just someone to monitor workhours and make sure people are at work. There are no Emiratis trained as plumbers, electricians or other skilled trades; very few professionals as doctors or engineers; they favor getting general business degrees and becoming managers. It's not a culture that rewards hard work."

Bob shook his head, "We have a Syrian lady, a secretary in the Talon offices, early sixties she has been in the UAE for more than thirty years. She said that Zayed used to meet with the people and would help those in need and help people get started, but he believed in hard work. She said he would be disgusted to see how lazy the society had become and how out of touch the current Royals are with the people."

Byron took a drink, "When the oil turns off, they are going to have big problems. Most of the Emiratis who enter our program look for every opportunity to avoid the physically demanding work. It is beneath them to run 5 kilometers, climb walls, move silently at night on the ground; they want to stand in the shade and shoot guns and play with their mobile phones."

They talked about sports a little bit, and then Michael started the business conversation. Mel was pleased Tom and Michael had a coordinated plan. Michael asked Bob, "You know we are trade representatives; you remember we are interested in sugar products and artificial sweeteners."

Bob remembered their cover was the nuclear program. He knew what Michael was doing, using an alternative code language for the business. "I remember, I still have your business card."

Michael threw a dart, "Have you three had any experience over the years with enrichment of sweeteners and fabrication and processing into final products, you know the ones with the explosive taste in your mouth."

Bob nodded, "We have some training in this kind of equipment used for enrichment and the production of treats and candies. We visited facilities in the US just in case there was ever the need to visit a foreign site to collect information or carry out some other business."

Tom could see that Keith and Byron were carefully following the conversation as everyone continued to play darts. Bob was concerned he had no interest in taking his team to Iran, that was the only game in town, he was irritated that Mel would push this on them.

Bob glanced around as he went to the bar to order another beer, no one was close by, and as he walked back, he said quietly "we aren't interested in Persian sweets, they are bad for your health."

Keith and Byron were relieved. They knew what Michael was talking about. They had no interest in going into Iran. It was one thing in Delta with the US Navy and Airforce in support, but the three of them alone, what was Mel thinking.

Michael shook his head in agreement, "I understand we weren't thinking of Persian sweets, there are some new processors in the UAE and Saudi Arabia a joint venture. We are pretty sure they have some finished treats; we haven't seen them yet."

Bob almost dropped his dart as he was about to throw, he paused and threw a bullseye. He looked at Mel to be sure. Mel had a big smile on his face, "Nice throw."

Bob sat down, "We would definitely be down to assist with that."

Michael reached into his dart case and handed Bob a dart, this one is a little heavier give it a try. Mel could not see but he was sure Michael had just handed off a USB. Mel was pleased, nice job Michael very nice. Bob set it up with the President of Talon; they would be working for the CIA station chief probably for the next month, they would work out of the Villa down the road set up for covert support and from the Embassy. The USB showed a simple map, with the locations of the sugar enrichment processing locations. They would check their contacts quickly and carefully and see if anyone had heard anything unusual about any of these locations.

Chapter Seventeen
Snipe Hunt

The next Sunday three server repair technicians, Bob Franklin, Keith Sampson, and Byron Hilliard, started working in the CIA station. Everyone met in the conference room. Jamila reported, "Tim and I have a new asset, a Saudi Captain responsible for base maintenance and repair."

Mel was pleased, "Let me guess photos with a Pakistani man."

"No, two young Bangladeshi men, he is anxious to help us."

Mel shook his head smiling, "I'm going to be a little more involved, this has grown into a more complex project. Craig is still the project lead and Michael is the overall director as the investigative lead. I just want to make sure I know the scope of what we are doing."

Craig was relieved, "Mel your direction and guidance would be very much appreciated."

Bob asked, "Michael and Tom, they aren't operators you said investigative lead?"

Mel smiled, "State Department Office of Inspector General investigators, Tom is a LEO Michael is an engineer and lawyer, pretty good meet on Thursday don't you think."

Bob laughed, "Very nice, you two ran that clandestine meet and brush pass very well; looks like the team here has taught you well."

Michael gave the Talon operators a high-level overview of what they had found so far, an outline of the briefing they had given to Mel.

Bob spoke for the Talon team, "We have not heard a whisper about any of this, and we did a little checking. Nobody knew anything unusual at the locations on the map Michael gave us on the USB. So, what you have sounds solid. Now you want physical confirmation of what is actually there, to nail this down tight right. We can help with that; one rule we play darts every Thursday and we expect you two along with Mel. Helps with morale and teamwork."

Mel laughed, "Good for me. You two better tell your wives you're booked Thursdays evenings for several weeks."

They decided to work out a plan one facility at a time. Starting with the most difficult, the enrichment cascades deep under the air force base. This was going to take some careful planning. Craig created a master task (Snipe Hunt) with subtasks based on the matrix they worked out with Michael. Michael started writing on the white board as Craig began to build the matrix; Michael outlined the flow of materials; "Okay, the low enriched UF6 comes in and the outgoing product is UF6 highly enriched, incoming and outgoing in large cannisters. We want visual evidence of cannisters coming in and out with trace samples of what they have inside. These are pictures of the types of large cannisters that will be filled with UF6 gas. The input for the centrifuges is coming from the Al Jabeer munitions facility that is manufacturing UF6 gas. The highly enriched UF6 gas from the centrifuges then goes to the Al Jabeer metal factory next to the munitions plant. We want visual evidence of the UF6 cannisters moving into and out of the cascade loading and unloading in the back of the warehouse and visual evidence of the cascades themselves."

Craig went next, "Okay let's talk about the collection methods and assets for these elements of evidence. Global Hawk surveillance of cask movement to and from the airbase to Al Jabeer for the entire month of November. The Saudi maintenance Captain will be given environmental swiping kits. He will have maintenance staff swipe every cask while they are in the cask loading-unloading area. Jamila and Tim say he has crews that operate the cranes and work to support those operations."

Michael showed them a picture of the cask, "They need to take the swipes on the casks after discharge or receipt of gas here on the upper lids. There are nozzle connections just under the lid; I have information from technical sources that there is always some small trace residue there."

Craig was typing in the task descriptions, "Got it, and they will need to date the samples, and the captain will bring these back to Abu Dhabi. Tim will work out a delivery protocol. They will get shipped to Langley for analysis."

Bob went next, "Let's talk about photographic evidence throughout the cascade. Based on the description from Michael, it will take about four hours. The radiation risks are low; Michael tells us only two times above background."

Michael confirmed, "That's right, the radiation from the uranium inside the cascade components cannot penetrate the walls of the pipes or centrifuges. It's low energy alpha and beta. Small leaks can create some risk, but you will hear alarms if there are leaks."

Bob continued using a map, "We will cross the border and go to this village about 30 km north of the base. The captain will meet us at this restaurant in his SUV. The security forces do not search the officers' vehicles. He will drive us onto the base, covered over in the very back seat and in the hatch. He will take us inside the "warehouse," he has the operating key for inner doors and elevators to move through all levels of the facility. He will drop us back at the restaurant in the village, and then we will cross back into the UAE."

The pace of work was intense. Craig, Tom and Jamila worked to develop assets for each facility, someone that could get the Talon guys inside to collect photographic and physical evidence. Shane and Lisa were collecting and collating everything being brought in from each task. Michael and Tom were reviewing the evidence collated and summarizing it in the Cross-Cut investigative database, with references to documents and records in the intelligence database. They began to organize findings and summaries for each facility as the evidence came in. The plans for the UF6 plant and metal fabrication plant were very much like the enrichment cascade, an asset with access getting the environmental samples and access for the Talon team to get inside for photographs and the global hawk for truck movements. Things proceeded smoothly; the Saudis were pretty lax with security, a victim of their own success at keeping the facilities covert for several years. After working at a furious pace for several weeks, they had collected all of the physical evidence in Saudi Arabia.

The warhead design and fabrication required a different approach. The other facilities had involved the movement of relatively large amounts of bulk materials; there was a clear trail of breadcrumbs, tons of uranium ore, large cannisters moving into and out of these facilities and the trace samples of uranium. The final nuclear warhead core only needed a few hundred pounds of uranium metal and was smaller than a basketball. The small metal ingots came into the fabrication facility for the final complex fabrication and assembly over several months before a finished warhead would be sent to Saudi for safe storage. The level of security was very high and the building was small; they had tracked shipments of what they believed to be ingots from the metal fabrication facility in Saudi Arabia, so there must be a warhead in some stage of fabrication inside. The small office building next door was where the design work had been going on for some time; the engineering work was being carried out by North Koreans. They would need photographs of the fabrication and machining operations, but these were small buildings surrounded by a security fence. They also needed to get access to the design information on the computers. Demonstrate what was being designed and what was being built next door, if they could get trace samples of ingots and other uranium in process that would be useful. They could not be sure what work was underway. They didn't yet have any asset on the inside, and the computers being used for design were separated from the internet. Shane and Lisa had tried for weeks to find a way in through Blackhole; they could find emails to and from the facility, but it seemed like they had created an airgap between the nuclear design computers and the network.

Craig invited Mel to attend a planning session they were struggling with the last facility. Craig laid out the challenge, "Michael has described what we need; there is a lot of evidence we need to collect. This isn't anything like these large remote industrial facilities we dealt with in Saudi Arabia. There are small buildings with a lot more people inside. We haven't come up with a collection plan. We could use some fresh ideas."

Mel thought for a moment, "Do you have any form of organizational chart for the people working in the fabrication and design in these two buildings?"

Lisa brought it up on the computer display.

Mel looked at the chart, "Kim San-do, what do we know about his level of involvement in day-to-day work?"

Michael answered, "From the emails he is a micromanager, he is involved in security, the physics and design of the warhead, and he is on the fabrication floor. He is very abrupt in his email communications with his staff."

Mel sat back and took a drink of coffee, "Kim is at the top of this small organization, has full access and maybe is a bit of a bully running the entire show. Kim has to be our asset, any means necessary within the guidelines and limits of the Agency and this station, we will not torture him, but if we need to scare him, make him think that Bob and

Keith are going to cut him up and throw his testicles into the Persian Gulf. Find a lever to control Kim; we may need coercive means."

The end of the week they invited Mel back for an update, Shane and Lisa had worked through the intelligence community and all the black-hole monitoring of his communications and movement, including his phone, laptop and internal security cameras in the buildings at Musaffah.

Shane briefed the team on Kim San-Do, "Fifty-five years old, a Ph.D in nuclear physics from Sung-Il national university in North Korea; his entire career in the North Korean nuclear program, married, no children his wife is in North Korea. We don't know her name or location, parents dead and no information on siblings. In Abu Dhabi more than five years setting up the warhead fabrication and design organization from the ground up. He lives in the building where they do the design work, a top floor penthouse apartment built for him; he does not go out much. The Emiratis find women for him a few times a month; he likes women from Thailand, they seem to stay one night and leave on their own the next day. He orders takeout several times a week and meets the delivery boy outside at the entrance gate. He doesn't socialize, spends his time watching television, and he likes to play video games. He goes to Yas Mall to buy video games a couple of times a month."

Mel thought for a moment, "He speaks English, right; he will under-stand a face-to-face message?"

Shane nodded, "Yes, all the Koreans there speak English, their work-ing language is English, just like the local legitimate enterprises."

Craig knew where this was headed, "I don't see much in the way of leverage with this guy. It's going to get dirty. Lisa, we are inside the cameras, cellphones and laptops there correct?"

"Yes, everything is covered including security systems. We can con-trol anything. The only thing we could not penetrate were the nuclear design computers."

Craig went to the white board and spoke as he wrote bullets for a plan. "Next week Lisa and Shane are going to film and record Kim everywhere. When he is on the toilet, turn on the camera and microphone of his cell phone, use his laptop, his smart TV. You are going to make a video and photo library of Kim, and his emails and text messages."

Shane understood, "You want to be able to show him he can't so much as piss without us knowing about it."

"That's right. Michael will give a list of everything we want from Kim: photographs, computer files, material reports on the warhead metals, everything. Next Saturday Talon will enter the penthouse, in full black Ninja wear and weapons. They will show Kim segments of his personal home movie, let Kim pick a day and time and show him what he was doing at that exact moment, sex with his Thailand girl, on the toilet taking a dump, spend a few hours showing him his life on video, his texts, his email at home and in his office."

"The Talon team will give him a clear message; he has two days to deliver everything on that list, half on the first day the remainder on the second day. A USB each day. He will order food for delivery each day and meet the delivery boy at the gate. The USB wrapped up inside a roll of bills for the food, Tim will be the delivery boy."

Bob understood, "We tell him he is a dead man if he opens his mouth, tries to write a note, send a text to get help or fails to deliver. We will assassinate him, maybe in a day maybe in a week, maybe on the drive to Yas Mall, maybe with one of his girls, he will believe us."

Craig asked, "What about entry into the building. Shane bring up the pictures of the building exteriors."

Bob looked at the pictures. "Shane and Lisa have the security systems, so they deal with these cameras and any detection systems on doors. Okay bring up the first picture, that shows the overview."

Bob used a laser pointer, "We take this streetlight out. It will be dark in this area. We park a van here, we have two small bed mattresses inside. Byron and I will jump and roll the fence using a mattress to cushion the drop and protect us from the razor wire. Keith will secure the van and we go in through this back door. It's probably not locked, but we can break the lock if we need to it is a cheap door, looks like they spent their money on perimeter security and the fabrication building, not the building with the design organization. It would be good to have one of your operators nearby with a small drone monitoring the local area if a local cop or someone appears headed toward the van."

Craig picked up a laser pointer, "We will have Tim back here in another van here on the far side of the parking lot, operating a drone with a camera; it has 4 hours of flight time."

Bob looked at Keith and Byron, they were shaking their heads in agreement, "Okay we need to work out a detailed timeline and communications plan. Mel, what are the rules of engagement if we encounter problems? We haven't had any problems at the other facilities, but there are a lot of people in these buildings, and this is on the edge of Abu Dhabi."

"If it's someone inside, I think you are going to have to quietly deal with them and pack them out and cleanup; someone sees you inside the small warhead fabrication facility or the design building will set off alarm bells. On the outside, a local cop, maybe you can justify it like you are doing night drills for the Emirati trainees; they know you guys are out and about wargaming sometimes."

Bob agreed, "That will work and if that turns sideways on the outside, Tim can help our outside coverage. Drug the cop and put them into the van and develop a disposal plan later. We put the police vehicle in the back corner locked. Shane and Lisa scrub Abu Dhabi security and police video to make sure the last image is the car just as it turns into the parking area."

Michael was silent during the planning session; he had never been involved in any discussions like this. Now this was really getting dirty. He nodded his head to prepare the list. He hoped it would not result in anyone getting killed; he wasn't worried about their guys just some poor fool who stumbled onto them.

Mel was satisfied with the plan, "We need to move fast on Kim and make sure he delivers quickly. He will be under stress, coercion is not the best means of getting something from an asset. If he senses the pressure lifting, he will not deliver, and if it is applied for too long, he could breakdown or try to escape."

Late Saturday night, two vans came into the parking area parked far apart, no one could see the two men quickly go over the fence and hide mattresses in the stair well. Kim woke up, he was terrified; he knew these people were American special forces, he knew the accents. He could not see their faces only their eyes.

The white man spoke, "Shut your mouth and listen. We know you are here designing and fabricating nuclear bombs."

They knew his name, where he went to school, and they had videos of him having sex, eating lunch at his desk, everywhere.

The white man spoke again handing him a sheet of paper, "Here are your instructions. If you try and communicate to anyone, we will know and you will be dead, maybe not in a day or a week, maybe while you are sleeping or in the parking lot at Yas mall."

Two hours later they were gone, and he started drinking to calm his nerves thinking about the long list of instructions they gave him. Kim had never wanted to come to Abu Dhabi in the first place, having been replaced by Park Yo San because his team was not making progress on miniaturizing the bomb for a Korean missile. The capability was beyond them; they didn't understand the core, tamper interaction well enough and needed better computer tools. Most of the people here were in the same situation not from the top team in Pyongyang.

Kim delivered both USBs wrapped inside money for delivery food, handing the rolled-up bills to Tim who took off on a scooter from Lebanese Grill after delivering mixed grill, Kim's favorite. Michael and Tom didn't know about the next part of the plan, the Talon operators and Mel's team worked this out as additional insurance to make sure that Kim did not talk; it would only take 30 minutes not exposing them for long. Three nights later the two men were back while he was sleeping; they woke him up. One of them was restraining his wrist to the bed and one of them was putting tape over his mouth. Byron put the gun in the center of his forehead. Kim's heart was racing. He had done what they asked, why were they going to kill him? Byron pulled the trigger, Kim shuddered, but there was no shot.

Bob pulled the tape off his mouth, "We will be watching for a long time, keep your mouth shut, and you wouldn't want the Saudis to know what you gave us, they would also kill you."

They cut the wire ties holding his wrist to the headboard and left. Keith was in the van as Byron and Bob got in; they put the mattresses in the back and waited for Tim to secure the drone in his van. Tim signaled thumbs up and drove off followed a few minutes later by Keith.

As Keith put the van into drive, he asked, "So, tell me, did he or didn't he, I bet Mel twenty bucks he wouldn't."

Byron laughed, "Sorry dude, Mr. Kim wet the bed big time. You owe Mel twenty."

"Crap, I figured if he didn't piss himself the first time, he would be okay."

Chapter Eighteen
Phantom Team Closes Shop

The last three months had gone by quickly. December the Phantom team worked collating and analyzing, writing summary papers of intelligence and looking for any gaps in the intelligence. Michael and Tom worked to import the summary papers into the investigative platform. It would take one or two months back in DC to prepare a complete report and briefing. By the end of the month the intelligence database and summaries were complete, and the database was ready to be locked down. The synthesis and analysis of a final report was necessary to draw the full picture of what the evidence meant for decision makers. The Phantom team and Mel Randolph knew they had nailed it shut, complete with photographic evidence of a partially assembled warhead in Abu Dhabi. To someone not directly involved, it just looked like thousands of unconnected dots in the intelligence database. Mel Randolph had watched Michael Case work for the last three months and read a couple of the reports Case had done in the State Department OIG. He was confident they had given him the evidence to confirm the presence of the nuclear weapons program and that he would organize the information into a clear and coherent report that would satisfy the decision-makers and intelligence officials.

The second week of December the database was locked down by Shane and Lisa; Craig completed all the Project closeout paperwork for Phantom and Mel Randolph signed off. Michael and Tom had an access code for the database, they could access it from Washington DC for a few months. Any access beyond that date would require approval of the Director of the CIA. Michael and Tom took the whole team to a late lunch at the Mazi Restaurant on Saadiyat Island. Everyone said their goodbyes; Michael and Tom talked to Mel before they left.

Michael got up, "We cannot thank you enough for the support; it stretched you all, and we know it was awkward to have investigators working out of your shop."

Mel smiled, "It's been a pleasure working with you both. You have some skills in the field, and this is one of the most important projects the station has worked on."

Michael stopped before they went outside, "We talked to our wives, and we would like to invite you and Don-Don to dinner at The Saloon at Danara this Friday night and then play some darts."

Mel had told them that Fridays were pretty much like Thursdays, not quite as big of a crowd.

Mel was surprised, "You sure you want to bring your wives to meet me and Don-Don?"

Tom shook his head, "We are sure. We told them we were working for a really good boss, we told them what kind of place it is the whole story. They are game."

"Well, I'm not your guys boss. But it would be nice to meet your wives."

Michael shook Mel's hand, "You are in charge of Abu Dhabi station, we worked in the station, so you were our boss."

The previous week the Bradleys and Cases had their usual weekend dinner together; Michael and Tom decided to tell the full story about their boss and the Danara Hotel. After Dinner Michael explained their idea for a dinner and darts, he said that Mel is a good man.

Amanda was upset with Michael and Tom, "Michael you are justifying what this man and woman are doing; she is selling her body, I am disappointed in you and Tom."

Marion put her hand on Amanda's shoulder, "Michael didn't say he was justifying anything, he said he would not pass judgment on his boss or the lady that lives with him. Michael and Tom believe he is a good man, and I trust them."

Tom could see Amanda struggling. He wanted her to think and use her big heart, "And the Pharisees brought the adulterous lady to Jesus asking if she should be stoned according to the rules of Moses, what did Jesus say?"

Amanda thought about the woman and Mel; what would she do if her children were hungry, she had no money, no education or job, no family to support her. How would she support her mother and a child? Tom said Mel had supported the woman and her family in Malaysia for several years. She was not about to cast a stone.

Amanda smiled at Tom, "John 8:7 if any one of you is without sin, let them be the first to cast a stone. If you both say Mel is a good man, I accept that, it is not my place to judge either of them. I am in, it will be fun getting a new sexy dress and shoes, get all dressed up for the night."

Tom was shaking his head no, "You don't need to get all dressed up, just some jeans and a nice top."

Amanda laughed, "No darling, you and Michael are not going to want to take your eyes off of us. I know you Thomas and your wandering eyes. What do you think Marion, want to get dressed up a bit?"

"Absolutely."

Friday night they met Mel at the restaurant and had dinner. Mel told Michael quietly that Don-Don felt self-conscious, maybe the women would not be comfortable with her. The five of them went to play darts. The working women were arriving and looking at the two new girls playing darts. Probably a Russian and Nigerian lady working together. Mels friends have wives; they must have gone back to America. Those women don't look like wives; they were definitely working girls, nice bodies and sexy shoes, they could use a little more makeup. Michael saw Don-Don come in looking from the far end of the bar, she was trying to hide just wanting to get a look at them. Michael quietly told Marion, "The woman back there in the dark green dress, that is Don-Don. She is embarrassed about meeting you and Amanda."

Marion looked at Mel "We need another player for three even teams, go get her," Marion waved at Don-Don.

Don-Don was smiling as Mel walked with her towards the group. She introduced herself in halting English, "Your husbands are fine gentlemen. They did not say how beautiful their wives were; it is my honor to meet you both," she said with a slight bow.

Amanda looked at the elegant lady, beautiful face and kind and sincere smile and shook her hand, "It is our honor to meet you."

Mel took a picture of the two American couples together at the dart board and one with the three women together, using Amanda and Marion's cell phone. Mel enjoyed the evening, these girls were not what he expected, he didn't see a hint of disapproval. Mel started to wonder maybe he should make things even more permanent with Don-Don, something to consider.

Chapter Nineteen
Two Fools and Three Stooges

The first thing they needed to take care of when they got back to work in DC was close out the investigation of Williams and Harrison and whether they were being directed by the Secretary of State or other senior officials to provide sensitive nuclear information. They had both left their jobs in late December. Michael and Tom interviewed the chief of staff for the Secretary of State who was also gone knowing that the President was on his way out. The chief of staff told them what he knew, "I was in three meetings with them, and the Secretary and he had asked them to support US companies seeking to get nuclear business for Saudi Arabia. The Saudis were making noise they might build fifteen or twenty reactors; they wanted a fuel cycle because they had uranium. I don't recall the exact directions for Williams and Harrison, it was possible that the Secretary said something like give them all the support they need; the Secretary did believe they should be allowed to get enrichment technology, but he had tasked his legal counsel to try and find a legal route to give Saudis access so US companies would get access. The Secretary could be bombastic, but he is smart, a Yale educated lawyer with a long record of public service. He is not going to direct criminal action. The Secretary never directed Williams and Harrison to give documents or information to the Saudis, not in my presence, and I am not aware of any meetings they had with the Secretary other than the three I attended. It became clear after a while that the Saudis weren't serious. The Secretary told me to leave the two fools alone, maybe they would find some small business opportunities."

Michael thought, yes two fools met three stooges in Abu Dhabi thinking of Aziz, Waddah and Salem. He started drafting a report for the weapons program as they finished this work. Tom pulled down the emails and backups of the hard drives, for Williams and Harrison. There were no emails from the Secretary or the chief of staff to either man. Several from them to the Secretary with the chief of staff on copy. Vague and general, nothing about providing classified information; just claims they were making progress with Saudi and UAE contacts. There were dozens of emails between Williams and Harrison discussing the documents that Williams was retrieving. Tom could not believe how careless the two of them were in the electronic communication, their emails were admissions they were passing secret and confidential documents to Saudi and UAE officials. Tom found the list of documents they provided on Shawn Harrison's hard drive. An index of the documents on four different hard drives he had given to the Saudis, with the full title and the classification. There were thousands of documents, concerning a few marked Secret and most confidential. Tom and Michael met with an expert at DOE NNSA with the index. They told him they suspected someone had passed these documents to a foreign government; they needed his assessment of the damage posed by such a leak. He reviewed the list for about 30 minutes, "These are support systems, general arrangement drawings, manuals; most of them are for a pilot project that was never built. There is nothing here on the inner design of the actual centrifuge or key components, that information is Top Secret. It's useful information that a competitor would like to have, but there is no national security risk posed by these documents."

Tom worked on a draft report and briefing for Andrea and IG Ross, summarizing what they found about Williams and Harrison. Michael had pointed Tom to several criminal statutes involving classified information, nuclear restricted information and giving classified information to foreign governments. Tom and Michael agreed the easiest was 18 USC § 798, *"knowingly and willfully communicates, furnishes, trans-*

mits, or otherwise makes available to an unauthorized person, or publishes, or uses in any manner prejudicial to the safety or interest of the United States or for the benefit of any foreign government to the detriment of the United States." Tom evaluated each element and laid out four counts of violations of 798 for both Williams and Harrison, one for each hard drive they had delivered. They knew that a prosecutor might want to bring other charges, possibly conspiracy, but they decided to make the report simple until they got some direction regarding prosecution. Michael reviewed the report, made some edits, tightened up the analysis especially of *mens rea* criminal intent, knowing and willfully. Michael made the final edits as Tom prepared the briefing slides. They had not interviewed Williams and Harrison; they would wait for a decision of a prosecutor before approaching the subjects. The report and briefing would be used to get an initial view of a prosecutor before going further. Tom could see Michael was tired, he had been working long hours on the final Saudi-UAE report. Tom was helping Andrea direct the X-ray team while Michael focused on the final Saudi-UAE report. Tom saw that Brandon Eller had become a good investigator on X-ray.

In late January they briefed IG Ross and Andrea Jacobs on this part of the Saudi investigation, conduct of Williams and Harrison and allegations implicating the former secretary of state. Tom gave the briefing with Michael in support for questions.

IG Ross was satisfied, "Good job. A couple of fools enjoying taxpayer funded trips to party in Abu Dhabi, who thought they were doing a great deed for our country. Clear violations of law but no impact on national security."

Andrea nodded her head in agreement, "It's clear they were acting on their own. They are no longer in the federal government. We need to give the Assistant US attorney this briefing, but they are not going to prosecute. If we get a declination, then we will prepare memos for their personnel files referencing the OIG Case number. They will never be able to get a security clearance again or be employed in the federal government."

IG Ross got up to leave "Sounds good. Michael you look tired, the final report on Saudi-UAE nuclear program is important, but not more important than your health."

Andrea and Tom met with the on-duty Assistant US Attorney Christy Taylor the next day, "Good work, solid case, but not worth prosecuting. I agree Andrea, it is a good idea to put memos in their files to keep them out of government or from getting another security clearance. That will cost a lot less than a prosecution and stop them from causing any further damage. It doesn't seem they are the sharpest tools in the shed, not likely they have hidden jewels they are trying to sell right?"

Tom agreed, "There are no indications they kept any other files or accessed information beyond what we found. Not a big market for this kind of information, and like you say, not the sharpest tools in the shed."

Michael called the contact number for Arthur Larson, the secretary said he was now working in the DC office; she connected Michael.

"Arthur Larson, JAG Naval Operations."

"Arthur, it's Michael Case. We have closed the case you brought to our attention, I will give you a little more information, given your security clearance and position as a JAG attorney. They were acting on their own in giving sensitive information to foreign officials, but none of it was of any value. There will be no prosecution. Thank you again for coming forward, and congratulations on your father's election. That must be exciting."

"Still sinking in to be honest. Thank you for closing the loop Mr. Case and for keeping this confidential."

Chapter Twenty
A New President—A New Team—Old Threats

President Larson sat down to read the report Andrew Friedman had gotten him on nuclear proliferation. It was his first week in office. It had been a long road since Larson's announcement to run for president the previous February. Simon Tomas and Richard Larson had to quickly adapt to their very new professional assignments starting election night last November. Simon Tomas had done a yeoman's job during the transition period; the two "professors" Larson and Tomas were surprising early critics. Tomas was a masterful administrator, organized and knew the importance of clear decision-making process, orderly flow of information and schedule efficiency in Office of the President of the United States (POTUS). Simon had emphasized the importance of early staffing; they would need to hit the ground running at full speed. The cabinet selection was complete before inauguration day. Larson did not really follow the government players when he was at Yale, not interested in politics. That was ironic as they began the process of filling out the cabinet. Simon had brought in a deputy Chief of Staff during the transition, Allison Bronson; she had worked as senior adviser in a presidential transition and had advised on all major appointments and selections for a presidential cabinet. Ms. Bronson built an effective selection, vetting and staffing system; she had a small staff of political operatives working as consultants that built out the resumes, with summaries for each position. They would then go to VP Packard and Simon Tomas to select the top three.

President Larson did not give them a long list of criteria that were necessary. He trusted them, but he gave some direction. He insisted that political party have no weight; diversity of thought and culture should be considered, and they should look for people respected in the organizations they would lead to help build morale in the institutions. Packard and Tomas would meet with Larson for the final selection. They were amazingly successful. Only one top candidate did not accept the position when approached for an interview due to a recently discovered cancer. Vice President Packard emphasized three positions, Director of the CIA, Secretary of Defense and Secretary of State; national security issues involving foreign powers and governments could emerge quickly and require urgent action within the direct control of the president. They pushed and had the three top candidates for those positions in place approved by the Senate in early February. People were anxious to get onboard the new administration sensing a renewed positive atmosphere in Washington DC. The Larson cabinet would be one of the most stable in modern history.

Charles Sweigart was the choice for Director of the CIA. "Chuck" Sweigart had an undergraduate degree in theology from Notre Dame. He had been on the football team as starting linebacker. Sweigart had grown up in a large Catholic family in South Bend, Indiana, not a wealthy family, three brothers and two sisters. Chuck was the oldest; his parents had not gone to college, they were fourth generation Irish immigrants and worked hard to make ends meet. They hoped their children could make it to college, but the dream of going to prestigious Notre Dame in their own hometown was not a possibility for a family of such modest means. It turned out that skill on the football field would get Chuck into Notre Dame on scholarship along with top grades in high school. He studied Theology thinking he might even be a priest, until he met Cindy his sophomore year; she attended St. Mary's College. He served in the US Army after college wanting to help improve the Army after the debacle of Vietnam; he worked in the Pentagon. He and Cindy got married when they graduated, and she would travel the world with him over the years during his career overseas. He went into the intelligence service and developed profiles to be used in analyzing guerilla warfare to help the country with the asymmetric warfare in the future. He developed characteristics of guerilla fighters occupying villagers' homes; he believed these general profiles could be used by unit commanders to identify threats hidden in communities and could be applied to other circumstances. He applied the framework to experience in Vietnam and wrote detailed analytical papers describing how the methods could be generalized to other circumstances. The morale in the Army was terrible, and senior commanders could not see value in the work he was doing, too theoretical to be applied in the field. His work caught the attention of clandestine service officers of the CIA, who saw them being circulated for comment. He was recruited into the clandestine service out of the army, first working in Washington DC developing frameworks he believed could identify "terror cells," he was way ahead of his time. He used methods similar to what he had used in his earlier work; "terrorists" were like guerrilla fighters trying to hide in the shadows.

The work he was doing got the attention of the Director of the CIA, a legendary figure in the history of the CIA. The Director had Sweigart come to his office, he wanted to hear about these methods that Sweigart had been using. He put Sweigart in charge of a new branch to develop the methods for identification of terrorist threats. He had only been at the agency for a few years, and the line managers were not happy with this decision to create a new position. Then he sent Sweigart into the field to prove the methods would work. He served all over the world. In middle east and Europe there were many early failures. His methods in the identification of identifying "cells" became the primary method used across US intelligence agencies. The methods became the standard because they also resulted in many successes, but nobody ever read about those in the newspapers. After years in the field, Sweigart came back into Washington DC and had moved up the ladder in the Clandestine services serving as deputy director of Clandestine services before being selected as Director by Richard Larson. Vice President Packard knew that there was something in particular that would catch Richard Larson's interest when he was briefed about Charles Sweigart; he had received a master degree, history of religions at Catholic University while he was working as a division director at the CIA in his mid-50s. Packard smiled as Larson commented, "Very interesting. I wonder if he wrote a thesis project, maybe Simon Tomas could find me a copy."

Henry Travis was born in rural Georgia north of Savannah; his father Franklin had become wealthy growing cotton on farmland owned by his family for generations. Most of the supervisors and managers of the property were African American; he built them comfortable homes the same as all of his workers, regardless of race. He worked to get good educations for all of the workers' children, including personal tutors. His employees were about eighty percent African American, and he provided all employees the same benefits and salaries regardless of race. Franklin Travis was ahead of his time and sought to do his part to undo years of racial injustice in the rural south. Franklin was Henry's hero and a role model. Henry graduated top of his class in high school and went on to get a bachelor's degree in political science from Princeton. Henry attended St. John's College, Oxford University, on a Rhodes Scholarship. At St. John's, he completed a master's degree in international studies and continued there as a research assistant for two years. He came back to Yale and got a Ph.D. in History and then a law degree.

Henry Travis went to work in the US State Department, Office of the Legal Adviser, starting with assignments reviewing bilateral agreements mostly related to defense and national security issues. He became the senior legal adviser to the Secretary of State who saw great potential in Henry and got him a job that changed the trajectory of his career. Travis moved to New York City and worked as the Director of Executive Support for the US Mission to the United Nations as a primary strategic advisor to the US Ambassador to the United Nations. Travis served in the position for a series of Ambassadors and his skills as a future diplomat were recognized, and he served in a series of Ambassadorship's of progressive importance including Brazil, Germany, France and Russia. He was named Deputy Secretary of State, the principal deputy to the Secretary of State, the position he was in when President Larson was elected. He was well respected in the employee ranks at the State Department having served his entire career in Washington and in embassies around the world.

Loretta Bird Cox changed the looks of the biography photographs of Secretary of Defense, the first African American woman. There were no questions about her qualifications. She was born Loretta Bird in Dallas, Texas, the daughter of a commercial airline pilot and schoolteacher. A good student and volleyball player, Loretta graduated third in her class in high school and went to the Air Force Academy, getting top grades in Aeronautical Engineering, and the Air Force paid her to go on for her Ph.D. at Texas A&M in aerospace-aeronautical engineering. Her graduate school studies were in advanced control systems and man-machine interface, making aircraft easier for pilots to control under the stress of combat. Lorretta "Falcon" Bird served as a test pilot at Edwards Airforce base putting theory to the test with new control system designs and adaptions for the F-16 Fighting Falcon. Loretta left military service at the rank of Captain and went to work as a project manager at Defense Advanced Research Projects Agency (DARPA) the high technology research arm of the Department of Defense. Loretta served in a series of senior appointments in top positions in the Department of Defense, Assistant Secretary of Defense for Research, Assistant Secretary of Global Security and Assistant Secretary of Defense Policy.

Loretta left the Pentagon reluctantly three years before Larson was elected. She was opposed to new drone technology under development and resigned to avoid a public confrontation within the Department of Defense. Loretta got a position with the Rand Corporation in the Pentagon City offices as a senior policy analyst. Loretta was resigned to the fact she would finish her career in think tanks and universities. Her husband told her the money was better, and she could relax and enjoy life a little. She had gotten married later in life, to Bradford Cox, a lawyer specializing in securities and finance. They didn't have children, and he told her they could start travelling more after she left government. Maybe Bradford was right, this wasn't such a bad life. Loretta was surprised when Richard Larson won the election, but she had lost interest in the machinations inside government. She did not know who Simon Tomas was when he called her at home in that evening in December after the election. He told her she was on the short list for Secretary of Defense; they were going to cancel the research into the new drone technology she had opposed. He wanted to know if she was available for an interview with President Elect Larson and Vice President Elect Packard. She instinctively said yes. She went into the kitchen, Bradford was making pot roast with mixed vegetables, she said they might need to delay the trip next month to Spain. She expected he might be angry. Bradford was ecstatically happy for Loretta; he knew that she loved working in the pentagon. He got out a bottle of champaign; he said Spain will always be there. Brandon toasted Loretta "*Falcon*" Bird-Cox, first African American woman Secretary of Defense.

Loretta said, "Well it's just an interview."

"You know better, if the President is interviewing you, that means you are at the top of the short list."

He was right, his wife was about to make history. The employees and senior officials in DOD and the pentagon were happy to hear that the

Falcon was coming back home and would be the new Secretary of Defense. There was of course service rivalry, the army and navy questioning an air force bird at the top. Loretta understood the rivalry and spent the first two months going to as many army and navy bases as possible, meeting and talking to soldiers and sailors in uniform. She went to air force bases last, the airman saying the *Falcon* saved the best for last.

As national security adviser, Andrew Friedman was charged with organizing national security briefings for President Larson. His position did not require Senate confirmation, he was on the team before inauguration day. The planned briefings involved the preparation of detailed briefing documents that would run anywhere from 50 to 100 pages. NSC briefings were sometimes necessary based on emerging issues anywhere in the world, at any time on any day. These briefings varied in the level of formality and documentation, but long briefing books were not available. Andrew had the critical job of triage, what was important enough to take the time of the NSC principals, especially the president and vice president. Their schedules were planned in fifteen-minute segments. It was important to know the fine line, when to disturb that schedule or work an issue into a routine briefing.

Along with the briefings, the President and the NSC principals along with a few other senior officials received the Presidents Daily Brief (PDB), a daily high-level summary of all sources of intelligence on national security issues. The PDB is collated and prepared by the Office of the Director of National Intelligence, most presidents ordinarily receive a verbal briefing along with the PDB at the start of their business day. The President and another larger group of select senior officials receive a daily publication from the Office of Analysis of the CIA, the "World Intelligence Review" (WIRe) covering a wider range of topics than the PDB. Both documents have very restricted distribution and are classified, the WIRe is Secret and the PDB is Top Secret. Andrew Friedman studied both documents carefully each day and used insights from these documents to determine whether an NSC briefing is necessary. The NSC principals did not need to be briefed on the exact same thing they have gotten from the PDB or WIRe.

President Larson had asked for a set of "orientation" briefings for the new principals of the NSC in the administration. The President wanted to make sure he was familiar with high-profile national security issues the administration would likely face over the next few years. It was also a means for President Larson to build rapport with these senior officials, and Larson had a particular interest in framing certain high-profile issues in a historic context. Friedman thought Larson had a good point; most of these more difficult issues had long histories. Friedman was developing the agenda and scope of the briefing topics for the "orientation series." The scope and schedule were reviewed first by Simon Tomas and Vice President Packard and then the President before the schedule was locked in. The President had already put some topics onto the agenda including two involving potential nuclear conflicts: the Kim Regime in North Korea and Iran-Saudi relations. As a professional historian, Larson knew that historical context was important and would play a role in some of the difficult geopolitical questions they would face in the coming years.

Andrew Friedman had access to an electronic library of NSC briefing documents that went back twenty years, anything older than that was in an archived library. The day after the inauguration Simon Tomas asked Friedman for an existing recent high-level historical overview on Nuclear Proliferation, the President wanted to read a full briefing paper. Tomas said, something off the shelf, don't task anyone to write something new. The President did not want an NSC Principals briefing on this historical overview, he felt they already knew the history. The

President told Tomas this was remedial training for the President on the subject, Tomas did not tell Friedman that comment. Friedman remembered there was a paper from Steve Thomas in the NSC files, it was only a few years old. He emailed it with Thomas's cover memo describing the briefing paper.

Steve Thomas was a senior adviser on nuclear proliferation at the State Department when he prepared a background briefing paper for the NSC files. A historical overview of how nuclear weapons had seeped from the New Mexico desert in 1945 to small nations around the globe and offer insights where proliferation might go in the future. It was not a detailed technical paper or legal analysis of policy. President Larson sipped his green tea, in the easy chair in the small private office next to the oval. It was early evening, Amanda was out of town, so he stayed a little late for some quiet reading time. He saw the cover memo for the report written by Dr. Steve Thomas at the State Department. The cover memo described the structure of the report, *a historical overview but focusing mainly on the recent history of the Pakistani program and the unique form of proliferation that emerged from that program.* He scanned through it. It appeared to be well written. It was a historical overview, focused more on the recent history, just what he wanted. Not a technical or policy jargon report; he could get that from other sources.

Larson glanced out the window, took another sip of tea and began reading. The paper covered three different periods of proliferation, the major powers period, age of proliferation and finally marketplace proliferation. The report explained, *the major powers period began with the original three countries, US, USSR, UK in a period of only seven years (1945-1952) essentially based on work done in the Manhattan Project with the UK stealing from their ally the US and the USSR getting missing details they needed from their spies in the Manhattan Project. The major powers period is characterized by the revolutionary science and physics that occurred in a compressed time period; the internal structure of the atom was still being discovered; James Chadwick discovered the neutron in 1932. The lack of electrical charge of the neutron meant it could easily enter into a nucleus, leading to unstable nuclei. The fission process and the possibility of a nuclear chain reaction induced and sustained by neutrons demonstrated in 1938 and 1939. Then the first sustained chain reaction in a graphite and uranium pile built on abandoned racket courts under Stagg field at the University of Chicago in December 1942. Only advanced countries with large scientific communities, access to resources and manufacturing capability along with the breakthrough discoveries of the scientists of the Manhattan project could enter the nuclear weapons community in the early major powers period. France and China joined the other major powers in 1960 and 1964 respectively.*

The proliferation of nuclear weapons required three separate capabilities: first, the production of high-grade fissile material; second, the sophisticated design allowing weaponization using the fissile material and third, the manufacturing capabilities to assemble a weapon that could be delivered by some means. The production of high-grade fissile material could proceed either by the enrichment of uranium or the production of plutonium in a reactor; either route required substantial resources and large engineering projects, but the technologies were largely known. The weaponization required the detailed understanding on the neutron physics and complex detonation process that occurred in microseconds. This required sophisticated engineering and physics knowledge or access to the work of others who had already solved these complex puzzles. Finally, the equipment and processes to fabricate the high purity precisely manufactured components and assemble them within exacting tolerances. The hurdles of weaponization and manufacturing capabilities have substantially been reduced over time as secrets of warhead designs had been shared or stolen and as general technology and manufacturing had greatly improved especially since the emergence of digitally controlled manufacturing equipment. Production of the fissile materials required large scale and expensive programs, generally requiring the resources of a nation state, but these activities can be and have been carried out covertly for periods of time.

The controls on proliferation were almost nonexistent in the 1950s and 1960s, the major powers were using nuclear technology to spread their influence without fully contemplating the consequences until it was too late. President Eisenhower wanted to expand US nuclear capability but wanted to focus efforts to use atomic energy on peaceful purposes; many viewed the civilian focus as an effort to conceal the US work to expand military capabilities. In 1953 Eisenhower gave the famous Atoms for Peace speech at the United Nations advocating harnessing the atom for peaceful purposes and included a proposal to create an agency under the sponsorship of the UN to promote safe and peaceful uses of atomic energy. The International Atomic Energy Agency (IAEA) came into existence in 1957. Interestingly, the proposal for the IAEA was a late addition to the speech and not considered a central point by the Eisenhower administration. The administration was caught off guard by the enthusiastic international response to this proposal and found itself needing to develop a proposed charter. The US began providing small reactors to allied countries, Israel, Iran, India, Pakistan and South Africa, to sustain alliance relationships. During these early years, US intelligence agencies began issuing classified papers cautioning that these small reactors and associated technology transfer could be diverted to nuclear weapons programs.

Next, the "Age of Proliferation," beginning on May 18, 1974 when India conducted an underground nuclear test estimated to have a yield roughly that of the Hiroshima weapon. Indira Gandhi's statement regarding the test announced it as a peaceful nuclear explosion, very ambiguous as to what that meant. Most experts conclude the threat of nuclear China was India's primary motivation for developing nuclear weapons and then in falling domino's fashion, India became the motivation for a nuclear Pakistan. This was another aspect of proliferation for nation states; proliferation tends to beget more proliferation in response to the threat of a hostile nuclear country. India used a civilian nuclear program to divert resources and materials to a covert weapons program, including plutonium from a reactor provided by the Canadians. This diversion of "civilian technology" was a watershed moment in proliferation circles, supposedly civilian equipment and technology could be used to develop weapons. The phrase "Age of Proliferation" has been used for the period inaugurated by the Indian test. Following the Indian test, the IAEA sponsored meetings and participating countries worked more closely to develop controls to try and prevent similar proliferation. These proliferation controls include the "trigger list" and "dual use" lists of equipment and systems that proliferation regimes seek to control. Other countries followed the model of India, using and adapting technology from existing nuclear sponsor countries along with indigenous development to develop nuclear weapons, Pakistan, Israel, North Korea and Iran, all with known capability or expected capability in the near term.

The major portion of the report described the details of the recent history of AQ Khan and marketplace proliferation. Larson found this particularly disturbing; he did not know any of the details although he remembered the name and some of the media coverage. He finished reading the report in the residence early the next morning during breakfast before going to the office. Amanda was in New Haven with Barbara Tomas for two more days hiring a caretaker for their homes, so he had time to read at the breakfast table. He read the final portion of the report

Damon Nomad

as he finished his coffee, *The AQ Khan network developed a free market for nuclear weapons proliferation; it was effective and difficult to detect. It operated for twenty years before being discovered, and when it was revealed, investigators realized there was missing enrichment equipment, precision tools and design information and suspected unknown additional customers. There were also missing copies of nuclear warhead designs that were stored in apartment buildings where AQ Khan was known to stay. The materials and equipment were being traded in commerce like a plumbing supply house, with warhead designs given as gifts to customers. The full extent of the diversion of technology and design of the AQK network remains unknown. The only progression beyond such a network would be a service providing full assembly and delivery of a warhead through a network. Although not likely it was possible, the greatest difficulty would be the acquisition of the fissile material. Such a network could deliver everything as a kit in pieces over time on an installment plan, with a customer support representative showing up for assembly later. Proliferation in the future would follow models based on the AQ Khan procurement network, purchasing and bringing the pieces together using the sophisticated tools available on the worldwide internet.*

The experience of the Khan network was troubling. This was his first detailed exposure beyond the little he remembered from press accounts. He knew that more recent development of the Internet and electronic platforms, including encrypted platforms, could make such a network even more difficult to detect now. He hoped this old threat was being closely monitored; people needed to keep their eye on the ball in the nuclear area.

It was late February; Larson had a meeting with Vice President Packard and Andrew Friedman to review plans and schedules for the NSC principals' briefings. President Larson thanked Friedman for the historical proliferation overview paper by Dr. Steve Thomas. Vice President Packard knew about Thomas, "Steve Thomas is well respected in the intelligence community and in diplomatic circles, a straight shooter."

President Larson asked them, "What are your views about the so-called missing customer and the missing shipment discovered during investigations of the AQ Khan network?"

Friedman responded first, "When the investigations were underway, it was most likely thought to be more scope of supply for the Iranians or possibly the North Koreans. There were rumors that it could have been Saudi Arabia, but that died away."

Vice President Packard nodded in agreement, "That is my recollection as well; nothing ever came of the Saudis, seems most likely it went to Iran. There were lots of rumors and concerns about the warhead designs, but it was anyone's guess as to who else may have gotten those, AQK handed them out like customer gift packages."

Larson sighed, "Yes, that was disturbing."

Vice President Packard continued, "You know what happens, it was on everyone's radar screen for a few years after the Libyan program was uncovered, but that's a long time past. The focus moves on to other more pressing matters."

President Larson looked at the schedule of briefings developed by Friedman, "So, the first briefing in the orientation series is the first week of March. Good I am anxious to hear what Dr. Wallace has to say especially given the bits and pieces we are hearing about this Saudi nuclear investigation and what I just read about proliferation."

Gulshan Wallace was born in the US, her mother Bahar immigrated to the US having worked for the United States government first working at the US Embassy in Tehran as a translator. Bahar was engaged to Gulshan's father, Walter Wallace, who worked for the US State Department in the Embassy. He was involved in development of electrical power generation, transmission and distribution development assisting the Iranian government. Walter was born in Saudi Arabia; his father was a mechanical engineer who worked for Lance Engineering & Construction. Walter's father was from Idaho and converted to Islam so he could marry a Saudi girl; almost unheard of at the time, but she was an orphan, and her uncle was happy to get a $1000 dowry in exchange for his written approval for the marriage. Walter grew up Muslim, his mother was religious his father was agnostic. Walter spent the first fifteen years of his life in Saudi Arabia, and he had grown up speaking Arabic and English. Gulshan's parents came to the US just to get married, but returned after the honeymoon to Tehran to live and work in the Embassy. They left Iran with signs of trouble growing especially for those who had worked to help the Shah and the Americans. Bahar had one brother; they were able to get her parents and her brother out of Iran; her father was a supporter of the Shah and the US Ambassador helped with immigration to get them out of the country.

Gulshan was a small child when the US embassy was overtaken by Iranian students. She grew up speaking and writing English, Farsi and Arabic. She had a doctorate in middle eastern studies from NYU. She was raised as a Muslim, but her parents allowed her to attend Christian churches with her friends and to be exposed to Christian teachings and ideals. In high school she went to Church and bible studies most every Sunday with one of her best friends, Mandy Hewett. Mandy's parents knew that Gulshan was Muslim, and they checked with Bahar and Walter to make sure it was okay for Gulshan to come to church and go to bible studies. Mandy also came to the Wallace house and went to Friday prayers with Gulshan and Bahar, there was a Muslim ladies' group that did Friday prayers in English. Mandy's parents thought it was a good opportunity for their daughter to be exposed to another faith; they knew

Gulshan and her parents well, they were good people. Walter and Bahar believed the Quran was the direct word of God. They believed that the words and teachings of the Prophet Muhammad were helpful in interpreting the Quran, but neither of them believed that Imam's were infallible. They didn't believe any human being was infallible. They also believed that Jesus was a prophet and that only good could come to their daughter from studying the Holy Bible and his teachings.

Gulshan focused her dissertation on American Iranian policy during the Kennedy Administration as American intervention in Iranian domestic policies grew. She grew up in Franconia, Virginia and her parents remained lifelong employees of the US State Department; their good reputations helped her get a job at the Department of State where she worked since getting her Ph.D. She loved her work, and now she was a senior policy advisor and considered the authority at the State Department when it came to Saudi— Iranian relations. She worked in the same building as her parents when they returned to Washington from Tehran. They were very proud of their daughter's accomplishments at the State Department. She went to work in the Office of the Secretary of State, the pinnacle of national diplomacy days after Secretary of State Travis was appointed to office. Gulshan Wallace had briefed Travis several times when he was Deputy Secretary of State. Gulshan's husband Geoff Peterson was an attorney with the State Department, he didn't mind Gulshan keeping her maiden name, it was an old-fashioned practice as far as he was concerned. He was Christian, that was not a problem for her parents, the Quran did not prohibit interfaith marriage, the only prohibition was marriage to those who worshipped multiple Gods and pagans. They had studied the Quran and what the Prophet said, regardless of what some zealots would claim about their interpretations. Geoff's parents struggled a little bit at first, but when they got to know Gulshan and her family, they were happy to have Gulshan in the family.

Gulshan thought Geoff was having a friend prank her when she answered a call in late February. He said his name was Andrew Friedman, she knew the name of the new President's national security adviser. He said the secretary of state had recommended her for a briefing of the NSC Principals, historical overview of Iranian-Saudi relations. She almost laughed. She looked down and saw the caller ID listed US GOV West Wing Operator 2, maybe it wasn't a prank. Mr. Friedman said the briefing would be scheduled for 90 minutes; he would email her a briefing template and presentation template. Gulshan had written a paper two years ago, the nature of a regional cold war between Iran and Saudi Arabia pushing both towards nuclear weapons. Some of the views in the conclusions of that paper were out of the mainstream of US intelligence, one of the reasons the secretary of state recommended her for the briefing. The briefing paper should be between 80 and 120 pages and submitted the day before the briefing. A few minutes later she got the meeting invitation for Thursday, the first week in March in the West Wing, Situation Room—Conference Room along with the templates from Friedman's executive assistant.

She called her mom at home, her parents had both been retired for several years. It was exciting news for her parents. The Wallace family had been in public service in the state department for more than 40 years now, a white house briefing was the mark of a brilliant career. Mr. Friedman had given her a good sense of what the President was looking for, framing the current state of relations between Iran and Saudi Arabia in a historical context and how historical influences may drive future behavior. The details of the nuclear program would be covered in another briefing, she only needed to cover the nuclear program as it was relevant to the overall historical relationship. She titled her briefing paper, Regional Cold War Iran and Saudi Arabia. Geoff was excited for her when she told him that evening, Geoff had joined a large firm the year after they got married and was a senior partner now. He knew this was a big deal for a State Department employee, recognition of the high value the State Department had in Gulshan's opinions.

Andrew Friedman tried to meet people before giving the briefings, the ones that had never been in the West Wing for a briefing; he wanted to set them at ease. He could see Dr. Wallace was a little nervous, he explained the NSC Principals were smart people who ask difficult questions, they are also respectful and not harsh in their questions. He told her to feel at ease and enjoy her first briefing in the West Wing. She did feel better, when she got into the room there was an assistant to show her how to navigate her presentation. The slide deck was loaded and ready to go, she had coffee and water at the table. Soon the Principals arrived and then the President, she saw they all had copies of the briefing book in front of them. Secretary of State Travis was a familiar and friendly face, he gave her a wink and a smile. Andrew Friedman introduced her, President Larson nodded his head, "You have the floor Dr. Wallace, your title is intriguing."

She introduced the general thesis at the beginning of her briefing, with the presentation filling in the details before she reached her conclusions. Saudi Arabia and Iran each saw themselves as the natural regional power in the middle eastern region from the Mediterranean in the west to Afghanistan in the east. Iran's national identity built on their great Persian history, one of the great ancient empires in the world. Saudis' national identity was much different, a short history of Bedouin cunning and survival and their relationship with the world's superpower the United States. Gulshan was relaxed once she got into the briefing, the NSC Principals seemed interested, and they were not peppering her with constant questions. She moved through the recent history of Iran, Saudi Arabia and the historical development of their rivalry and conflict and the complex relationship with the United States.

Gulshan was wrapping up near the end of her briefing, introducing a view that she knew was controversial, especially for the CIA director. "A final factor in the degrading relations with Saudi Arabia and Iran, was the announcement that Saudi Arabia would follow the United Arab Emirates as a nuclear energy country and that they intended to have their own fuel cycle. The Iranians believed the Saudis had finally decided to develop their own nuclear weapon, no longer trusting in American support. This was the final nudge for weaponization of the Iranian nuclear program, development had been underway for more than forty years putting the pieces together over decades. The only remaining decision was how to make the Saudis, Americans and Israeli's fully aware of their capability. They could test a weapon underground and announce the nuclear weapons program. I think the more likely route for Iran is to come to the United States secretly confirming they have fully weaponized the nuclear program. The Iranians will seek an elimination of all sanctions and promise a no first use policy. The Iranians know the American's will share the information with the Saudis and Israel, that is what they want. The Iranians want to achieve a similar status as Israel, nuclear ambiguity."

"The unintended consequence will be Saudi Arabian nuclear weapons development; this will be the final push they need to go nuclear; either through direct purchase of warheads from Pakistan or the development of nuclear weapons through the acquisition of technology. The Saudis will not tolerate a nuclear threat from Israel and Iran, their trust in the United States has fallen steadily for decades. It is likely that Saudi Arabia has already moved down the nuclear weapons path. I know this opinion is not the current position of US intelligence. This will transform the growing regional cold war into a potential nuclear conflict."

President Larson smiled at Gulshan, "Very interesting briefing Dr. Wallace, I agree with your assessment. There are forces driving Saudi

Arabia towards nuclear weapons, although I understand we have no direct intelligence of this at this time, it would be interesting to know how far down the path they may have gone. I recently read a paper that makes the point, proliferation tends to beget proliferation, that is what we have learned from recent history. Any views Director Sweigart?"

"Dr. Wallace's views are known in the intelligence community, her analysis and opinions of the conflict between the Saudis and Iranians are widely used in our intelligence analysis. With all due respect, her views on potential nuclear weapons in Saudi Arabia are highly speculative and a bit ambiguous. There are certainly forces pushing the Saudis down the nuclear path, but likely not more than some clandestine research projects. That is the assessment of all intelligence agencies in the US government as well as our closest allies." Sweigart knew he would hear a briefing on the Saudi investigation in a few weeks, but the Deputy Director of Intelligence had assured him it couldn't be much more than some small-scale enrichment experiments, possibly a small pilot cascade.

Vice President Packard intervened, "Dr. Wallace, it is a fair point, moving down the path is a bit ambiguous; can you add more?"

"Well madam Vice President I am not a technical analyst, I look to the experts to make that determination, but I do believe they have been on the path for many years." Gulshan remembered a similar conversation with Steve Thomas last year on this exact point during a meeting at the OIG.

President Larson nodded, "Dr. Wallace, turning our attention to the Iranians. What Iranian reaction would you expect if we were to preempt them and confront them publicly with evidence that they have nuclear weapons? Just off the top of your head, go with your instincts."

Gulshan had not considered this before, she thought it through as she answered, "The Iranians will feel cornered, the route of nuclear ambiguity taken away and confronted with decades of deceit, they will fear more severe sanctions, possible military action by the United States or Israel. They will start with denials and retreat further from international engagement and begin to strike out, more strikes against Saudi oil installations seeking some way to get a stronger negotiating position."

President Larson continued, "Same scenario but we give them a public ultimatum that we will take unilateral military action unless they dismantle the nuclear program."

"If it is a clear credible threat that the United States will take strong military action, they will slowly comply, and they will seek some financial benefit, asking for relaxed sanctions as they make progress. There also is some small chance they could strike out, but not likely; they know the power of our military. If they were to strike out, it will be due to the fragmented nature of their decision-making; the role of the clerics and revolutionary guard could cause a radical element to strike out, it likely would be reflexive and not sustained. If we were to give a direct and credible ultimatum, a stick as they say, it would be best to offer it with a credible carrot, reduced sanctions or the release of assets on some reasonable time frame. This would likely avoid a potential reflexive strike, seeing there is a benefit in advance."

Chapter Twenty-One
Final Report Arabian Nuclear Weapons

Preparing the Final Report was a massive task, between Russ Nixon's database and the blackhole database; there were millions of documents and records. But they had been organized into relevant evidence during the course of the investigation; still Michael had to select from more than two hundred thousand pieces of evidence to reference in the final report. He narrowed the relevant evidence down to more than twenty thousand individual pieces of documentary, photographic and scientific evidence (results of material samples). Now this evidence had to be described in a coherent manner describing the nuclear weapons program. He followed the outline of the briefing they had given to Mel Randolph. He was working on the report every day putting in ten-hour days and working some Saturdays.

Before he was done, there was a new president in office, new Secretary of State, Secretary of Defense and other major cabinet posts. The final report referenced 22,350 pieces of evidence, and it was organized into Three Parts; Part One covered the first fifteen years of the program, when Sheikh Zayed and King Fahd agreed to collaborate concerned about Iran and Israel, the division of labor between the two countries like the Manhattan Project; the Saudis to produce the fuel and the Emiratis to design and fabricate the warheads. It described the Emiratis monitoring AQ Khan and stealing the initial warhead design from his Dubai Apartment and the early operations of the enrichment cascade, where they struggled to produce enriched uranium.

Part two of the report covered the activities starting with development of the Hidden Nucleus procurement network based in Dubai, a modern and upgraded version of the AQ Khan network. The report described in detail the construction and design of all of the facilities in Saudi Arabia and Abu Dhabi. Part three of the report traced the movement of uranium and how the different facilities had operated together over the last several years. The report described the flow between the facilities, ore to the UF6 facility, the low enriched UF6 cannisters from Al Jabeer to the enrichment cascade, highly enriched UF6 cannisters from the enrichment cascade at the airbase to the metal fabrication facility where HEU ingots were produced and sent to the Musaffah facility for fabrication of the warhead and then transport to a safe storage facility in Saudi Arabia on an air base.

Part three also described the final warhead design, clearly a derivative of the plans stolen from AQ Khan as modified and enhanced by the North Koreans who had a similar design. The final paragraph in part three described the final results; the first warhead was shipped to Saudi Arabia in August and referenced a picture from November of a partially constructed warhead and the core assemblies, expected to be complete in December. The final report was 265 pages long, the separate index listing the evidence was in a separate volume listing the titles, description and the database index number was another 530 pages long. The report included maps, facility pictures, facility diagrams, graphs of material flows, isotopic trace plots and an organizational chart of the enterprise, Hidden Nucleus.

Andrea Jacobs had been reviewing the report and spot checking references as Michael developed it working in parallel. She had never seen such a long and complex investigation report. She reviewed the final draft as Michael prepared a briefing. They had a final version and a briefing package ready for the IG and CIA Director in the third week of March. It has taken nearly three months of full-time writing, editing and reviewing to finalize the draft report and prepare the briefing. The briefing was scheduled for two hours at CIA headquarters, Andrea and

IG Ross had agreed the report was too sensitive, complex and large for indexing and referencing. They would need another means of independent review and validation. The report was Top Secret and not suitable for public release it was developed for national security decision-makers.

CIA Director Sweigart invited Scott Fonda, a Division Director from the intelligence branch, to the briefing. Fonda was representing the Deputy Director of Intelligence who was overseas on travel, Fonda had the lead for the middle east nuclear assessments. Director Sweigart had read the OIG into Blackhole months ago when he was Deputy Director of Clandestine Services, he was skeptical about the investigation at the time. Sweigart was thinking of Dr. Wallace's NSC briefing only two weeks ago as Case was getting his presentation loaded onto the computer. Sweigart remembered what Wallace said about the Saudis moving down the path; he was about to hear how far they had gone. Fonda was aware of the scope of what Michael Case had been working on with the blackhole team in Abu Dhabi. He knew the evidence came from the Russ Nixon database and a databased developed by blackhole specifically for this investigation. He was not read into blackhole, but he knew they had human and technical assets to collect intelligence in the middle east and they worked out of Abu Dhabi. He was skeptical, a nuclear weapons program in Saudi Arabia was very unlikely; if there was one it would likely be at the research stage with small scale enrichment, possibly a very small pilot cascade. He knew about the power analysis; he believed the team in Abu Dhabi had made errors in laying out the grid topology. This is what all of the analysts believed, there were a group of large factories north of the base, they likely got the topography of the grid wrong. Where could the Saudis have gotten 20,000 centrifuges? Fonda was ready to punch holes through an assessment based on a power flow analysis filled with uncertainty and potential errors.

Michael went through the briefing in about 90 minutes; IG Ross, Director Sweigart and Scott Fonda listened and did not interrupt. Michael saw that Fonda was taking extensive notes. Director Sweigart was surprised and impressed; the briefing was very well laid out. He saw the citations to pages in the report; it looked like the report was over 260 pages in length. He knew the entire intelligence community had missed the covert nuclear program he had just heard described to him. "Michael this is much more than I expected to see and hear, very comprehensive. It is beyond compelling, obviously we have all missed this for years but let's not dwell on that now. The team in Abu Dhabi station has a lot of good things to say about you. I have only been director for about a month. Honestly, I thought this was most likely a waste of time when I was Deputy Director. As I heard the updates, I knew there was something there, but I did not expect to see evidence of an entire weapons program and actual confirmation of a warhead. There will be some lessons learned in the intelligence community for missing this for so long; seems like we took our eyes of the ball."

"The support we got from the CIA station was first class; it was an honor to work with them. It was a team effort. Steve Thomas told me we would need overwhelming evidence; he suggested a picture of a warhead with a Saudi flag on it might be needed to convince some people."

Sweigart laughed, "That sounds like Thomas. What about the two Americans alleged to be acting on senior government direction to assist the Saudis?"

"There is a separate report close to file; the senior official had never given them any direction to disclose classified information. The two Americans did give the Saudis some relatively useless Confidential and Secret information, and they have left government. We had someone at NNSA look at the document listing. The US Attorney's office declined prosecution, and we closed it to file. There are memos in their personnel files referencing the OIG case number if they ever seek a security clearance or government employment again."

Sweigart looked to Fonda, Fonda was trying to organize his thoughts, what he had just seen and heard was beyond his comprehension.

"How many cited pieces of intelligence were used in the final report?"

"There are 22,350 from the MissingLink and Blackhole databases."

"You drew that from what population of intelligence records relevant to the findings of the report?"

"A little over two hundred thousand records."

"Is there any indexing?"

"Yes, a separate index volume to accompany the full report; the index includes a title, sequential evidence number, short description from the database, and the database reference point if someone wants to go back to the raw intelligence."

"That must be a long index document."

"The index document is 530 pages. I thought it was important that someone could read the report with only the index as a reference, not requiring constant access to the intelligence databases, but it is just cut and paste to create the index."

"So, the index is extracted directly from the intelligence collation, and you did not alter anything other than adding a sequential evidence number."

"Of course, the index is essentially a form of evidence; the report turns this evidence into a narrative. It would contaminate the evidence if I altered the information in the index."

"The final report must be around 270 pages?"

"265 pages."

Fonda could see Michael was tired, he understood why. "Michael, I came here expecting to hear some half-baked theory extrapolating beyond a limited set of evidence. To convince people there is a Saudi nuclear weapons program requires massive evidence, detailed analysis and clear and coherent reporting. I have no doubt there is a covert weapons program from this briefing, if your written report is like this briefing presentation people will be convinced. This is some impressive intelligence analysis; you didn't take any shortcuts." Director Sweigart admired how Fonda responded, very professional knowing he would take some of the heat for missing this along with others. Sweigart knew this had been missed for a long time; it was the leadership and politicians that would need to answer for this not Scott Fonda and his staff.

"I just wrote the report, a summary of what CIA and NSA staff collected and collated working with us."

Sweigart shook his head, "No you did a lot more than that, that's a lot of dots to extract and connect. Michael, this is really impressive to organize so much information into a coherent report in this time frame. You must have put in a lot of hours. Scott is right if you would have taken some shortcuts, people would punch holes in it."

Director Sweigart continued, "IG Ross, this is a sensitive and complex report, significant policy decisions will be made using this report and I understand you have not had time to follow the rigorous review processes that you would use for OIG reports. I recommend that this be reviewed by a small CIA and DOE-NNSA team this month, a RED challenge team. A group to go back to the raw intelligence and scrub down the full report. Michael will brief the team and answer any initial questions, and they will review the final report and index, we will give them access to the databases and in March they will come back with their views on the report. Then we can make a decision on briefing the

NSC and the President. We should place this report under a special access program, under custody of the CIA."

IG Ross was in agreement, "I agree, if a form of public report is developed, we can derive a version following our processes."

Michael smiled, "how about Sakar for the name of the SAP."

Sweigart laughed, "Ok Arabic for candy or sweets, does that mean something from your time in Abu Dhabi?"

"Yes, it reminds me of some things I learned working with Mel Randolph during a covert meet."

"Okay Sakar, yes Mel Randolph a good man indeed."

Michael Case briefed the red team members two days later and they were all read into SAKAR, Scott Fonda another CIA analyst, two experts from Los Alamos and an NNSA Division Director. He used the same briefing that Sweigart and IG Ross had been given. They were all in shock. Brent Thomas from Los Alamos broke the silence, "This is for real, right not some kind of drill or practice to see how we work together to handle something like this. They have operated under our noses for more than two decades and have built these facilities and have warheads sitting in Saudi Arabia and Abu Dhabi as we speak."

Michael nodded, "Yes, that's exactly what they have done."

Scott Fonda was the leader of the red team, "Okay as you can all see Michael, and the team he worked with built an absolutely overwhelming case. But we have to go through the raw intelligence and see if there is something missing. and thoroughly review the written report. We need to review this carefully and look for flaws in the report, evidence not considered or contradictions. You all know if the report stands, it will be going to the President and the National Security Council as actionable intelligence; it needs to be scrubbed down hard. It will likely change the diplomatic and military posture of the United States in the region, and you all know it will shock the intelligence community. We have all missed this for years, what is important is getting this right now. If there aren't any more questions for Michael, let's get to work. We are on a tight schedule; we only have about a week."

Scott Fonda sent a classified email with a detailed report attached to CIA Director Sweigart and copied IG Ross and Michael Case. *The red team has finished the review of the report and index for SAKAR against the two intelligence databases. Attached is the full team report. The team confirms all findings of fact and supporting analysis in the report and report index as reflective of the underlying raw intelligence. No recommended modifications or changes to the report. The red team endorses the report and index as final intelligence products for use by senior decision makers in the US government. The conclusion of the red team is the report provides extraordinarily high confidence that the Saudi-UAE government have engaged in a covert nuclear weapons program since 1995 with two confirmed operational warheads and likely a third by this time. We did find one typo, misspelling of nuclear on page 85 in a footnote, but we found the error was in the index, I'm sure Michael preserved the error as appropriately reflecting the integrity of the report as reflective of the evidence.*

April 8 at 10:00 Michael Case was in the conference room next to the situation room at the White House, to brief President Larson, Vice President Packard, Secretary of Energy Emmanuel Gibbs, Director Sweigart, IG Ross, Secretary of State Travis, Secretary of Defense Cox and National Security Adviser Andrew Friedman. It was the first time he had ever been inside the White House, and he was nervous; he woke up at 4:00 am. and he could not go back to sleep. Michael was told to trim his briefing down to 60 minutes, the essentials for the President and NSC. Michael saw Director Sweigart walk towards him; he gave Michael a pat on the shoulder, "Good morning Michael; just relax. They have an idea of what you are going to tell them, but the details will knock their socks off. I have your back on this okay."

Director Sweigart introduced Michael, "This report is the result of a collaboration between the CIA, NSA and OIG State. The work originated with alleged misconduct of government officials working in the state department and disclosure of classified nuclear technology. The actions of the officials have been found not to be significant, but OIG investigators and CIA and NSA staff led by Michael Case did uncover a covert nuclear weapons program, a joint venture between the UAE and Saudi Arabia. A red team of CIA and DOE NNSA experts reviewed the report developed by Michael Case against the raw intelligence databases. The red team has validated the findings and the CIA endorses the report and index as intelligence for use by senior officials of US government. We have missed this for years; we have time to review what went wrong, that is not the subject of this briefing."

Sweigart then handed the briefing over to Michael Case. He took the President and senior officials through the history of the Saudi-UAE nuclear program. President Larson spoke when Michael finished, "Extraordinary narrative, how long have you been investigating this?"

"Since February of last year, a little more than a year based on a tip from a whistleblower, a naval officer." He couldn't tell the president his own son was the one who had brought this to his attention; he asked to be a confidential source.

"You started working on this about the time I announced I was going to run for President, quite a long journey for both of us. Thank you Mr. Case and congratulations on finding AQ Khans missing customer. Andrew, I want to read the full report. Vice President Packard, where do you recommend we go from here?"

"The information is endorsed by DOE NNSA and the CIA, Mr. President; this is actionable intelligence; we need an intervention and response strategy to deal with the Saudis and Emiratis. They have warheads, we don't know what they intend. We need to develop a tasking working through Andrew Friedman for review by the NSC principals. I think we can wait to formulate a detailed plan; I do not see any need for immediate action."

The President went to Secretary of Defense Cox, "I agree with Vice President Packard, let's not do something rash. There is no reason to think this is an imminent threat. We should not alter our defense posture. I think this information should be embargoed with the NSC until we have a plan."

President Larson went to CIA Director Sweigart and Secretary of State Travis, they were in agreement with Cox. Larson closed the meeting, "Okay, we will keep this information at the NSC for now and Vice President Packard and I will work on a tasking with Andrew Friedman for an intervention and response proposal."

Andrew Friedman and Director Sweigart had known each other for years. Sweigart saw Friedman walk his way as everyone was leaving, "I don't want to hear it Friedman, not a word."

"I was just going to offer to send some flowers to Dr. Wallace on your behalf, maybe chocolates."

The President, Vice President and Andrew Friedman had received briefings since the election that there was an ongoing investigation into a potential Saudi nuclear program, but the reports were that the intelligence community was very skeptical. Freidman thought something might be there when he was briefed about the power flow analysis from last October. None of them expected to hear about a full-scale weapons program with warheads. Vice President Packard and President Larson met alone after Michael Case finished his Saudi investigation briefing. They were in the Oval office, Larson took a drink of green tea, "Well the honeymoon is definitely over. That was a lot more than I expected to hear; I didn't anticipate operational warheads. We need a plan."

Larson had only been in office a few months, no experience in national security issues and no history with the people in important positions. He looked to Vice President Packard, "Christina, I need your recommendation on how to proceed. This is going to require sophisticated analysis, weighing the delicate balance in the middle east, there are geo-political and military considerations that must be taken into account."

Packard was surprised by the briefing as well, "First, this needs to be managed in a very tight circle, currently this information is known by a limited number of people; Michael Case and the team he led in Abu Dhabi, NSA and CIA and another IG Investigator. There is the red team from DOE-NNSA and CIA that reviewed the evidence collected by Case and those in the briefing today. This is not an imminent threat targeting us, we have some time to do some careful planning. I recommend that Andrew Friedman take the lead to develop a strategy. He will brief us on a concept. When we approve the concept, Friedman will develop a full briefing for the NSC principals on an intervention strategy. I will update Simon Tomas; he needs to be in the loop as well, nobody else."

Larson agreed on the course of action, they had some time. As Packard said, there were no indications of an imminent threat from the weapons. Andrew Friedman was the only choice they had considered for National Security Adviser, Vice President Packard asked for this position to be filled shortly after the election and put his name at the top of the list. That was the other key national security appointment along with the CIA Director, Secretary of Defense and Secretary of State, but they did not need Senate approval for his position. He was on the job the moment President Larson was sworn in, he had gotten daily briefings and updates all through December from his predecessor. Andrew was born and raised in Racine Wisconsin, on the western shores of Lake Michigan. He got his undergraduate degree in History with a focus in International Relations at University of Wisconsin and then went into the US Army Officer Candidate School and served six years, with an honorable discharge at the rank of Captain. In the Army he was assigned to a strategic planning position, in US force HQ in NATO. He used money saved from his spartan lifestyle and GI benefits to pay for law school at the University of Virginia Law School and passed the Virginia state bar exam. He took a job in a DC law firm, but he was searching for a career in the government; he was interested in the international law of military operations. He worked a little over a decade at the State Department and then years at the Department of Defense, including time as a policy and legal adviser to the Joint Chiefs of Staff, and he served as Chief of Staff to two Secretaries of Defense; he was working for the Carnegie Endowment as a National Security Fellow when he got the call to serve in the Larson administration. He lived in the same small apartment not far from Dupont Circle for the last fifteen years, staying physically fit hiking and walking. He had been working on a book about International Security and the Rule of Law for the last five years, he was searching for a publisher. He had never married; he wasn't gay but there were rumors, he just never found anyone that seemed the right fit for his monkish lifestyle. Vice President Packard had been around Friedman in a variety of circumstances over the years; he was usually working quietly behind the scenes, never seeking the limelight of praise, even when he was the leader of a project, he kept thing's low key, not barking out orders; but nudging and facilitating, driving consensus; but not afraid to push and make a decision when the time came.

Friedman had been considering the difficult task of responding to a Saudi-UAE nuclear program ever since his first briefing after the election by his predecessor, when he heard about the power flow analysis.

He knew that a covert uranium enrichment program was the most likely explanation although there were others floating around, high powered laser weapons or EMP weapons testing among them. He knew that the intelligence analysts believed the power analysis was flawed. They suspected bad data from the field description of the grid. He was not so sure that it could be that flawed, but he never expected to hear that they had operational nuclear warheads. The President and Vice President tasked him with the lead for a response strategy after Case's briefing. He was excited to take on a project that would allow him to do some research and use his skills at developing complex strategies.

Chapter Twenty-Two
Designing Checkmates

Andrew knew he had time; this was not an imminent threat. First, he needed to have a concept, and it was important not to treat the Saudi nuclear weapons in isolation, the geopolitical considerations of this complex region were important. Andrew played chess at Dupont Circle on most weekends during nice weather, a local legend. The word would spread when he arrived, and the best players would start queuing up on the old decaying public tables. He would play three games at a time moving from table to table; he had not lost a match in the last three years. A visiting Russian Chess master ranked 25th in the world heard about the matches when he was on tour in the area and beat him. The Russian thought he was lucky to beat Andrew quite a good player for the public parks. Friedman realized the Americans could not deal with the Saudis in a vacuum, there was a triad of secretive nuclear weapons programs in the middle east Israel, Iran and Saudi. The strategy would need to take all three into consideration, the outline of the strategy came to him one day after playing chess at Dupont Circle; a series of moves on three tables and three checkmates.

In late April Andrew went to Langley HQ on a Thursday, he went to the basement archives to do some background research. He spent all day the next three days in an old hard copy storage area in the subbasement going through the *Vela Flash* Files. He carried his lunch with him and had a thermos of coffee; working in the small research office, the hard copy files were a throwback that looked like something from the 1960s. The files covered a period starting in 1976 and the final information was from the early 1990s, classified information the CIA got from an asset in South Africa. The story started in 1976 when the President of South

Africa and Israeli Prime Minister entered into a secretive nuclear cooperation agreement. The first exchange was 30 grams of tritium from the
Israelis, a weapons booster (code named tee blare Afrikaans for tea
leaves) in exchange for 50 tons of uranium from the South Africans
(code named mutton). In September 1979 US technicians were reviewing traces from a Vela satellite; the Vela satellites were deployed at an
altitude of 70,000 miles to monitor the surface of the earth for nuclear
detonations, mainly to detect testing in violation of the international
treaty against atmospheric testing. The satellites became well known
because of the array of things they detected over the years, not nuclear
detonations, especially information that was of interest to astrophysicist
and astronomers.

The primary detection device on the Vela was called the "bhang meter," fast responding photodiodes that could detect the visual signature of
a detonation and estimate the yield. Signals from multiple photodiodes
could allow triangulation and location of a blast to be determined
accurately. The Vela satellite that provided the signal being reviewed in
1979 had been in service for seven years, they only had a trace from this
one "bhang meter", the electromagnetic pulse (EMP) detection equipment was out of service. This bhang meter was functioning perfectly and
had never provided any false signals. They reviewed the trace several
times, it was the unmistakable trace that had been detected by similar
devices during US atmospheric testing in the 1960s. When a nuclear
detonation occurs in the atmosphere, the initial intense fireball begins to
grow, but the hydrostatic atmospheric shockwave overtakes the fireball,
acting like an optical shutter obscuring the intense light behind the fast-
moving shockwave. The result is an unmistakable signal trace from the
bhang meter, a short 1 millisecond peak the initial brilliant flash of the
detonation, then a dramatic decline as the shockwave attenuates the
light, and then a lower and longer peak as the shockwave passes allow-

ing the light from the cooling fire ball. Because they only had the one signal, the exact location could not be determined; it was somewhere in the southern part of Africa and areas of the surrounding Indian Ocean. Later narrowed down to a large area of the southern Indian Ocean.

President Carter was briefed along with the principals of the National Security Council, they assigned senior staff to evaluate the event. Experts from around government and the national laboratories reviewed the data, searched for other confirmatory data, seismic data and other signals that might confirm the test. There were 22 WC-135 "Constant Phoenix" flights, collecting air samples throughout October. No atmospheric samples provided any positive results for a nuclear test. A New Zealand nuclear laboratory reported trace increases in Barium isotopes in rainwater samples in October in comparison to August and September that indicated the potential of a very low yield nuclear test in the atmosphere. American Scientists at the Arecibo radio telescope in Puerto Rico reported the observation of an ionospheric disturbance captured at the same time as the bhang meter indications. The size of the disturbance is believed by some experts to be consistent with high energy electrons from the gamma and x-rays of the nuclear blast impacting the ionosphere, like small pebbles hitting the surface of a pond.

The experts across government were conflicted. There were theories that it is a malfunction, a micro-meteor strike, even high-altitude ball lightning. The controversy spilled over into the media and reports about the possible nuclear test were in newspapers, people pointing fingers mostly at South Africa, but their nuclear program was clandestine. There were also stories about the possibility of Israel wanting to test a small yield tactical weapon. The final classified NSC briefing paper in 1983 laid out all the possible explanations. The final position taken by the lead author, a Los Alamos expert, was summarized in the conclusions. *The Vella signal in September 1979 was a small nuclear device (estimate 2 KT) exploded in the southern Indian Ocean. The conclusion is based on the following key factors: the signal was a classic atmospheric detonation signature for a device of that size; no known device malfunctions display this trace. Wind modeling showed none of the aircraft samples after the blast would have been able to detect this small blast in the collection locations, the high reliability of this bhang meter, the Barium results in New Zealand and finally the timing of the ionosphere disturbance monitored at Arecibo.* Since it was believed to be an ocean blast, there would be no evidence to allow for forensics to determine who was responsible for the weapon test.

There was no more information until 1992, CIA clandestine officers had developed an asset in the South African intelligence services. He sold them classified documents related to the secret South African nuclear program, and they included documents about the cooperative agreement between South Africa and Israel. There were some documents from the September 1979 detonation of a 2 KT Israeli warhead. The Israelis needed exact performance data; they intended to use the device as an initiator for a thermonuclear device. The test was monitored with test equipment on four boats with South African and Israeli scientists and naval officers. There were also atmospheric isotopic samples, collected by the South Africans. The South Africans had deceived the Israelis keeping copies of all the documents and tests records for themselves; they were supposed to hand everything over to Israel in exchange for more tritium. The CIA information from South Africa was Top Secret and controlled under a special access program, the information from years before analyzing the bhang meter was Secret and some of it was publicly known. Everyone had forgotten about the 1979 controversy when the files were archived in 1992. Andrew had his notes reviewed and classified on Monday morning in the Langley Office of Classification, this piece was done. He had a clear idea of how to use this, he had some other work to take care of that was more pressing.

Chapter Twenty-Three
Exposed King

The Saudi Arabian Ambassador to the United States had always felt his country was making progress too slowly on social issues, but culture changed slowly. On defense issues though, he had been frustrated by America and he knew that the Iranians had some small number of warheads, either operational warheads or ready for final assembly, capable of being operational in a few hours. He was one of the few senior officials who knew that Saudi Arabia had full nuclear capability late last year and would pursue a nuclear ambiguity policy. He did not have a problem with the strategy. He knew the discussions with the Americans later this year would be difficult, when Saudi Arabia revealed their secret to the Americans. He was worried when his brother, the foreign minister, called him for an urgent visit in late April. The trip was urgently arranged claiming family issues to his superiors, he knew there were no family issues.

He could see his brother was disturbed when he arrived, he came straight to the Embassy. Neither of them liked the aggressive and abrasive King Rashid, the Ambassador was sure the problems related to Rashid. Threatening Turkey and Iraq with military action, openly talking about the need for chemical weapons capability. His brother insisted they should go for a walk; it was a nice day outside. They sat near the Kennedy Center for the Performing Arts not far from the Embassy, on a bench looking out on the Potomac River.

The Ambassador was stunned, "Rashid could not be this reckless, are you sure?"

"I was working in my office after a meeting two weeks ago, I opened a file folder from the meeting. There were papers from General Abdul

Latif. They had gotten mixed in with my papers. We sat next to each other in the meeting. The papers provided details of the plan, exchanges between a small group of military advisers and King Rashid. I quietly returned the folders to General Latif's office, putting them on his assistant's desk discreetly while no one was around."

His brother looked at the river, "You know what we must do. The Americans will figure this out. It may take them time, but they have enormous technical capabilities."

The Ambassador shook his head, "Yes, I know what needs to be done. I must betray my country and tell the American President about our nuclear program and these plans of Rashid." They both knew he could be executed for treason.

Vice President Packard joined President Larson. The Saudi Ambassador had urgently requested a private meeting, entering the White House outside the view of the press, the last week in April. They both knew there was a possibility that he was going to present them with a demand for nuclear ambiguity; they would defer the decision and tell him they needed to discuss the matter with the NSC and the group of eight in congress. Michael Case's report may have come too late. There had not been enough time to develop a strategy to deal with the Saudi Arabia-UAE nuclear program.

The Ambassador sat on the sofa opposite Vice President Packard on the matching sofa, President Larson was in his side chair close to Packard. The Ambassador began, "I come with a heart filled with remorse. I must betray my country, and I pray that you never expose my deed. Saudi Arabia has a nuclear weapons program; we have produced warheads." He then went on to describe the plans his brother had discovered in Riyadh.

The President had talked to Vice President Packard about the Ambassador at length before the meeting; she held him in high regard, "He will not directly lie to us, he will withhold information, he will use deception like any diplomat. He is honorable and he is a good and faithful public servant to his government."

The President asked the Ambassador, "Who knows about these plans?"

"Only myself and my brother, the foreign minister. He agreed we needed to contact you."

President Larson calculated how difficult it was for the Ambassador to share this with the US President, the President went with his instinct. "The US has already discovered the covert Saudi-UAE nuclear program; we know the enrichment facility is hidden in the airbase southwest of Riyadh and we know the warhead is designed and fabricated in Abu Dhabi; we know that you call the warheads al-badhour. We were reviewing our options to intervene; we were not aware of this plan for a test. I have just revealed state secrets to you, and you have revealed state secrets to me. You should rest your mind at ease. I promise you the United States will not reveal that you have disclosed information and you will not reveal what I have shared with you. We will intervene in a way to minimize the risk; now the timing is difficult."

The Ambassador agreed to keep the mutual secrets, he felt relieved the Americans already knew about the nuclear program. All he revealed was this preposterous test scheme. He would wait and be quiet, there was nothing more he could do.

Andrew Friedman answered the phone. It was Simon Tomas, "Andrew, the VP and the President need to see you in the Oval office immediately."

Andrew Friedman walked into the Oval Office, the President spoke as he sat down, "Andrew we don't have the luxury of time. We need a plan much sooner than we thought." The Vice President described everything they had heard from the Saudi Ambassador.

President Larson was surprised by his reaction, "Andrew why are you smiling? The pressure is on and we have just given you a difficult deadline because of the Saudi plans."

"No, Mr. President, they have just exposed their king for a check-mate, I will have a plan in a few weeks."

Andrew Friedman was at CIA HQ the next morning working on the Iranian piece of his strategy. The Deputy Director of Clandestine services met with Andrew Friedman to brief him on the *Imam*, very few people in the US government knew about the asset and even fewer knew his identity. "He is Feisel Mohammad Ramul, has a doctorate in Physics from Tehran University. His father was a supporter and organizer for Ayatollah Khomeini and had run the southern Tehran Imam network. His father was killed in a mugging when Feisel was in graduate school. He is officially listed as the Director of Research in the Iranian Nuclear Organization. The position he actually holds is the Director of Applied Physics in the weapons division, the Iranians referred to it as the Mirage Division. He managed the entire design of the nuclear warhead effort, taking the Iranians to nuclear capability about six years ago. Before the *Imam* became our asset, we were still grasping at the capability of the Iranians. The official classified evaluation was they were nuclear capable, but there was no precision in the evaluation, beyond the capability to design and fabricate a warhead. That all changed with the *Imam*, he has delivered extensive information on the designs of the weapons, the throughput of nuclear materials, the actual inventory of nuclear warheads and locations of all key facilities. He even delivered physical material samples that had been given to his organization for analysis for weapons design purposes. Instead of destroying the samples, he stored them in a vault and passed them to an asset in Tehran. A very difficult exercise from the point of clandestine tradecraft."

"He had already been trained in clandestine tradecraft by the Iranians when he made the first contact with one of our operatives. He must have had information from the Iranian security services that one of the Americans in an IAEA delegation was actually a CIA clandestine officer, posing as a low-level US State Department nonproliferation expert. During the meetings, he cleverly passed a message to our officer using an Ottendorf cipher. Our asset found the cipher in a book he was reading and quickly worked out the message. There were several rounds of preliminaries before we worked out an agreement and protocol with him; his tradecraft is good, and he is very cautious. He has passed information and made clandestine meetings in Vienna and Tehran. He has never engaged in long conversations and refused meetings and interviews. He is not interested in telling us his story and avoids any opportunity of being recorded or photographed with CIA operatives."

Andrew Friedman was impressed, "What does the *Imam* get in return for his cooperation?"

"This is the curious part; do you know about M-I-C-E?"

"Only the rodents or the mouse for the computer. I don't know the relevance in this context."

"It is an acronym for the motivation of spies when they betray their countries, money, ideology, coercion and ego. For example, John Walker was the classic pure money motive. He walked into the Soviet embassy in 1967 with specific information on encryption device keys and a specific amount of money he wanted. Then there was Robert Hansen, an FBI agent that betrayed FBI counterintelligence sources for decades. Hansen was brilliant, but he was also abrasive and had poor social skills, limiting his upward mobility in the FBI. His lack of career progression frustrated him, and his ego drove him to betray his country. He saw colleagues move up the career ladder, people he judged lesser than himself. He evaded detection for 22 years, even when it was well known that there was an FBI counterintelligence leak. The *Imam* has only made one request at the very beginning, a promise that the US would use his information to reveal the Iranian nuclear program. We gave him the promise as having been endorsed by the director of the CIA. His response was that if we did not reveal the information, he would out himself and reveal the evidence that he has given to the CIA and reveal the US government's failure to act."

"Interesting, and we conclude what ego or ideology?"

"We are not sure, but everything he has given us that can be validated has been validated, and he has given us the crown jewels."

Andrew Friedman outlined what he wanted from the *Imam*.

The Deputy Director nodded his head, "This is definitely in the skill set of the Imam and the CIA. There are IT and security hacks the CIA has used in the past that can do this, no problem. We will send you detailed plans next week."

In May Andrew Friedman briefed the NSC principals on his plan, SMOKESCREEN.

Chapter Twenty-Four
Son of a Martyr

Feisel Mohammad Ramul had graduated with top honors, his doctoral dissertation addressing fast neutron transport at the interface between metals and low-density materials. The topic of the doctoral work came directly from the president of the Atomic Energy Organization of Iran (AEOI). Feisel Ramul was the son of a martyr, his father a great Imam who had helped the founding of the revolution. The neutron behavior at the interface, between a bomb core, tamper and the low-density explosive lenses was an important area of physics for the nuclear program. The President of AEOI was sure that Feisel Ramul would do great things and transform the nuclear program and Iran. He was brilliant, a dedicated and hard worker and the son of a martyr, willing to do anything for the Islamic Republic. He was sure this young man would do great things for the program. Feisel had read the Fatwahs of the clerics and the Ayatollah and read their public speeches targeted at western audiences. Nuclear weapons were an evil of the great Satan America, they were not in the interest of Iran and not consistent with Islamic teachings. In smaller gatherings, off the record they would preach the opposite, nuclear weapons were justified by the Quran for use against infidels, fire against the unbelievers. When he was the design team leader, he listened to a cleric from the office of the president of Iran at AEOI imploring them to push harder for a nuclear weapon. He remembered one of his mother's favorite quotes from the Quran; it was still in his change purse in his mother's handwriting; *Do not confound the truth by mixing it up with falsehood and do not knowingly conceal the truth.*

Feisel became the director of the Applied Physics division after years of hard work, they called the division the Sarab (Mirage); he had 6 managers and nearly 100 engineers and scientists working under his direction. He was barely fifty years old, and the position was so important the Iranian President and Ayatollah were consulted about his selection; his division was responsible for finalizing the design of the warhead. He had a nuclear physics group, high energy dynamics group predicting behavior of warhead assembly through energetic high-explosives, and a detonation sequence electrical engineering group. Feisel Ramul would be the one to finally lead Iran to a functional nuclear warhead that could be carried on a missile. The President of AEOI knew that decades of research and development of engineering and scientific talent would pay off for the Islamic Republic. The next several years Feisel proved him correct. He became expert in high-energy explosive lenses, and he recognized the key to the design was in the efficiency of the explosive lens, the detonation timing, timing of the neutron burst and sophisticated modeling of the physical and nuclear behavior between the core and tamper prior to detonation. The young engineers and managers called him the "monk-genius." It was a compliment, an attribution to his hard work and brilliant mind. He was enormously respected, working longer hours than any of them. The senior officials could see the progress being made as they proceeded toward warhead manufacturing.

They knew he was deeply religious, and a brilliant scientist would make them all proud, if only his father was here to see what he did for the Republic. He was often seen in his office late in the early evening, reviewing the last of the paperwork submitted for his review and approval, lying under his justice paperweight. Many of them sensed he was lonely, living alone in his flat, no siblings, and his mother had died of cancer the year before he had become division director. The President of AEOI wished he would enjoy life just a little more; he had kept the same small apartment he had since he was first hired out of university, a one-bedroom flat with a study. He spent some time exercising; he liked

---

to jog, a bit unusual, he would jog in the morning before work and then walk on the weekends. He visited a few cafés to drink tea and read on the weekends. Besides that, he spent his time in his study. The security services had monitored him closely the first few years after he was selected director, but they found no reason to waste resources; they judged him no security risk and would support his elevation even to the President of AEOI if selected, but he did not seem ambitious.

It took several years but the breakthrough design was complete. The advanced computer models predicted the warhead would have nearly 100 KT yield and would fit into the RV design the Chinese had sold to Iran. The Chinese would not give the Iranians a warhead design, but they would give them the RV that fit on the missiles they had purchased from the Chinese. A year later the first two warheads based on this design were produced, small 10 KT devices configured for a testing platform. There was a governmental debate on whether to test. Feisel's decision was for the first two warheads to be built as a testing configuration waiting for the government to decide. The next eight were configured for the RV warheads, around 100 KT. After several years they had an inventory of ten warheads and decided to maintain that inventory for a year until a decision was finalized on the way in which they would make the program known. There were ongoing debates. Ayatollah's circle of advisers favored an underground nuclear test, followed by an announcement and a stern warning to any country that would attack them. Even the Ayatollah was skeptical of this; it would further expose them to international criticism. The moderate clerics and the president's advisers favored a covert approach. They favored approaching the Americans in Vienna through their interactions at the IAEA and establish a secret dialog. They would give the Americans a briefing just enough to demonstrate they had a small nuclear stockpile and tell them that they intended to follow a policy of nuclear ambiguity; the Americans would leak this to the Saudis and Israelis. Publicly they would claim that their program was a peaceful civilian nuclear power program and demand sanctions to be lifted. The President's advisers believed the potential threat of nuclear weapons would give them leverage and the Americans would placate them by slowly removing the sanctions so long as the nuclear weapons program was never publicly acknowledged. A decision would be made in August next year, and the Majli senior leadership would be notified.

The president of AEOI came to Feisel's office one morning, gestured and took a seat in the side salon. Feisel got tea for the two of them and sat down with the president. He wanted to try and sway Feisel to support him for testing a weapon. He heard the Ayatollah was very skeptical about supporting testing.

"Feisel, what are your views on underground testing? I believe we should support testing. It will confirm our designs with real data; it would be a day of great national pride. I still remember the celebrations they had in Islamabad when they conducted their tests."

Feisel was sure that nuclear ambiguity was the most rational and likely decision for the government. He also knew the president was an ally of the Ayatollah, "Sir, this is a political decision not a scientific matter. I frankly do not have an opinion. Your opinion is the one that matters, and the leadership will listen to you, not me."

"Well, since you have been representing us with the IAEA in Vienna, I have noticed you have quite the diplomatic skills. Maybe there is a future for you in politics. You know if the leadership chooses the nuclear ambiguity route, we will need you to lead the negotiations with the Americans."

"Me, are you sure? This will be a most delicate matter."

"Yes, I have already discussed this with the Supreme leader and the president. They both agree that you are the best suited and importantly can be trusted; they have heard of your skills in Vienna over the last few years."

Feisel Ramul had been Iran's primary delegate to the IAEA meetings for several years. In those meetings he went by the title of Director of Research, and he was quickly noticed for his diplomatic skills. The President of AEOI was surprised when Feisel approached him to become the lead representative. Feisel told him he would like to see some of Europe. He had been working hard for several years and now the difficult design work had been completed; this would allow him to develop some other skills. The President of AEOI was very happy to give Feisel this small reward for his service. He spoke excellent English and the security service had already cleared him years ago for high positions in government. He confirmed the decision with President Ahmadi and Ayatollah Emami. They both agreed Feisel was an excellent selection for this role representing Iran as their senior nuclear official; he could provide intelligence on what he thought the Saudis or Pakistanis were up to through his interactions in Vienna. If they moved forward with the nuclear ambiguity plan, he could be trusted with the delicate negotiations.

Feisel had other reasons for pursuing the assignment to make frequent trips to Vienna, an environment to carry out his retribution against the clerical establishment. He had been working on his plans for years in the evenings in his study. He developed a strategy and detailed plan and studied references from the security services about covert communication and how to protect information from spy networks. When he was selected for the IAEA assignment, he requested the security services give him training for countermeasures against foreign spies, electronic or human surveillance. The President of AEOI and the head of the intelligence and security services thought this was an excellent idea; Feisel was indeed a true patriot. In reality he really wanted the training to develop his skills to operate clandestinely to avoid Iranian security services as much as the foreign services. Soon, he was ready to move forward with the first phase of his retribution plan, providing the Americans with detailed information on Iranian nuclear warhead designs, nuclear production capability in exchange for an American promise to expose the program. Feisel made his first trip to Vienna at a leadership meeting for heads of delegations on nuclear safety, a look back at the Fukushima accident and lessons learned and improvements in safety. The meeting was a planning session for a planned plenary meeting later that year. This was his first trip to Europe, and he was anxious to see Vienna. He knew that the spring weather could be a little bit wet, but the weather should be quite comfortable. He thought it was funny that the Iranian foreign ministry would recommend he stay in an American hotel. He got there on a Friday. He wanted to see Vienna before the meetings started the next Monday. It was a compact little city, very attractive buildings. He had not treated himself to a single vacation in ten years, and he felt he could actually relax this weekend. A chance to see the city and he also used it as a chance to reconnoiter Vienna and the IAEA for locations to pass information to the Americans sometime next year. He didn't think he was being followed by the Iranian government, but possibly they would as well as the Americans or others. He assumed that an entire army of spies was shadowing him and monitoring his communications.

The concierge gave him a walking map. The first Saturday he walked down to Stephanplatz, he knew that was German for Stephen's Plaza; there were many Platzs in Vienna. It was a long walking street, with tourist shops and restaurants; he had also been cautioned by the security services that there were prostitutes along the walk looking for single older men. St. Stephens cathedral was beautiful. He bought one of the small picture guidebooks in English of Vienna, they did not have

Farsi. He read that the Church was built in the 13th century. He admired the beautiful spire reaching high into the sky and the intricate carvings all over. He walked down the street, a sign for Bingo Burger not far from the cathedral. He wanted to try this American fast food, just to see what all the fuss was about; he decided on the original big burger and French fries. It was okay. He could not understand why they were so wildly popular. He stopped in several of the tourist shops; lots of things with Mozart on them, music boxes, candies, coasters, scarves and umbrellas, and small models of pianos. There were also lots of images from an artist he had never heard of, Gustav Klimt, some were quite provocative showing a woman with her breast exposed. The images were on everything, not in very good taste. He walked to the Albertina, a former palace with a renowned art collection he had read about. The lines were very long, and he decided to go to the café across the corner. The Mozart Sonnet Café had outdoor seating; the weather was nice it didn't look like a cheap tourist stop. He found a small table outside and relaxed as he read through the guidebook. The Mozart Sonnet Café became his favorite spot to people watch while eating a few pastries, and he even found he was developing a taste for coffee; he had always been a tea drinker. The whole morning he had been looking in store front windows, looking in the reflections and stopping occasionally to look around at the scenery, he didn't see anyone following him.

The next day he took the subway towards the southwestern edge of the city center to see the Schonbrun palace. He spent nearly half a day there with the walking tour on the inside, then on the surrounding grounds through the gardens up the hill to the Neptune Fountain. The rooms inside the palace were grand. They looked like the pictures in the guidebooks. What he most enjoyed was the view of the palace on the high ground near the fountain. He looked back towards the skyline of Vienna in the background and the beautiful St. Stephens cathedral was visible. This was the most beautiful view of Vienna in Feisel's opinion. He didn't see any signs of surveillance during his sightseeing.

He got back into town and got off the subway late in the afternoon, he went into the small shop across from his hotel. There was no one else inside the shop. He bought a small bottle of wine. He told the clerk he wanted something not too sweet. He carried it back to his room in a bag a German Rhine wine along with some croissants and sausages. He had two glasses of wine as he snacked on the sausages and bread. It was good, but it would be his first and last taste of alcohol. It was not because it was a sin, but he couldn't risk being seen drinking. Alcohol consumption was another false teaching of the Shia Imams but also Sunni clerics; the Quran said never go to prayer intoxicated, and it said that alcohol has evil and good effects, the evil greater than the good. The word of Allah was a warning to be careful, but it was not an admonition not ever to drink alcohol.

Over the next few years Feisel came to like Vienna; he visited many of the old churches dotted across the downtown. His favorite St. Peters. It was not the grandest, but he liked its small footprint and appealing outer design with the middle dome and two small spires; the outer design was nearly perfectly symmetric when looking at the front door from the street. He enjoyed the cafés and small restaurants, and he liked to sit on the walking street at Stephanplatz and people watch, the street musicians. He liked the Natural History Museum and the Museum of History and Art. The two buildings sat right across from each other, impressive symmetrical buildings. He visited the art museum on every visit; he was especially drawn to the work of the Italian master Raphael. The vivid facial expressions and provocative displays, many women with exposed breasts. They would never display these in Tehran. He liked to go on weekdays when it was not so crowded. There were also many sculptures, but for some reason he was drawn to the paintings. The inside of the building itself, the murals and statues and high ceilings, were nearly as impressive as the artworks.

He was disappointed when he first went to the IAEA in the Vienna International Center (VIC) called UNO-City. It was more modern looking, finished in 1979; he thought it was quite ugly and not keeping with the beautiful architecture of the rest of Vienna. Across the river from the old central city, it was a short 5-minute metro ride from Stephanplatz. Immediately after coming through the security building were the buildings where the IAEA was headquartered. Two tall buildings, each one in an arc shape with a short squat cylindrical building between them. The exteriors looked industrial; all concrete, steel and glass. It must have been popular in 1979, but it looked cold and sterile to Feisel. In front of the buildings, a circular stone and concrete courtyard with national flags surrounding a pool and fountains that didn't seem to be operating half of the time. Most of the interior was unattractive, small meeting rooms and hallways connecting the three buildings. There were some interesting features. There was the certificate of the Nobel Prize to the IAEA in the hallway in an open foyer area. There was a small gift counter in the main hallway with IAEA gift items, writing pens, everything a logo could be placed on. He bought several sets of pens as gifts for the managers who worked for him, they had all done well in their assignments. The large plenary meeting room had the appearance of a large diplomatic meeting room, with old wood paneled walls with the IAEA Symbol between the large display screens behind the slightly elevated speaker's table. The speaker's table faced the auditorium of delegates. The delegates were seated at tables each with small microphones and headsets for translation. The meetings are conducted in English, but translation is available in the official languages for the meetings: English, Arabic, Chinese, French, Russian and Spanish.

Feisel found the IAEA meetings tedious and boring, the small meetings of executive officials as well as the large conferences and their plenary sessions. Scientists and engineers who acted like they were diplomats making decisions affecting world affairs. He knew better, these meetings were a waste of time and money; the countries acted in their best interest and were not about to be bound by any substantial decisions made in these meetings in Vienna. Every document and decision was muddled and watered down by compromise. By the end of the day, there was no practical consequence to anything. Many of the officials seemed most interested in the evening wine and cheese social gatherings at the end of the day, free wine and beer. He had been to only a few, many officials drinking a little too much, sloshing their wine out of the glass as they criticized their colleagues from other countries, their weak safety culture or poor funding for research.

The first year, Feisel went to more meetings than he needed to attend or even wanted to attend. He knew there would be no complaints from the AEOI president. He knew the President saw it as a reward for Feisel's years of hard work. He went to six meetings that year, scoured Vienna and the IAEA. He expected that maybe the Americans or Saudis possibly even the Iranians had followed him on the first few trips. But they surely had gotten bored. He didn't do anything other than shopping on Stephanplatz and visit tourist sites. The next year he was ready to make his first contact with the Americans to begin a covert delivery of information and materials on the nuclear weapons program in Iran and get a promise they would expose the program to the world.

He had selected his methods of passing messages and information and his locations. Early that next year he was at the IAEA for a large conference, the plenary meeting hall in building M. There is a large coffee area immediately outside the meeting room and seating with tables in the area. He found one of the bookstores on Stephanplatz sold

English language popular science and technical books. There was a large display of books written by two Americans about the Fukushima nuclear accident. The American he had been watching at the conference was reading the book at lunch and at the coffee break area outside of the plenary meeting hall. The evening before, Feisel had generated a simple cipher using the book, a series of three numbers: page number, then line number, then word number counting over from the left-hand side. It was simple and impossible to break unless you knew the book that was the key. He crafted a simple message for the Americans. He wanted to provide information on the Iranian nuclear weapons program and he wanted a promise that the Americans would expose the Iranian nuclear program. The message instructed the American to go to the café in the Kunshistorisches art museum the last day of the conference at 2:00 pm, have a green umbrella as a signal of American interest.

He had the cipher on the back of a bookmark in his copy of the same book the American had been reading all week. During the afternoon coffee break, the American left the book on the table with his coffee, and he went to the men's room, the same as he had done every day. Feisel went by the table accidentally knocking the American's book to the ground. He picked it up, but he subtly placed his copy of the same book back on the table and walked away. The Iranian security service had told Feisel the man was a CIA operative working undercover as a US State Department employee. The man came back to the table and saw the bookmark, he casually looked. He knew it was a cipher. He expected it was from the Iranian, but he waited to check when he got back to the hotel.

The next day the American was at the museum café with a green umbrella. He saw Feisel but sat down far away just barely making eye contact. After Feisel finished his coffee, he went upstairs to the third floor and walked slowly through the galleries. The American was shadowing him but not too close. Feisel went to the gift shop before he left, purchased a few bookmarks and postcards. He wrote a short message onto one of the post cards, Vienna Sonnet Mozart Café with a date and time. He left the card on the bench. He saw no one was nearby other than the American who was "reading" a magazine. Feisel left and did not look around; he knew the American would retrieve the card. The American contact read the card. This man was cautious, that was good. Someone had taught him some tradecraft.

He had the necessary tools and methods. It was not so difficult to pass on USBs around Vienna and at the IAEA, the cafeterias, hallway seating areas and the small coffee nooks across the buildings and the museums and cafés across Vienna. He provided the Americans with substantial evidence, including warhead design, predicted capability, production records, facility locations and actual warhead locations. They also worked out a difficult and more dangerous set of transfers in Iran, including materials sample from the laboratories, the Iranians had used the samples for warhead design, analysis of exact isotopic composition. The Americans had asked for the samples to establish isotopic signatures of the Iranian materials, claiming the American tests were more detailed and reliable. Feisel received a delivery of groceries, the delivery man had slipped in four cans of white beans; the cans had been fabricated in the United States and had a storage receptacle inside to place the stainless-steel tubes with the samples. There was a thick lined plastic bag enclosing beads and a fluid that gave the right feel, weight and sound of a can of beans. Feisel placed the tube inside and put the top back on, sealing the top in place with a clear resin. He left the can on the deck outside his second-floor bedroom in the evening, in the back of the building; no one could see it was there. The can was gone in the morning. The same was repeated three more times for three more samples, the same way each time.

The Americans had everything to expose the program after three years. He was growing impatient, but finally he had some instructions. He wasn't sure exactly what was going to kick everything off and how it would play out, but his actions were not difficult. The first week of June he got what he needed at the café near his home, he could see the purpose of the strategy, but he did not know how it was going to be used, he would play his part. The next day at work he inserted the USB into his computer; he typed in the encryption code allowing access. He knew the virus would alter all of the plutonium and uranium inventories, manufacturing records, memos and orders, throughout the nuclear files and email and other IT systems; it will appear as if there were one additional test warhead under his custody. There was never a warhead in his vault, but he did have a nuclear storage vault, he had stored samples, samples he had passed on to the CIA. Officers in the Revolutionary Guard also have access using general access codes. They can access any of these government secure vaults with the same code. The vault had been there for several years; he was the only one who had been inside the vault. The virus altered the records and documents to appear that a test warhead was placed in storage two years ago with no other author- ized movements of the warhead since that time.

He had also been given a very small thin device he attached to his security access card, when he used his access card that morning it inserted a small virus; a piece of software to hack the security system. The vault access security files were stored in the same security system as the door access controls; the vault access records were altered to indicate the vault was opened once using his access code to store the phantom warhead, and it recorded another access when he was on business in Vienna in April. The April phantom access showed a general access code of the Revolutionary Guard. The USB virus and the security virus deleted and purged themselves from the IT systems without a trace. He removed the small device, about the size of a postage stamp, from his access card and put it in a bag with the USB. He burned them to ashes in his back garden that evening. He knew he would be confronted about a missing warhead. He would say he never opened the vault since placing the warhead in storage. There will be small remaining trace amounts of nuclear materials from the samples supporting the idea that a warhead had been stored in the vault, if the security services take samples. The American instructions said something would happen that would be a signal for him to be ready for the confrontation, and he was then to send a message the Iranians were searching for a missing warhead. He wasn't sure how long he would need to wait.

PART THREE

Darkness Before the Dawn

Chapter Twenty-Five
Nuclear Explosion in the Indian Ocean

A few minutes after 5:00 pm on June 9 phones started ringing all over federal national security offices in Washington DC. The NSC duty officer contacted Andrew Friedman at home around 6:30. "Sir we have confirmation of a nuclear detonation in the Indian Ocean shortly after 1700 Washington time. Far from land, initial estimate is 2000 miles due east of Madagascar. We also have confirmation with the British that the platforms they operate with the French have detected a nuclear detonation a few minutes after 2200 in London. We have high confidence this is not a system malfunction. We have DOD confirmation it is not a US nuclear device."

Similar notifications to government officials were also underway in England. The same was happening in Beijing a few minutes after 5:00 am on June 10 Beijing time, The Chinese President was contacted by his director of national security, they have detected a nuclear test in the Indian Ocean; they are also hearing chatter that the Americans and British are responding as well.

An hour later the Chinese President placed a call to President Larson through the translator, "We have detected a nuclear detonation in the Indian Ocean, it is not a Chinese device. I am seeking confirmation from the United States."

Larson spoke fluent Mandarin but replied in English, "We have also detected the detonation. It is not a US device, and we have been told it is not British or French."

An hour later the US President has a similar conversation with the Russian President. Within three hours all of the major confirmed nuclear powers are sure that there was a nuclear detonation in the Indian

Ocean, and they are all sure it was not them. They knew the likely suspects, Iran or North Korea, or someone they do not know about.

The US National Security Principals met at 8:00 pm with Andrew Friedman. The duty officer gave a short briefing, "The satellite signature was at 17:01:05.1 EST this evening on two separate satellites, bhang meters, infrared and EMP. Analysis is underway to determine the size of the detonation, initial assessment appears to be a relatively small device, less than 100 KT. Because we have multiple detections, the final location determination should be rather precise. The current estimate is here S 18^0 54' 22" and E 79^0 51' 18" almost equidistant between Madagascar and the west coast of Australia. Strong indication that it is a test in this remote area of the Indian Ocean."

The watch officer was excused, there were no questions, he saw their expressions not the slightest sign of nerves, those are some cool customers.

Andrew Friedman brought up high-resolution satellite video and a map showing the location of a ship moving slowly in the Indian Ocean. The video had been edited already for the NSC principals for the key segments. Andrew Friedman reported, "No damage to any civilian airline or commercial ships from the nuclear blast."

CIA Director Sweigart reported next, "No indication of any military movement across the world. We have focused on Russia, North Korea and the Middle East. No unusual communications beyond what we would expect in these circumstances."

Secretary of Defense Cox reported, "The same as Director Sweigart from military channels focusing on the same theaters; nobody seems to be moving troops or missiles and no unusual naval or air force movements. No damage to military aircraft or naval vessels. We were well out of harm's way."

A few minutes after Cox finished, her NSC phone rang. She picked up, the liaison officer reported "The Defense Minister from the Republic of South Korea is on the line with a translator."

"Minister Kim. You are on the speaker phone with President Larson and the National Security Council; we are in the White House Situation room. How may we assist you this morning?" Loretta Cox knows it was mid-morning in Seoul.

She can tell the Defense Minister is excited, his voice is high and he is speaking rapidly. She waits for the translation, the Minister is upset "The US Commander in Korea is refusing to raise the readiness and alert levels of US forces. Why hasn't a command been given to increase the alert level?"

"Why would we increase our alert level sir. There have been no movement of North Korean troops, no movement of missiles or any sign of aggression from North Korea."

She responded to the excited reply, "Sir the nuclear test may well be a North Korean nuclear test, that is yet to be seen; but it would not seem a good military strategy to initiate an attack on the ROK by setting off a nuke in the middle of the Indian Ocean, don't you agree. If we start to increase our alert level that might make the DPRK a bit nervous, probably not a good action at this time."

There was a long pause, then a more calm response and translation. "Yes, we agree, please inform us on any updates of the nuclear test."

The President took a drink of green tea, "We all know what needs to be done next, the action is with Director Sweigart. I'm going back to the residence and watch one of my favorite television shows on BBTV Entertainment; it's on in ten minutes. Good evening, everyone."

Within 24 hours news outlets across the world were saturated with stories about the nuclear detonation detected in the Indian Ocean. It is not one of the major nuclear powers. There are investigations underway worldwide, in the US the talking heads were already pointing the finger at the Iranians. There was a debate amongst "two experts" on BBTV, one made the case for North Koreans.

The other "expert" responded, "That is absurd; you should consult an Atlas. Why would the Koreans go all the way to the Indian Ocean?"

"To throw suspicions off of themselves, of course, and fool people like you; we don't even know that Iran has a functional nuclear weapon."

Others were saying it could be the Israelis maybe testing a new small tactical device or a totally new player. On and on they went, what kind of investigations were underway, what would President Larson do, his first major international crisis.

Michael didn't understand the reason, but the direction came in May he was to produce and finalize a report for public release on the UAE-Saudi nuclear program. It would describe the enrichment program and not discuss the information related to warhead design or construction, making it clear that the Saudi-UAE were working together to produce HEU, which can only be used for a weapons program. The report would say it takes several years to weaponize the HEU into a nuclear weapon. It was not exactly a lie, but it was misleading. It would take years; in fact, it did take years to weaponize. The direction was clear from Andrew Friedman to IG Ross by direction of the President; they needed the final report approved for issuance by June 1. The IG would approve it and hold the report until instructions came from the President to release it. It would go directly to the Secretary of State, Congress and President.

Michael went to IG Ross shortly after completing the public report. He found IG Ross in his office, and he waved Michael in, "Sir, what is going on? This is very awkward. It makes me uncomfortable to write a misleading public report."

243

"I'm in the dark Michael, the directions came directly from the President through Andrew Friedman. There is something going on that we don't know about. We need to trust the chain of command. I know a bit about Friedman, I trust him. What you wrote is only part of the picture. There are no false statements, but it's not how we usually do business. This is much bigger than anything we have ever dealt with before."

Michael saw the news on WNN, Breaking News late around 9:30 on June 9, he was stunned. Was it one of the Saudi devices? What were the President and the NSC doing with his reports? The original classified report and public version of the report they had him create later. Marion came in from the kitchen and sat down on the couch beside Michael, "My God a nuclear test in the Indian Ocean. What is going on? Do you know anything about this?"

"No, I have no clue. The talking heads are pointing fingers at the Iranians."

Michael was confused. Had his report been too late, and this was some sort of smokescreen, or maybe it was the Iranians. He had seen the summary of their nuclear capability, weaponization was the classified conclusion. Why would they covertly test the device? They might think they could get away with it staying covert while seeking nuclear ambiguity. He was worried about the public report he was asked to prepare. Was he being set up by someone working for the President as having done an inadequate job, maybe the Saudis tested a warhead? They will say he underestimated the risk of the Saudis, showing the public the modified report. Surely not, the IG was right, he would have to wait things out to see what happens.

Mel Randolph and the rest of the Blackhole team that had worked with Case and Bradley were confused by the news of the test. They met and talked in the conference room. Shane said what they were all thinking, "The Saudis could have used one of the nuclear devices, and what was going on with the report from Michael Case? It should have been done months ago."

Mel was thinking the same thing, "I'll send an email to Michael, something vague about the status on the report."

Mel understood the short response from Michael, "In the dark here."

Mel got the group together, "Michael doesn't know anything. He is a good guy. I am sure he finished the report, the big dogs are in control; he is probably out of the loop. It's in the hands of political decision-makers now. It could be a while before we know the full story of what was done with the report. Hopefully someone eventually tells us something." Mel could feel it, there were some major political wheels turning.

Chapter Twenty-Six
Iranian Response

President Ahmadi in Iran began to suspect that some members of the Revolutionary Guard may have acted beyond what was formally authorized. The stories in the US media were starting to get very specific and the French, British and even the Russians were now confirming the narrative. A warhead detonated at the location of a Revolutionary Guard boat under US surveillance. He remembered the reports sent to him, Iran had ten warheads, eight in storage for missiles that could be deployed and made operational within hours of an order. The other two were configured as test devices if the country ever made the decision to test. He was concerned that some extreme element of the clerics had gotten Ayatollah Emami to issue an order to the Guards to use one of the test devices. There was still no public confirmation that Iran had an operational nuclear weapons program. He was sure the Americans knew it was operational even if they had not established the exact details with high confidence in their intelligence community.

The American report on the Saudi enrichment nuclear program was released June 15, just days after the test. This was the next shock. The President of the United States calling on the Saudis to admit the enrichment program in a press conference the same day. Ahmadi was fluent in English, and he listened carefully to President Larson when he was questioned, "The report is clear about the Saudi enrichment program; it took years for full weaponization after enrichment. Given this finding, they could not have been responsible for the test. The US was investigating the origins of the test, there are reports indicating links to Iran."

The Saudis and Emiratis issued their press release acknowledging the enrichment program on June 18, and the Saudi intent to cooperate with the Americans and the IAEA to shutter the program, but again pointing fingers at Iran for the nuclear test. The Emiratis had helped fund and deliver equipment for the centrifuges in Saudi Arabia. It was difficult to take in everything that had happened in the last eight days.

Days after the nuclear blast, the President went to Ayatollah Emami's office; they sat in the side salon. "I assure you President Ahmadi, there was no such order, but I will have the Revolutionary Guard conduct a physical confirmation of each warhead and a member of your Office can participate in the physical inventory. Maybe the Americans did this to implicate us, or the Americans and Israelis together."

They both knew that the Americans would not take such a risk, too likely it would eventually be discovered by the Russians. The Ayatollah didn't remember the exact count, less than fifteen, he was sure. There was confusion when staff began reviewing records within the Revolutionary Guard. The memos and records indicated three test warheads, even the memos that went to the Ayatollah's office, most everyone remembered it was only two, others said their colleagues have faulty memories it was three test warheads, why were some people so absent-minded. There were no hard copies, orders were strict, any hard copy was to be destroyed the same day, too easy to get into the wrong hands. They contacted the AEOI staff, the same response, production records indicate three test warheads and eight for the missiles; the AEOI staff did not admit to their own confusion, people seemed to recall only two test warheads.

President Ahmadi was contacted by his Military Chief of Staff, he was accompanying the Revolutionary Guards as they physically verified every warhead in inventory. "The eight missile warheads were all accounted for, but only two of three test warheads."

Ayatollah Emami's chief of staff rushed into his office, "There is a missing warhead, a test device under the custody of Feisel Mohammad Ramul a senior official of Atomic energy organization AEO."

The President asked his staff for copies of his reports, why did he remember two test warheads. They printed and brought him hard copies of the reports sent to the president's office the last several years, three test warheads for the last three years, there had been two for the previous five years. His staff shredded the hard copies, according to protocol. Maybe that's what he remembered, two test warheads when he first came into office; it must be three the same as the Revolutionary Guard Records and AEO.

The Revolutionary Guard and Presidents Military Chief of Staff interviewed Feisel Ramul in his office. He was very calm. "Yes, I remember taking custody of the warhead two years ago."

He had the delivery record on his computer; the Revolutionary Guard signatures were not clear as to who made the delivery.

"I have not accessed the safe since it was placed there for safe storage. It would not be appropriate or necessary. If the warhead was missing, someone else had gotten access and stolen it. I am sorry I cannot offer any more assistance. This is a terrible thing, but I cannot be held responsible for the actions of others."

They knew this man was very well respected, the son of a martyr, could he be involved in the theft wanting to show his warheads would work?

The Presidents Military Chief of Staff and Revolutionary Guard Officers reviewed the security records based on their interview of Feisel Ramul. Security records indicated the last access to the vault was this past April using a general access code of the Revolutionary Guard. There was only one other access, two years ago on the date of Ramul's paperwork when he said the warhead was put into storage. They con-

firmed that Feisel Ramul was in Vienna representing the Islamic Republic of Iran at the IAEA in April when someone accessed the vault. They
directed, technicians to take swipes on the inside of the vault; the next
day they had the report of traces consistent with Iranian test warheads.
June 15th the Iranian President and Ayatollah received a preliminary
briefing of the investigation, a test nuclear warhead went missing in
April, someone with a common Revolutionary Guards access code. It's
not the warhead custodian, Feisel Muhammad Ramul they both know
him. He has an excellent reputation and has been cleared through
numerous security reviews. The security records verify he had not been
in the vault for two years and was in Vienna when the vault was accessed in April.

Later that same day President Ahmadi heard reports about the Saudi
Arabian enrichment program. There was no time to worry about this.
He had a bigger problem on his hands. They started an intensive hunt
for the missing warhead. On June 20, ten days after the nuclear test and
two days after the Saudi acknowledgement of their enrichment program,
President Ahmadi knew the search had run out of time. Word came that
the US President was on the phone. President Larson spoke, there was a
Farsi interpreter, but Ahmadi understood his English clearly, "The US
has conclusive evidence the nuclear warhead test is Iranian. We will
show you the evidence in a direct briefing, or we will go to the United
Nations and present it to the world."

It was agreed that CIA Director Sweigart would secretly travel to
Tehran and present the evidence to the Iranian President, select staff and
officials. CIA Director Sweigart landed at Imam Khomeini International
Airport southwest of Tehran in a small, unmarked US government jet.
He had a five-person security detail and no other personnel. They were
quietly escorted from the airport to a secure building in Tehran a few
blocks from the presidential offices. Sweigart started his briefing,

presenting evidence of isotopic profiles collected by environmental sampling programs from Iran for the last several years. He had maps and satellite images of key nuclear facilities located around Iran.

Sweigart said "The classified US analysis before the test was that Iran had weaponized but no high confidence estimate of the inventory of warheads, the estimated range was 10 to 20 warheads." This was a deception, the CIA had more accurate information, but the deception had a purpose, protecting an important asset.

Next, Sweigart presented tracking information of a ship as it moved from the Strait of Hormuz to the location of the detonation. Photographs of the small ship, in Iranian waters and in the Indian Ocean with Revolutionary Guard markings, but no clear ship number. Sweigart said the photograph came from US naval assets, meaning a submarine. This was true a submarine had taken the photographs, but they were more than a year old when they were tracking another ship. President Ahmadi knows there are hundreds of small boats like this one, a typical vessel used by the revolutionary guard.

The next statement from Sweigart is false, "We suspect that the occupants on the ship sacrificed themselves and were onboard when the nuclear device detonated."

Sweigart tells the Iranians the Americans were tracking the ship because of intelligence that the ship might have nuclear materials or chemical weapons being smuggled to another country. There were also aviation assets available. When the flash was spotted, the Americans were able to capture air samples in the plume and develop isotopic signatures. Sweigart showed these samples overlaid with the environmental traces, the weapon signature was nearly identical to environmental samples. Sweigart concluded, the evidence is overwhelming. It was an Iranian nuclear warhead detonated on a Revolutionary Guard ship in the Indian Ocean. In reality, all of the data came from the *Imam's* samples.

The Director of the CIA had a letter from the President of the United States; he handed it to the Iranian President and Sweigart departed; he did not take questions. President Ahmadi reviewed the letter with the Ayatollah later in the day. Ayatollah Emami had already been briefed on the information from the American CIA Director, by members of his staff in attendance. The letter said the Iranian government had until June 27 to announce their responsibility for the nuclear test or the Americans would go to the Security Council of the United Nations. The Americans would lay out the same presentation that had just been given to the Iranian president on television at the United Nations. The Iranians would also commit to dismantling the nuclear weapons program under the supervision of the IAEA. President Ahmadi knew the Americans had made a similar UN presentation years before confronting the Soviets over nuclear missiles in Cuba. The letter also required that the Iranians allow IAEA access beginning June 30. The letter from the US President clearly stated the consequences if the Iranians did not take these actions on schedule and continue cooperation with the IAEA. The US would move with deliberate speed taking unilateral military action targeted at all nuclear weapons sites throughout Iran, precise strikes intending limited collateral damage, no warnings would be given. The US would also be monitoring Iranian military assets, if any offensive moves were detected the US would strike. The President's Letter closed, if the Iranians did disclose their program and allow in IAEA teams to secure the program the United States would immediately begin actions to eliminate sanctions, unfreeze Iranian assets and relax the military posture in the region as they monitored Iranian actions.

President Ahmadi and Ayatollah Emami knew what it meant for this to be in writing from the US President, it was not posturing or diplomacy, if they did not comply the Americans would strike. During that week, US forces were on heightened alert, with intense monitoring of communications within Iran for any indication of military movement. The Revolutionary Guard was getting nowhere in their investigation. These access codes were readily available to hundreds of guards, and they may have given the code to others. The information about the test warheads locations were not as carefully guarded as they should have been. President Ahmadi knew someone had done this from inside. It would take them months or years to find out who it was and why they had done this reckless thing; the government should have made the decision. Whoever it was had died on that boat in the middle of the Indian Ocean, and their accomplices would feel safe remaining silent.

President Ahmadi and Ayatollah Emami knew they had only one rational choice; they would pay a price for losing control of a nuclear warhead. The silver lining is they believed the US President would honor his promise, the removal of sanctions and unfrozen assets would be a great benefit. The expensive nuclear program had become more of a burden than it was a benefit. The Saudis had already announced they were giving up their program under IAEA monitoring. On June 27 a written statement was released from the Office of the Iranian President acknowledging the test was an Iranian nuclear weapon; however the test had not been authorized by the government. There were still investigations to find those responsible. The country was going to abandon the nuclear weapons program and allow it to be dismantled under IAEA observation. The first IAEA team entered Iran on June 30 to receive a briefing on the weapons program and agree to an inspection and dismantling schedule.

The lead Iranian representative to meet the IAEA team was Feisel Mohammad Ramul, he had gone to a café after being interviewed about the missing warhead days earlier, just after sending a text message to the office supply shop; he needed toner cartridge, please deliver as soon as possible. This was a message for an immediate meeting at the café, and the shop would also deliver the toner the next day. Feisel wrote a short note on a napkin. When he saw the man arrive, he got up and offered the man his table. The man sat down and read the note in Farsi, "Looking for a lost football." This brush pass to the CIA handler was immediately transmitted back through secure channels. This was Feisel's last instruction from the Americans. The Iranians thought they had a missing warhead; a few days later CIA Director Sweigart was on a plane to Iran for the briefing accusing them of conducting the nuclear test. Andrew Friedman's Iranian chess moves were complete.

Chapter Twenty-Seven
Israeli Response

The day after the Iranian announcement, President Larson invited the Israeli ambassador to a meeting with Vice President Packard, they were also joined by CIA Director Sweigart. Director Sweigart summarized the evidence showing a 1979 nuclear blast in the southern Indian Ocean was an Israeli test device and the most recent intelligence estimates of Israels nuclear forces. President Larson handed the Ambassador a copy of the letter signed by Gola Maier and President Nixon, a promise of the US not to disclose the Israeli program unless the Israelis tested a weapon.

Larson told the Ambassador, "We want Israel to take action to create a nuclear free middle east, the Syrian nuclear threat is gone, the Iraqi nuclear threat is gone, the Iranian nuclear threat and Saudi nuclear threat will be gone. I expect an announcement from Israel, acknowledging the nuclear weapons program and a plan to eliminate nuclear weapons on a timetable to match the Iranian timetable under IAEA oversight. I expect the announcement by July 30; this gives you time for internal deliberations. If Israel does not do these things, I will declassify the Israeli agreement letter and authorize publishing an assessment of the 1979 test and current Israeli nuclear capability. The United States will call for a UN security council resolution for Israel to eliminate its nuclear weapons or be subject to sanctions. I do not enjoy threatening a close ally, but it is time for changes in the dangerous situation in the middle east, nuclear weapons just make the situation more unstable."

The Israeli parliament held several classified sessions with the Prime Minister. There were heated debates but in the end they all knew these weapons were no longer needed; created in a different era more than forty years ago, so much had changed since then. The approval was

unanimous the middle east would be nuclear free, with the announcement from Israel on July 29. Given developments in the region, the
Israeli government acknowledged its nuclear weapons program. It
would cooperate with the United States and IAEA on a schedule to
dismantle the program, matching the schedule in the Islamic Republic of
Iran. When Andrew Friedman saw the Israeli statement, he smiled three
checkmates.

Chapter Twenty-Eight
Saudi Arabian Response

On June 10th King Rashid's inner circle were gathered in the Erga Palace in a large private sitting room. They were all seated on a massive lavish rug and floor cushions, Arabic traditional seating. There were tables of fruits, snacks and fruit juices and sweet Arabic tea. Word had just been received by radio, "The seed had been safely delivered and blossomed." This meant the three Saudis were safe and on their way home, successfully detonating the device with the timer. Rashid's inner circle was celebrating. It had worked just as they planned.

The three men were speeding back towards the coast of the Emirates taking the smaller and faster boat they had lowered by crane from the larger slow-moving boat. It would take more than two days to get back; they had fuel and food. They left the big boat moving slowly on auto-pilot in the middle of the Indian Ocean. The Saudi King and his advisers were sure the Americans would not be able to detect this small vessel. Only their most advanced satellites could possibly see such a small boat; they would not deploy these platforms to track a large slow-moving smuggling freighter. The scientist told the three men they would be safe 250 km away from the blast, not to look in the direction of the blast, and stay inside the cabin to avoid any fallout depending on wind. The weapon detonated 5 hours after they left it, and they continued speeding along. They had seen the great multi-colored fire ball rising above the ocean, lighting up the entire Ocean and felt a strong harsh shock wave rattle the boat minutes later. They were amazed even from that distance it was frightening. They slowed down when they got near the Emirates, put on their Saudi Uniforms and took down the Iranian flags and raised the Saudi flag on the small military boat. They changed direction heading for the strait then home to the Saudi base.

The next day the Saudi King and his circle watched the international news: first WNN as the stories began to come in, rumors and then leaks from unnamed US intelligence officials a nuclear test in the Indian Ocean suspected to be Iranian. Then BBTV was reporting the same; soon everyone was pointing the finger at the Iranians. King Rashid was so excited he could not sleep for the first twenty-four hours. He had a call from Sheikh Abdullah in Abu Dhabi. ABZ was surprised by the Iranian test; Rashid agreed, "We were smart for building our nuclear arsenal. It seems the Iranians had gotten caught. Hopefully the Americans would finally go after them."

Rashid laughed to himself. Only a small group of his most trusted military advisers knew what had really happened and none of them would ever reveal the secret. They feared what would happen to their families and loved ones. It was a wonderful weekend in Riyadh. Rashid spent the time with his youngest wife, drinking South African chardonnay and relaxing, two televisions on WNN and BBTV as the stories continued speculating about the Iranian nuclear program. Sunday he was back to his office and had a call from the US CIA Director Sweigart. They had information about the nuclear test in the Indian Ocean; they would like to brief King Rashid and ABZ from Abu Dhabi on June 14 in Riyadh. King Rashid was excited. He welcomed Director Sweigart to come. Rashid intended to press him about an American response against the Iranians when he finished his briefing.

Director Sweigart arrived in Riyadh with a small security detail and no other staff. The briefing would be given by Sweigart to the senior Saudi and Emirati officials. ABZ had brought a small staff, including his nuclear expert Faisal and his military chief of staff. King Rashid had assembled a large group most of whom knew nothing of the Saudi role in the nuclear test, including his nuclear adviser Haitham. He wanted a big audience when he gave his ultimatum to Sweigart for the Americans to respond. Then he would call President Larson and repeat the demand to attack the Iranians. The small circle of military advisers who had coordinated the test were waiting excitedly to hear the Americans finger the Iranians. Director Sweigart started, "I have troubling information."

Sweigart started with the tracking of the large ship with Iranian Revolutionary Guard markings from the strait into the Indian Ocean, just as Rashid had expected. "We also tracked a small rapid moving vessel leaving the larger ship. It was 248 km away 5 hours later when the weapon detonated. We believe the three men placed the large ship on Auto pilot with the warhead on a timed detonation. They lowered the smaller ship into the water to escape the blast." King Rashid was getting nervous.

"We tracked the vessel all the way to this Saudi naval base." He showed a series of satellite still shots of the three men leaving the ship and a Saudi Flag on the vessel. ABZ was confused, "Are you saying that Iranian agents are operating inside of the Saudi Navy?"

"No Sheikh Abdullah that is not what we believe happened." Sweigart realized the Saudis must not have involved the Emiratis in the testing plan.

The next image from Sweigart was a map taken from the classified version of Michael Case's report, showing the location of UAE and Saudi Arabian nuclear facilities. He described each facility marked on the map; the procurement operations in Dubai, the enrichment facility southwest of Riyadh, the UF6 and metal production facility at Al Jabeer and finally the warhead fabrication facility on the western edge of Abu Dhabi. Sweigart showed a spectrum representing Saudi produced HEU collected by Americans through environmental sampling around the enrichment cascades and the metal fabrication facility. Finally, a slide showing the isotopic and chemical signature from the blast compared to the environmental samples.

"It is conclusive and absolute, the device detonated on June 10 local time was fueled by Saudi produced highly enriched uranium and fabricated into a warhead in Abu Dhabi. We discovered the Saudi-UAE nuclear program months ago and we were suspicious when the Saudis suggested this Iranian boat might have nuclear materials. We thought maybe you were trying to lure us to intercept it with planted nuclear materials on board to implicate the Iranians. We deployed high resolution platforms to monitor the boat. We never imagined you would be so reckless to actually detonate a device in the atmosphere."

ABZ could hardly contain himself but remained silent. He knew that Rashid was dangerous, but he never imagined something like this. He waited to hear what the American government was going to do to them now.

Director Sweigart laid out what would happen next, "We are going to release a nonclassified report tomorrow describing the discovery of a Saudi Arabian-UAE enrichment program intended for a weapons program. It will not disclose the progress on weaponization and warhead production, implying you are years away from that point. The President of the United States will give a press conference later in the day, confirming that the Saudi-UAE program was a weapons program, again suggesting you are years away from a warhead. The US will support the story that the test was an Iranian nuclear device leaking that we have tracking data of an Iranian Revolutionary Guard vessel and later leak we have samples matching Iranian weapons. The President expects the Saudi-UAE governments to publicly acknowledge their covert enrichment program by June 18. If this happens, the US will take custody of the warheads and the other assets and materials associated with the weapons program, other than the enrichment cascade, the records will be altered in material balances to match the inventory of HEU you currently have in containers. You will open the enrichment program to the IAEA for dismantling on a schedule to be determined. If you do not acknowledge the program by June 18, we will introduce a resolution to the UN national security council for immediate access by the IAEA and the full scope of what you have been doing will be discovered, including your responsibility for the test."

ABZ stood up, "We will acknowledge our role supporting the enrichment program at noon on June 18 along with our Saudi colleagues by Press Releases." The Emirati delegation left along with Director Sweigart and his security detail. King Rashid would not last much longer. He had assembled a room full of witnesses to his irresponsible behavior. The Press Releases came from Abu Dhabi and Riyadh on June 18, admitting the Uranium enrichment program reported by the Americans and their decision to abandon the program under US and IAEA oversight. The first checkmate of three designed by Andrew Friedman.

Chapter Twenty-Nine
Confusion Then Recognition

Michael Case was in shock when he heard the news on June 15. There would be a Presidential news conference at 3:00 about the Saudi nuclear weapons program following the release earlier in the day of the public version of his report. Michael left work early; he took a half day of sick leave and took the metro back to Bethesda. He got to the townhouse and went to the family room and turned on WNN, it was 2:15. The reporter was talking, "World News Network has confirmed the report was prepared by Michael Case, a State Department OIG investigator who has a reputation for uncovering nuclear proliferation. It looks like Case and his team in the State Department have made one of the biggest discoveries in decades."

The reporter was summarizing the report. Michael checked to see the British take on BBTV; it was the same. The frenzy about the Saudi nuclear program was building and his name was being used on every channel. This is not what he wanted, and he especially did not like the deceptive nature of this report. Around 2:30 his cellphone rang, it was Marion, she was excited, "Michael they are talking about you on the news. I am so proud. This must be the project that you were working on in Abu Dhabi with Tom."

"Yeah, I am at home watching the news. I took the afternoon off."

"Good idea. I will come home early; we can have a celebration."

Michael listened carefully to the president's statement and his answers to questions. The President's statements were carefully crafted, he did not lie but he did mislead the American people and the world, and he used Michael's report. He did not say the Saudis had not gotten to the warhead stage. He just said that the report says it takes years to go from enrichment to the warhead stage. If the Saudis had not gotten to the warhead stage, they could not be responsible for the test. The President responded, yes, he met Michael Case. He had briefed the President and other senior officials on the Saudi nuclear program. He understood Case had a solid record at the State Department in a number of important investigations.

Michael muttered, "Not a direct lie in a single statement, but misleading beyond comprehension. What the hell is going on?"

Marion was home about 3:30. She was surprised Michael did not seem happy at all and was not in the mood for a celebration.

The confusion continued for Michael on June 18 as the Saudi and Emirati governments admitted to their uranium enrichment program and they would give it up. Then on June 27 the Iranians admitted the nuclear test was one of their devices, an unauthorized test, but they would dismantle their program under international oversight. Michael was confused. What had happened to his classified report and what about the Saudi nuclear warheads, was it really an Iranian test? Finally, the Israeli decision to give up their nuclear weapons the end of July. By the end of July, he figured it must have been an Iranian test, why would they admit it if it wasn't, but he remained concerned about the Saudis. They had a lot more than an enrichment facility. Michael got answers in August, starting with a request for a meeting in the White House on August 14, an invitation from Andrew Friedman.

After President Larson had read the full report by Michael Case in April, he asked Simon Tomas to put together a profile of Michael Case, education, work history. He talked to Director Sweigart. What did he think about the full report and Michael Case's work. "Case started with an allegation that Americans were giving some nuclear enrichment information to Saudis in Abu Dhabi. He dug through years of old evidence and worked systematically with others to discover this entire program. He found AQ Khan's missing customer, doggedly digging through old evidence. He pursued the evidence of a Saudi weapons program, when the community said it was not possible. I was astounded by what Case was able to do putting that report together in a few months, drawing from a sea of intelligence and citing more than 20,000 pieces of individual evidence. Michael Case has a unique gift, an analytic mind that can quickly make connections and see patterns in evidence and he communicates clearly in briefings and in formal written reports."

After the Iranians admitted the nuclear test was theirs, President Larson discussed his proposal with Vice President Packard, a new assignment for Michael Case. Use him to probe the hidden corners of the intelligence community. The meeting was in the same room Michael had given his briefing in April. President Larson came in with Vice President Packard at 10:00 am, Michael had arrived escorted by Andrew Friedman a few minutes earlier.

President Larson smiled and shook Michael's hand, "I hope you have been well; you probably have been a bit confused about the happenings since you briefed us in April."

"Confused, but things seemed to have worked out well, now I'm suspecting there is some intelligent design behind all of this."

"Yes, there is indeed. Andrew is going to let you peek behind the curtain at his project."

Andrew read Michael into SMOKESCREEN. "I will give you a high-level summary to understand how your work has been used in SMOKESCREEN."

"First, the blast in the Indian Ocean was a Saudi warhead. They had not told the Emiratis about their intent to test a device disguised as an Iranian test. They wanted to see that the device worked. More importantly they wanted us to go after the Iranians. We learned about the plan for a test after we had your report and used these circumstances to develop a strategy to get all of the nuclear weapons' programs out of the middle east. We used the information in your classified report to force the Saudi-UAE to give up their weapons. We used your public report limiting the scope of the Saudi program to enrichment to help deceive the Iranians. We also had other evidence, real and deceptive, convincing the Iranians the nuclear detonation was one of their warheads gone missing months earlier. The missing warhead was a canard, created through some IT mischief. We had substantial intelligence from inside the Iranian nuclear program. Finally, we used Iran and Saudi giving up their nuclear programs as leverage, along with some breaches of old promises by the Israelis to convince them to make the middle east nuclear free."

Michael leaned forward looking at the President, "You knew they were going to detonate the bomb, and we watched them do it?"

President Larson smiled, "Well yes, we planted information about severe weather along the route of the ship to ensure ships and planes were clear. Sorry you were out of the loop, you didn't have a need to know. We knew your reputation might take a hit if things went badly, we would have done all we could to limit the damage."

Michael wondered, "Was the yield of the Iranian missing warhead the same as the Saudi device? What if the Europeans, Chinese or Russians were to compare the detected yield from their satellites to the Iranian test warhead design?"

Friedman marveled at how quick Michael was. He had found the one gap in the story where this might unravel, "We are the only ones who have all of the information in hand now and are burying that. Never mention that to anyone, you understand."

Michael sat back and nodded, "Yes sir. I know you are not obligated to brief me. I am honored you have shared this information with me;

very clever and the results speak for themselves. It looks like a chess match."

President Larson laughed, "Yes it reminds me of the same thing. There will be Presidential Commendations Ceremony for the Saudi Report in August for you, Tom Bradley, Andrea Jacobs and the CIA and NSA team in Abu Dhabi including the station chief."

Andrew Friedman explained, "The CIA and NSA staff would be announced as State Department employees in the Abu Dhabi embassy. I will provide all of them a limited scope briefing on SMOKESCREEN, so they understand how the team's intelligence was used in the project."

"Could Steve Thomas be added to the list? He was instrumental in the first phase of the investigation and has spent his career on non-proliferation."

President Larson responded, "Absolutely, is there anyone else we missed, who contributed substantially to this effort?"

"Do you know the story of Russ Nixon?"

"No, I don't know about Mr. Nixon."

Michael explained his dogged pursuit of the development of the database that they used to uncover the original enrichment program. A database that no one wanted, and he pushed to finish in the basement of the CIA as he was dying of cancer.

Andrew Friedman spoke up, "I know about Mr. Nixon. He had a long career in the shadows with several important databases. The analysts across the CIA hold Russ Nixon in high regard. He built the backbone supporting several major intelligence breakthroughs. I have another idea about Russ Nixon, to recognize him for a lifetime of achievement at the CIA, we need to get the approval of Director Sweigart."

President Larson moved on to another topic "We want to discuss something else with you. I have already discussed this with IG Ross, he is not particularly happy, but he agrees it is a good opportunity for you. There is a new position, senior level advisor in the IG in the Director of National Intelligence Alejandro (AJ) Reyes. We want you to fill that position covering the entire intelligence community. I have an agreement with IG Reyes that I can occasionally task you for special assignments."

Michael was surprised. He knew that he was being told this was his new job, in a nice way. "Thank you Mr. President, I appreciate the opportunity."

"You are expected at OIG DNI in September."

In August a private award ceremony was held at the State Department, with family in attendance. Andrew Friedman read all of the team into SMOKESCREEN and gave them a summary briefing. Marion was proud of Michael. He told her he was just a member of the team and the one who wrote the final report. He seemed much happier about the work now, more so than when the media was talking about him. She knew he had mixed emotions about his new assignment. He would miss Andrea and Tom and the State OIG team.

The President stayed a while for photographs, and there was a small reception, Steve Thomas found Michael at the reception; "I told you, crap I told everyone there would be another use of a nuclear weapon in my lifetime."

Michael laughed, "Wait a minute, you always said that in reference to the use in war not for a nuclear test."

Steve Thomas smiled, "Well maybe you have me counselor; man this is a great way to go out. I can retire on a positive note."

"Retire, I'm surprised. What will you do with yourself?"

"I've been thinking about writing novels. To be honest, it has been a little frustrating, trying to make progress on something like nuclear non-proliferation. It moves like a glacier, and it really had been mostly downhill until you and Andrea opened shop. But this, what happened these last few months, this is a reversal of direction in a good way, maybe it can stop the advance, maybe the dominoes will fall the other direction."

"You mean nonproliferation might beget nonproliferation, if my neighbor gives up his weapons, I can give up mine."

"Well, it's an optimistic view, but North Korea should keep us all up at night, who can predict what they might do with their nukes."

Marion and Amanda were very excited; Mel Randolph had brought Don-Don to the United States. They all met later at a restaurant for lunch. Mel explained; "I have taken a month of leave, Don Lau and I are going to get married, Don-Lau Zhang is here on a fiancée visa. The state department fast tracked the Visa for us. It turns out my brothers have cleaned up their acts, they are running a couple of fishing boats together in Port Angeles and my mother is living with one of my brothers. Don-Lau and I are going there to visit and get married in Port Angeles. Then we are traveling to Malaysia and meet her mother and her son. They are coming to Abu Dhabi as dependents, the Secretary of State has worked that out for us."

The next day at a private ceremony at CIA headquarters, Russ Nixon's only living relative, a younger brother, received the Honorable William H. Webster Distinguished Service Award posthumously on behalf of Russ; Steve Thomas and Michael Case attended along with the President and Vice President. The CIA reception Hall was filled with employees glad to see that Russ Nixon had finally received recognition for his decades of quiet dedicated service. The CIA webpage published pictures from the award ceremony later that day, detailing the lifetime of service of Russ Nixon in building databases for the US intelligence community.

Chapter Thirty
Message from the *Imam*

Things were calming down in the aftermath of the nuclear revelations in the middle east, there were plans for awards for key players involved in the Saudi investigation and planning was underway on dismantling the nuclear programs. The last two weeks had been relatively quiet in Langley, Director Sweigart was reading the WIRe early in the morning as he drank his coffee. He shook his head, the grammar in the section on North Korea needed polishing. He sat back and looked out the window on the wooded low hills surrounding Langley headquarters. It was going to be hot and humid, early August was usually like this in DC. The Deputy Director of Operations came in, "Good morning Director. A bit of a surprise, we have a message from the *Imam*."

Sweigart, took his eyes away from the window and leaned forward as the Deputy Director sat down.

"The *Imam* passed a message in Vienna yesterday along with a USB during the negotiations on scheduling to dismantle the Iranian weapons program. A simple Ottendorf cipher using the same book he has always used with us, but it is a long message, unusual for the *Imam*."

Director Sweigart read the message and immediately contacted Andrew Friedman on a secure line. Friedman listened as Sweigart read the message.

Sweigart finished the message, "You're the strategy man Andrew, what do you think we should do?"

"How about we have Gulshan Wallace come to your shop, study the message and the USB and be briefed on the background of the *Imam*. She will brief the NSC Principals and provide a recommendation."

"Sounds good to me; she is going to need to work fast given the Imam's request. She needs to give a briefing the first week of September, and I understand there is a lot on that USB. I will confirm her security clearance and have her State Department ID cleared for Agency access for the next several weeks."

Gulshan saw the caller ID, it was Andrew Friedman; they didn't need another historical briefing on Iran. She felt like she had been vindicated on her views of the Saudis and their nuclear aspirations. She wondered what Mr. Friedman might want as she answered the phone.

"Dr. Wallace, I hope you are well. I have just gotten off the phone with Secretary of State Travis. He is aware that you will be detailed to the CIA for several weeks, this is urgent. You need to report to Langley on Monday and meet first thing with Director Sweigart, he will brief you. You need to have a briefing ready the first week of September for the NSC principals. By the way, good call on the Saudi nuclear program. Good luck Dr. Wallace."

Gulshan Wallace had never been in the CIA headquarters; she had met analysts and senior CIA officials over the years. She looked at the stars on the wall as she waited in the lobby, heroes who had died in the service of the country. She was nervous, unsure of what she was expected to do. She was told her ID authorized entry, but she did not know the way to the Directors Office. She was escorted to the office and was met by Director Sweigart and his chief of staff.

"Dr. Wallace, good to see you again. Please have a seat over here; coffee or tea, anything to drink?"

Gulshan sat down in the comfortable sofa, across from Director Sweigart in a leather side chair. "Coffee Director, thank you and please call me Gulshan."

Director Sweigart smiled, "Okay Gulshan it is in this informal setting, first things first, just get it out before we get started. Go ahead."

She was confused, "I am sorry, Director Sweigart, I am not sure what you are looking for."

"Just say I told you so about Saudi Arabia, so Andrew Friedman will stop teasing me."

She laughed, "Just my instincts that their motivations would force them down that path."

"Instinct informed by years of hard work and intelligent thought."

Director Sweigart briefed her on the history of the *Imam*, "We didn't expect any more messages, but we received a message from him last week with a USB. There is an office set up for you next to mine, my Chief of Staff and my executive assistant will give you anything you need; study the message and the files on the USB. You will not have time to read all of them; you will need to get a sense of what is there. You will see that the *Imam* is requesting US assistance; your briefing needs to cover the contents of the message, the USB and make a recommendation regarding his request."

Gulshan felt a bite of nerves, "Will the recommendation on his requests be based on my analysis alone?"

Director Sweigart sensed she was nervous, "Don't worry Gulshan, there is no one more qualified for this task than you. The Secretary of State is sure of this, Andrew Friedman is sure, I am sure. Trust your instincts, there is a bit of time pressure, but you have the entire resources of the CIA behind you."

The text of the Cipher was in the office, along with a desktop computer connected to the CIA and State Department Networks; she had a separate computer for reading the USB file. It was never to be connected to the network and the wireless chip was physically disabled; a so-called air-gapped computer. Her heart was racing as she read the message, what she was reading was almost beyond comprehension; the *Imam* had plans far beyond his betrayal of the nuclear program. She worked long hours combing through the thousands and thousands of files, emails, text messages, police reports, witness statements, meeting summaries that Feisel Ramul had been collecting for at least the last thirty years; that was the oldest document she came across. He organized the documents into three main folders, Nuclear, Moral and Religious lining up with the requested support he wanted from the United States. The chief of staff provided her with a CIA evaluation of the files, an analysis of the meta-data and other descriptive features. They concluded with high confidence they were legitimate, not fabrications.

Director Sweigart suggested she not get his opinions and views before the briefing; go with her instincts; he was confident in her abilities. They ate lunch together twice a week in the large employees' cafeteria, just the two of them. They talked about family life and growing up, not about work. She was proud to sit with this American hero, tremendously grateful that he took the time. She also knew that he chose the large employee cafeteria for a reason. Director Sweigart knew it would benefit her career, word would spread across the intelligence community and the State Department. Gulshan Wallace was working in the CIA Director's suite and having lunch with him twice a week. Her mother heard the news through the rumor mill, her mother's friend Beatrice said people were saying she was a Secretary of State in the making. Gulshan didn't have those aspirations, but she was happy that her parents were proud. Gulshan emailed the briefing presentation and briefing paper to Andrew Friedman the first week of September. The briefing to the NSC principles was the next day.

Gulshan Wallace was much more relaxed for this briefing, which was strange, the previous briefing was mostly informational. This time she was required to make a critical recommendation to the NSC. The President came into the room; he smiled and nodded her way, "Dr.

Wallace good to see you again. I hope things went well in your temporary assignment at the CIA."

"Director Sweigart and the CIA staff could not have made me feel any more welcome, and they were all incredibly accommodating."

"Very good, I understand you will describe an interesting message from the *Imam* asset in Iran; you have the floor."

Gulshan started with her narrative, first giving a short biography of the *Imam*, the NSC principles were already aware of the role he had played in providing details of the nuclear weapons program and his assistance in "SMOKESCREEN"; she mentioned these points briefly for completeness. She noted that his only request previously to the US was for us to disclose the Iranian nuclear weapons program. It was Gulshan's understanding from Director Sweigart that they did not expect to hear from the *Imam* again and were going to avoid contact so as to not compromise his safety. She moved to the cipher message and the USB. She referred to the *Imam* as Feisel Ramul for the remainder of her presentation.

"The message in the cipher is longer than any previous message sent. First, Feisel Ramul thanks the United States for honoring the promise to reveal the Iranian nuclear program. He says it was an elegant and bold strategy. He also says that many of the problems between our countries started with our meddling in domestic relations and supporting a coup in support of the Shah and supporting the Shah's abuses of power when he was in office. Feisel says it is time for those things to be forgotten, but the United States should stay out of Iranian domestic affairs. He does request US intelligence technical support only to distribute information he has collected; he wants us to dump it on the internet and provide supporting social messaging on Farsi social media through hacking to promulgate these materials. He is emphatic that there be no US fingerprint and no other actions, there will be no further communication."

"He has amassed evidence in three areas which he refers to as three betrayals by the religious clerics. The evidence appears to have been collected for at least thirty years and is composed of emails, text messages, police reports, witness statements, meeting summaries and other documents. The USB has a little more than 35,000 files. CIA analysts have high confidence the documents are legitimate."

"He has organized the distribution of materials and social messaging into three stages, in sequence Nuclear Betrayals, Moral Crimes and Corruption and the last Religious betrayal. Each of the three stages has a set of folders with the collected files and evidence and a detailed description of the messaging campaign for social media. He requests that there be a covert dump of the files on a certain date, followed by a social media campaign promoting the messages. For the nuclear betrayals he has collected evidence that prominent Ayatollahs and Imams including the Supreme Leaders have all privately supported, endorsed the nuclear weapons program; while they issued Fatwah's and made public speeches that Iran did not have a nuclear weapons program, that it was opposed to Islamic values and nuclear weapons were the product of perverted western colonial powers. The social messaging campaign is designed to illustrate the hypocrisy and misleading speech from religious leaders in the now disgraced nuclear program. The nuclear betrayal sequence is supposed to begin with the document dump on September 11 with social messaging through October 10."

"Moral Crimes and Corruption files are mostly police records and witness statements along with emails and text messages. They implicate six very senior Imams in the Tehran area who have been accused of sexually assaulting multiple women, four to seven women each. The text messages and emails point to two senior aids and advisers in the office of the Supreme leader who directed the suppression of the allegations, planted rumors about the women as sexually deviant and pressured police to close down the investigations. There are another ten senior Imams across Iran with multiple accusations of accepting bribes and using religious funds to their own personal benefit. There is supporting evidence in emails and documents and records of financial transactions. The social messaging campaign points to the criminal behavior and the hypocrisy of these religious leaders. This stage begins with a document dump on October 11 with social messaging through November 10."

"The religious betrayal is the boldest of the three stages, there are a series of documents, not evidence in this stage. The first is a lengthy, detailed and complex essay, titled "Khomeini's Deception," it dissects and discredits Ayatollah Khomeini's 1961 book "Clarification of Points of Sharia." This book generated a large radical following for Khomeini earning him the rank of Ayatollah and also laid the foundation for the supervision and guidance of government by the religious clerics. Feisel's essay analyzes the contradictory evidence in the Quran and other religious texts and demonstrates how Khomeini and his followers used it to gain power for themselves, and how they have used the revolutionary guard and other instruments of government to enforce their extreme moral code. There are a series of four short papers that summarize key topics in the essay; the social messaging campaign calls for the essay to be released on November 11 and one of the topic papers each week until December 11. The messaging campaign in this period draws together the moral crimes' corruption, nuclear lies and the harm it has caused the country and the religious betrayal, a condemnation of the radical clerics, their hypocrisy, rigid moral views and interference in government. The last two weeks of the social messaging is a call for justice and accountability. That concludes my summary of the message and the contents of the USB." She took a drink of coffee waiting for comments and questions before she moved to her recommendation.

President Larson took a drink of his warm green tea giving her a moment, "Remarkable he seems to hope for a new revolution to transform the Islamic Republic. Do you have any assessment of his motivations and what he would want it to look like at the end of the day?"

"His motivations are difficult to judge. There are insights mostly through the way he has structured the social messaging and his reasoning in the essay. I also came across some circumstantial evidence that is interesting, of course this is quite speculative. We know he led the intensive efforts to finalize the nuclear warheads, yet he had no problem destroying his life's professional work. Clearly, he had a longer agenda planned many years ago, well before he became the Director at AEOI. He is meticulous and mastered clandestine tradecraft; I believe he has been developing this longer-term plan since his graduate school years. He has not requested money, there is nothing indicating he is seeking political power or fame, much the opposite. I believe he is deeply religious and is highly skeptical of the infallibility of Imams. His religious views are not clearly Sunni or Shia, I suspect he dislikes the extremist on both sides. He supports a partial separation of "church and state" to use an American analogy. The role of the government would be to provide financial support for Islamic mosques and institutes as the official state faith but would allow for other religious practice without efforts to convert Muslims. The clerics should have no role in government, if they choose to run for the Majlis, they must temporarily abandon their religious postings. I conclude he is fundamentally religiously and patriotically motivated. He believes the Americans damaged Iran, but he also believes Khomeini's radical Islam and the clerics role in government has damaged the State and the people."

"I also believe there is personal motivation, and this is quite speculative, his father was murdered while Feisel was in graduate school. His father was an Imam, a supporter of Khomeini who preached primarily using the "Clarification of Points of Sharia", the book that Feisel now attacks in his essay. Several years before his father's murder there is a police report, an anonymous tip that his father assaulted Feisel's mother Afshan. That document is in the files collected by Feisel Mohammad Ramul. I believe that he is the one who called the police to report his father assaulting his mother. There is another police report from an anonymous caller regarding Ayatollah Rasmani, one of the clerics accused of sexual assaults. This report does not name a victim just a claim that he is sexually assaulting women in Tehran. The police file indicates they traced the cell phone number to a woman Jasmin Ganwar. They filed the document as not credible, too vague from an unreliable source living 300 km away from Tehran. The caller's sister is Afshan Ganwar, Feisel's mother; the report was made years after his father was killed, about the time Feisel finished graduate school and started work. I don't know exactly what happened, but I believe he feels betrayed by his father's abuse of his mother or sexual assault of his mother by Rasmani, or both. He has linked these personal betrayals to the hypocrisy he sees in the clerical system which both men belong; this might explain the emotional energy needed to drive him so hard for so long to seek retribution. In the last stage of his social media campaign, he refers to it as a campaign for justice, the first delivery date to initiate the entire campaign September 11 is the date his father was murdered, but maybe a coincidence."

"On the second part of your question, Mr. President, what does he want the revolution and the new Iran to look like? Again this is informed speculation. I believe you are correct. He seeks a new revolution, peaceful and from the middle class like the first one, but this time with no foreign demons to punish but corrupt clerics. The end result for him is the clerics and Imams preaching a more moderate form of Islam, sticking more closely to what is in the Quranic text and allowing for alternative reasonable interpretations, especially regarding personal behavior and morality. He seeks government support of Islam through financial support and fundamental values, but no role for the clerics in supervising and guiding the government. He will want to see the dissolution of all entities that involve the Clerics in government, the elimination of the Supreme Leader and the elimination of the Revolutionary Guard."

President Larson nodded sitting back in his chair, "Interesting Dr. Wallace, thorough and well-reasoned and what is your recommendation?"

"It is easy to see this as a wild pipe dream, but recall the first Iranian revolution, how quickly that happened, fueled by the rhetoric of Khomeini and tapping into the emotion of the middle class about foreign influence and abuses of the Shah. I believe the Iranian middle class is frustrated by the government, a depressed economy and intrusions into their personal lives. Many Iranians will blame the radical clerics who have wielded power over government for these problems. Feisel Mohammad Ramul has the energy, intellect and motivation to stand up and lead this effort. The essay he requests be published on November 11 has his name as the author. He intends to stand up then or before that time to be a voice of what he sees as justice. I see a sense of justice in his cause, he seeks to remove an oppressive force that has brought harm to the Iranian people, the region and international relations. President Ahmadi and his senior advisers are not big supporters of the Clerics and Ayatollah Emami, they would be happy to see them eliminated as supervisors of government. If the effort is peaceful, the President will quietly try and support him, keep the internet from shutting down. If a clear majority of the public support change, the President will find a legal means to support the revolution. My preliminary discussions with the staff in the Directorate of Intelligence indicates we have the tools to provide the support requested by Feisel Ramul. Success is uncertain, but my recommendation is to deliver the requested document postings and social media campaign ensuring no American footprint."

President Larson nodded, "Thank you Dr. Wallace. He must know that he is putting his life at risk, do you agree?"

"Yes, Mr. President, he is ready to die for his cause and knows that is a possibility, and he will go forward with or without our support."

President Larson looked to the CIA Director, "Director Sweigart can we hear your views?"

"The analysis and reasoning of Dr. Wallace is clear and convincing. I support her recommendation that we provide US support. We have quite the toolkit we can provide to keep these documents available on the internet and generate thousands of supporting social media messages and amplify messages of those in support and quash any counter attempts to block or create a counter campaign. Nothing will be traceable to the US. Everything will appear to be coming from Iran, Turkey and Qatar; the sources bouncing around the internet and changing every minute. We will monitor efforts to freeze his assets, access to funding, interference with his computer and cell phone and attempts to discredit him; we can deploy these countermeasures as well."

The President went to Secretary of State Travis, "I want to thank Dr. Wallace for her years of service at the State Department. Mr. President you might not know but both her parents spent their entire professional careers at the State Department. I believe it's more than forty years of continuous service from her family. I find her reasoning sound and compelling; Feisel Ramul has proved a reliable source and he has also shown himself to be resourceful and able to work under duress in a covert manner. A peaceful transformation of Iran along the lines of Dr. Wallace's analysis are to the benefit of the United States and would likely result in better relations between our countries. I support Dr. Wallace's recommendation."

The President smiled, "I was not aware of Dr. Wallace's parents service; thank you for noting that. Secretary of Defense Cox, what are your views?"

"I endorse Dr. Wallace's recommendation; I would like to expand on it, Mr. President. We should honor his request to avoid American interference in domestic politics, but he has asked for our technical help; so we will be involved. I believe we should take some actions to protect Feisel Mohammad Ramul. I agree with Dr. Wallace, he is in pursuit of a just cause and I believe it is in our interest. He will not want to leave Iran, so taking him out of the country to safety is not realistic, but we can covertly offer some protection in Iran."

Director Sweigart was shaking his head in agreement, "I agree with Secretary Cox, he could use some guardian angels. I believe DOD and CIA should develop a protection strategy. If he fails and they jail him, we will have to stay out of it, even if they execute him. We should certainly try."

The next day the President signed the Presidential Directive with the tasking developed from the recommendations of Gulshan Wallace's briefing document and the recommendations of the NSC. Andrew Friedman distributed the Top-Secret directive to CIA and Department of Defense, codeword ARCHANGEL.

A week after the meeting, Gulshan's mother called her at home. "You are not going to believe what we just got in the mail, a letter from President Larson thanking our family for years of service to the US State Department. It has details of many of your father's assignments and mine and yours. You need to see this; we are going to get it framed. What prompted this?"

"I don't know mother, sometimes the rumor mill has good things to say about people."

Chapter Thirty-One
Exposing the Hypocrites

Feisel only needed limited assistance from the Americans for the next part of his plan, and he did not want them involved in Iranian Domestic Politics. The Iranians had trained him in covert and clandestine counter-measures, he also had some electronic software the Americans had given him; he could use it to get into email accounts and computers without detection. He was happy his mother would not be around for this; he would soon become a pariah in Iran and be labeled a traitor. He had saved his money, he kept cash and valuables stored around Iran and his home was paid for; he expected that he would end up dead or in prison; he would accept the consequences. He was working on his backup to the Americans. He had devised a crude system of posting and was developing some social messaging robots, but it would not be anything compared to what the Americans could do, and it increased the likelihood he would be caught before he could finish his campaign. On September 11, he saw the social media messages and links to websites take off. The traffic was slow at first, but it was building; he wasn't sure how much of it was the Americans or actual real social media. It was clear the messages were angry at the clerics. He checked later in the day; there were many links, and the documents could still be accessed. The Americans must have a room of ten or twenty people working to support him. He was impressed with the support.

He was wrong, ARCHANGEL was much bigger than that; there were more than 120 "analysts" working in support of the internet and social media campaign and on countermeasures and the protection of his IT and finances. They had been working nonstop set up on 24 hour shifts for more than a week. They were mostly in NSA headquarters, but there were also groups in Istanbul and Doha; the staff had also been increased under Mel Randolph in Abu Dhabi. They intended to exploit the Emiratis assets in Tehran for monitoring, using the Blackhole platform. There was also a group of five men in Tehran. They had arrived in the city on a bus from the southern city of Borazjan looking for day work in the city. They had actually been deployed on a small boat from the USS Albany, a Los Angeles class submarine, 3 CIA covert service operators and 2 delta force operators. Some days they were cleaning up trash in the street; some days they worked on the underground piping near the apartment of Feisel Ramul. They were telecommunication workers, gas company, electric company. A crew had proceeded before them, with a large delivery smuggled into the country a week earlier to set up their operation. The apartment was outfitted with personal gear and uniforms and communications. They had two large storage garages with vans and large equipment for their covers. They looked a little different each day depending on the role and location they were in that day. They were Feisel's guardian angels; they had constant intelligence feeds of what was happening across the city, any indicators of threats against Feisel. Their orders were clear, intercept any threats without blowing cover; if they could not avoid their cover being blown, then Feisel Ramul's life would be lost. They were not about to let that happen.

The citizens in Iran were getting angry. The religious clerics had lied about the nuclear weapons program for years, telling them and the world it was a sin, saying it was a peaceful program. They were secretly advocating and pushing the weapons development, pouring billions of dollars down the toilet, and then they lost control of a warhead that exploded in the middle of the Indian Ocean.

President Ahmadi's chief of staff consulted him, "What should we do? Ayatollah Emami is angry. He wants us to shut down the internet and find who is doing this."

President Ahmadi had detailed reports on what was going on; a focused media campaign critical of the clerics not the government, that was fine with him. There were no calls for violence, a few small rally's; he was not about to shut down the internet for this. "Tell the Ayatollah we are doing everything we can, but it would make things far worse if we shut down the internet."

President Ahmadi didn't know who was behind this. The Americans could do it but what possible reason, the nuclear weapons program dismantlement plans were progressing, and the US had honored their promises beginning to release assets and lift sanctions. It must be a grass roots campaign, people with dirt on the clerics fed up with their hypocrisy.

The media and government establishment were reeling when Feisel Mohammad Ramul announced his resignation from the Atomic Energy Agency on October 1. His statement was released on his social media account, "The betrayal of the public by the clerics and my role in the development of the nuclear weapons program forced me to be accountable for my actions. I encourage the clerics to take responsibility for their actions and resign their role in government as well."

The message was picked up on social media. The clerics responsible for the deception should resign from government. Ayatollah Emami was angry. He believed in this man, he was a fool with such an idealistic childish view of the world. President Ahmadi smiled when he read the message, more fuel for the fire.

President Larson was briefed the next day by Andrew Friedman, "Ramul seems to have taken a first step towards going public, and the social media campaign is working. A majority of the messages now were from legitimate accounts, the CIA and NSA are reducing the stream of messages from their assets, but they are closely monitoring.

There haven't been any attempts by the government to interfere on the internet or with social media platforms."

The next bombshell dropped on October 11, a new batch of files on the internet and social media messages from the US assets. Six senior Tehran clerics sexually assaulting women, another ten senior clerics across the country taking bribes and stealing funds from the Mosques. The senior clerics were covering it up and pressuring the police. By the middle of October some of the women were coming forward along with their families, two police chiefs admitted to being pressured by the senior clerics. The public rage was growing on social media, along with the messages planted by the CIA and NSA, the clerical leadership was corrupt and evil. There was a march on October 20 in Tehran, 200,000 people calling for the clerics and the Ayatollahs to be held accountable.

Ayatollah Emami came into President Ahmadi's office without an appointment interrupting a discussion with his chief of staff, "This needs to be stopped, these riots and reckless accusations. Why aren't you doing anything?"

"What should I do? I had state prosecutors investigate these claims and review these documents. Do you say these are all false claims? The prosecutors say the police complaints are real, the emails and interference by some senior clerics are real. Why shouldn't the clerics be the ones who get arrested and those hiding their crimes?"

Ayatollah Emami was caught off guard, he had heard the rumors; he did tell his staff to keep it all quiet, and he suggested some pushback; he walked away. "Do what you must."

State prosecutors announced indictments of four clerics for sexual assault; investigations continuing into two additional clerics, they also announced a tip hotline for additional allegations. The next day they announced indictments of five clerics for public corruption, and two senior Ayatollahs for corruption and conspiracy. President Ahmadi's office issued a press release. There would be no interference in peaceful demonstrations, and there would be no curfew. However, in the interest of public security, a website was being setup to request permits for planned marches, listing the locations. These would be authorized in less than one hour and police and security services could then act to ensure everyone's safety. It was a brilliant move. It appeared to be in the interest of public safety. It was in essence an endorsement of the public's outrage of these transgressions. The President secretly put the military on alert to monitor the revolutionary guard. He met with Ayatollah Emami and the head of the revolutionary guard, the military would move against them if they went after Iranian people peacefully protesting.

On November 10th Feisel Mohammad Ramul appeared in an interview on Tehran television. He was asked about the nuclear program and the recent corruption of the clerics. Feisel Ramul had never been on television, he appeared calm and credible, "I was deeply troubled during the nuclear program about the hypocrisy of the clerics. I had listened to the Fatwah's and public statements and then sat in private meetings where they told us the weapons were imperative to our safety. I was wrong for participating in the development of these evil weapons, and I regret my actions and will have to face Allah for what I have done. These clerics have violated the Quran's admonition to not confound the truth by mixing it up with falsehood and not to knowingly conceal the truth. They are religious leaders and now we see evidence that they also covered up sexual assaults and corruption, what kind of leaders are they? I have closely studied the Quran and Khomeini's "Clarification of Points of Sharia" for many years. I have written an essay against the "Clarification of Points of Sharia" and also some short study papers that I will post to my social media account over the next few weeks. I invite the good people of Iran to see if what I say is true, and I will be judged on my written words."

The postings went onto his social media accounts by the American assets. Ramul believed he would be immediately arrested or assassinated. He knew that the American postings would look like supporters were using his social media if he was not able. This was followed by the social media messages, a call for justice, a call for reform, get the clerics out of government and into the Mosques.

Chapter Thirty-Two
Assassinate the Traitor

The heat shot up in the general public, protests and marches were underway. Feisel was on radio and television for frequent interviews. He agreed to lead a march on Saturday, November 20, planned to attract one million people. It was estimated there were almost two million marching North to South along Khordad Avenue, past the national museum, then passing the Golestan Palace. Marchers were carrying signs with quotes from Feisel's essay, there were signs calling for the constitution to be modified and clerical forces to be taken out of Iranian government; there was a chant "teach and pray in the Mosque, stay out of the capital," the Farsi version had a melodic sound.

The police and security forces were distributed along the route, it had been peaceful when it started at 9:00 am, it was a cool and clear autumn day. Just after 11:30 the front of the march led by Feisel passed the intersection beyond Golestan Palace was when things spun out of control. Counter protesters came out from between buildings, with smoke bombs and firecrackers. The police in the area moved towards the small group causing the disturbance. They were a diversion. Three men were moving towards Feisel from the opposite direction at the leading edge of marchers. Someone yelled gun! People began to scramble wildly, Feisel felt two strong men grab him and lift him off of his feet moving towards the side of the road. By the time things got under control, police found three men on the ground screaming in agony unable to even crawl away from their guns. The police found Feisel on the side of the road sitting on a bench. They saw two men run away as they approached. He said they told him just to wait for the police, they would not harm him.

General Khoram, the director of internal security services, came to President Ahmadi's office a few minutes after 4:00 pm. He had a laptop and connected it to the display in the Presidents conference room. "We have reconstructed and enhanced videos from several cell phones at the time of the attack, all of the CCTV cameras had gone down; we do not know the cause. You see these three attackers, coming towards Feisel from this direction."

General Khoram paused the video, using a laser pointer as he spoke. "Watch these five men as the attackers approach, they appear to have firearms under their cloaks, but we cannot be sure."

He played the rest of the video in slow motion, "Our analysis is that this intervenor yelled gun just moments before a gun was visible. At the same time these two intervenors immediately took Feisel in the other direction. You can see the other three intervenors rapidly move one towards each attacker. They take them to the ground in a smooth sweeping motion, see holding the wrist on the hand with the firearm so they cannot pull the trigger slamming the hand to the ground. Each attacker has cracked bones in their wrist. Then two rapid strikes, you can see their arms moving, but it is just a dark black blur in their hands, we believe those were tactical batons, rupturing the tendons below the kneecaps on all three men. It took less than ten seconds for all three men to be incapacitated. These were not just good Samaritans wrestling attackers to the ground. This was a highly professional coordinated protective force, and they knew the attack on Feisel was coming."

"What about identification of the intervenors?"

"None of the images are good enough for facial recognition. They pulled their head coverings down around their faces and kept their heads down. If we had higher quality CCTV footage then maybe we could identify them."

The general continued, "One hour after the attack, we received this USB from a courier service. We cannot identify who sent it. It has an audio recorded from cellphones of Ayatollah Emami and General Khatamen of the Revolutionary Guard during a meeting and then another audio recorded from General Khatamen instructing his chief of staff."

President Ahmadi listened to Ayatollah Emami talking to General Khatamen, "Stop Feisel during the march tomorrow, plan this carefully, no one can trace the killing back to us."

"Are you sure, Supreme Leader, is this the only way?"

Ayatollah Emami screams, "Assassinate the traitor."

The next conversation has some video, they could see General Khatamen's face from his mobile phone camera as he talks to his chief of staff, as he searches his contact list on his phone, "I know someone who can help us, a former revolutionary guard officer."

The video is shaky, but it shows General Khatamen's face as he tells his chief of staff, "The supreme leader has ordered the killing of Feisel tomorrow during the march; here, this is the one who can lead this."

Khatamen finds the name and address, the video stops as he puts his cell phone back on the table. The audio continues, "contact this man Colonel Rumiara and work out the details, talk face to face no cell phones."

General Khoram continued, "Colonel Rumiara is one of the three we have in custody, one of the attackers from today."

President Ahmadi sits back taking it in, "Who has heard and seen the video and audio?"

"Only the two of us."

"This has to be Americans, special forces or covert operators, intervention in the attack and these recordings from cell phones. Destroy the enhanced images of the attacks showing the ones who saved Feisel. I don't care why the Americans protected Feisel or why they are giving us this evidence. Let's keep our eyes open to make sure they are not up to some mischief, maybe they just want to give us a helping hand. We are going to use the evidence as if we have collected it ourselves. We have the ability to collect video and audio remotely, from cell phones from short distances. We will say we suspected General Khatamen of some crime. Destroy the recording from the Ayatollah's phone, it just duplicates what came from the general."

The chief prosecutor and his leading state prosecutor for national security were called to President Ahmadi's office. He gave them a USB, "This comes from state security. The sources and methods are classified. You will find that the device number from which the recording was made is General Khatamen's cell phone."

Before leaving the president's office, they watched the video and audio, one conversation of the Supreme leader with General Khatamen and the General Khatamen with his chief of staff. The chief prosecutor and lead prosecutor confronted Colonel Rumiara and offered him a slight reduction in sentence for his testimony. Colonel Rumiara confirmed it was the chief of staff for General Khatamen who directed the attack, and he was told they were acting on orders of Ayatollah Emami. The testimony of the Khatamen's chief of staff was the same. News that Ayatollah Emami and the leader of the revolutionary guard had been arrested for the attempted assassination of Feisel Ramul was international news.

Feisel Mohammad Ramul was on prime-time television in Iran the evening of the attack, being interviewed about the attack on his life. It was reported that it was one of the most watched television broadcasts in Iranian television history. There was grainy cell phone video that the news channels had been showing, three men moving toward Feisel, you can see what might be a gun at one point in a man's hand. People are running and two men are pulling Feisel away and three men have quickly thrown the attackers to the ground and appear to strike them in the legs, maybe walking sticks the reporter guesses. Then the three men who saved him are gone as well as the other two men, who had carried him away. The reporter asks, "what was it like for you?"

"It happened so fast, I heard someone yell gun and then many people screaming gun and the next moment my feet came off the ground. They were two very powerful men, moving me rapidly away from the crowd. I must be honest, I thought they were going to kidnap or kill me. One of the men whispered we are here to protect you on the command of Allah, he quoted the Quran about angels sent to protect. They sat me on the bench and when we saw the police coming, they said you are safe, wait for the police. I do not know who they were or who sent them, but they seem to have disappeared, maybe they were guardian angels from Allah."

The reporter asked, "Do you think the attackers might be Shia radicals angry about your essay and criticism of Khomeini's book?"

Feisel thought for a moment and said something no Iranian had ever dare say in public much less on national television. It was instinctive and from his heart and his personal views of religion.

He looked into the camera, speaking calmly, "When did we come up with this sick and twisted competition between Shia and Sunni, spewing hatred and lies about each other. I have studied the Quran my entire life and the messages and Hadiths of the Prophet Muhammad. There is no Shia and Sunni to be found in the sacred text or the words of the great Prophet. What would the great Prophet say about Muslim speaking against Muslim? Arguments about doctrine and the role of religious leaders a division into two competing groups. I believe in my heart he would be angry with all of us and tell us there is no Shia and there is no Sunni, he would say we are all Muslims, there is one God, Allah, and one message in the Quran. I do not see myself as Shia, I see myself as a

Muslim, and I try to be faithful to the Quran and be informed by the messages of the Hadith. These men who attacked me will have to answer to the law and to Allah, I do not understand why they did this, but I will try and forgive. I think the last few months has revealed that the myth of infallibility of Imams or Ayatollahs is what it has always been, a myth to give power to a few over many."

Feisel was surprised by the positive reaction over his public statements, first from the general public, a simple message reverberating across Farsi social media, "I am neither Shia nor Sunni I am Muslim", it was even being messaged by moderate Imams and he heard it was making its way in the Sunni world. Taped replays of this segment of his interview played around the world.

Chapter Thirty-Three
Reformation

There were two things Feisel Ramul wanted to avoid with his campaign, violence and American interference in Iranian domestic politics. The Americans had honored his request; they had given technical assistance but were not interfering. The official comments from US government officials he saw on the news were low key, the situation in Iran was being monitored. The attack caused him to rethink his public appearances and he decided he would avoid the media, and he stayed in his apartment for several days. He wasn't afraid for his life, he just wanted the temperature to drop down. He was pleasantly surprised at what he witnessed over the next several weeks, starting early the next week. A group of 50 moderate Imams in Tehran signed a petition directed to the acting head of Tehran's religious community, the petition endorsed Feisel's essay and it called for a condemnation of Khomeini's "Clarification of Points of Sharia." They called for a foundation based on the Quran and reduced emphasis on Fatwahs and secondary sources, careful study of the Hadiths and an open mind and debate on different interpretations.

The movement grew, across Iran it was clear by the end of the week that the moderates were the vast majority and that they enjoyed broad support of most of the public. The next Saturday there was another march, the same route as Feisel's; the central message a need to reform the clergy and get them out of government. A new leader was emerging, a forty-one-year-old energetic Imam from just north of Tehran once imprisoned by the Revolutionary guard for preaching messages critical of Khomeini. His name was Aahil Shadpour, his name meant gift from God, he was energetic and enthusiastic. He was on television every night that week calling on the people of Tehran to participate peacefully in the march that Saturday.

The night before the march, he spoke to a large television audience, "I would like to thank Feisel Ramul for lighting the spark for this reform movement, placing his life at risk let us continue the message. It is time to heal the Shia and Sunni divide and to put government back in the hands of secular powers, supported by Islamic values but tolerant of other views."

Aahil gave a sermon the Friday before the march, the television stations broadcast it live in Tehran. It was estimated there were 300,000 people gathered around the mosque with large screens and speakers around. It was a message of peace, peace between Shia and Sunni, peace between Christians, Jews and Muslims. Those who used Islam as calls for violence and attacks were not true believers, those who sought division were not true believers; he said they should focus on the better angels of our nature, lets again see dance and music, not debauchery but things that enrich our souls and give praise to Allah. Women are equal to man; they should not hide in the shadows or be ashamed to show their face. The march the next day was estimated to be a little more than two million and was peaceful; the zealots who had supported Khomeini were moving into the shadows, they could see change was coming, they would need to adapt or disappear. Feisel watched on TV, happy that the torch had been picked up, there was a new generation of religious leaders. There was something else he could focus on to try and help his country, something which he was competent and capable.

President Ahmadi carefully watched the media and monitored security reports. The movements were peaceful, and the messages were clear and popularly supported; get the clerics out of government. He was happy to offer the legal framework for this to become a reality. The intelligence services and security services reported there were no signs of foreign actors in the marches. There was some unusual social media traffic from Turkey and Qatar early in the month but nothing of note now, this seemed to be a home-grown middle class revolution. No signs of any American forces or covert operators since the attack on Feisel.

In the middle of December, President Ahmadi announced that the ministry of justice had drafted reforms to the constitution. They would be published for public review and there would be a voting referendum next March. These modifications would not result in a purely secular Islamic Republic but would remove the clergy from governance and supervision of the government. Government would support Islam as the national religion and provide funding for mosques and clerical education and programs. If the public majority of at least 55% approved the reforms, governmental restructuring would be undertaken throughout the next eighteen months. The President also announced that Feisel Mo-hammad Ramul had been named the new head of the Atomic Energy Organization, and he would pursue a new peaceful nuclear energy program working with the international community. The details would be announced by the Atomic Energy organization.

Feisel Ramul had contacted President Ahmadi with his proposal to try and resurrect the nuclear power program, a truly peaceful program to develop electricity, produce isotopes for medical treatment and save the enrichment facilities from destruction. President Ahmadi immediately recognized the potential economic benefit to the country, and there was no better candidate to lead the effort than Feisel, but he knew it was a "long shot," The Americans would likely kill the idea before it got off of the ground. Why would they ever trust us after the years of lying, loss of control of a warhead and an illegal nuclear test. Feisel also knew it would be difficult, but he thought there might be some chance to get American support. The Americans knew they were not responsible for the nuclear test, but the President was right the Americans would likely kill the idea before it could get off the ground.

In early January President Larson was briefed along with Vice President Packard, Andrew Friedman, Director Sweigart and the Secretary of State Travis by Heather Moss of the State Department. Moss summarized a proposal that Feisel Ramul intended to present at the IAEA Board of Governors' meeting the last week of January.

Moss summarized in closing, "The proposal is radical, it called for the middle east to be a new pilot for monitored enrichment and fuel fabrication plants. Any country in the region who wanted to have enrichment or fuel fabrication plants would agree to full-time IAEA resident inspectors on site with full access to facilities and records and laboratory resources for independent sampling by the IAEA. The countries would also agree to allow the resident inspectors to go to any suspicious locations in the country without prior notification. The countries would pay fees to fund the IAEA resources; the maximum enrichment for Uranium would be limited to 5%. They could manufacture and sell nuclear fuel for research, medical or power reactors anywhere in the world. Feisel Ramul has developed a model country agreement for participation that would be submitted by any country in the region, describing the facilities and the agreements for access. He has already developed a proposal for the Iranian enrichment and fuel fabrication plant as a proposed approach under this model, approved by President Ahmadi. I will be representing the United States at the IAEA Board of Governors' meeting. I need direction how to proceed before that time."

President Larson didn't follow his usual formula and quickly closed the briefing, "Thank you Ms. Moss. Very good briefing, you will get directions through Secretary Travis."

Feisel Ramul was pleased the Board of Governors had put his paper up for discussion for the meeting on January 27. They allocated more than two hours and then there would be discussion time. He knew the critical person was Ms. Moss from the United States. She would have the Saudis and British along with her and others that followed. If she killed it, the proposal was dead; his only help might be an alliance led by the Chinese and the Russians. Ms. Moss was an experienced diplomat, he could not read her expressions or body language; she was waiting to speak letting the Russians and other countries aligned with the Russians go first.

The Russian representative spoke excellent English, "The Russian Republic strongly endorses the proposal of the Islamic Republic of Iran, and we strongly urge approval of the Board of Governors. Allow the Iranian people a chance to go forward and build their economy, it is the responsible and ethical thing to do."

All eyes went to Heather Moss, "This is a most interesting proposal." She went through the parade of horrible things the Iranians had done in the nuclear weapons program for years leading up to the dangerous nuclear test in June of last year. "According to US legal counsel for the IAEA mission, the proposal was beyond the authority of the IAEA Board of Governors; the board does not have the legal authority to approve such a proposal. The US has consulted with the Chinese, UK and France and other countries. There is agreement that this would need to be presented to the UN permanent members of the security council for approval before the IAEA could even vote on the matter."

Fiesel knew this was beyond dead, there would not even be a debate. What was the point in going to the permanent members. It was already clear that the US already had four of the five on their side, even the Chinese had joined the Americans.

The Russian foreign ministry told the Iranians it was a waste of time, the Americans would kill the proposal along with the other permanent members. The Iranian foreign ministry pushed, President Ahmadi was insistent the Iranians understood this, but they needed to let the world and the Iranian people see that the Americans were blocking this chance at development, continuing to harm their economy. In reality, the Russians did not really support the program either. For economic reasons they wanted to sell fuel and nuclear reactor technology in the middle east including to Iran, they did not want any more competition. They agreed to help their friends. They would introduce the measure on behalf of the Iranian government and endorse it for approval at the meeting of the permanent members of the Security Council in early February.

The Russian representative introduced the proposal that had been circulated to the other members, "This is a reasonable proposal; it allows for full time monitoring of the fuel enrichment and fabrication. There is no possibility to cheat the system. Let the Iranian people build a peaceful nuclear program to recover some of the investment they had made in this technology; there are jobs at risk and families' futures. What harm can come from allowing them to operate enrichment facilities and fuel fabrication equipment under constant IAEA supervision. The Iranians acknowledged mistakes have been made in the past. To vote against this is petty and spiteful; I urge the support of all members. I give the full support of the Russian Federation for the proposal and cast our vote for approval. I request a recorded vote from the other members of the security council, so we have everyone on the record."

He sat back and waited for Secretary of State Travis to crush the Iranian peoples dreams of a commercial nuclear power program. He looked at Travis and smiled, as he took a sip of water.

Secretary Travis smiled and nodded to his Russian colleague, "The United States of America strongly supports this initiative. It allows the IAEA Board of Governors' majority vote to put in place controls for Iran and other countries in the region with existing enrichment and fabrication capability using the model proposal developed by Iran. The United States has already been advised that Saudi Arabia would also join the initiative with their enrichment cascade to operate under IAEA oversight, allowing them to also convert their weapons enrichment facility to peaceful purposes. The United States agrees it is best to forgive past misdeeds and support the jobs and economies of the region. The United States votes yes to the proposal."

The Chinese foreign minister then spoke, "China supports the proposal, and I would like to announce a trilateral initiative with United States and France in further support of this development. The development of 15 power reactor projects over the next 15 years in Iran and Saudi Arabia with loan guarantees to assist in construction. Five reactors from each of the supplier countries, with an agreement to purchase fuel from the Saudi and Iranian fuel facilities made possible through this proposal. Any other countries in the region who would agree to use the monitored fuel enrichment facilities would be offered financing and loan guarantees for power reactor construction. The Peoples Republic of China votes in favor of the proposal."

The French and the UK gave their endorsements and votes of support. The Russian representative was scrambling, "Point of order, we should have more time for open debate and formal motions and filings, then have another vote in a few days."

Secretary of State Travis laughed, "You must be confused sir. Don't you understand we all supported your proposal. It's approved unanimously by the security council by a recorded vote, no need to do it all again. You won sir a good day for everyone." The Russians were left holding the bag, 15 nuclear power reactors in the middle east and none of the business would go to Russian suppliers.

After Heather Moss made her presentation in early January, President Larson continued the discussion with Vice President Packard and Secretary of State Henry Travis, Andrew Friedman and Director Sweigart. Vice President Packard thought it was unusual that the President did not ask for discussion and comment while Ms. Moss was there, but now she understood. The President had already formulated a plan. He contacted President Chou in China on his proposal to support the Iranian plan and his distrust of the Russians. President Chou agreed to the proposal and then the French President was brought onboard by President Larson. Secretary of State Travis and the Chinese Foreign Secretary spent the next several days lining up support of all the parties on the Security Council to receive full support for the proposal.

The Russians were the only ones out of the loop. The trick was to get them to make the proposal and cast their positive vote first, sure that the Americans would kill it. Andrew Friedman had the idea of how to do that and Director Sweigart sent directions to an asset in Vienna.

Feisel Ramul was setting in the Mozart Sonnet Café in Vienna late in the afternoon on January 27th, the day could not have gone any worse. He had killed the nuclear program in his country. He knew it was dead after listening to Ms. Moss kill any further consideration of his proposal to the IAEA Board. He had been arrogant when he developed his retribution strategy, not thinking about all of the lost jobs, thousands of engineers and technicians who were patriots working for their country. Their efforts wasted along with the money invested in education and research. These people and their families would be justified in hating him; he had not thought about all of the consequences of his actions. If he had planned better, he could have worked with the Americans to try and convert the program to a peaceful program at the beginning.

He heard an American accent, "Excuse me sir, I think you dropped this."

The man was holding out a bookmark, Feisel didn't have a book with him. "I don't think so."

"The man smiled, "I'm sure I saw you drop this."

"Thank you," he saw the book in the man's hand the Fukushima book.

He watched the man as he walked away, just now noticing he had a green umbrella, Feisel smiled there was no sign of rain today. He turned the bookmark over there was a cipher. When he got back to Tehran, he found his copy of the book, the message was short and simple. *Go to the Russians and have them get the proposal before the UN Security Council. The outcome will be even better than you can imagine.*

Epilogue

The Iranian people overwhelmingly approved all of the proposed modifications to the constitution, with 76% of the vote well beyond the mandate of 55%. President Ahmadi moved quickly operating transparently, he knew that would keep the pressure on the legislature to honor the public vote. By the end of March the next year, the modifications to the constitution were ratified by the legislature and President Ahmadi signed the order executing the will of the people. The first institution to be dissolved was the Revolutionary Guard. Officers below the rank of Colonel were offered equivalent positions in the military, and all soldiers were offered positions in the military; they were however required again to take an oath to the new constitution. The senior officers, the top 50 lost their jobs in the military, President Ahmadi asked that middle ranking positions be found for them in government, and that they be separated from each other in different institutions. The other organizations filled with clerics in the government directing government affairs were dissolving almost on their own; the clerics understood the vote of the people, many of them wanted to go back to religion, their original vocation in the first place.

After the arrest of Ayatollah Emami, there was no new Supreme Leader named. The clerical officials were reeling from the revelations involving corruption and sexual assaults. The movement favoring moderate Imams was reducing the following of Khomeini's disciples, and the senior officials in the office of Supreme Leader were told they no longer had positions in government. A new institute of Islamic Affairs was formed. It focused on publishing religious texts and religious scholarship and teaching it was fully funded by the Federal government. The leader of the institute was appointed by a vote of a council of 20 clerics. The original selection of the clerics was made by recommendation from Imams in Tehran to President Ahmadi, he approved all nominations wishing not to interfere in the selection of religious leaders. They selected Aahil Shadpour as the leader of the institute, the Director of Religious Affairs. Aahil contacted President Ahmadi. He wanted to confirm that the proposals he wanted to make to the council would be accepted by the government, since their funding was coming from the government. The President thanked Aahil for the call; he preferred for the government not to interfere with the decisions of the clerical council. He had no concerns with the proposals of Imam Shadpour.

That Thursday in mid-April Aahil gave a televised speech and press conference to announce the formation of the Islamic Institute and describe its mission of religious publishing, research and the development of clerics and enforcing ethics in the clerical ranks. The first thing the TV audience noticed, Aahil was not wearing any head covering. He spoke to that immediately, the day of white and black turbans was gone for him, he wore simple clerical robes. If others chose to wear the turbans that was their decision. He said the governing council of the Institute had abolished the use of the term Ayatollah, they would only use the term Imam, and there were no ranks other than institutional rank of the council and his position as director. These ranks had no religious connotation, his sermons carried no more weight than any other Imam. He thanked President Ahmadi and the Majli for funding the organization and giving it institutional freedom in decision making. He said his term as Director was for five years, council members were also on five-year rotations and would be voted on by clerics across the country in the future. He announced that there would be no doctrinal prohibition in research, Imams who endorsed the views of Khomeini were invited to join the institute, but all published works would be subject to rigorous peer review and comment.

What Aahil said next was revolutionary for religious leaders in the middle east. He said the council had also approved the establishment of an interfaith office. They were seeking applications for Sunni scholars, Christian and Jewish scholars all people of the faith. The institute would publish texts from this office in Farsi, Arabic, Hebrew and English after review and approval by the Council. He closed saying they would have a website, their electronic publications would be free of charge, the government was providing the budget, there would be a small printing fee for hard copies, their financial reports would be published on the website for transparency. Aahil closed, this is a religious institute. There would be no role in the government. He did not anticipate any more television announcements after this, they would speak through their religious mission. The next Sunday was Easter Sunday and Pope Francis had a large gathering and a television audience for mass. His message was from Peter Chapter 3. "Having compassion for one another, love all as brethren" and "give an answer to every man that ask you a reason for hope," messages of tolerance Pope Francis said, something most needed in these times. At the end of his sermon, he asked rhetorically, who can we look to in these times for words and actions of tolerance. He answered, there are many including a young Imam Aahil Shadpour, standing up for faith without division and his recent establishment of an interfaith religious office in Tehran. The Vatican will follow his lead and establish a permanent interfaith office of Protestant, Muslim and Jewish scholars, and we will publish works from this office in Italian, Farsi, Arabic, Hebrew and English. The first director of the interfaith office in Tehran was Reverend Paul Bundy, an American and former President of the World Methodist Council. His wife was born in Jordan, and he spoke and wrote Arabic and had published a book, a comparative analysis of the Bible and Quran based on his doctoral theses in religious studies. The book emphasized themes and principles in common between the two faiths.

In May that year, President Ahmadi was in Washington DC and held a joint press conference with President Larson announcing the restoration of full diplomatic relations between the United States and the Islamic Republic of Iran. President Ahmadi's statement was honest and complete. The United States had made mistakes interfering in domestic Iranian politics and Iran had made many mistakes including the clandestine nuclear weapons program and allowing protestors to overtake the US embassy in Tehran and hold captives in 1979. The international behavior of Iran has not been what it should be. He said it was time to forgive these past transgressions. The Iranian people looked forward to seeing American tourists in Tehran, American businesses operating in Iran and for peace to come between our people and the middle east in general. President Larson spoke after Ahmadi. He agreed there were old transgressions from both sides, and it was time to forgive and forget those matters. All Iranian frozen assets had been released over the last several months and all trade sanctions and embargoes lifted on Iranian officials and companies. President Larson noted that the revolutionary guard restrictions had not formally been eliminated, it was not necessary, the March vote of the Iranian people for changes in the constitution and elimination of the guard made this matter moot.

Three years later the warheads were completely gone from the middle east, in the possession of China and the United States and the former nuclear weapons facilities were well on their way to being fully dismantled under the watchful IAEA inspectors. There were full time IAEA resident inspectors in Saudi and Iranian enrichment plants; they had enrichment contracts for nuclear power plants in Slovenia and Hungary, much to the anger of the Russians. Nuclear power plants from China and the United States were under construction in Saudi Arabia and Iran, the

French had yet to approve the loan guarantees. President Larson and Vice President Packard had easily won their second term. The threat of nuclear weapons greatly reduced by the actions across the middle east. Steve Thomas had been right in what he had told Michael Case, the Kim regime in North Korea and their nuclear weapons would be on everyone's mind in President Larson's second term. The President would call on Michael Case to get to the bottom of the threat.

Coming Soon!

DAMON NOMAD'S

A DANGEROUS TEST
NUCLEAR PROLIFERATION TRILOGY
BOOK 2

**Ripped from today's headlines,
a series of missile tests by North Korea.**

President Larson knows their longest-range missiles can reach all the population centers on the west coast . . .

What if they have a nuclear-tipped missile on a launch pad? What if they launched that missile, is it a test or targeted at LA, Seattle, or San Francisco? President Larson would have less than thirty minutes to decide what to do, and the technology to shoot it down does not exist.

A dangerous tipping point, that could lead to global nuclear war.

**For more information
visit:** www.SpeakingVolumes.us

www.ingramcontent.com/pod-product-compliance
Lightning Source LLC
Chambersburg PA
CBHW020226260626
47156CB00002B/553

*9 7 8 1 6 4 5 4 0 6 4 0 2 *